CW00495300

THE SECOND VERSE

ONKE MAZIBUKO

THE SECOND VERSE

Published in 2022 by Penguin Random House South Africa (Pty) Ltd
Company Reg. No. 1953/000441/07
The Estuaries No. 4, Oxbow Crescent, Century Avenue, Century City, 7441, South Africa
PO Box 1144, Cape Town, 8000, South Africa
www.penguinrandomhouse.co.za

© 2022 Onke Mazibuko

All rights reserved.
No part of this book may be reproduced or transmitted in any form or by any means,
mechanical or electronic, including photocopying and recording, or be stored in any
information storage or retrieval system, without written permission from the publisher.

First edition, first printing 2022
9 8 7 6 5 4 3 2 1

ISBN 978-1-4859-0472-4 (Print)
ISBN 978-1-77638-012-1 (ePub)

Cover design by Ayanda Phasha
Author photograph: Tarryn Goldman Photography
Text design by Fahiema Hallam
Set in Granjon LT Std

Printed and bound by Novus Print, South Africa

For Yaya, who taught me how to see myself

Book I
April 1998

Book 1

April 1998

One

Mr Knowles's suit looks like it's made from the same material as a seatbelt – cheap, dark-brown and faded – probably as old as he is.

'Bo-gang. Talk to me.'

He looks at me as if I owe him something. After all this time at this school, and still this fool can't say my name right. No surprise. They all like this.

'Look, Bo-gang, I'm here to help you. This is about what's best for you. I can't help you if you won't speak to me.'

Right. The only thing that matters to him is the school's reputation. He cares about me about as much as a butcher cares about animal rights. His eyes give him away; the stretched skin under one of them twitches.

He waits.

Silence is golden and patience is a virtue. Let's do this thing, then.

His office really sucks for a deputy principal's. It's not much of an office actually, but then again, he's not much of a deputy either. I bet the head and the other deputies laugh at his punk ass. Punk-ass Knowles. That's what they should call him. His office is all the way at the back of the school, in the dead zone, where nobody ever goes. There's barely enough space for the two of us in here, with his long legs and all. The walls aren't even the same colour, and it stinks of boiled cabbage and old newspapers. Ten bucks says this used to be a cupboard or something.

Someone's stupid laugh comes from outside: loud and carefree. Other boys out there enjoying their break-time, while I'm stuck in here, dealing with this petty nonsense.

Mr Knowles holds up the essay. 'Help me understand this, Bo-gang, *please*.'

He must think he's talking to one of his sorry-ass kids when they step out of line. So lame. 'Sir, I don't know what to say.'

'This essay is, well ... what can I say? *Shocking*, to say the least. Don't you think?'

'It's just an essay, Sir.'

'Just an essay? No, Bo-gang. This is ... a lot more, I think.'

He can believe what he wants. This fussing is way overboard. I actually thought I did pretty well on this one.

'You've written here about suicide, Bo-gang, in great detail. We're concerned about you.'

Why can't this damn chair swallow me whole and save me from this grief? Punk-ass Knowles, with his punk-ass questions. Best for me? What the hell does anyone know about what's best for me?

Mr Knowles goes on to ask me questions about my school subjects. I tell him. He asks me about my teachers. I tell him that, too. He asks me about English and my teacher, Ms Hargreaves. I tell him what he already knows.

He wipes his hand across his spotted forehead. 'Talk me through this essay. Why suicide?'

'It was the topic, Sir.'

'No. The task for Ms Hargreaves' essay was to design a project to address any social issue. You chose suicide. Not as the social issue, but as a solution.'

The man has interesting books on his shelf, the titles running along the spines. One of them is really thick: *Diagnostic and Statistical Manual of Mental Disorders*. It's like a bible of the things psychos suffer from, I bet. Probably has mad-parables and verses of the ins-and-outs of insanity, people's shortcomings and suffering, definitions of oddballs, treatments for the marginalised and normal run-of-the-mill shamefaced losers. But what does it say about the society that created them?

'People should not be stopped when they want to kill themselves,' Mr Knowles reads from my essay. 'They should in fact be encouraged.' He looks up briefly before continuing. 'Every person has the ability to make decisions. This should be respected. Suicide is a person's prerogative. People should not say it is a wrong act or a cowardly decision. People should not even say it is a brave decision. It is only a decision, made by a person for themselves.' His eyes trail out the window. He turns back to me with an expression I don't get. 'What are you really trying to say here?'

'Maybe you should read the whole thing, Sir.'

'I have, and I must say, I am not only appalled, but greatly disturbed.'

Trust Mr Knowles not to get it. 'I thought shrinks weren't supposed to be judgemental, Sir.'

Mr Knowles's brow drops. He tries a smile, but his clenched jaw undermines any friendliness he might be trying to fake.

'Bo-gang.'

'My name is Bokang, Sir.'

'Bo-*kang*. Look, as I have said to you already, your well-being is our greatest priority. You must appreciate the fact that you're part of this exceptional college, and everything that affects you affects us too. I'm trying my level best to ensure an amicable outcome for everyone concerned.'

Yeah, right. And I'm Bishop Tutu.

Back to the waiting game, then. Shrinks are supposed to be good with that. Mr Knowles seems to be struggling, though. He checks his watch, then the clock on the wall. He sits back in his chair, his foot resting on his knee, revealing a hairy shin the colour of mozzarella cheese.

'Okay, fine. We have informed your mother. We don't want misunderstandings; by giving you an opportunity to talk, we hoped to avoid any further unpleasantness. But if—'

'Sir, it was just an essay, honestly. Suicide is not such a big deal, when you consider other areas of society that need attention. As I said in my essay, suicide can be used to generate income to solve problems.'

'How exactly?'

'Well—'

The bell rings. It sounds like the damn thing is right inside this office. Mr Knowles smiles like he's used to it, like his ears and eyes aren't about to bleed. The sound stops, but something still rattles in my ear. Voices and footsteps get louder as boys move towards the buildings. What a shame, it's such a dope day to be outside.

Mr Knowles is saying something.

'Sir?'

'I said, you don't have to go back to class right away. Your mother is on her way, and I think it best we reach some sort of conclusion, and consensus, on where we stand, before she gets here.'

'Suicide clinics, Sir. The world needs lots and lots of suicide clinics.' Mr Knowles lifts an eyebrow. 'Imagine if, for a hundred bucks, a person could go to a clinic and be put down peacefully. No mess. No trauma. Perfect for the family. All the person's affairs put in order before they die. Right?'

Mr Knowles stares at me.

'All the depressed people out of the way, and they pay for it. I mean, it's their decision to die, right? *And* for a good cause. Think of the numbers, Sir.'

Mr Knowles rubs his chin.

'Imagine all those hundreds of rands. That's mad-cash, Mr Knowles Sir, by anyone's standards. And the world is already overpopulated, right? Now we solve that problem too.'

'Bo-gang. Bo-*kang,* I don't think—'

'I'm just saying, it's a win-win situation. So many problems solved. Imagine what we could do with the organs of all those dead people, Sir. Think of the long-ass organ transplant lists out there—'

'That's enough!' He wipes his forehead again. 'Surely you know that suicide – the taking of one's own life – is morally wrong?'

'I'm not so sure about that, Sir.'

He clears his throat, his Adam's apple flexing like a knuckle. 'Might I remind you, Bo-kang Damane, that this is St Stephen's College, an institution with a great history and strong traditions. It is incumbent upon you to speak in the proper manner, as you have been taught, and as expected of you as an ambassador of the school. Arguing and cutting me off is highly unbecoming. You might also want to mind your language when addressing a senior staff member. I don't need to tell you that.'

'Yes, Sir. Absolutely.'

Punk-ass Knowles.

He lectures me about the morality of suicide and Christian values and the school's expectations and blah blah blah.

The phone on his desk rings. Mr Knowles ignores it for the first couple of rings, then answers with his eyes still on me. I can't hear the person on the other side. Mr Knowles nods and speaks in short sentences. 'Well, it seems your mother is here. Let's take a walk to Mr Summers' office, shall we?'

It takes us less than ten minutes to get to the principal's office, where his secretary, Ms Tudhope, a woman who reminds me of a white-headed vulture, ushers us in. Ma is already there, grinning awkwardly at something Mr Summers has just said. Poor Ma, she don't need this drama. Everything's been blown way out of proportion. Mr Summers, with his I'm-scared-to-get-old hairstyle, tells me to wait outside his office while the grown-ups talk.

Ms Tudhope won't stop eyeballing me. I swear if she keeps it up, I might just bust her a good one in the beak. She picks up the phone and starts squawking.

A kid walks in. Ms Tudhope points him to a seat with one of her talons. He slouches in the chair with his hands pumping into each other. His grinning face is an explosion of zits, as if he downs a huge smoothie of steroids every morning for breakfast. I don't make eye contact, even though I know him. Well, I don't know-him-know-him, but I know *of* him. Everybody knows Randall Leonard. And everybody knows that Randall Leonard spends more time in the principal's office than any other kid. He's been in the school just over a year, he's two grades below me, and yet he has one hell of a reputation. Now they got me up in here with Randall Leonard, like we 'Delinquents ʀ ᴜs' or something.

Twenty minutes later, the door busts open and Mr Knowles waves me in. Now *this* is an office, not like that shoebox Mr Knowles works in. This one is worthy of a man like Mr Summers, who sits behind his perfect desk, with his perfect hair and his perfect teeth. Ma and Mr Knowles sit in chairs next to each other in front of the desk. I'm offered one on the other side of Ma. She still hasn't looked at me.

Mr Summers addresses us like a man used to an audience. He explains what Mr Knowles told him about our little chat, and what the three of them have discussed. It doesn't sound like Mr Knowles sold me out too badly. Words like 'concerned', 'well-being' and 'effort' fly around the room. The old lady studies him with blinking eyes.

'Thank you, all,' Mr Summers says, 'for pulling together to ensure the well-being of Bokang. Mrs Damane, I applaud you. Your effort as a parent is appreciated.' He gives her a politician's smile. Turning to me, he says, 'So, Bokang, we are all in agreement. For your well-being – and considering the context your mother has just shared with us – you will see Mr Knowles for at least three more sessions ...'

Oh Lord.

'... redo Ms Hargreaves' essay ...'

Christ on a bicycle.

'... and write an extra essay on morality.'

Strike me down now, Lord, *please*.

'Okay, Bokang?'

'Yes, Sir.'

Back outside, walking towards the school gates, Ma keeps up a mean pace. I feel like I used to as a toddler following her in a supermarket when she was fed up with me. Why would she be fed up with me now?

It isn't until we're in the ride and the school is out of sight that Ma finally says something. Typical: she's concerned about what people will think. She waits for the traffic light to turn red. 'You know how far away my work is, my child?'

'Yeah, Ma, I know.'

'And still I have to come out here for this.'

What does one say to that?

'You know I can't be doing this, Bobo. I've got too much work.'

'I know, Ma. But it isn't what you think.'

'What do you mean?' She grips the steering wheel with both hands. 'Tell me. What is all of this?'

'There's no problem. It was just an essay.'

'I saw it. It was embarrassing. Do you really want to kill yourself?'

'No, Ma.'

'Then what?'

'The light is green, Ma.'

'I don't care about the light!' Somebody behind us hoots. 'Go to hell!'

It's not every day you hear the old lady cussing. This is bad. But tough titty. It's not my fault everyone is losing their damn minds.

She pulls off and I'm sitting here wishing I was in another place, in another time, and in another life. Good God, the D.R.A.M.A! The stupidity of it all!

Ma takes the off-ramp onto the North East Expressway from Pearce Street towards Beacon Bay.

'What is it you want me to do for you?'

'What do you mean?'

'Do we need to take you back to Dr Schultz? My medical aid is used up, but—'

'Definitely not.'

'At least they said you can see the psychologist at the school.'

'Yeah, thanks for that. Why'd you have to go and tell them?'

'Everyone is trying to help you.'

'Trying to help me? They're making a big deal about nothing. No, I don't want to kill myself. No, I don't need to see a psychologist. I'm fine! Sheesh! Why can't you just get that?'

'Bobo, we don't want this to be like last time.'

'This is *not* like last time! I'm fine, Ma. For real.'

It's a quiet-ass ride to Beacon Bay, which suits me just fine. We drive over Batting Bridge; the murky waters of the Nahoon River beneath are dull like the sink water in an art class. A dude on a speedboat causes ripples across the surface. I wonder what his problems are, and how they ripple into the rest of his life.

Ma makes a stop by KFC to grab some grub. She knows it's my favourite, so I guess this is some sort of peace offering. She can barely afford these takeaways.

We pull into the driveway to the crib. Ma doesn't open the garage door. Instead, she switches off the engine and places a hand on my arm. She removes it when I stare at it.

'You know I love you?'

I don't say anything.

'You can always talk to me.'

Yeah, that's what everybody keeps saying.

She turns towards me and takes my hand in both of hers. 'Do you remember when we used to go to Bonza Bay? On Sundays, just the two of us? We'd get up early to catch the sunrise, but we'd always miss it.' She laughs, but it isn't a pretty sound. 'Do you remember, Bobo?'

'Yeah.'

'It was so lovely. Do you want to go there? Now?'

'Nah, Ma. It's okay. I'm good.'

'Come on, Bobo. It will be like old times.'

I pull my hand away.

'Bobo, your teachers gave me your essay. It's in my bag. We can forget this whole thing. Your father doesn't need to know. We'll be quick.'

She starts up the ride.

'Okay, whatever.'

But our progress back down the driveway is halted by another ride pulling up. The back doors open and my younger siblings, Israel and Sizwekazi, tumble out, all smiles and giggles. Ma switches off the engine and gets out to join the other driver. Nice. Fat chat and big laughs. Perfect.

I grab my school bag and head into the crib.

Yeah, so much for old times.

Two

Sketching is life. I have a bunch of pads filled front to back, top to bottom and side to side with outlines, characters and mad-ideas. Dark pencils are my favourite medium, but highlighters, markers and coloured pens also play their part.

Israel rumbles into the room we share and finds me at the desk. 'What up, big bro?' His hug damn near crushes the breath out of me. The kid is only eleven and he's built like Booker T. He's obsessed with bulking up through exercising and eating. I don't know where he gets it from; both our parents are short and lean.

'I'm all good, Izzy.'

'Why you back from school so early?'

'Ag, nothing. It was just an early day for some of us.'

'What about rugby practice?'

Israel is also obsessed with rugby; not only that, he's mad-obsessed with St Stephen's College. He and Sizwekazi go to Chesterfield Primary.

'I'm not in any team yet. I'll sort of fit into the one that needs extra players.'

'Come on, bro! You should be going for the first team.' He lugs his bags onto his bed and starts ripping off clothing.

'Naaaah, I don't know about all of that. Anyways, what's up with you and your team?'

'I made the A-team again. I'm still the captain.'

Of course he did, and of course he is. Israel is a mad-likeable kid. He excels at everything he does. He'll fit right in at St Stephen's College when his time comes.

'Bobo!' Sizwekazi, or Sizwe as we call her, comes bouncing into the room. She's on my lap before I know what's up.

'Hey. What's going on?'

'Guess what Teacher Lyndsay said to me today?'

'What, Siz?'

'She said I'm an angel. She gave me a gold star.' She grins, exposing the adorable gaps between her teeth.

'Ag, that's lame,' Israel says.

'*Haaayi!*' Sizwe swipes a fist in his direction.

'Easy there.' I blow air on her neck and she giggles. Sizwe kills me; she's a real riot. The six-year-old princess of the family. 'What was the gold star for?' I ask.

'For ballet. Teacher Lyndsay says I'm the best. She says I'll be the best in the recital.'

'Haaaaaaaaaa! You such a liar!'

'Ah, aaaah!' Sizwe tries to wriggle off my lap to smack Israel.

'Yo, chill, yo.'

'She's lying! Who's Teacher Lyndsay? There's no one with that name at school.'

'It's Ms Miles, stupid! She said we can call her that!'

'Rubbish! Ha, ha. You such a liar!'

'I'm not!'

'Yo, easy.' Sizwe wriggles out of my arms and we try tackle Israel onto his bed. Even with Sizwe's pint-sized help, it's a mission. The three of us tumble onto the bed in a heap of laughs. 'Get him, Siz!' The little one lays her fists into Israel's hard muscles.

The old lady calls us to come grab something to eat.

'Sit with us,' she says, when she sees me turning towards the passage once I've got my plate.

'Nah, it's okay. I'll sit in the room.'

'Come, Bobo!' Sizwe says.

What do I say to that? Her cuteness is deadly.

We take our plates to the dining room. Ma doesn't have a plate. She could really do with a bite, though.

'When's MaMvundla coming back?' I ask. That's the lady who's been helping us around the crib since Israel was little. She usually does the cooking during the week.

'Next week some time,' Ma says. 'Her child is still sick. I told her to take as much time as she needs.'

'What happened?' Sizwe asks. A piece of chicken flies from her mouth.

'Hayi, wena! Don't make a mess.'

'Sorry.' She giggles. 'What happened?'

'Nothing happened. Her child is sick.'

'From what?'

'Eat your food.'

'So I know where we can find those Adidas rugby boots,' Israel says. His chow is already done, and he's reaching for seconds. 'They have them at Totalsports.'

'Okay, my child.' The old lady definitely ain't down with this. But what can she do?

'Did you leave some food for Tata?' Sizwe asks.

Ma doesn't say anything. Israel watches for my reaction.

'Don't worry about that,' I say. 'Worry about your own stomach.'

'When's Tata coming back?'

Who knows? Who cares? Ernest – that's the old man – has been MIA for two days.

'Don't worry about that either, Siz. Are you done eating?'

'Yes!' Grease covers her hands, fingers and cheeks.

'Good girl.'

'Is Tata at work?'

Good God, Siz, give it a rest already.

The gate intercom buzzes. Thank God for that.

'I'll get it.' Ma makes a beeline for the front door. She says something, laughs, and a man's voice responds. They enter the dining room.

Nice. Pastor Mzoli, just the bastard we need to see.

'Hello, children.' He holds up his hands, grinning as if he's some sort of celebrity.

None of us respond.

'Hawu, don't be rude, guys,' Ma says.

'Hello, Pastor Mzoli,' Israel and Sizwe mumble at the same time.

I get up and start clearing the plates.

'You two get cleaned up, then come back and do your homework,' Ma says.

'Yes, Ma.'

'Bobo, please make us a cup of tea.'

Great. A cup of tea for His Holiness. Ma and all this church business.

I bring the tea in a pot on a tray with the cups. Ma and Pastor Mzoli are sitting in the lounge. Pastor Mzoli sits in Ernest's chair – we kids are not allowed to even dream of sitting there – and Ma sits on the sofa next to him, looking like a TV talk-show host interviewing her guest:

Ma: So, Your Holiness, tell us what makes you such a douchebag.

Pastor Mzoli: Oh thank you, thank you, sister. I'll tell you, yes. It takes years to cultivate this level of doucheness, yes. Not just anybody can achieve it, yes, yes. It needs just the right kind of integrity.

Ma: Oh, wonderful! Can you share your secret with our viewers at home?

Pastor Mzoli: Well, I shouldn't be giving away the secrets, but because I'm such a douchebag, I'll go ahead and share, yes. The integrity of a douchebag requires consistency in three key things: inflexibility, yes; dullness, yes; and arrogance, yes, yes.

Ma: Oh, wonderful, wonderful! Studio audience, give him a round of applause. You can also clap at home!

Placing the tray down on the table in front of them, I turn to leave.

'How are you doing, son?'

I give it a moment before responding. 'I'm not your son.'

'Bobo!' Ma covers her mouth.

Pastor Mzoli looks at me, smiling as if we cool like that. 'That's okay. The boy has been through a lot, yes.'

'Apologise, Bobo.'

'It's not a problem. The boy is just expressing how he feels. You're right, I am not your father. Where *is* your father, by the way?'

I don't say anything; probably best I stay quiet.

'Please sit with us for a while,' Ma says. She pats the space on the sofa next to her.

'Nah, I can't.'

'Please. I asked Pastor Mzoli to come by, after what happened today.'

'I have homework.'

'It's no trouble, sister Khensani. Let the boy go. We'll have plenty of time to talk.' He gives Ma's hand a squeeze.

Sneaky bastard!

'I'll stay. Just for a few minutes.'

'Thank you. Just for a short while.'

The priest is amused. 'Your mother told me about your trouble at school. She didn't tell me the details, but she did say you could do with some support, yes. Do you know the name of Jesus Christ?'

Christ, who doesn't?

'And do you know how much He loves you?'

Oh, boy. Ma watches me closely. My response matters to her. 'I don't really go to church or read the Bible.'

His Holiness nods. 'Jesus loves you, regardless. He waits for you, yes. He is always there, even when you don't know it, waiting for you to acknowledge Him, yes.'

Wow. Sounds a lot like a debt collector to me. We've seen plenty of them around here. 'And what does he want in return?'

'Very good question. Our Lord Jesus Christ wants nothing from you. Nothing at all.' He smiles and I get the sense that he's laughing at me.

'Nothing at all?'

'Nothing, my son ... I mean Bokang. Nothing at all. Except your devoted love and recognition of Him as the one, true Son of God and the Saviour, yes.'

'Oh. Right.'

'To receive all of His love, you must repent for your sins, call Him your Saviour and pray for forgiveness. Hallelujah.' He raises his hands with the fingertips touching. The nails on each pinkie finger are long and uncut. Nasty.

'Wait, I thought you said He loves me no matter what?'

'He does, yes.'

'So then why must I repent?'

'For your sins. So He can welcome you into the Kingdom of God, yes. Where you can live in grace and glory. Bless the Lord. Amen.' He spreads his arms open like wings.

'Amen,' Ma says, clasping her hands and bowing her head.

Yeeeaaah, this is where I get off this ride. The old lady will have to understand. 'Okay, thank you very much. But I do have plenty of homework, sooo …'

'Are you ready to become a man?'

The old lady glances at me, her eyes pleading.

'Well, yes, I am, but probably not this year.'

'No, no, no, son. I'm not talking about outdated, barbaric practices. You don't need to sit in a hut in the bush to become a man. I'm talking about becoming responsible and mature in the eyes of God.'

'I don't think going to bush is outdated; it's our tradition as Xhosa people. I don't understand how you, somebody who's been through it, can say that.'

'Bobo, please.' Ma reaches out a hand to me.

'We will all be answerable to God one day, so the scripture says. There's only one true path to salvation. To become a man of God.'

'Yeah, okay. I'm just gonna go, for everyone's sake.'

This is such trash. The old lady can explain my departure.

In my room, Tupac Shakur gazes down upon me, feeling my pain. The poster of the cover of the *All Eyez on Me* album hangs on my wall. Other posters of rappers: Busta Rhymes, Wu Tang Clan, Keith Murray and EPMD fill up the rest of the space. Israel's side of the room is full of posters of wrestlers – Shawn Michaels, Bret Hart, Macho Man Randy Savage, Stone Cold Steven Austin and of course Hulk Hogan – but my side is the shrine to dope hip-hop. Tupac's music speaks to me on so many levels. The track 'Hit 'em Up' bumps from the Walkman. I roll myself a joint and take it up onto the roof where I sit and smoke, enjoying the loneliness.

Pastor Mzoli eventually leaves. Israel and Sizwe are in bed when I come down. I do some sketching while I'm still mellow from the joint, and get stuck into some homework afterwards. I hit the sack just before midnight.

> I've been here on this farm; I recognise it from my childhood. A nasty wind blows, ripping through everything: branches fly from trees, foreign objects tumble through the air, and farm animals twirl upwards as if riding a whirlwind. People stand everywhere, unmoving like statues. They disintegrate like sand particles, forming clouds that blind my vision. Where is my family? They can't hear me screaming out to them; there's laughter in the wind.
>
> Falling. It's raining. I'm in the back seat of a long black car. A driver with a black hood sits in the front seat. He's saying something, but the deafening sound of grinding metal muffles his words. We're speeding on a highway. Other identical black cars weave in both directions. The rain falls so hard, our car slips and slides. What are we doing? The driver turns to speak: 'You must find it, Bokang.' What must I find? He will not tell me. Why isn't he watching the road ahead? Watch out!

The time is 3.08 a.m. when I check the digital clock next to the bed. Israel snores like a champion. He won't mind me switching on the bedside lamp. The bathroom seems a world away; my legs are sacks filled with cement. I rummage under my bed and pull out my Suicide Manifesto. Inside is a list of different kinds of suicides. For example, Suicide #7 is jumping off Steve Biko Bridge. A lot of people have tried this one, even though it has a low rate of success. Suicide #3 is gassing myself in the old lady's busted-up Hyundai, and Suicide #11 is swallowing fifty marbles. There's no ranking to them, I just randomly list them as they come into my head. Some of the things from my discussion with Mr Knowles earlier in the day are still on my mind, so I put them down in the Suicide Manifesto.

Thirsty. Light filters down the passage from the kitchen. Ma is sitting at the table staring into a half-empty tea cup. It takes a moment for her to notice me.

'Hey, Bobo. Why are you awake?'

'Why're you sitting here?'

'Ag … I'm just … I wanted a cup of tea, then …' Her voice is barely a whisper.

I take her hand. 'You shouldn't be here.'

'You shouldn't be out of bed. Why are you taking care of me, when I should be taking care of you?' She lets out a low laugh.

'Let's get you to bed.'

'No, I'm waiting. I'm waiting for …'

'Waiting for what?'

'Waiting.'

'Ma?'

She stares off at something behind me. She could drop a tear at any moment, but even that seems like an effort. She smiles again. It's not pretty. 'Bobo, it's you.' She places a cold hand on my cheek. Recognition crosses her face, like she's seeing me for the first time.

'Are you okay?'

'Of course I am, my baby. Come with me to the beach, Bobo.'

'Not right now, Ma.'

'Of course not now, silly. But will you come with me? We can go on Sunday, like we used to, just the two of us.'

'Yes, fine. We can do that.'

'You know I think of you as the man of the house?'

'Come on, Ma.'

'I do. I know you're no longer a baby. You're becoming a man. I know your father makes you angry—'

'Ma, stop.'

'I know, my child, I know. It's okay. This is growing up. I'll always be there with you, but there are the little ones. You must take care of them. They look up to you.'

'Okay, Ma.'

But who will take care of me?

Three

The old lady needs my help getting Israel and Sizwe ready for school. She leaves before us since she has a long-ass drive to work in Bisho. The three of us kids mission to the taxi rank. Siz is her usual bubbly self in the taxi, prattling on in English. I catch more than one person staring. I don't pay them no mind, though; if they knew anything about anything, they wouldn't be riding in a taxi.

'I have ballet after school,' Sizwe says as they climb out, 'so we'll see you later. Okay?'

'Yeah. Bye, Siz. Easy, Izzy.'

Outside the St Stephen's College main gate I check my boy, Senzo Fihla, stepping out of his old lady's ride. He gives her a kiss on the cheek.

'Yo, what up, Big Bo?'

'Yo, Enzo. Easy, man.' We shake hands and embrace. 'What's going on?'

'Nothing, dog. I'm all good. Yo, what up with you, though? You pulled a Houdini yesterday.'

'Yo, you won't believe what I've been through, for real.'

'I already heard, dog – *everybody* talking about it.' He shakes his head, flapping his elf ears.

'Talking about what?' We stop walking.

'About you wanting to off yourself, man.'

'Off myself? *What*?'

'Yo, man, peeps are talking. Crazy shit. So, what's up?'

'With what?'

'With yo mentals, nigga. Are you tryna off yourself or what?'

'Goddammit, you know me better than that. What you think?'

'Man, I don't know nothing. You're a teenager fool, I don't know what be going on in yo head.'

'Man, shut up. You're a teenager, too. Talking like you don't know what's up.'

'Yeah, whatever, dog. Look, Imma check you out break-time. I got mad-stories for you, yo.'

'All right, cool. One.'

'One.' He gives me dap before taking off.

There's no assembly on Friday mornings, so it's straight to class. Senzo and I don't share any classes. He's a bit of a dumb-ass, but he's still cool peeps.

The quad is a sea of maroon-and-navy blazers, the St Stephen's College uniform. Privileged kids shuffling in droves towards their preordained futures.

'Hey, Dama-nee!'

Damn. Gotta get out of here.

'Hey, Dama-*nee*!' A second voice calls.

Goddammit.

A hard hand grabs my shoulder and spins me around. 'Dama-nee. Are you bloody deaf or something?'

Duncan Pederson and his trusted sidekick Chad Peinke; the Batter and Brawl Twins, as I like to call them.

Duncan shoves me up against the wall with one hand. 'Why you ducking when I'm calling you? You soeking for trouble?'

'Nah, man. I didn't hear you.'

'Didn't hear him?' That's Chad, the dumber one of the two. 'Kak, man.' He places a hand on my other shoulder.

'What's this kak I hear you tried to kill yourself?' Duncan asks.

'I didn't.'

'What?' Chad says, putting pressure on my shoulder.

'I said I didn't.'

'You see,' Duncan says, turning to his mate. 'I told you it was kak. Listen here, Dama-nee bru, you don't ever kill yourself without my permission. Otherwise I'll kill you myself. Okay? Say okay!' Chad crushes me harder against the wall.

'*Okay*, I get it. Don't kill myself without your permission, otherwise you'll kill me. Right.'

'Lekker. Because I need you to do another project for me. I got a kak mark in my last science test. You gonna score me a lekker mark, neh?'

'Yeah, whatever, man.'

'Meet me at the end of second break, outside Barnes's classroom.'

'Sure.'

They take their grubby hands off of me. Chad feigns a punch, which makes me feel stupid for flinching, and they stomp off cackling like retarded hyenas. Every day this same nonsense. A few kids watch me. Some of them snigger. Bunch of punks.

Outside Mevrou De Lange's Afrikaans class, some of my classmates ask me stupid questions about yesterday. I ignore them.

'Yo, bra, what kind?' Roscoe Munsamy approaches. Outside of Senzo, he's the only one of the fools in this place I consider a friend. We have a few classes together.

'I'm all good, man.' I take his hand. Roscoe is straight peeps, I don't like keeping things from him. When he asks how you doing, he really means it.

'Are you sure?' His eyes are serious behind his glasses.

'Yeah, man. Don't even ask.'

During Afrikaans class, Mevrou De Lange calls me outside.

'Is jy all right?'

'Ja, Mevrou.'

'Is jy seker?'

'Ja, Mevrou.'

She gives me a hug. WTF?

In third-period Biology, Ms Meadows leans down by my desk and asks me how I'm doing. What the hell is up with everyone today? Can't they just back off? I'm nice to her, though, cos she's one of the few teachers that's good peeps.

During first break I skip out the main gate. I know I'm supposed to chill with Senzo and Roscoe, but I just need a minute. Up Plum Street, past Wallace Hospital and across Main Road. Leaving the school grounds during school hours is not permitted, but what the heck, these are extenuating circumstances. Meredith House, our sister school, is here. On the other side of the fence, girls in their yellow-and-brown uniforms frolic and do whatever the hell girls do.

The Westwood train station lies beyond the school. I go through a hole in the fence and find a spot under some trees to spark a blunt.

It's an unremarkable day, overcast. The grass is inviting; I could catch up on the zzzs I missed out on last night. Two men sit under some trees on the other side of the fence, nicely soused on cheap liquor. One of them waves a dirty hand. I ignore him.

The walk back to school takes forever. The weed wasn't good, but it's better than nothing. I'll need to mission for something fresh soon.

I can't remember if I left my schoolbag outside my last class or the one I'm going to. Roscoe brings it to me outside our next class.

'What happened to you, bra?'

I say something back.

'What?' Roscoe eyeballs me suspiciously over the rims of his glasses.

The teacher does his thing at the front of the classroom; all of it goes over my head. Someone taps me on the forehead; apparently I passed out. Everyone is staring at me. Roscoe isn't pleased. Mr Coleridge stands over me, also not pleased. Or is that concern on his face? 'Damane, I think you should take some time out.' He sends me to Mr Knowles in his small shoebox office.

'How have you been sleeping at home?' His suit is a dull navy today. Not much of an upgrade.

'Fine, Sir.'

'What time do you generally go to bed?'

What time does *he* go to bed? Dude is like seriously pale, as if he goes to bed when the sun comes out. 'Nine. Ten.'

'And wake up?'

'Six-thirty.'

'What about last night?'

'What about last night, Sir?'

'What time did you go to bed?'

'Ten, Sir.'

'Did you sleep through the night?'

Did you drink someone's blood? Or fly with some bats in a cave? 'What do you mean, Sir?'

'Did you sleep uninterrupted for a full eight hours?'

'Yes, Sir.'

'Are you sure?'

'Yes, Sir.'

He stares at me. He doesn't want to do this today any more than I do. After a few more lame questions, he schedules our appointment for next week and gives me permission to go home. This is earlier than yesterday. Me, Senzo and Roscoe are supposed to chill at Senzo's spot after school, but that will have to wait.

Instead of catching a taxi at my normal place at the rank, I take a walk towards Westwood Shopping Centre. Fresh air will be good, the brisk walk is better. I catch a taxi on Molineux Avenue and sit somewhere in the middle row between a fat woman and a skinny man, the former digging into some greasy chicken while the latter stares past me at the chicken. Caught in the middle: the story of my life.

Back when Ernest still had his ride, taxis were foreign to me. This was before the debt collectors came to relieve him of the burden of car payments. Not many kids at my school who live in the suburbs take taxis to school. I guess I'm one of a kind. (Yay!)

The taxi drops me off before my usual spot so I can walk some more to clear my head. The front door is wide open when I get to the crib. The fridge in the kitchen is also open, exposing the empty shelves, except for a carton of beer that wasn't there this morning. A couple of cupboards are open. I head down the passage to the folks' room. Ernest is passed out on the bed, fully dressed, like Attila the Hun after a marauding mission.

I lie on my own bed and count the holes in the pattern of the ceiling. Sometimes it helps when I can actually count beyond two hundred and sixteen. Today I quit at eighty-three, after losing count three times. I'm tired, but sleep is damn near impossible.

Israel and Sizwe come home and find me lying on the bed.

'How was school, Bobo?'

'Fascinating, Siz.'

'What does fas-nating mean?'

'It means exciting, interesting, great.'

'Why was it so fas-nating?'

'It just was.'

Israel strips down and flexes his bare torso in homage to the hall-of-fame wrestlers on his wall.

'School for me was also fas-nating today.'

'Great, Siz.'

'You want to hear what I did?'

'Not particularly, but go ahead.'

'Okay, so ...'

Her words are a rambling blur. Israel does push-ups between the beds to her cadence. Where has Ernest been these past couple of days?

Israel goes out the room and quickly returns. 'There's no food in the kitchen.'

'Yep.'

'There's beer in the fridge.'

'Yep.'

He scratches the side of his head. 'When's Ma coming back?'

'Not sure, but I doubt it'll be long.'

'I didn't finish my lunch today,' Sizwe says. 'You can have my sammich.'

She scoots out the room and returns holding a tightly wrapped sandwich. Israel devours one half of it in two bites, as Sizwe and I watch in awe from my bed.

'Tata's back,' I say.

'Really?' Sizwe says.

I nod.

'Where's he?' Israel asks.

I tilt my head in the direction of our folks' room.

'When did he get back?' Israel asks.

I shrug.

'Can I go see him?' Sizwe asks. Poor thing really wants to see the old man but she knows better than to go stepping up in the folks' room without permission (one of Ernest's rules).

'He's probably still sleeping, Siz.'

'When will he wake up?'

'Don't know.'

'Can I see him?'

Cradling Sizwe in my arms, we stand at the doorway to the folks' room, peering inside; Israel leans in too. You would swear we are looking at something special like a damn unicorn or freaking Big Foot. But all we're staring at is T Ernest Damane, beloved husband and father.

'Okay, Siz. Enough?'

'Wait ...'

She stares at him a little longer before we shuffle back to my room. We sit around talking sweet nothing. The food situation and the return of Ernest have Izzy and Siz uncertain. They cling to me for reassurance or something.

Not long after, Ernest appears at the door, barefoot and still in his crumpled suit, as jaded as a grizzly bear who missed his wake up call after a long hibernation. Wordless, he grinds his back teeth.

Sizwe jumps off the bed and runs to him. 'Hello, Tata!'

Ernest the Bear grunts. He hugs her tiny frame to his skinny body. He holds out his other hand towards Israel. The big boy goes to his daddy's embrace. Ernest stands there in the doorway, his two babies clutched on either side of him. Daddy of the Year.

'Are you good?'

'Yes, Tata,' they respond in unison.

He gives them a squeeze and growls. Izzy and Siz giggle in delight.

'You're my babies,' Ernest the Bear says.

More giggles from the babies.

Ernest the Bear, aka Daddy of the Year, looks over at me. 'Are you too old for a hug?' His face stretches in a gruesome grin. My silence sends the three of them lumbering off down the passage, Israel and Sizwe asking their father mad-excited questions.

With an 8B pencil in my hand, I turn my attention to the sketchpad in front of me.

Barely twenty minutes later, Ernest summons me: 'BO-KANG!'

He sits in his favourite seat in the lounge. Sizwe kneels in front of him while Israel sits on the armrest.

'Get me a beer, boy.'

Great. 'Yes, Tata.'

In the kitchen, I tear out one of his Black Labels from the packaging.

The garage door opens electronically while I'm rummaging for a bottle opener. The old lady's ride hums inside. She comes into the kitchen empty-handed, carrying only despair across her sagging shoulders. She sees the beer bottle in my hand and her shoulders appear to sag even more. 'Hello, my child.' The wind swallows her voice as she closes the door behind her.

'Hey, Ma.'

She doesn't say anything else. What is there to say?

We hear the old man's laugh coming from the lounge. The two youngsters also laugh. I take him his beer and head back to my room. Not long after, Ernest calls again. 'BO-KANG!'

This time he sits alone. 'Cut my toenails. And bring me another beer.'

I bring the beer and get to work on Ernest's spotted yellow feet. The TV is on a news channel. A woman reports in isiXhosa about Bafana Bafana's preparations for the Soccer World Cup in France.

'Ha!' Ernest exclaims. 'Bloody fools don't stand a chance. Just because they have a French coach, they think they're going to win.' He does the chesty laugh again. 'What do you think?'

'I don't know.'

'You don't have an opinion?'

'Not really.'

He grunts, takes a long sip of his beer. 'Ah! That was good.' He places the bottle down. 'You must have an opinion.'

'I don't. It's not a big thing.'

'Not a big thing?' – cocking his head dramatically – 'Hawu, don't you think it's significant that this team, from this deeply challenged country, has achieved something that has put us on the world stage?'

'I don't know.'

'I don't need to remind you how things were in this country just four years ago, do I?'

'No, Tata.'

'So how can you not care?' He claws at his raggedy beard.

'I'm just not a soccer fan.' Finished with his left foot, I move to the right.

'But this isn't about soccer. It's about more. Can't you see that?'

I struggle with the big toenail and squeeze the clippers so hard I catch a bit of his skin, and he winces.

'Sorry.'

Israel comes back into the room and heaves himself onto the sofa.

'This is a big deal, my boy, make no mistake. The world is always watching us, and we as South Africans should be aware of this. Not so?'

'Yes, Tata.'

'You need to be aware of things, know what's happening around you.'

'Are you watching this?' Israel asks.

Ernest laughs. 'Yes, of course we are.'

Israel pulls a face.

'Get my briefcase in my room,' Ernest says to Israel. 'You see what you're teaching your brother?' he says to me. 'He doesn't care about the news because his older brother's indifferent. Have you been following the news?'

'Not really.'

'Why not?'

'There's just too much happening out there. I can't know it all.'

He smacks his hands together. 'But you need to watch the news to stay informed and have an opinion on things. Not so?'

'I can't really have an opinion about everything.'

Ernest whistles, shaking his head. 'You're wrong. Opinions define character and show maturity.'

I pause from working on Ernest's nasty feet to think about this. This is what Ernest does at his best: he tosses up head-scratchers. But in my essay I expressed an opinion, and that didn't work out so well. 'Having opinions gets people in trouble.'

'What do you mean?' He folds his arms.

Israel returns with the briefcase. Ernest pulls out a wad of cash from inside. Surprise, surprise, the man is flush. He instructs Israel to give the old lady some cash to get some food for the house. 'What do you mean?' he says again, turning back to me.

'Adults don't allow kids to have opinions, especially if those opinions differ from theirs.'

'Yes, surely. I agree that happens.'

'Also, opinions are just opinions; they don't really matter.'

Ernest claps his hands. 'It's not about being right or wrong. It's about coming out of yourself, engaging with what's happening around you, taking a stance on things. You get me?'

'Sure.'

'Opinions mature, just like you mature. When you're a Xhosa man, this will be expected of you.'

'When is Bobo going to bush, Tata?' Israel asks, returning to the room.

Good freaking question, Izzy.

Ernest tries to take a swig from his bottle, frowning when he realises it's empty. 'Go get me another,' he says to Israel. The boy hesitates but Ernest's stare makes him move.

'So, when will I be going to bush, Tata?'

Ernest stares out the sliding door. 'When you're ready.'

Right. More like when your broke ass has the money. 'But I am ready.

Most of the boys at school go in Grade 11. Senzo's going now in June and it would be nice if I—'

'You're not ready.'

'Say thank you to your father,' Ma says, standing in the doorway with Sizwe.

'Enkosi, Tata,' Sizwe says.

'We just going to the shops to get something to eat.'

Israel brings the old man's beer.

'Izzy, are you coming with us?'

Israel looks over at the old lady and then to me. I nod. The three of them leave.

'Tata, I really think—'

'Leave it alone, boy.'

'But—'

'I said leave it alone.'

In one long pull, he gulps down half the beer. His glazed eyes stare at the TV screen, the cheerfulness gone from him. Yep, this discussion is definitely over. I finish clipping his last toe, clean up the mess, and stand up to walk away.

'Have you seen what the garden looks like?' he says.

Oh-oh.

'It's a bloody mess, boy.'

Of course it is. Somebody – no names – hasn't paid their garden-service bills.

'How can you live in this house with a garden like that? It doesn't look like the garden where a man lives.' Still staring at the TV screen, he takes another sip. 'I want you to clean it up. Cut the grass and trim the bushes.'

'I'll do it tomorrow.'

'No. You will start right now.'

'But it's getting dark out.'

'You better hurry, then. You want to be a man, you better start learning about responsibility.'

* * *

I'm out in the yard hacking at the bushes with a bush knife and garden shears. It's slow going. This is beyond whack. Thinking about it fuels me into slashing harder. I work up an impressive sweat, despite the chill in the air.

By the time the old lady returns with the youngsters, I've made an impressive mess in the back yard. There's still plenty to do, but it's a start.

'Come get something to eat,' Ma says.

'Just now.'

The slashing and clipping continue. I don't feel like being with all of them right now, sitting around a table, eating like some sort of TV sitcom family.

Israel comes out after a while and helps bundle the leaves and branches into plastic bags.

Sizwe sticks her head out of the sliding door. 'Bobo, you have a phone call.'

Ernest watches me walk across the TV room.

'Hello?'

'Yo, nigga, what's up?'

'Hey, Enzo. Nothing much.'

Ernest watches me.

'Yo, you making a habit of this disappearing thing, dog. I'm starting to worry about you.'

'Nah, it's nothing, man. I'm good.'

'Come on, Big Bo. Talk to me, dog. I know shit ain't right.'

'I'll tell you, just not now.'

'A'ight. Well, check it, why don't you come over tomorrow. We can work on the comic. Big Ros is coming through. We'll make up for the time we lost today.'

'Sounds like a plan. Only after midday, though.'

'That's perfect.'

'A'ight, check you tomorrow.'

'Cool.'

Ernest catches me halfway across the room. 'You're not going any-where until the garden's finished.' He burps.

I don't say anything. I stand in the back yard looking at the work I've already done. It's a lot, but there's still plenty to do. Ernest won't get the better of me. I can push some more tonight to leave as little as possible for tomorrow. The bushes will be done tonight, the grass can wait until tomorrow.

Ernest will not get the better of me, that's for sure.

Not now, not ever.

Four

Sleep is hard to come by when the body is fatigued. A tingling sensation courses through my aching joints. The house is quiet except for Israel's gentle snoring nearby and Ernest's louder snoring further away. Willing myself to sleep is a hopeless joke. Reading, writing or sketching require too much effort.

The sun rises to a Saturday morning. Ah, but there's nothing like the sound of Ma and Ernest arguing to remind me it's time to get up. Their loud-ass voices are a serious temptation to stay buried under the covers for longer, but I got moves to make today.

The grass is still wet with dew when I begin mowing it, disregarding the possibility of being electrocuted. (That would be sweet, though: Death by Electrocution, Suicide #22.)

By the time Israel gets up to come help me, it's almost ten o'clock and the lawn is just about done. All that's left to do is the clean-up. Not long after, Ernest steps out the crib as we carry the last plastic of grass into the garage.

'I'm done,' I say, sounding both defiant and triumphant.

'Good. Now clean the garage.' He doesn't stop to debate the point or inspect the work. He strides down the driveway towards the gate, where Tata uMfene, an old buddy of his, just pulled up in a battered bakkie. Ernest climbs in and the bakkie backs up in a cloud of filthy smoke. They drive off without the courtesy of a goodbye.

Whatever.

The garage can wait.

Within the hour, I'm done washing and chowing; I head out the door with my backpack strapped on and beats bumping from my Walkman. I mission on foot to the other side of Beacon Bay, to my man JP's spot. He's this cool Afrikaans kid I get my blunts from.

His mom lets me in and tells me to go through to his room. She's always nervous when she sees me, like they don't get many of my type around here. Their little dog follows me, snuffling suspiciously.

JP sits on his unmade bed, strumming a guitar. He holds up a finger to silence me as I enter. He strums a few notes with his head bent over, his long hair hanging like the strands of a mop. 'Whooaaaa ...' he says. Then laughs. He strums a single note. 'Whooaaaa ...' He laughs again, leaps up, taps something on his keyboard, then sits back down and begins playing. A few seconds later, he's tapping the keyboard again. He listens to the playback of what he's just recorded, nodding his raggedy head.

'Whatchu think?'

'Sounds dope.'

'Raaaad, bro.' He stands up to give me a sliding handshake. 'What's going on, bro?'

'I'm all good, man. I see you doing your thing.' I point to the guitar.

'Yeah, man, the sound is essential to the oneness.'

I'm not sure what he means, but this is how he always is: full of wisdom cooked up from the smoked pips of the finest weed.

'Listen to this.' From the PC comes the sound of the guitar segment he just recorded, layered on a drum pattern.

'Yo, that's banging, son.'

'You think you could rip to this?'

'Hell, yeah!'

'All right, then. Let's do it, man.' We both take hits from his bong, which makes him cough like he's about to hack up minced bits of his lung.

I spit a few bars on the mic, just some freestyles and a few lines from my black book, nothing serious. It's dope to get it out there.

'You really sick with the rhymes, man,' JP says, moving from his desk chair to a bean bag in the corner. The little dog immediately jumps onto his lap. 'Now I know why they call you the Supreme Khon.'

'And you nice with the beats.'

We both laugh. It's a moment. We silent. But it's good.

'You got any more blunt?' I ask, taking a chance.

JP nods sagely, but doesn't move. He holds up his hands as if he's touching an invisible wall in front of him. The dog lifts its head, curiously watching his hands. 'You got really great energy, bro, when you smiling.'

'What?'

'Come on, I wanna show you something.'

It's crazy that I've been to JP's place so many times before, but never actually checked it out in its entirety. But now he takes me through the crib. The little dog, Rasta, follows us; long hair covers its body, even its eyes – the same way JP's hair covers his face when he bows his head.

Different-sized family pictures line the passage walls. Both his parents are giants in every photo, which would explain his height. He also has a little sister I've never met. I tuck my elbows in as we walk through a dining room full of ornaments. The TV room is full of latest-model appliances. Back at our crib, we have a VCR and an M-Net decoder that don't work. Only two out of five of our hi-fi speakers work. But everything stays on the room divider, just for show.

We exit into the back garden with its neatly cut lawn. From the front, you'd never say there's so much space out back. Cutting this lawn would be a bummer, for real. Neatly trimmed bushes line two of the walls and two huge pine trees, one of which has a swing hanging from it, stand close to the third wall. A covered pool takes up one side.

We walk all the way to the end of the garden, under the trees with white flowers (JP tells me they're magnolias) to a pond with dark waters. We stand on the bridge peering down at the fish swimming below.

JP points.

'What?'

'Koi, bro.'

'Yeah, I see them.'

Red-and-white fish, or koi, swim down below, maybe eight or nine of them. We stand there staring, not saying much. I'm not sure what we supposed to be seeing. The fish are pretty and all, but I don't get why we out here. JP stands leaning on the wooden rail smiling down at the water; his eyes are slits.

'How many do you see?'

'Er, nine. No. Eleven?'

JP's smile widens, his eyes thinning even more. 'Twenty-one, bro.'

Down in the water, the fish swim in constant motion, moving over one another in slow and steady rhythms. They're pretty big. Some are as long as my forearm and hand together. While some are white-and-red, others have black-and-gold patterns. Some have more than three colours. The patterns on the koi are startling; they make me grin. 'Well, I'll be damned.'

JP laughs. 'Do you know why people keep koi?'

'Nah, bra.'

'They're peaceful creatures. They don't get diseases like other fish, and don't fight among themselves, or with other fish. Having them around brings a lot of feng shui.'

'Fun *what*?'

'Feng shui, bro: peaceful energy.'

'Oh.'

'Yeah. That energy spreads to those that spend time with them.' He nods like a kung fu master.

'Right.'

'I've never brought anybody back here, man. This place is sacred. The way you flow with those rhymes, it reminds me of how the koi swim.' He uses his hand to make the motion of a fish swimming. 'Don't ever stop your art, bro. Not for anybody. Stay true to the spirit of the Supreme Khon.'

He taps me on the shoulder and gives me a stiff smile. With that simple action, the moment changes; the magic is broken.

We head back to his room in silence. When we get there he doesn't sit down. Instead, he opens his cupboards and drawers as if he's looking for something. He searches the pockets of a pair of pants he picks up off the floor. I know these signs. When JP is restless, it usually means he wants his visitors to leave.

'Yo, man, I think I'm gonna go.'

'Cool, man.' He pulls out his stash – the good stuff – and gives me a fat head wrapped in a piece of paper. 'That's for your journeys. Safe travels and respect.' He bows to make his point.

We walk to the front garden, outside the kitchen. 'You know my friend Gert?' he says. 'He has this chick, Carla. Real Afrikaans meisie. They've been together forever. She doesn't really dig me, and I don't really dig her.' JP's mom watches us through the kitchen window. 'She has this swak energy, you know. When you around her, it just takes over everything. You know what I mean?'

'Nah, man.'

'Everything with her is like hectic. She never knows when to stop; kinda kills the mood. Know what I mean?'

'Why you telling me this, man?'

'Just don't give up your art, bro.' He gives me another shoulder tap. 'And know your limits.'

The taxi ride to Vincent Heights is a short one. It takes about fifteen minutes to walk from where the taxi drops me to Senzo's house.

His twenty-one-year-old sister opens the door for me.

'Hey, Lulama. What up?'

She gives me a smile, still fine as ever. One day, man, one day … she will be my woman, for real.

'Yo, what up, cats?'

'Yo, Big Bo.'

I dap Senzo.

'Hey, Bokang.'

I dap Roscoe.

'What y'all punk-asses up to?'

'We waiting on yo punk-ass,' Senzo says.

'You late, bra.' Roscoe adjusts his glasses.

'Late? Come on y'all. It's freaking Saturday. How can I be late for anything on a Saturday?'

'We said twelve, bra.'

'It's like five to one, yo. Chill.'

Roscoe shakes his head.

'Whatever, nigga,' Senzo says. 'You got the sketches?'

'Hell, yeah. But since y'all tripping, I ain't so sure about showing y'all.'

'Come on, man.'

'Okay, okay, okay.' I pull out my sketchpad from my backpack.

'We've been going over the first three scenes of the second act,' Roscoe says, getting straight to business. 'Everything is cool, except here' – pointing to a sketch – 'we think these need revision.'

'Say no more, Big Ros. I got you.' I hold up one of the recent sketches. 'I wasn't feeling that layout, either. So I came up with this.'

'Yoooooo!' Senzo says. 'This is ill!'

'Wow.' Roscoe says. He's mostly responsible for dialogue and plot in our comic series, while Senzo does themes and anything else Roscoe assigns to him. All animation is my responsibility.

'What you cats think?'

'This is sick, dog. It really works.'

'Hmm, nice.'

'Just nice, Big Ros?'

'It's nice, bra. What more you want me to say?' He moves his fringe back with a flick of the hand.

'Well, if you think those are nice, then you gonna love these.'

'Yo! What are these, son?'

'These, my nigga, are the latest mark-ups for the Kujalla Death Squad.'

'They off the chain!' He taps his hand over his heart. 'I'm loving this one. Is this the new Sharique Hammer?' He grabs the sketch pad from my hands.

'You know this, man.'

'Wait, wait, wait.' Roscoe shakes his head. 'New mark-ups? I thought we already agreed on the final sketches for the KDS. We spent enough time doing those.'

'I know, Big Ros, but I took an executive decision.'

'An executive decision?'

'Yeah. I was inspired – and you know you have to act on inspiration.'

'When were you gonna tell us?'

'I'm telling you now.'

'These are kinda nice though, Big Ros,' Senzo says.

'I didn't say they weren't nice. But we agreed on everything as a caucus.'

'What?' Senzo says. 'What the hell has this got to do with dead bodies?'

'Not carcass. Caucus. As in c-a-u-c-u-s.'

'What?'

'Forget him, Ros. The decision isn't made. I came up with these last week, after our meeting. I was gonna show them to y'all yesterday, but we didn't meet up. So here we are.'

Roscoe goes through the sketches again. 'So it's new sketches for the entire KDS?'

'Yeah, man. Sharique Hammer, Lons Krispen, Dak Dreggen, Spoce Ke Hemet, Lilak Shreng and the Supreme Khon. I still need to do a few touch-ups on the one for Les Farok, though.'

'Damn, son, this is a lotta work,' Senzo says. 'I'm mad-impressed, yo. For a while there, we was thinking …'

'You was thinking what?'

The two of them exchange a glance. 'We've missed enough deadlines, that's all.'

'Deadlines? What goddamn deadlines, cats?'

'We discussed the timeline a few weeks ago,' Roscoe says. 'We have to stick to it.'

'What about us just spending time together? Remember that?'

Senzo avoids eye contact.

'Yeah,' Roscoe says. 'We need to take it seriously.'

'I do take it seriously. I take y'all cats seriously.'

'Pssss. Really?' Roscoe lets out a sarcastic-as-hell laugh.

'Yo, what's that supposed to mean?'

'Yo, cats, can you chill out?' Senzo whines.

'Nah, nah, nah. Let this cat say what's on his mind, yo. What's going on, Big Ros? You got something to say?'

'Actually, I do. We both have something to say.' They exchange another look.

'Okay, spit it out.'

'What happened with you this week? You write an essay about suicide and freak everybody out, but you don't want to talk about it. You say you take us seriously, but we don't even know what's going on.'

'Jesus, Ros. It was nothing. I already told this dude.'

Senzo stares at the ground.

'But that's not what everybody's saying.'

'Forget what everybody's saying. Listen to what *I'm* saying.'

'What *are* you saying, Bokang?'

This is some bullshit. 'Cats, I'm fine. Everything's fine.'

'No, you're not. We see what's happening. Falling asleep in class. Forgetting to do homework. Getting kak marks for tests you could do in your sleep. Spending less time with us. Showing up to class goofed.'

Now for that, I don't have a response.

'When did you start smoking, bra? Do you hang out with Randall Leonard and those guys now?'

'No.'

'Then what, bra? You can't even deny it.'

'I don't even smoke that much.'

'You see,' he says to Senzo. 'I told you, bra. Why you even smoking? I thought we said we would never do that stuff.'

'Man, come on, Ros. It ain't even that bad. Just chill out, man. This is so childish.'

'Childish? I'm trying to show you how much we care.'

'Yo, cats, can we just squash all of this, for real?' Senzo says. 'Let's just get back to what we came here for.'

Roscoe shakes his head. 'Look at him, he's goofed right now.' He grabs his things, packing them into his bag.

'Come on, Big Ros,' Senzo says, tossing my sketchpad on his bed. 'Don't leave.'

'Can I use your phone to call my mom?'

'*Come on*, Ros.'

This is whack. Depressing-as-Aids whack. 'Nah, you cats chill and do whatever. I'm out.'

'Nah, not you too, Big Bo. Come on.'

I waste no time: I pack my stuff and leave the two of them to figure things out.

Ernest isn't home when I get there (surprise, surprise). Ma, Israel and Sizwe chill and watch TV; I decline the invite to join the family moment. My stomach hasn't seen much food all day, but I'm not feeling Ma's attempt at supper. I go straight to my room. I don't even bother sketching. Buried deep under the covers is the only place to be.

Five

'Bobo, wake up.'

No, I don't want to wake up.

'Bobo.'

This is my dream.

'Wake up!'

Leave me alone.

'Bobo!'

The old lady eyeballs me, looking goofy as hell.

'Ma. Is it time for school?'

'No, it's still Sunday. Let's go to the beach. We can catch the sunrise.'

Oh, God. Sleep was damn near perfect. My dreams were mashing it up. But now it's done; there's no plugging back in.

'Come, let's go. Don't wake your brother.'

We drive down Bonza Bay Road in the Hyundai. Barely saying a word, still half-asleep, I keep rubbing my eyes and stifling yawns. The old lady takes her eyes off the road to peek at me. She grins like an idiot.

'We not gonna make it,' I say through another yawn. 'The sun is already almost out.'

'Yes, we will.' She pats me on the thigh, then accelerates.

We drive downhill on the final stretch of Bonza Bay Road, which ends in a parking lot. The pathway leading down towards the beach runs alongside the Quenera River. It's semi-dark, but my eyes adjust. It's high tide, and the river mouth is a swirling mass of waves where the silently flowing river meets the loud frothing ocean. The sky towards the horizon is already turning orange through a mesh of low-hanging clouds.

'Come on! We don't want to miss it!' The old lady breaks into a fast walk.

'Aah, Ma.'

She goes ahead.

It's been a minute since I was last out here. Ma is right when she says this used to be our thing. Once Ernest used to join us, but that was an eternity ago.

Ma takes off her sandals. She points at my flip-flops. I take them off. The sand is cold but soft between my toes. It gives me a boost. Ma walks away ahead of me. I walk towards the water's edge, splashing seawater onto my face and tasting salt as the water trickles down.

Ma points towards the horizon where an orange sun rises. She seems taller, even as a silhouette in the distance. She walks with freedom out here. I'm glad to see her happy. Even though I wouldn't tell her, for whatever it's worth, it was a really great idea to come out here today.

We sit on the rocks at the far end of the beach. 'You know you didn't cry when you came out,' Ma says. She has to speak loud above the wind and the waves.

'What?'

'When you were born, you didn't cry. It was so scary. I thought something happened to you.' She stares off towards the horizon. 'But everything turned out okay. The birth was so easy, and you were a good baby. As a first-time mother, I wanted to do everything right, and you made it easy.' Goosebumps appear on her skin. 'Being a mother made me so, so proud.'

People walk dogs on the beach, confidently ignoring the *No Dogs Allowed* signs.

'It was different with your brother and sister. Do you know that I almost lost my life giving birth to Izzy?'

'No.'

'You wouldn't remember. Even though you were six years old, we didn't tell you. I spent a few days in hospital. Thank goodness we both survived.'

We listen to the sounds around us. Spray from the waves hits my face.

'Sizwekazi's was also a tough pregnancy. But you never gave me trouble. You never give me trouble.'

'Ma …'

'I know you've been through a lot.' She wipes a tear from her cheek. 'I feel so guilty. Things were so different for you.'

'It's not your fault. It's just, things happen.'

She smiles, reaching out a hand. 'Come on, let's go home.'

We pass by Spargs on the way back to buy groceries.

'Have you been thinking about university?' the old lady asks, as we head back to the ride carrying shopping plastics.

'Nah. Not really.'

'You should give it some thought.' She unlocks her side. It takes a couple of jigs of the key. She reaches across from inside to unlock my side.

'What's there to think about?' I say, slamming the door harder than I intended.

The old lady sits still, watching me. 'You should think about what you want to do. I know your father wants you to follow in his footsteps but—'

'Come on, Ma. We both know that's a done-and-dusted topic.'

'No, it's not. Your father will not be paying for your university education so he can't tell you what to study.'

Why isn't she telling *him* that? Is she gassing me up so I can take the fight to Ernest myself?

'All I'm saying is: think about your options.'

She starts up the ride and we head back home.

Six

I'm in soldier mode for the first two days of the following week. Not much talking to Senzo and Roscoe. School work takes priority. I even find time to redo Ms Hargreaves' essay and write the lame-ass morality one for Mr Knowles. Some of my teachers show genuine concern for me, but that doesn't last long, since there's always something going on around here requiring their attention.

On Wednesday morning, the Batter and Brawl Twins unfortunately intercept me at the school gate. I wish *they'd* forget about me.

'Dama-nee, Dama-nee, Dama-nee,' Duncan Pederson says. 'Where have you been?' He puts his arm around my shoulders. 'You were supposed to meet me last week and sort out my science project.' He squeezes my shoulder.

'I was off sick last week.'

'He's lying,' Chad Peinke says.

'Just ask anyone in my class.'

'Did this have anything to do with you killing yourself?'

'Nah, man.'

'Well, the project is due tomorrow, so you do it tonight, china.'

Chad chuckles like the moron he is.

'I want it done nice and pretty, you check. You better impress Mr Barnes. You hear me?'

'Yeah, man.'

At the end of third-period Biology class, Senzo intercepts me. 'Yo, my nigga, we gots to talk.'

Roscoe comes out of the classroom after me and Senzo intercepts him too. 'Yo, cats, can we talk?'

The three of us head to the cafeteria and grab a table. The place is a circus: long queues and rowdy boys.

'Look, cats, I say enough of this,' Senzo says. 'We need to get past it. So what y'all say? Big Ros, you cool?'

'Ja, I'm fine, bra.' Something in his voice is far from convincing.

'Big Bo? We all boys?'

'Yeah, man.' I take Roscoe's outstretched hand.

'Well, all right then,' Senzo says, relieved.

Honest to God, I'm glad we speaking again, even though I know the tension isn't entirely gone. Trying to ignore these cats is a lot of frustrating work.

My next appointment with Mr Knowles is at break-time. I don't mind seeing him today; I feel like talking. I still think it's kind of whack that a school deputy is the school psychologist. Why would any kid in their right mind speak to him? Everybody would think you're a snitch – snitching on your damn self. Anyways, I figure this is the second-last session, and if it goes well, he might make it our last.

We shoot the breeze for a while before he gets to the heavy questions, a typical strategy that I see right through.

'So tell me about your father.' He sits with his hands on top of his crossed legs.

'He's a father. What can I say?'

'What does he do for a living?'

'He's a lawyer. Runs his own firm.'

'What kind of law does he practise?'

'I don't actually know, Sir. We don't really talk about it.' What I do know is that it's pretty much a failed business. I don't even know if Ernest has any clients left.

'What do you talk about?'

'Everything and nothing. He knows a lot, since he reads a lot. But I can't say we talk about anything in particular.'

'So you do talk?'

'Yeah, mos def.'

'How would you describe your relationship?'

'It's cool, I guess. I mean, he's a father. What do fathers talk about with their children?'

'You tell me.'

I shrug.

'Okay. Tell me about your last conversation. When was it?'

'I can't say, Sir. Maybe some time over the weekend.'

'That's three to four days ago. Is your father a busy man?'

'I guess so.' Yeah, Ernest is busy all right. Only he knows with what.

'What do you want to study after school?'

Is this all grown-ups ever think about? Jesus Christ. 'I'm not really sure, Sir. I still need to decide.'

'Well, you're in Grade 11 now, you should have some idea.'

'Right.'

'How do you feel about law?'

'It's not for me, Sir. The old man would be pretty happy, though.'

'Why?'

'He has this idea that I'm going to study law at Rhodes University, here at the East London campus, and then work with him at the firm. I'm not so sure about that.'

'What's your plan, then?'

'I don't know, but I know it ain't law.'

'Does your father know you're not interested in law?'

'Not really.'

'You haven't told him?'

'He doesn't listen too good.'

'I see.'

He asks me more questions about the fam. It's funny how much a session with a shrink is like a boxing match: jabbing, deflecting, bobbing and weaving. You need strength and good speed work. Some of

Mr Knowles's questions are teasers, like he's jabbing, then out of no-where he throws something serious like an uppercut, a hook or a real powerful-ass haymaker.

'So I read through your two essays. I'm glad to see a change. How do you feel now about your original submission?'

'It affected people around me. My moms, my friends, and I suppose the school.'

'How did they react?'

'Disappointed, mostly.'

'And how does that make you feel?'

'Whack, Sir – I mean not so good. I don't want people upset on account of me. People are dealing with their own dramas, you know. They don't need me adding to them.'

'So what would you do differently?'

'I don't know.'

'How about telling them what you're going through?'

'Oh, yeah. Definitely.'

'Or telling them regularly what they mean to you?'

'Yes, of course, Sir.'

'What was your father's reaction?'

Bob and weave, bob and weave, avoid those powerful-ass hay-makers. 'He was surprisingly okay.'

'Explain.'

'He didn't make a big deal about it. They spoke, he and my old lady, and I guess they came to some sort of agreement.'

Mr Knowles watches me closely. He wants to say something, but he's trying to find a nice way of doing it without upsetting the to-and-fro of the conversation. 'Okay. Who would you say you're closest to?'

'My friends Roscoe and Senzo.'

'What is the greatest thing you've done for either of them?'

'Um, shuuu. I don't know, Sir. What do teenagers really do for their friends?'

'I'm asking you.'

'I've known them since primary school, Sir. There isn't much we don't know about each other. We've helped each other grow, I guess. That has to count for something, right?'

Mr Knowles nods. 'Okay. So, since all of this unfolded, what has been your lowest point?'

Hmm. How do I respond to that without snitching on myself? 'Disappointing everyone, I guess.' This sounds lame, but yeah, whatever, he caught me off guard. 'Like I said earlier, I don't like to bother people with my stuff. I know life is tough for everyone, and we have to learn to deal with it appropriately.'

The twitch under Mr Knowles's eye is back for the first time this session. He stares at me, his eyes narrowing in the bony structure of his face.

The bell rings.

Thank goodness.

Mr Knowles glances at the clock on the wall and checks his watch. He eyeballs me hard for a minute. 'I guess you're free to go.'

'Great. So we done with these sessions, right?'

'Would you like another one?'

Jab, jab.

'Er, it would be great and all, but I actually think I'm fine now, Sir. You've been a great help. Thank you.'

He gets up and moves to the chair behind the desk. 'I think we should have another session, and see from there. Maybe even another, after that. Same time next week.'

Wonderful.

Victory by TKO to Mr Knowles.

Goddamn rugby practice. There are a lot of better things a person could do with their time. Unfortunately, rugby is the Gospel around here, and those of us who suck at it are the sinners. I'm in the ninth team, the lowest team in our age group. It's filled with no-hopers. Senzo's in the same team, which I don't get because he loves rugby, but I guess he sucks at it, regardless. He plays scrum-half and, fortunately for him, he suffers from short-man syndrome, which gives him the right degree of belligerence needed for that position.

Someone throws the ball in my direction. I reach for it. It hits me on the head.

Laughter. Ha, ha. Funny.

'Catch a wake-up, Dama-nee!' That's Mr Stevens, our coach. He's the worst kind of coach. I guess you have to be if they assign you to the worst team. We don't do much, except run, run and run some more, until we almost drop our guts. Mr Stevens is sadistic. He's an overgrown version of the boys at this school. I don't get these teachers who think they're funny, and act like they're the same age as the boys. What they don't get is that when they make their lame-ass jokes, the boys aren't laughing with them, but laughing at them.

'Gather around, losers.' Mr Stevens grins like a bastard.

Some of the boys laugh.

'Easiest game of the season this weekend, hey. Are you ready?'

'Yes, Sir!'

'Good, boytjies, good. We gonna klap them a good one, hey.'

'Yes, Sir!'

Laughter all round.

'All right, bugger off. All of you.'

Thank God that's over.

'You okay, Big Bo?' Senzo comes over.

'Yeah, I'm all good.'

'You sure? You don't look too hot.'

'For real?'

'Yeah, you ugly as a mug.'

I swipe a hand at him. He ducks, laughing.

'Whatever, man.'

'But for real, jokes aside. You don't look so good, dog.'

I rub a hand over my face. I don't know how I feel. I hope that isn't a sign of anything.

MaMvundla is chilling with the kids when I get to the crib. She's such a happy woman. She just gets on with it. Here she is back at work when her kid is sick. It must take some toughness to look after other people's families when yours is struggling.

In my room, I get stuck into some homework. The old lady arrives not long after.

MaMvundla heads off after she's finished cooking supper.

'Bobo, come get something to eat,' Ma hollers.

Meat, rice and veggies, that's the daily staple. MaMvundla's cooking is great, *much* better than the old lady's. Ma can cook, but I don't think she gets any joy out of it, and that comes through in the taste.

'How was your day?' Ma asks, passing me the butternut.

'All good.'

'How was practice?' Israel asks.

'Cool.'

'What position are you playing this year?'

'They got me on the wing.'

'Nice.'

'What does a wing do?' Sizwe asks. A spoonful of rice falls back on her plate.

'They catch the ball and run real fast, Siz.'

Sizwe isn't convinced. 'Don't they all do that?'

'I play eighth man,' Israel says. 'You have to be strong for that. Wings have to be fast.'

'Are you fast, Bobo?' Sizwe asks, perking up.

'Probably not.'

'So why are you the wing?'

'Never mind your cute little head. So, what's up with your recital?'

Her face brightens. She puts down her spoon. 'It's great. We ready now. Next week Thursday. Will you come?'

'Of course I will, baby girl, I wouldn't miss it for the world.'

'We'll all be there,' Ma says.

'Aaaah, do I have to be there?'

'Yes, Izzy, you do. You must support your sister.'

'But she never comes to my rugby games.'

'Don't be like that, my child.'

Sizwe can't stop smiling. Israel is trying real hard to look upset.

Ernest comes home. He takes one look at us sitting at the table, grunts – his way of greeting – and carries on down the passage.

After supper, I retreat back to my desk. I haven't sketched in days. The inspiration isn't there, even tonight. I focus instead on my homework. Duncan's science project. The bloody thing is due tomorrow and there's so much to do. It will probably take me until the early hours of the morning to complete. I don't want that. These past two days at least, I've had half-decent sleep.

Ernest appears at the door. He's holding something in his hand. 'What is this, umfana?'

'What is what?'

He glares at me. 'Is that how you speak to your father?'

'I'm just asking what you want to know.'

He throws a piece of paper at me, and I glance at it. Oh-oh.

'It's my essay.'

'What garbage is this? Heh?'

What has Ma done? 'Um, it was for school.'

'This is bullshit! How can you submit something so stupid?' He walks up close to me. He reeks like a sewer beneath a beer factory. 'Heh, boy? Say something.'

What more is there to be said?

'Speak!' He shoves me on the shoulder.

I stay quiet and avoid eye contact, trying not to provoke him.

'Not so clever now! You have nothing to say. What kind of son are you?'

'One that's nothing like you.'

'What did you say?'

'Tata, just get out. *Please*!'

'Hayibo! What did you say? You listen here ...' He lunges at me, but my counter move sends him stumbling to the floor.

We've never had this kind of beef before, but it's been coming, and I'm not backing down now.

He struggles to his feet. 'You want to fight me?'

Ma shows up at the door. 'Tata, what is happening here?'

The old man points a finger at me. 'You think you're a man?'

'Tata, please stop this.' Ma steps between us.

The old man cackles like a pirate, a real mean over-the-top laugh. 'What kind of man needs his mother to help him?'

Ma pulls him out of the room, pleading. He doesn't stop laughing.

'Bobo.'

'Just leave me alone, Ma.'

She's done enough. Betrayal is her name. How could she sell me out?

Seven

Walk. Walk. Walk. Don't stop. Find the edge of the earth. Drop over it. Don't stop falling. Scream. There's nothing to return to in that madhouse.

The old lady is a real piece of work. Just when I thought we were getting along, she goes and rats me out to Ernest, who is a straight-up son of a bitch; nothing he does is ever a surprise. But the old lady? Pretending to care about me? Taking me to the beach as if I'm still a kid, making me feel like she actually cares, and then selling me out! Yeah, she doesn't deserve any nominations for Mother of the Year.

The Caltex garage a few streets away from our crib is brightly illuminated. A petrol attendant who's half-asleep on his feet attends to the solitary car. The bright emptiness is a startling reality check, like staring into a fridge with only one item in it.

'Dammit!' A girl using the payphone to my right slams the receiver down. She could be my age. She's wearing a navy-and-white tracksuit, hair styled in a huge afro crown. 'What are you staring at?' she says.

'Nothing.' *Just your ridiculously awesome beauty.*

'Well, then, keep moving.'

'Are you okay? I mean ...'

She clicks her tongue.

Inside the store, I buy a lighter and a packet of chips. The lady at the till hardly acknowledges me; she's distracted by a small TV high in the corner.

When I walk past the payphone again, leaving the garage, the angry girl hollers. 'Hey!'

'Yo.' I stand there, fidgeting in my pockets.

'I need you to do something for me.'

'What do you need?'

'Cigarettes.'

Is she for real? 'You need me to go into the store and buy you cigarettes?'

'That's right.'

'Sure, but I don't get it.'

'Are you gonna do it or not?' She turns away.

The petrol attendant stares at me. *What's wrong with you?*

I turn back towards the store.

'Here's the money.' She holds up a R10 note.

'Nah, don't sweat it. I got it.'

Back inside the store, the lady at the till barely registers me again, her eyes still glued on the screen in the corner. She completes the transaction quickly.

'Thanks,' the girl says, snatching the cigarettes off my palm.

'Do you need an escort or something, to get home?' Is this the right question?

'No, dude, I'm fine. I live around the corner. Light?'

'Yeah, I got you.'

I spark the lighter.

'Not here.'

We walk away from the garage, towards the street. She's taller than me, and I'm not even close to being short. When we stop, she offers me a cigarette.

'Oh, no. I'm good.'

She lifts an eyebrow. 'What's the lighter for?'

I pull out my pipe and the stash from JP.

'What's that?'

'Blunt.'

'Blunt?'

'Weed.' Now it's my turn to look at her like she's the lame one.

She struggles to light a cigarette. Pretending not to notice, I take a hit from my pipe. The autumn breeze wraps itself around us. The ocean is a distant drum rhythm: kick, snare, kick-kick, snare; kick, snare, kick-kick, snare. I close my eyes and imagine a ship floating away towards the horizon in perfect time to the beat: Ernest strapped to the mast; the old lady about to walk the plank; Pastor Mzoli, Mr Knowles, Mr Summers, Ms Tudhope, Mr Stevens, the Batter and Brawl Twins, all below deck, chained to oars they use to row the boat away to infinite hell ...

'What's so funny?'

'Nothing.'

'Why do you smoke that stuff?'

'What's up with the cigarettes?'

'I asked you first.'

'Nicotine will kill you. You know that, right?'

'Drugs will mess with your head.'

I laugh. She smiles. My insides tingle like hi-hats under the rattle of drumsticks. 'But seriously, no disrespect. Smoking is not for you.'

She doesn't respond. Instead she tosses away what's left of the cigarette, pulls out some bubble gum and pops a piece into her mouth. The smell of strawberries is intense in the crisp air.

'I know you,' she says, making it sound like an accusation.

'Oh, yeah?'

'You go to St Stephen's.'

I brush my foot across the gravelly surface of the pavement.

'You walk past our school, most days, looking like the world owes you an apology.'

And there it is, her comeback. She really doesn't like being on the back foot, not even for a moment. 'So you be checking me out?'

'You wish! Why don't you try smiling sometimes?'

'Do they teach you to over-analyse people at Meredith House?'

She laughs. 'No, I just know what I see.'

'And what do you see?'

She's bored now. Her face shifts impressively fast from one expression to another in a matter of seconds.

'So, what's your name?'

'Nokwanda.'

'Hi, Nokwanda.' I stick out my hand. 'I'm Bokang.'

She leaves me hanging, just long enough. 'Thanks for the cigarettes, Bokang.'

'The pleasure is all mine.' Her hand is so warm, I don't want to let go.

'Your name isn't Xhosa.'

'Nah, it ain't. It's Sotho. My mom is from Gauteng.'

'Ooh, exotic.'

'Glad you think so. Why couldn't you buy your own cigarettes?'

'Are you a momma's boy or something?'

'What? Nah, hell no! I'm just ... me and my moms ... hey, it ain't like that.'

She grins. Her eyes press the advantage.

We watch a car drive by. The empty road leads away into the darkness.

'You look a little stressed there,' she says. 'You okay?'

'Yeah, I'm good.'

We keep our heads down as another car drives past from the opposite direction.

'So, do you often hang out in the streets after dark?' I ask, not sure what else to say.

'What kind of question is that?'

'It's a real question. I mean, what are you doing out here? These streets ain't safe.'

'Please. This is the suburbs. What can happen out here?'

'You never know.'

'Yeah, whatever.'

'So what was that phone call about?'

Her face changes again. 'It was nothing.'

'Sorry, I know it's none of my business.'

'What are *you* doing out on the streets so late?'

'I needed some air.'

'Right.' She does the bored look again.

'I'm glad I came out, though, for real. You've been worth it.'

We stand around for a bit, not saying much. I want to say more, but I'm not sure what, so I keep quiet. I figure if she wants to leave, she will.

'Well, I have to go,' she says, right on cue.

'Yeah.'

'It's been pretty cool.'

'Don't go slamming phones no more, okay?'

'Yeah. Don't go losing your mind.'

'Word.'

She disappears into the night.

I'm sitting in a small room, on a small chair. It reminds me of Mr Knowles's office. My hands are tied behind my back. Something covers my mouth, preventing me from shouting for help. Dark stains, like oil spills, run down the black and brown walls. It reeks to high hell of rotten mushrooms and months-old, soap-scum-polluted water.

Something sits in front of me in Mr Knowles's chair, shifting form like a shadow, with tiny red eyes. Every time it opens its mouth to speak, waves of something foul hit me, making my eyes water. Its voice is too loud for me to make out the words.

Other voices echo around. So many voices. One of them is the old lady's, another is Senzo's and yet another is Roscoe's. They're all trapped in the walls, the shapes of their faces making the plaster bulge.

Falling down in the dark.

Eyes open. In a classroom. Everybody staring at me.

'What. The. Hell. Is. Wrong. With. You?' Mr Stevens asks, his voice echoing.

The other kids laugh, even Senzo and Roscoe. They point at me. I'm naked.

I stand up in disbelief, knocking the desk over. My skin is pale yellow. I try to move around the desks to get away, but the other kids surround me. They chant, 'Mellow-yellow Ultra-mel! Mellow-yellow Ultra-mel!' I swing my arms, but my punches are useless. I shout at them to stop, but the words don't form.

Something falls from my mouth. I reach up. My teeth are falling out. Every single one of them dislodges from my gums and falls into my hand. I cry like a baby. I sink to my knees, covering my head, teeth scattering on the floor.

Falling.

I land on something soft.

Nokwanda's hands.

Her huge face looks down at me. Her lips are red with strawberry lip balm, the smell makes me hard. It feels so good to be in her hands. She's smiling at me. She's coming closer to kiss me.

I sit up in bed. There's a mess in my boxer shorts and some of it has spilled onto the sheets.

I rummage under my bed and pull out the old washing rag, stashed there for such incidents. I clean up the mess as best I can before storing the rag away in its secret place. The time is 3.03 a.m.

I scribble a picture of Nokwanda in my sketch pad, desperately trying to preserve that smile of hers. I can't let it fade away.

Eight

The next day, I'm chilling with Senzo and Roscoe. Today we're not in the cafeteria, where we usually spend first break. I suggest we sit all the way out on the grandstand, by the rugby fields. I don't tell them I'm on the run from Duncan Pederson, since I didn't complete his stupid project. I don't need that drama, especially not today.

'So, Enzo, you know quite a few girls at Meredith House, right?'

'You knows I'm a straight baller, pimping all them hoes. Don't be shy with yo questions. I gots you.'

Senzo is the furthest thing from a player, but he does have his ears close to the grapevine. 'Her name is Nokwanda. Know her?'

He rubs his chin like a magic lamp. Then, as if a genie has appeared from somewhere deep within his mind, he says, 'So, you've decided to up yo game. A'ight, cool. So, there's Nokwanda Mkiva, who I'd say is a six out of ten at best. She the one in Grade 10, and was with that fool, Dumisani Booi, a while back. A psycho from what I hear. You want nothing to do with her – trust me.'

'That's not the one. I know her.'

'Then there's Nokwanda Sithole – no, Dlamini. Some Zulu-ass surname. She the yellow-bone one – kinda like you.' He giggles like an imp until he notices my glare. 'But she kinda young, dog. She only in Grade 9. She may be a seven out of ten, or even an eight, but damn, son, that's a bit young, even for you. You not that desperate, are you?'

'Nah, man.'

'Cos I can hook you up, for real.'

'I said nah, man. She's not the one. The one I'm talking about is tall, with long legs and a lot of hair – all natural in an afro.'

'Ah-ha! Brother Damane, Brother Damane! Looks like you been struck by the love bug. You got it bad, dog!' He indulges himself in laughter.

'So you do know her?'

'That lovely young thang would be Nokwanda Bilitsha, a definite ten out of ten and definitely out of yo league, Brother Damane. I love you, man, but I can't let you commit suicide like that.'

Suicide. *Suicide*. SUICIDE.

'So what do you know about her?'

'Shuuu, you should be asking what I don't know about her. She in Grade 12, plays first-team netball, been at Meredith House for over a year now. Lives with her pops and stepmom and a couple of raggedy-ass siblings. Stays out there in Beacon Bay, where yo ass be at. Her pops supposed to be some big-shot doctor and all.'

I stare at Senzo.

'What, man?' He holds his hands up in innocent protest.

'How do you know all of this?'

He rolls his eyes. 'Because, dummy. I be the s to the E to the N to the Zee, and if you wanna feel me, then you add an o, cos you gots to know. You feel me?'

'Whatever, man.'

'Don't be hating on me cos I knows my shit.'

'Are you going to tell him,' Roscoe says in a bored voice, 'or should I?'

'Tell me what?'

'Nah, you tell him that part, Big Ros.'

'What part?'

'No, you tell him, bra, since you the s to the E to the N—'

'Man, shut yo curry-eating ass up!'

Roscoe takes a swipe at Senzo, barely missing his head.

'Cats, could one of you level with me, please?'

'A'ight, a'ight. Easy, Big Bo. But if you thinking what I think you're thinking, and feeling what I hope you ain't feeling, then you ain't gonna dig what I gots to say.'

'What, dog?'

'Nokwanda Bilitsha is not only out of yo league, son, but she be Napoleon Dikembe's woman. They have this non-stop, on-and-off, psychopassion thing going.'

Napoleon Dikembe is in Grade 12 at our school and plays eighth man for the first rugby team. He's the size of a minibus and the shade of oil in a drum kept in the boiler room in hell. Nobody comments on his skin tone, though – to his face, anyway – because of his size and reputation.

'How do you know all of this?'

'Again with the stupid-ass questions,' Senzo says. 'Everybody knows, man.'

'Except you, bra,' Roscoe adds, 'cos you mos busy.'

'Why you even asking about her?'

'I met her last night. We had a dope time.'

Senzo and Roscoe exchange a look.

'Stay away from her, dog. I don't know what happened last night, but I do know that nigga Napoleon crazy as a mug. He be jealous and having mad-issues.'

'Don't you remember what he did to Tulani, bra?' Roscoe asks, shaking his head.

'Nah, what happened?'

'Jesus Christ, Bo, where you been, dog?'

'He's always distracted, with his head in the clouds.'

'For real, this shit's gotta stop. Come back to us.'

'Whatever. I don't know what you cats on about.'

'Come on, you know you have your moments. Where you disappear? And nobody knows what's up with you? We here for you, man.'

The bell rings.

We head off back to class, Senzo to lower-grade Maths and Roscoe and I to English. This class sucks since the drama with my essay; Ms Hargreaves is always mad-twitchy around me now.

'So have you decided on your options?' Roscoe asks.

'What?'

'University.'

'Oh. No, not yet.'

I hate this topic, it's all Roscoe ever wants to talk about these days. We barely through our Grade 11 year and he's already talking about careers. He already knows he wants to do accounting at UCT or Wits.

'I've been checking out the res options, eksê.'

He goes on and on, in every class after English. By the time second break comes, I want to be as far away from him as possible.

We track down Senzo. I'm hoping he can help me change the topic.

'Yo, Enzo, what the deal?'

'Eyo, cats.'

'What up?'

'Nothing.' Senzo avoids eye contact.

'Are you sure, man?'

'Yeah, it's just, I can't hang.'

'What?'

Two boys approach us from behind: Siyabulela Rulashe and Kenneth Mahlathi. 'Eksê, Senzos, you good?'

'Yeah, I'm good, bras.'

'Let's go.'

Senzo walks off with these two fools as if he doesn't know us.

'Yo, what kind? This bra is friends with Siya and Kenneth now?'

'Yeah, Big Ros, that's what time it is.'

Roscoe laughs. 'Since when?'

'Since now, Big Ros. The three of them going to bush in June. Remember?'

'Oh, ja.'

'So now they can't be seen with us boys no more, since they becoming men and all.'

'Eish, you bras and your manhood. When are you going?'

'I don't know.'

'Let's go sit by the hockey fields.'

'I can't. There's something I gotta take care of. I'll catch you after break.'

I sneak out the front gate, and head for the spot under the trees by Westwood train station. I spend the entire break there, thinking about what Senzo and Roscoe told me about Nokwanda. Napoleon Dikembe. Really?

The last two classes of the day are a breeze. There's no rugby practice today, thank God.

After school I pass Meredith House, hoping to see Nokwanda, but that doesn't happen. She's on my mind all the way home.

Nine

Friday is usually one of my favourite days of the week – there's nothing better than spending the afternoon with the cats, working on the comic book. This Friday, though, is just lame. It drags on and on, and I can't wait for it to be over. Not only do I spend most of the day avoiding Duncan, but I'm also avoiding Senzo and Roscoe. I don't sit with them during break, and I barely say a word to Roscoe when he's next to me in class. After school I don't explain to them why I can't hang.

As soon as school is out, I head over to the Meredith House gate, scanning the area for Nokwanda. I don't see her, so I catch a taxi to Beacon Bay. I hope to see her as I walk towards the crib, but that doesn't happen.

The best part of this Friday is that Ernest isn't home. The old lady has church things to attend to, while Sizwe is away at a sleepover. I kick it at the crib with Izzy, and that's nice and peaceful.

Saturday morning comes. The old lady drops Izzy and me at our respective schools for our rugby games. I catch up with Senzo at our team warm-up.

'Well, well, well. If it ain't Bokang Houdini.'

'Come on, man, get off it. What up?'

'All good, dog. What up witchu?'

'I'm all good. Thought you didn't have time for us common folk.'

'Whatchu on about?'

'You hanging with the big boys now, or should I say the big men.'

'Don't give me grief. You know how it goes.'

'Whatever.'

The game against Sandhill High goes well, and we win comfortably. Mr Stevens is happier than a maggot in a dead dog's eye socket.

I leave the change rooms with Senzo. 'Nice one, Big Bo, you actually caught a ball or two.' He gives me dap.

We run into Roscoe coming from his hockey game. 'Yo, Big Ros, what the deal?'

'Eksê, bras. Did yous win?'

'You know, mos,' Senzo says.

'And you?' I ask.

'Two-one, easy.'

'Nice.'

'Yo, cats, what time's the first-team netball game at Meredith?'

Senzo and Roscoe stop walking, eyeballing me like I lost my damn mind or something.

'Whatchu just ask, nigga?'

'Come on, man, you heard me.'

'Please tell me you ain't going over there for this chick? Pleeeease.' He begs with his hands clasped together.

'Why else would I go there? Come on, cats, what time's the game?'

'What about our first-team game?' Roscoe says.

'Come on, you cats know the netball ends way before the rugby. We'll be back in time.'

'*We* ain't going nowhere, man.'

'You can't let me go over there on my own.'

'If you dumb enough to go over there in the first place, then yo ass deserves to be alone.'

'Is that so? Is that how you really feel?'

He holds his hands out. 'You leave me no choice, dog – that girl comes with mad-issues.'

'Big Ros? What about you?'

'Going there's stupid; we've told you why. Forget about this girl.'

Roscoe stares at me while Senzo looks away. We've been here before. We keep coming back to this same point, again and again, the intervals getting shorter. Something has got to give.

'I can't believe you cats. What ever happened to one for all and all for one?'

Roscoe laughs. 'Yeah, you tell us.'

'Whatever. I'm not gonna stand here debating this. Peace out.'

I head out the school gate towards Meredith House. I've never been there before in my eleven years at St Stephen's. Can you believe it? They do a good job of segregating us, something I've never truly understood. I know at our school it's certainly not helping us mature. A concentration of boys brings out the worst qualities of masculinity: aggression, immaturity, pack mentality and small-mindedness, to name a few. The school keeps on churning out more of what the world doesn't need.

Outside the Meredith House gate, I take in the scene: girls everywhere, frolicking and chatting. This is it: I can't chicken out now. The layout of the buildings is confusing and I have no idea where I'm headed. The sound of cheering leads me to the netball courts, where a big crowd is gathered.

Nokwanda isn't part of the current game on the court. The rules of netball are beyond me. Screaming, shouting, jumping, clapping, all meaningless excitement. The game ends, and I think Meredith House has won because they scream the loudest and do some chirpy war cries. New players take the court and the singing from the stands gets crazier. This must be the first-team game. Nokwanda is there in the middle, her huge afro making her look like some sort of African goddess. I clap loudly, as if she can hear me.

The game starts and again I find myself wondering what the heck is going on. The ball flies around, the girls run, but whoever has the ball stands still. It's quite a trip. Nokwanda has a huge *GA* written on her back. I don't even know what that stands for. Girl Avenger. Girl Awesome. Go Away. All I know is I'm glad I'm here. Every time she gets the ball, the crowd goes nuts, and I can tell she's the star of the team. She does plenty of scoring.

At half-time, I move a little closer. Nokwanda must see that I'm here.

The second half is as frenetic as the first. Meredith House must be winning because the home crowd is going bananas. I'm standing as close as I can to the court without actually being on the court. Nokwanda doesn't see me, though.

The game ends and Meredith House girls swarm the courts. More cheering, screaming and singing. I have to move back not to get trampled in the mad-rush. Nokwanda is surrounded by the crowd. This is as close as I'll get to her. That's all right, though. I sit on the fast-emptying stand and watch from a distance. Everyone walks off towards the buildings. I stay until I'm the only one left by the courts. Leaves fall from the surrounding trees, mostly missing the netted hoops on poles, like aimless shots or misdirected hopes.

I take a taxi home. I figure nobody's going to miss me at the St Stephen's College first-team rugby game. At the bottom of Old Transkei Road, just before Batting Bridge, the taxi stops. A lady with a head wrap and a quiet toddler get off. She's carrying shopping plastics. She places them on the side of the road and fiddles with the sliding door of the taxi. It comes off its hinges, almost knocking her over. One of her shopping plastics spills, sending groceries scattering on the side of the road.

Nobody in the taxi moves to help her. I'm all the way in the back; no chance of me being a hero. Everybody watches the taxi driver giving the woman a death stare.

'Fix it,' he says, looking like a guy who's not shy with his fists.

The poor woman struggles hopelessly before two random cats walking by stop to help. Lucky for her, because the taxi driver is for real ready to give her a serious beatdown.

On the other side of the taxi, a black car drives by slowly. It's the same one from my dream. It's the one that had the dude in a black hood who kept saying *Find it, Bokang, you must find it.* By the time I look ahead again, the taxi door is back in place and we moving.

When I get to the crib, I kick it for a while on my own, before the old lady returns with the kids. Sizwe can't stop babbling about her recital and Israel wants to know all about the rugby.

Late in the afternoon, the old lady hollers. 'Bobo, phone call.'

I take it in the dining room.

'What you up to?'

'Er, excuse me, but who's this?'

'It's the girl who walks the streets at night.'

'Oh, snap. Yo, I'm good. Nokwanda, damn. What up witchu?'

'I'm good, thanks. What you doing?'

'I'm talking to you.'

'No, dummy. I mean what are you up to?'

My brain is in overdrive, I want to say so many things. 'Nothing much. Why? You want to take me out?'

'As if you'd be so lucky.'

Ouch.

She laughs. I laugh too, even though I feel as nervous as a comedian with no jokes.

Silence.

'I saw you at the game today.' I can almost hear her smile. It feels like she's laughing at me.

'Oh, you did?'

'Yeah. Thanks.'

'For what?'

'For coming to watch, support or whatever. You were there for me, right?' She's chewing something.

My laugh sounds stupid. 'Yeah, maybe I was.'

'Good.'

'I didn't think you checked me, though.'

'Of course I did. In case you didn't notice, there weren't many boys from St Stephen's. Everybody saw you.'

Everybody? That can't be good. 'Oh. Right. So why didn't you acknowledge me or something?'

'I was in the game.'

'You quite the superstar.'

'I am, actually. I thought I'd see you after.'

'Sorry, I had to be out. You really are a star though.'

'Yeah. Whatever.'

'For real.'

'Thanks.'

Silence.

'Hold up. How'd you get my numbers?'

'Duh. Telephone book.'

'But how did you get my surname?'

'What difference does it make?'

'None, I guess.' Dammit. She probably thinks I'm an idiot – *which I am*.

'Good. Just be grateful you got a call.'

'Yes, Ma'am.'

'So, now I got your numbers, and I know where you live.'

'I guess you do.'

'Well, I have to go.'

'Wait. Is that it?'

'Yeah, what more were you expecting?'

An invitation? A declaration of love? A touch from that warm hand? 'Nothing, I guess, but it's dope chatting with you.'

'Yeah. We'll do it again soon.'

'All right. Later, then.'

'Bye, Bokang.'

'Bye, Nokwanda.'

Ten

On Wednesday morning, the following week, I'm sitting in class writing Nokwanda a letter. I'll probably never give it to her, but that doesn't stop me going with the feeling. These days I've been sitting at the back of the classroom, away from Roscoe.

In fifth-period Biology class, Ms Meadows is more excitable than usual. 'Boys, settle down. Today we have a very special guest with us, all the way from the United Kingdom. He's an exchange scholar, here for the rest of the term. Boys, please welcome Humphrey Thorpe.'

A tall kid with a big-ass head comes into the classroom. Dude is seriously pale. His ears are a wonder. Some of the boys, including me, laugh. Embarrassment spreads like spilt ink across Humphrey Thorpe's pasty face.

'Come now, boys, settle down. Humphrey, tell us a bit about yourself and where you come from.' Ms Meadows sits on her desk, looking eager.

Humphrey is not having a good time up there. His accent is thick as hell, and I can't believe he claims to be speaking English.

'So what do you enjoy doing in your spare time?' Ms Meadows asks encouragingly.

'He spanks his monkey,' I chirp from the back.

The class goes bananas. Angus Mathews and Cyril January high-five me. I lay down on my desk, trying to hide.

'Hey! No, boys! That's not how we behave!'

The laughter continues; some of the boys clap.

'Who said that? Tell me now!' Ms Meadows is on her feet. She's so short she might as well be sitting.

'Bokang Damane, Ma'am.' The snitch can only be Rory Beard, sitting in the front.

The laughter dies down.

'No, Bokang, that's not nice,' Ms Meadows says.

Humphrey Thorpe from the United Kingdom continues his little talk.

When the double period ends, everybody shuffles out for second break.

'Bokang, can I see you for a minute?' Ms Meadows says.

Good grief. What now? Roscoe gives me a disapproving look on his way out. I almost stick my tongue out at him, but think better of it.

Ms Meadows closes the door, points to a seat in the front row and sits right up close to me. 'Bokang, what you did was really unkind. I'm really disappointed in you.'

'But Ma'am, what did I do?'

'Bokang, you embarrassed another boy who was already feeling nervous. Can you imagine what it must be like for him, being in a different country, and having people laugh at him?'

'But Ma'am—'

'What do you think he's going through?'

'I don't know, Ma'am.'

'What was it like for you, when everyone was talking about you? I bet that wasn't fun, hey?'

No, it wasn't, that's for sure.

'I can tell you, Humphrey is not feeling very happy right now.'

Ms Meadows is good peeps. I hate seeing her all serious like this. 'Yes, Ma'am.'

'Bokang, I know you haven't been yourself lately. But that's no excuse to take it out on others. I expect more from you.'

'Yes, Ma'am.'

'I don't know what's going on with you. Do you know what the teachers think of you?'

'No, Ma'am.'

She holds her small face in her hands. 'I'm tired of always defending you, Bokang.'

Defending me?

'You need to help me to help you.'

That right there is Mr Knowles-speak.

'Everyone is confused about you. You get good marks in class – or you used to. But then at times you're impossible – like today, showing complete disregard for everyone. Hey? Don't you care?'

This is killing me. I wish she'd quit already. 'Ma'am, I'm sorry you disappointed.'

'I wish you weren't sorry, Bokang. I really wish you could hear me.'

'I am hearing you, Ma'am.'

'No, unfortunately, I don't think you are.'

I could really do with a blunt, but my money is funny, and I'm hoping JP is feeling generous today. I mission to his spot after school. I'm supposed to be at rugby practice, but I give that a skip.

JP ain't home. Nobody is. I ring the bell until his little hairy dog, Rasta, barks so much it freaks me out.

Dammit.

Home doesn't seem like a great place to be right now, so I mission to Bonza Bay Beach, uniform, schoolbag and all. It's low tide at the river mouth today. I don't go near the beach sand; I can't exactly walk there in my school shoes.

Parked cars overlook the river. Two dudes sit in one, looking suspicious as hell. A group of other dudes stand next to their car, drinking beers. I sit on one of the benches and stare at the river water. I can see the mucky bottom; beer bottles lurk there like sunken battleships. More spill over from the bin next to me. Cigarette butts all over the place. Scribbles cover the bench I'm chilling on:

Stacy for Brad.
Ken and Roxy Forever.
There is no future.
Bugsy was here.
Eat shit.

I don't have anything clever to write. Not on the bench, anyways. I pull out my rhyme book and put some thoughts to paper. The rhythm is off today, the lyrics lacking.

The walk back home sucks. When I get there, the old lady hovers around me like she wants to talk, but I don't give her the time.

Ernest appears at the door while I'm sitting at my desk. 'I need your help, boy. Come.'

I follow him down the passage, dragging my feet. He's wearing his usual attire of three-piece suit, except now he's in his socks, with his blazer and tie off and the first couple of buttons of his shirt undone. He holds a lit cigarette and the smoke billows all around like some sort of essence of him. The old lady has asked him plenty of times not to smoke inside, but I guess he's the man of the house and does what he wants.

We step into Sizwe's room.

'I need you to go through this.' He points to the bookshelf. 'I'm looking for books on tax law and the South African Revenue Service. SARS. You got it?'

'Sure.'

'There are at least six books somewhere on this shelf. We must find them.' He pats me on the back before disappearing out the door, followed by his smoke.

Ernest loves his books; they take up so much space in the house. This shelf in Sizwe's room is the biggest one – it takes up the entire wall. The room divider in the TV room is basically a bookshelf. The dining room has two shelves on either side of the table. The garage is filled with boxes of books waiting to be placed on shelves. One of Ernest's father-and-son tasks we've yet to get to is building shelves in the garage for his books.

It takes me twenty-five minutes to go through the entire shelf properly. Four of the books fit the description.

The old man sits in the dining room, with open books covering the table. 'What did you find, boy?'

I show him.

'Well done! Yes, these are the ones. You checked the whole shelf?'

'Yes, Tata. What do you need all of these for, anyway?'

'I'm working on a new case. Check the year of publication on all these books. Then line them up in order, from the oldest, this side, to the most recent, this side. Got it?'

'Yes, Tata.'

We get to it, all while Ernest keeps chatting, truly in his element. It's not so bad being around him when he's like this; it reminds me of days when I was younger.

Eleven

'**B**allet recital!' Sizwe explodes into the room. 'Get up! Get up! Get up!'

'Damn, Siz, yeah, we up.'

Israel moans. 'No, we not.' He covers his head.

Sizwe jumps on top of me. I tickle her and she releases glass-shattering shrieks. She jumps on top of Israel. 'Get up! Get up! Get up!' She jumps off him and vanishes out the door like a tiny whirlwind.

It's not often Sizwe gets up before the rest of us. The old lady hasn't left yet – I can hear her chatting to Sizwe. There's something to look forward to today; Sizwe's excitement is contagious.

The old lady helps Sizwe get ready for school and leaves out the breakfast cereals. She takes off, leaving me to finish getting the kids ready. Surprisingly, Ernest is already up, sitting by his books in the dining room, eating something the old lady threw together for him. Sizwe sits next to him, eating her cereal.

'So my little princess is going to her first ballet recital.' Ernest laughs from deep within his chest.

'Will you come, Tata?'

'Of course I will, my little princess. I wouldn't miss it for the world. Not even a natural disaster will stop me from being there.'

'What's a natural disaster?'

Ernest himself could be defined as one. If he doesn't show up tonight, that could be considered another, for Sizwe anyways. 'Don't you worry about that, Siz. Finish up, we gotta go. Izzy, are you done?'

'Yeah.' He's in the kitchen, chewing and putting on his blazer at the same time.

Ernest calls Sizwe and Israel to stand one behind the other in front of him, lining up for kisses from Daddy of the Year. He starts with Israel, holding his ears out and kissing him three times on the lips. Then he does the same with Sizwe. (Being older suddenly feels like a blessing.) 'Shine today, my children.'

'Yes, Tata.'

'Come on, yo, we gonna be late. Bye, Tata.'

It's dark out as we head for the taxis. I'm under-dressed. Sizwe has a scarf that Ma insisted she wears. Israel, is well, Israel; the elements don't seem to affect him like the rest of us.

If Ernest still had his ride, he would be saving us a hell of a lot of time, not to mention discomfort.

'What time do you finish school today, Bobo?'

'Half-two, Siz.'

'Will you come home before the recital?'

'Yes, Siz.'

'Okay.'

'And you'll come to the recital with us, with Mama?'

'Yes, Siz.' I laugh.

We climb into a taxi, sitting in the row behind the driver. 'I'll be in the front row in the recital.'

'Yes, Siz, I know.'

She continues chatting about the recital as we head toward Chester-field Primary. She talks so much I can't tell if it's excitement or nervousness. Anyways, the poor thing deserves to be excited about something.

The taxi drops them off outside their school.

'See you later, Bobo!'

'Bye, Siz.'

Israel shakes his head at his little sister. People in the taxi find her amusing.

'Later, Izzy.'

I get off the taxi on Murray Road in front of St Stephen's College. Boys in their maroon-and-navy blazers get out their parents' rides and head through the gate.

Roscoe stands outside first-period English. He's trying to look hard but not pulling it off.

'Big Ros.'

'Bokang.'

'Why you over here looking like some sort of bum or something?'

'Whatever. Shut up.'

'Did you hear back from UCT?'

A smile spreads across his face. 'Yeah, actually, a guy called me back. Gave me all this info.'

It's great to be chatting with the big guy again, like things used to be. In class, we sit next to each other.

During second break I have a session with Mr Knowles. I'm very co-operative in the session. It works, because he tells me this is our last one. 'So how do you feel about the past few sessions?'

'Good, Mr Knowles, Sir. I mean, I've had the opportunity to open up about things, you know. At first it wasn't easy. I guess it's never easy, but if I try, then I can benefit.'

He nods happily. 'Always remember, you don't have to wait until things get really terrible before you seek help. I'm here for you. Mr Summers is here for you. The college is here for you.'

'Yes, Sir.'

'So the final thing I'd like to know: what are you looking forward to in the next few weeks?'

Hmm, that's an insanely good question. Seeing Nokwanda again, that's for sure. Sizwe's recital, believe it or not. Even Ernest's new tax case. After all the reading we've done together, I'm actually interested. Damn, that's crazy. Mr Knowles doesn't need to know all of that, though, but I do need to tell him something to keep him off my back.

'Well, Sir, Roscoe and I have been researching universities, and we've received some replies.'

This is not entirely true.

'We also working on a comic-book series together, with Senzo, and I always look forward to working on that.'

Well, that's very true.

'In fact, they've been helping me look at possibilities, of studying cartooning and drawing, at these universities.'

This is not exactly true, but it does sound like something worth pursuing.

'That's great, Bo-gang. I'm pleased to hear that.'

'Yes, Sir. Thank you. Also, this evening my little sister is performing in a ballet recital, and I'm really looking forward to that.'

Mr Knowles smiles like I've never seen him smile before. 'That's wonderful, really wonderful.'

Okay, I didn't mean to let him in on that, but it's a perfect way to convince him of my mended ways.

'Well, all the best, young man.' He stands up, sticking out his hand. I shake it and say goodbye.

After school, I head for Meredith House. Many cars are parked outside the school, and girls are pouring out the gate like ants from a flooding anthill. I don't see Nokwanda anywhere, but I figure she must be somewhere deep inside the campus. I'm not allowed to enter these hallowed grounds without an official reason, but today it's worth the risk.

I walk in, not sure where I'm going, but something draws me towards the netball courts. A few girls out there are practising, but they look way too young to be teammates of Nokwanda. If she isn't here, I'm not sure where she could be.

I head towards the buildings, which are similar to ours: two storeys high, red-tiled roofs, white walls and French-style windows. Again I wonder why they segregate us from the girls when so much about these two schools is the same.

The corridors are deserted now that school's out. That suits me fine. Of course, it could also mean that Nokwanda herself is not here. I walk through two floors of one building and move into the next. On the second floor of the second building, I pass a couple of girls who giggle at me like I'm a celebrity.

The letter I wrote to Nokwanda is in my blazer pocket. It's been chilling there since yesterday. Who knows, I might just give it to her after all.

I finish walking through the second building and consider giving up. This was probably a dumb-ass idea. A group of three girls in netball gear stand in the corridor.

'Sorry, do you know where I can find Nokwanda?'

'Nokwanda who?' the chubby one asks. She isn't pleased to be answering my question.

'First-team netball?'

'Oh,' the short one with braces says, giving her friends a look.

I wait, but she doesn't say anything more. 'So? Where is she?'

'What do you want with her?' the chubby one asks.

'Er, none of your business?'

'Pssss, you two deserve each other.'

The other two girls laugh. The third one, who hasn't said a word, high-fives the chubby one.

'Whatever. Are you going to help me out or not?' I say to the one with braces. She has the most innocent face.

'She's probably at drama. They have rehearsals today.'

'Right. And where would that be?'

'School hall. On the other side of that building.'

'Cool.'

I head off in the direction the girl points towards. I convince myself not to make a big deal about the chubby girl's comment. I approach the hall and peek through the double doors. I immediately see Nokwanda; it's hard to miss those legs and that afro. She's way up in front, and I know she can't see me from where I'm standing. Going inside is too risky; a teacher is with them, yelling instructions. If only I could sneak in and sit in the back and watch from there. If only there was some way of letting Nokwanda know I'm here. She looks happy fooling around with the other girls. I could stand here forever just—

'Excuse me, young man. Oi!'

A grumpy teacher has shown up behind me, a woman wearing a brown-and-green dress that makes her look like a giant bullfrog. 'What are you doing here?'

'I, um, er ... I'm looking for my sister.'

'You know you are *not* allowed here. What's your name?'

Stuff that. I bolt back in the direction I came from. She yells, but I don't look back.

Instead of running through the buildings, I run around them towards the front of the school. I don't stop when I'm in the front and it's clear the bullfrog lady isn't chasing me. I don't stop when the security guard at the gate looks at me funny. I don't even stop when I make it out the gate. I keep going, going and going, until I'm a good long way away. My chest hurts something awful. I'm laughing hysterically, bent over with my hands on my knees.

When I get to the crib, the old lady is already there with the kids. Sizwe is dressed in her pink ballet outfit, her face shiny with Vaseline.

'Looking good, Siz, looking really good.'

'Thanks, Bobo.'

'Hey, my child,' the old lady says, 'how are you?'

'I'm all good, Ma.'

I keep my distance. Ever since Ernest found out about my suicide essay and we had that showdown, I haven't been really chatty with the old lady. She tried to tell me she didn't snitch to Ernest, saying he must have found the essay in her bag when he was scrounging for loot. Whatever – either way he wouldn't have known had she not kept the damn thing in her bag.

After eating a quick supper, we prepare to leave. As we exit the crib, Sizwe stands frozen by the door. 'Where's Tata?'

'I don't know, my child. Come, we have to go. We'll be late.'

'Maybe he's already there?'

The look on Sizwe's face is a killer. I don't like seeing her like this. I lift her up and cradle her in my arms. 'Come on, Siz, you have a show to put on. I'm sure he'll meet us there.'

I don't know why I'm telling her this. I really shouldn't. I feel like a dodgy parent making empty promises. Ernest won't be there, she never should've expected him to be. Holding her in my arms and walking towards the car, I realise I can't protect Sizwe from the world – nobody can. Not me nor Israel as older brothers, not Ma, and certainly not Ernest.

A surprising number of people attend the recital. But then again, I suppose people will do anything for their kids. Fancy cars park all the way up and down Molineux Avenue outside Chesterfield Primary. I'm glad we on time for a change.

Every kid in a ballet outfit is accompanied by their family. Teacher Lyndsay – Sizwe's teacher – stands to one side collecting all her charges, a mother hen with all her little chicks.

'Good luck, Siz. Do your thing.' I give her dap. She runs off to be with her teacher and friends. They use a different entrance to the hall.

We join the queue of family members entering the hall. We find seats towards the front, on the left-hand side of the hall. We nine rows from the front. Israel sits between me and the old lady, bored and irritable.

The hall is bigger and fancier than the one at our school, which surprises me. The curtains on the stage are a dark velvety maroon. Colourful flags hang from the walls in between the awards boards. I'm sure some of them represent the different houses at the school. At least three galleries, two on the sides and one at the back, make up the additional seating areas.

In front, to the side of the stage, on our side of the hall, a lady sits at a piano. She smiles at the crowd as if she's a piece of art. Her cheeks wobble like that jelly the old lady used to make for Sunday lunch. She clearly can't wait for the show to begin.

Soon enough, Teacher Lyndsay comes on stage in front of the curtain, the humming voices in the crowd settle down, and she makes an opening speech. She explains the show and the journey to get the kids prepared. The endless hours, the joys and tears, and the support from families that made it all possible. She mentions something about clapping and no flashing cameras. After an enthusiastic round of applause, she moves off and the curtains go up. The lady on the piano does her thing – she clearly knows what she's doing. The crowd oohs and aahs, some people clap, and smiles fill the hall.

Sizwe and her crew are quite something, even I can admit that. Their outfits are enough to pull at the heart strings. Their movements are perfect, all the practice paying off. For kids this small, this is impressive. There's a bit of fun in it too; some of the movements cause laughter and clapping from the crowd. Even Izzy is smiling; I guess the tough-guy routine isn't for him.

The girls keep interchanging with every song; some go off stage and others take their places. Siz is in every song so far. I don't think I've ever seen her exert herself so much. She's really loving it.

'Go, girls! Ja!' Somebody in the back cheers and claps louder than anybody else. 'Ja! That's it!' His cheering and clapping is out of sequence with everybody else's. 'Go, Sizwekazi! Ha! Wonderful!'

Me and the old lady exchange a glance. She's too scared to turn around and check who that voice belongs to, even though she already knows. There at the back, standing under the lights, is T Ernest Damane in his trademark three-piece suit, looking marvellously sloshed.

The expression on my face confirms what the old lady already knows. Dark bruises instantly appear below her eyes as if she's taken a couple of jabs from Evander Holyfield. She looks back at the stage, shook. Israel is uneasy, too. He keeps looking back at his old man, and checking me for a response.

'Brilliant! Ja! Bravo! Bravo!'

One of the fathers at the back tries to say something to Ernest.

'Voetsek! Who do you think you are?'

A murmur ripples through the crowd. Heads turn. Hands cover mouths. Eyes look about.

'That's my girl! I pay fees here. You don't tell me anything!'

The happy lady on the piano is no longer smiling; her chubby cheeks flap as she snatches glances at the back of the hall, misplaying a couple of notes in the process. Little heads on the stage look uncertainly in every direction. Poor little Siz can tell that her daddy has made an appearance, but unfortunately she can tell it ain't the daddy she likes. The poor thing can't even keep in step with the dancing.

'Get your hands off me!'

One of the fathers and a security guard drag Ernest out of the hall. It's a pity they can't gag him, cos he's shouting and making a fool of himself, and everyone else too.

The show goes on, but it's not the same. Sizwe is in tears and barely moves. Her demeanour infects those around her, so a number of the girls look unhappy even though they don't know why. Teacher Lyndsay, standing to the side of the stage, tries hard not to look horrified, but it isn't working. The whole thing is a godawful mess.

The old lady can't even look at the stage, and stares at her feet. Poor Izzy has glassy eyes.

The show finally ends and people stand up to clap. They trying to be supportive, but there's definitely a bitterness in the air.

'Come on,' Ma says, pushing Israel towards the aisle.

We squeeze past people while they clap, forcing our way out one of the side exits. The cold evening air should be a relief, but it's more like a slap across the face, waking us up to a reality we don't want to face.

'Here,' the old lady says, thrusting the car keys into my hand. 'Find your father and take him to the car. I'll find Sizwe.'

'But Ma …'

'Just do it.' She sounds like she's been arguing with the devil about a bad deal made a long time ago.

I make my way through the crowd, Israel following me at a stuttering pace, a shell-shocked soldier.

We find Ernest arguing with a group of men. 'This is disgraceful! Don't you touch me with your filthy hands. Do you even know who I am?'

'Tata.'

Ernest stiffens in the grip of two men. 'These are my boys!' he says, turning to us. 'Ha ha! Come here, my sons!'

I nod at the two men. The one who is a father is mad as hell. The security dude is either amazed or dumbfounded, possibly both. They release the old man.

'Ha ha ha! Come here, boys!' He stumbles over to us, throwing his arms around Israel and planting a boozy kiss on his forehead. I manage to evade his grasp.

'Come, Tata, let's go.'

'Is this your father?' the angry man asks, his fists clenched.

'Yeah.'

He says something to Ernest, but Izzy and I drag the old man off, supporting him on either side. A response from him could prolong this scene. Fortunately the sun has set and all we have to do is move out of the lights into the shadows.

We move quickly through the parking lot towards the gate. Ernest's wobbly legs and swinging arms don't make it easy. It's like this is a fun game to him. Some of the people recognise the old man as the person who ruined the night for everyone. Some shake their heads, others whisper to their families. We keep moving, escaping the scene.

Ernest spits as we drag him along, laughing to himself, and every now and then saying random things like 'bloody fools' and 'do they know who I am?' and 'stupid' and 'bastards'. When we get to the ride, he refuses to get inside, his second wind coming at the worst possible time. This is what happens when he's level-five-disaster drunk: his energy surges up and down; one second you think he's about to pass out, then next thing he's on a tirade, making life miserable for everyone.

Now he insists on smoking a cigarette. Fortunately, we standing too far from the main gate for anyone to recognise us.

'Where's my light, boy?' he says to Israel.

Israel mumbles a response.

Ernest pats his own pockets. I reach for his waistcoat pocket and feel for his lighter; this is where he always keeps it.

'Aha!' He fumbles with the lighter, sparking the cigarette from the wrong end. I don't bother telling him he's smoking the filter.

Ma appears, carrying Sizwe, who has her face buried in the old lady's shoulder. The poor thing.

When Ernest sees them, he says, 'My little star! Come here.' He reaches for her, but Sizwe squeals. 'Whatever! You little baby!' He takes a long drag of his cigarette, then chokes, bends over, choking some more, and eventually spits and gags. He looks at the cigarette, pulls a face and tosses it away in disgust.

We all climb into the ride, the silence like an extra passenger. The old lady drives. Ernest sits in the passenger seat, Israel behind him, me behind the old lady, and Sizwe between Israel and me, her face moist with tears.

Ernest reclines his seat in spite of Israel's protests, laughing like a pirate lord.

The old lady doesn't say anything, not even when Ernest lights a cigarette in the ride, puts the air con on full blast – even though it's a coldish evening – and insists nobody opens the windows. She doesn't say anything either as Ernest goes on and on about the injustice of his being thrown out of the recital.

Sizwe's tears are contagious, cos pretty soon Israel's eyes are streaming too. I keep my arm around Sizwe. Israel also puts an arm around her, but I think it's to comfort himself rather than her. At this point I'm wishing I had eight arms, like Dr Octopus, even if they were mechanical arms. At least they would allow me to hug both Sizwe and Israel, wipe their tears, and still punch Ernest in the face.

All the way home Ernest blasts Teddy Pendergrass from the radio, the volume getting louder and louder as we get closer to home.

'Tata, please,' Ma protests.

Ernest ignores her, smirking. Nothing pleases him more than making someone beg. The old lady knows this better than anyone. She tries her best not to indulge him, but I guess that doesn't work. After all, she's a mother, and mothers are supposed to protect their children from everything, even their father. That last feeble resistance was her best effort to protect us. There really isn't any hope for us. She's as pathetic as he is.

When we get to the house, Ernest doesn't move. He just lays there reclined in his seat, playing dead. The old lady and I exit from our side,

I cradle Sizwe, and the old lady has to help Israel out from under the reclined seat pinning him down. We leave Ernest where he is, in all his glory, listening to his Teddy Pendergrass. Even though he's lying with his eyes closed, I'm not fooled into thinking he's passed out. The predator in Ernest is like a crocodile waiting below the surface for you to come too close before launching an attack.

The old lady baths Sizwe and starts to get her ready for bed. Israel looks better, and I'm grateful for that.

I lay on the bed counting the holes in the patterns of the ceiling, but I don't even get to fifty. I rummage under my bed for my Suicide Manifesto. It's on a day like this that I get why and how a person could end their life by throwing themselves into a volcano. The medium of death suits the mood of the person taking their own life. A person overdosing on pills feels numb inside, a person gassing themselves feels choked up, a person slitting their wrists is bleeding inside, a person jumping off a bridge is falling apart, and a person jumping into a volcano is mad as hell at the world.

Israel lies on his bed in a similar position to mine. I'm holding the Suicide Manifesto, he holds an old MAD magazine, one of mine from the collection I gave him. When these family dramas happen, Israel mimics my behaviour. He's noticing that things aren't okay, and he must figure I've been noticing for a while. You have to love him for that. I wish I could spare him growing up, I really do.

'Bo-kang!'

The crocodile stirs. If I don't move, maybe he'll lose interest.

'Bo-kang!'

Israel holds his breath. If I don't face the beast, it might want a piece of him. It might want a piece of Sizwe – what's left of her, anyways. It's long since destroyed the fleshiest morsels of the old lady.

Ma enters the passage carrying Sizwe wrapped in a towel. We exchange a look. Yeah, I know. I'm the sacrificial lamb. Somebody has to be.

The door leading from the garage into the kitchen is closed. Teddy Pendergrass's 'It Don't Hurt Now' blasts behind it – this is the fourth time this track is bumping tonight. This is all a trap, of course. How did Ernest turn the music down, open the door, scream my name and then close the door, turn the music back up and lay back down in the reclined seat if it wasn't him that did all of that?

Opening the door, I find him reclined back in the passenger seat – a maneater in waiting. A leg and an arm hang out the ride. A cigarette smoulders in the hand hanging out. The music is so loud I grit my teeth. 'Tata!'

It's pointless: he can't hear me above the music. The door, the music, it's all part of the trick. This is a cunning beast; even the smouldering cigarette is part of the elaborate trap. A nip of Red Heart rum stands next to the foot hanging out the ride. I don't know where that came from – probably a stash somewhere here in the garage.

I move slowly towards the car, thinking the loud music might mask my movements, but immediately knowing better than that; this creature is too cunning. Should I prod him? Or should I turn the music down first? I decide on the latter. Reaching inside, over his heaving body, I'm aware that at any moment he could make his move. My heart beats rapidly in my chest. I turn the music off. The silence is so sudden it almost echoes.

The beast before me rolls its head from side to side on the headrest. It grunts once, twice, then lulls back into its rumbling breathing.

I sigh. I wonder how many sighs it takes to get to the withered state the old lady has reached. 'Tata.'

Nothing.

'Tata.'

The cigarette between his fingers drops to the concrete of the cold garage floor. Am I supposed to think he's more asleep than before?

'*Tata!*' I prod him on the shoulder.

He moans.

Then, in an attack of my own, I shake him roughly. '*Tata!*'

Ernest the crocodile grunts like his liver has been pierced with a spear. He blinks a few times, looking around with unfocused eyes. He always looks more beastly without his glasses. His eyes home in on me, narrowing into slits; the cunning is there.

Yeah, I see you too, old man.

He hoicks something nasty from his chest, pulling a couple of times to get to the really dark matter. He spits it onto the windscreen. It's jungle green in colour and so thick it doesn't slide down from where it splats.

'Take me inside,' he growls. He holds up his hands for me to take.

I grab his dry hands and pull.

Ernest being who he is, leans his weight back and stiffens his body. He grunts. 'Come on, boy. Pull!'

Positioning myself better and leaning my own weight back to get leverage, I pull again.

Ernest does the same thing, grunting louder this time. 'Come on! What kind of man are you? Are you a sissy?'

I take up a sturdier position and stand squarely in front of him. I pull again, and again he stiffens his body and leans back, pulling in the opposite direction. This time I let go. With his counter-pulling, he flies backwards so the handbrake digs into his scrawny back. He howls, now more like a sheep being slaughtered than a predator. The blow stuns him.

While he's in this state, I grab both his hands and pull him out of the ride. He doesn't resist. He tries to rub the spot where he got it worst, but his co-ordination is so disrupted he can barely reach.

I take him into the house all the way to the folks' bedroom and sit him down on the bed, where he topples over onto his side. The old lady stands watching, doing nothing. I turn to leave.

'Bokang.' Ernest sits up, his eyes closed. 'Take off my shoes.'

The old lady says nothing, does nothing.

I reach down and take off Ernest's shoes and socks, then turn to leave.

'Bo-kang,' he growls in a slur.

'Yes, Tata.'

'Cut my toenails.'

'No, Tata.'

'Heh? What did you say?'

'No, Tata. I'm not your slave.'

I walk out, not waiting for his response. He shouts words, but I ignore them.

The old lady tries to intervene, but I don't care.

I am done.

Book II
May 1998

Book II
May 1998

Twelve

I don't really know when Ernest started drinking. I don't really know when he became a drunk. I don't even know if there was ever a difference between when he started drinking and when he became a drunk. All I know is, things were not always like this. I clearly remember him being part of my childhood, when it was just the three of us: him, me and the old lady. I remember us doing things, going places, and actually living a life together. Not like now, where he isn't part of anything we do.

Maybe Ernest has always been this way and I was too naïve to notice, sort of like Siz and Izzy now. The only person who could tell me this is the old lady. But she's changed too, and probably because of him.

The change was sudden.

The folks started arguing all the damn time. Israel and Sizwe came along. Cash dried up. Next thing there was this *thing* hanging about and tarnishing everything, never going away. It hangs over all our heads, clinging to the walls in every room, coming off our clothes as a smell, and leaving a nasty-ass aftertaste on everything it comes in contact with. It is just there. It is about us. It is a part of us. And it *is* us, no matter how much we fight it.

It's hard to put a finger on the *thing*. Nobody talks about it, even though it manifests differently through each of us. It was there in Ernest's crocodile eyes last night. It came in the form of the bruises that appeared under the old lady's eyes. It was Izzy's sad defiance at refusing to admit what he was seeing, and it was the innocent hurt in Sizwe's tears. It was with us in the ride home from the recital.

It is the *thing* that got me sent to Dr Schultz's office all those years ago, when I had to take those goddamn pills.

And now it's back.

This morning it's out in the open. I didn't sleep at all last night, almost as if I was waiting for the *thing* to turn up again this morning. Israel didn't sleep either; he kept waking up, choking, like he was forgetting to breathe. The *thing* has got Siz real good this morning. She hasn't made it out of bed. Ma says she's sick. Now the old lady is taking the day off work to take care of Siz.

The *thing* is heaviest in the folks' room. The door is half-open, the curtains still closed. Ernest sleeps with the *thing* in there.

I really couldn't be bothered with school today. There's nothing for me there. There ain't nothing for me here at home either – except the *thing*. If I don't go, though, Izzy may never snap out of the gloom he's in.

The two of us trudge towards the taxis. Today's a bitch of a day; the winter witch's nails scratch all the way down to my balls. The taxi's warm, though, with funky smells; too many bodies crammed together, but all of them grateful to be out of the cold.

When the taxi gets to Izzy's stop, I tap him on the shoulder as he's climbing out. 'Yo, Izzy, open a can of whoop-ass on 'em.'

He gives me a faint smile. It's something. Stone Cold Steve Austin always gets a rise out of him.

Paul Rogers meets me at the main gate. 'You're late, Damane.' He isn't even a prefect yet. His punk ass is in Grade 11 with me, but he's pushing hard to be one next year.

'Whatever, Rogers.'

Mr Coleridge doesn't make a fuss about me being late for his maths class. I take my seat next to Roscoe. My focus is not on the class; I just want it to be over.

When it ends, and we heading over to the next one, Roscoe starts his usual conversation. 'How's the studying going?'

'Studying?'

'For exams, bra. You do remember we start next week?'

'Yeah, of course. It's great.' Actually I don't remember. I can't believe it's already that time again. Where has my mind been?

A hard smack to the back of my head brings me blinking back to reality. I'm trying to figure out what just happened, when a hand rips my bag from my back. Tears blur my vision.

'Dama-nee, Dama-nee, Dama-nee.'

Duncan Pederson. Lovely.

He lifts me up with his full weight and bashes me against the wall. 'You been avoiding me, china?'

'Duncan, leave him alone.' Roscoe tries to intervene.

'Shut your mouth, curry muncher, unless you wanna die with him.'

Chad Peinke. Where would Duncan be without his retarded sidekick?

My vision starts to clear; Duncan is so close, his zits threaten to pop in my face.

'You're fucking dead, Dama-nee. I failed my project because of you. Now my class mark is so low, I need a miracle to pass. What the hell is wrong with you?'

He pushes me hard, then gives me a head butt for good measure. A bunch of rubberneckers gather around, sensing blood. Roscoe stands there, not sure what to do.

Chad the retard, giggling like a hyena on meth, spills the contents of my book bag on the ground.

Duncan grabs my chin and squeezes. It feels like my jaw is gonna bust. He gives me a good slap across the face, then sends me banging into the wall. 'I'm gonna get you, Dama-nee. You're dead, boy. This is just the beginning.'

My vision lasts long enough for me to see Chad stomping on my books, then the two of them moving on. My mouth is bleeding, my cheek is burning and the back of my head hurts. Everybody stares. Laughter. Pity. Hatred. Roscoe fusses over me. He's saying something, but none of it goes in. I wish I could close my eyes and lay here forever.

I wish I could melt into the cement, melt away as if I was never here in the first place.

Roscoe helps me collect my things, and takes me to the toilets to get cleaned up. We late for our next class, but Ms Meadows doesn't make a big deal. She does fret about the cut on my lip, though. 'What happened?'

'Nothing, Ma'am.'

'But your lip is swollen!' She holds my head with her small hands.

'It's nothing, really.'

'He bumped into the back of my head, Ma'am,' Roscoe says.

'Really? How did that happen?' She frowns.

'We were, um, running in the hall, then we collided. Stupid. Yes, we know.'

'But are you okay? Both of you?'

'Yes, we're fine, Ma'am.'

Ms Meadows gives me a long stare but I avoid eye contact. 'All right, then.'

Ms Meadows could never understand how this place works. St Stephen's College is an animal factory. Bullying is not just a word here, it's a way of life. That's what you get when you cram a bunch of boys together. Most everybody gets bullied at some time while they're here, all in the name of grade privileges and traditions. You can be teased, shoved around, or whatever. Everyone also has a nickname they hate. A nickname that usually has something to do with some sort of discrimination or humiliation. They call me Mellow Yellow or Butternut. They call Roscoe Charo or Durban Curry. They call Senzo Lord of the Rings cos he's short like a goblin or Cheese cos he's all pampered. It just happens. You have to give it as well as you take it. There's nothing to report to the teachers; snitching only makes it worse.

I'm glad I had my run-in with the Batter and Brawl Twins today. I'm glad to feel something other than the *thing* cloaking me. The taste of blood in my mouth and the pain at the back of my head give me satisfaction. People can stare and laugh, but at least they don't say anything to me. This allows me to be quiet the whole day, keeping to myself.

After school, I take a taxi to Beacon Bay. With exams starting next week, we don't have time to work on the comic; besides, Senzo is never available these days.

I head over to JP's spot and find a bunch of niggas hanging out, which is pretty cool. JP is in an excitable mood. We smoke mad-blunts. We have mad-laughs. Somebody even has a bottle of vodka. For the first time, I sip alcohol. I figure, what does it matter? Everybody's doing it, and it feels right to go along.

By the time I leave JP's spot, it's well dark. Ernest will have a fit if he's home. I don't give a damn. I feel dope right now. I can't stop smiling. I feel all warm inside even though it's chilly out. I even walk with a bounce in my step. I can't think too clearly, and that's good. I'm trying not to think at all. I'm just loving this feeling of nothingness.

Walking past the Caltex garage, lost in my own world, I come across Nokwanda and a friend.

'What's happening?' she asks.

'I'm cool. What up with you guys?'

'What happened to your face?'

'Yo, I'm fine. Just taking it easy. It's Friday and all.'

'Sure. This is Asanda.' She nods to the friend, who has really big eyes, like those aliens from *X-Files*.

'Cool. Nice to meet you.'

'This is Bokang.'

I wave like a little kid. Asanda's eyes narrow, but still manage to look big.

'Where you coming from?'

'From ... er ... a friend's. Niggas was just chilling, you know. What are you guys up to?'

'Nothing much. Asanda's sleeping over.'

'Oh, you having a sleepover?' For some reason, this makes me giggle.

Nokwanda frowns at me. She pushes me on the shoulder. 'What have you been up to, Bokang?'

'Nothing, really. I'm hundreds.'

'Hmm, I'm not so sure. We gotta go. Take it easy.'

'Yeah, sure. You too.'

They walk off, leaving me standing there, smiling like a fool.

As I turn to leave, Nokwanda hollers. 'Oh, Bokang?'

'Yeah?'

'Call me.'

Call her? When, exactly? When I get home? Tomorrow? Sunday? Next week? It doesn't matter. That was a crazy encounter.

At the crib, I avoid entering through the front. The fam is probably chilling in the TV room. I go around to the kitchen door, trying my best to open it without making a sound. I head down the passage towards my room.

The old lady calls my name. Ready to collapse, I ignore her. The gravity in the house feels ten times stronger. The last few steps into my room are an effort; they take every muscle in my body. Crashing onto my bed, the spinning world turns to darkness.

Bokang Damane: *What is it that you fear most?*

The Supreme Khon: *I am not possessed of fear.*

Bokang Damane: *How is that possible?*

The Supreme Khon: *It just is.*

Bokang Damane: *So how is it that you do not have any fear?*

The Supreme Khon: *Fear is the rough side of a smooth stone, or the smooth side of a rough stone, depending on how you see things. It is one side of a whole; it cannot exist in isolation. If its opposite does not exist in a singularity of time, then fear as a phenomenon cannot be. Ergo, I do not fear, because I am dispossessed of its opposite.*

Bokang Damane: *And what is its opposite?*

The Supreme Khon: *Love, young apprentice. Love. I do not fear, because I am not burdened with a heart. Rid yourself of love, and you shall be free of fear.*

Something violent is happening. Screams, movement, blood. I'm being chased. I'm chasing. The world has turned on itself. Everyone is a stranger here. Everyone here seems lost.

Still in my clothes and shoes, I wake up lying on my stomach. What time is it? The room is dark. Where is Israel? I can't hear his usual snoring.

I sit up and immediately bring my hands to my pounding head. The cut on my lip stings. I have to force something back down my throat. My bladder is on fire.

Izzy's bed is empty. Strange. He's always in bed by this time, and usually sleeps right through the night. Maybe he's in the toilet.

I wait a moment, until a moment becomes too long. Stumbling towards the toilet, I use the wall to balance in the dark. I drain my bladder without switching on the light. A lot of piss ends up on the floor. I'll clean it up in the morning. My stomach feels like it might come up through my mouth and splatter everywhere.

Israel isn't in here. Could he be watching TV? At this hour? That's insane. When I stumble back into the passage, I see a dark figure standing there. It's one of the figures from my dream. I almost scream. I come close to running into the folks' room at the opposite end of the passage.

The figure is motionless. I get closer and realise it's Israel. He's standing there with his body leaning to the left and his head tilted downwards. The kid is fast asleep on his feet.

'Izzy,' I whisper. The last thing I need is Ernest finding us here, if he's home. 'Izzy.' I put my hands on his shoulders. The kid truly is down and out for the count.

Something tells me waking him might not be such a good idea. I walk behind him with my hands on his shoulders, directing him back to our room. I tuck him back into bed before getting into my own bed.

Sleep doesn't come, though. Something keeps me up to look out for Israel.

Thirteen

The weekend is a blur. I'm sick for most of it. I can't even tell what kind of sick I am. All I know is being in bed is the only place for me. My throat is scratchy, my head hurts, my stomach is on fire and my veins are full of cement.

I spend most of my time in bed not only cos I'm sick, but cos I don't want to see anybody. Sizwe is away at a sleepover – thank goodness. Israel also leaves for a sleepover but only for the Saturday night. I don't mention anything to him about his sleepwalking. I'm in the house with Ernest and the old lady, just like the good old days – except it isn't.

This is the coldest weekend we've had all year. Everything is grey outside. The trees look all skinny, like wicked stick-men. The year is going on. I can't believe it's already exam time. Maybe I should be studying. I'll get to that when I feel better. English and Biology are my first two exams – I should be okay with those.

I wish it was the holidays already, then I could stay in bed like this all day and all night without having to explain myself. I don't have plans for the holidays – unlike Senzo, who's going to bush.

Scribbling and sketching. Writing rhymes. Bumping beats. This is my therapy.

Some time on Saturday afternoon, the old lady comes into my room. 'Hey, Bobo.'

'Hey.' I sniff, pulling the blankets over my shoulders.

'How're you feeling?'

I shrug.

'Can I get you anything?' She takes a hesitant step into the room, then thinks better of it.

'Nah.'

'You haven't eaten all day.'

I shrug again.

'You need to eat something.'

'I'm not hungry.'

She wants to come in, sit on the bed, and rub her hands all over me. But she doesn't. 'You should still eat. I was thinking, maybe I could make you a nice meal? What do you feel like?'

I shrug a third time.

'I'm going to the shops. I'll make you something special. Okay?'

'Forget about it.' I drag the covers over myself.

I wait for her to leave before I sit back up in bed. Why is she trying to make herself feel better through me?

On Sunday morning, she's back. This time I really am sleeping – more or less.

'Bobo?' she whispers. 'Do you want to go to the beach?'

Eyes, stay shut.

'Bobo?'

Mouth, stay shut. Not a single sound, not even a breath.

She eventually leaves. Why the hell would anyone go to the beach in this miserable weather? The old lady's losing it fast. Even the way she called my name, it sounded more like she was speaking to herself. These are the signs of the *thing* and how it affects the old lady.

Even though this weekend has been the three of us, with Ernest, it feels like there's something else with us – the *thing*. Every time I hear footsteps in the passage, I stop whatever I'm doing in my room to listen. The old lady's footsteps are like a ghost's shuffle. The old man's footsteps are heavier and more hurried. Both are followed by the echo of the *thing*.

Ernest usually blames the rest of us after his monumental benders. I'm not sure if he's sipping this weekend. Nonetheless, I brace myself for a storm within our walls.

We survive.

Late on Sunday morning, the old lady heads out to fetch Israel and Sizwe. Now might be a good time to get some fresh air. My head isn't pounding as much as yesterday, and my gut seems to be holding up.

I head over to the Caltex garage to buy a phone card, and use it to call Nokwanda. The phone rings four times before somebody answers.

'Hello?' A kid's voice. I can't tell if it's a boy or girl.

'Hi. Can I speak to Nokwanda?'

'Okay, hold.'

The kid screams for Nokwanda without moving the mouthpiece from her mouth. I guess it's a girl, probably younger than Sizwe. I hear Nokwanda saying something to the child as she approaches the phone. 'Hello?'

'Nokwanda, what up?'

'Who's this?'

'Bokang.'

'Bokang who?'

'Er, Bokang? Nokwanda, it's me ... um ... we—'

She bursts out laughing. 'Oh, you should hear yourself, dude! *It's Bokang!*'

'Ah, come on, yo, that's cold.' I cough to clear my throat.

She can't control her laughter. 'I'm sorry but that was *funny*.'

'No, that was mean.'

'I'm sorry. Don't be mad at me.'

'I'm not mad.' I clear my throat again.

'Yes, you are. But don't be. How ya doing? You don't sound so great, your voice ...'

'I'm chilling. Good.' The gunk in my throat comes up into my mouth. I spit it out away from the phone's mouthpiece. 'What's going on?'

'I'm good, just kinda busy with studying.'

'Oh snap, sorry. I just thought I'd check up on you.'

'That's nice of you. But you don't have to do that.'

The silence lingers.

'Yeah, well, I was wondering, when, um, I would see you again?'

'Oh, now isn't a good time, with exams and everything.'

'Yeah, I know. You're right. When do you finish writing?'

'In two weeks.'

'Cool. Maybe during the holidays, then?'

'Um, I won't be around much. I have a netball tour. I made the national team. Isn't that exciting?'

'Oh, yeah, of course.' I say this without much enthusiasm. 'I heard something about that. Congratulations.'

'Thanks.'

Awkward silence.

'Well, I guess I'll see you around then. Whenever.' I sound like a sick puppy.

'Yeah, cool.'

'All right, then.'

'Bye.'

I stand there a moment staring at the handset of the payphone after she hangs up. What the hell just happened? I thought she wanted me to call her?

Fourteen

There's nothing I hate more than people telling me how clever I am, going on about my potential and telling me what I should be aiming for. Ever since primary school, people have been losing their minds about my marks at school. Teachers going on and on about what a clever little boy I am. Other school kids making a big deal about it, wanting to know my marks, asking me what I'm aiming for.

Lately everybody is bugging out about my marks, telling me I'm not doing as well as I'm supposed to. Roscoe and Ms Meadows ask me endless questions about my exam preparation, as if they're freaked out that I might fail or something.

They need to chill.

Today is the last day of term. My last exam was two days ago. Since then, coming to school has been a waste of time. They'll let us go soon, at half-past ten; at least it's earlier than yesterday.

Roscoe walks over from his desk at the front to where I sit at the back. He gloats about his marks and his plans for some job-shadowing gig he got himself for the holidays. There ain't much else to say. He stands around as if there is. Eventually he walks off. He shares a joke with Warren Potter and Ishmael Moosa. He's been sitting with them cats a lot these days.

When class eventually ends a few minutes later, I head straight for the door. I don't want another awkward conversation.

The corridors are already filled with overly excited boys. Winter holidays. Five weeks of no school. A good reason to be excited for most.

At the end of the corridor, outside one of the classrooms, I see Napoleon Dikembe. I stop for a second to get a good look at him. So this is the guy who supposedly has an on-off relationship with Nokwanda. On the one hand, I get *why* a girl like Nokwanda would be with a chimp like Napoleon: the netball superstar and the rugby god (Beauty and the Beast). That's how things work around here. But, on the other hand, I don't get *how* she could be with a dude like that. I mean, he is literally a gorilla; as big and as muscular as one.

Anyways, what do I know about anything? Nokwanda can get her thrills however she wants.

Outside the building, I move fast through the grounds, headed for the gate.

'Heyo, Big Bo!'

Head down. Straight for the gate. Almost there.

'Yo, Bo! Supreme!'

Almost there. Just a few more steps. Push through the crowd. Disappear through the gate.

A hand touches my shoulder. 'Yo! Big Bo, wait up, dog.' Senzo. Smiling. Expecting me to smile back. 'Hey, what up, yo?'

'I'm good.'

'It's been a minute.'

'Look, I gotta go.'

'Hey, come on now, don't do me like that, dog.' He steps in front of me. 'Come on, Bo, let go of the hate, it don't suit you. Walk with me, bra. You can catch a taxi in Vincent.'

'Nah, I gotta go.'

He breaks out his widest smile. 'Come on, bra. Can you really say no to this?' He moves in for a hug. 'Come on, show me some love. Come on, yo. Yeah, there you go.' We embrace. 'There you go. Get some.'

We laugh. We head down Snape Road towards Westwood Shopping Centre.

'It's so good to see you, dog, for real.'

'Oh, yeah? Well, I thought you trying not to hang with boys and what-not.'

'Come on, Big Bo, you know I'm still a boy myself. Even when I do become a man, I'm still gonna be your boy.'

'So when do you go to bush, anyways?'

'Yo, like tomorrow, son.'

'Word?'

'Word.' He looks uncertain. 'Tomorrow we head out with the fam to Idutywa. We gonna meet up with my pops' relatives, and then do this thing.'

'You gonna be all on your own out there?'

'Nah, there's a bunch of us. I think, like, six or seven initiates. One of 'em is my cousin and another his friend. I don't know the other dudes; they from out there in the rurals.'

'Okay, so you should be all right, then.' If I know anything about Senzo, it's that he likes being surrounded by people he's familiar with.

'Yeah, I guess so.'

Cars line both sides of the street outside St Stephen's Preparatory, parents picking kids up from school.

'You know, I still wish we was going to bush together, right?' he says. 'For real. I remember when we was still here' – pointing to the St Stephen's Preparatory gate – 'we was boys for life. And I want you to know that no matter what happens, from here onwards, we will always be boys. Even beyond this manhood shit.'

He shakes my hand.

'Yeah, big up for that.'

'I mean it, dog.'

'So how do you feel about the whole thing? You scared?'

He doesn't say anything. He takes a few steps, looking at the ground, thinking. 'I'm scared and I'm not scared. I ain't scared of being there, going through the whole thing, you know. But I *am* scared of what comes with all of this.'

'You mean the expectation of being a man?'

He snorts. 'Yeah, something like that.'

I don't say anything, letting him work through his thoughts. We get to Molineux Avenue and cross. Pretty soon I'll have to get my taxi.

'You know all this almost didn't happen?' he says. He continues without waiting for my response. 'Yeah, my moms was against it, right from the get-go. Then last month she got this big job in Jozi, and she moved up there. She said I should join her. Said peeps up there don't care about all this bush, initiation and manhood business.'

'For real?' I had no idea Senzo might be leaving East London for good.

'Yeah. But my pops was all for it – *obviously*. I was kinda caught in the middle, but in the end I decided, let me do this bush thing, and then make the move to Jozi.'

'So you leaving?'

'Yeah.'

'When?'

'I'm not coming back after the holidays. It's three weeks of bush, then I'm off to Jozi.'

Senzo gone forever. I'm not prepared for this. I thought I was losing him temporarily while he was transitioning into a man before me, but I always thought I'd eventually catch up to him.

'Listen, dog, I want you to be there at my umgidi, when I get out in three weeks. It will be my last chance to see you. Please say you'll be there.'

I'm not listening. I'm still trying to see life beyond the holidays without Senzo.

'Yo, Big Bo. Please say you'll be there.'

'Yeah, man, of course I will. Nothing will stop me from being there.'

The taxi ride to Beacon Bay is like a dream, and not a very pleasant one. I'm in a daze. I hear the voices of the people in the taxi, I see their shapes, but I'm not here. I stare out the window, but I don't register anything. Senzo leaving: that's all I can think about.

I get off the taxi and realise I've missed my stop. Home is in walking distance, though. All the way I'm wondering what I ever did for Senzo to let him know what he means to me. (Mr Knowles once asked me this same question and I avoided answering then. I still don't have an answer.)

When I get to the crib, I notice another ride parked in our garage next to the old lady's. What is she doing here at this time? Whose ride is that parked next to hers? MaMvundla is off today, so I know she isn't around.

The TV room is empty and so is the kitchen. I check out the back veranda, but nobody's there. I walk all the way down the passage to the folks' room, where the door is half open. When I stick my head in, I see the old lady sitting on the bed with Pastor Mzoli next to her. Bastard Pastor Mzoli. This son-of-a-bitch has one monkey-ass hand on the old lady's thigh and the other on her chin. His face is close to hers, and he's whispering something in her ear.

The old lady's eyes go wide when she sees me. 'Bokang!'

'*Ma*!'

'No, Bobo. Wait!'

Turning to leave. Running down the passage. Dropping my school bag. Exiting the house. Straight through the gate. Blocking out sound. Heart thudding. Down the street. Running. Which direction?

Need to get away.

Fifteen

Waves rock steadily, coming and going, created by unseen forces. The view from the dunes at Bonza Bay Beach is amazing. The water's edge seems like a no-go area, since it's the place I usually go with the old lady.

People stroll along the beach, many of them with dogs. The sun will set soon, and yet I don't feel like moving. I could get sick again from sitting here.

When I do eventually get up, my legs ache from sitting. The mission up Bonza Bay Road is slow going. The headlights of the cars come on as the sun disappears from the skyline. I clutch my school blazer tighter around me. I have my school jersey on underneath, but it doesn't feel like enough.

Outside the crib, I stand by the front gate. Our house is similar to all the other houses on the street, except it has chips in the paint, the gutters are rotting and tiles are missing from the roof. The garden is a mess again.

Inside the crib is an even bigger mess – a world I no longer recognise. I'm tired of being the person I have to be in there. But Israel is in there. Sizwe is in there. I have to care about them. I don't know how I can make things better for them. It's been a fail for me. Words that Senzo once said to me in primary school come to mind: *This situation can't last forever.* But Senzo himself is leaving.

Are people defined by their problems? While we try tell the world who we really are, our character is expressed through what we experience.

The old lady's ride isn't in the garage. The house is too quiet for Israel and Sizwe to be here. Lights are on, though, so somebody is here.

The old man is chilling in the TV room, all laid back on his favourite sofa, like a tinpot despot.

'Hello, boy.'

'Hi, Tata.'

He has a half-smile that could mean anything. I can't look at him; I might just tell him what I know. But why would I do that? What good would it do me? I don't know if Ernest deserves any favours from me. He could react any way, and that might not necessarily be good for me. What if the folks divorce or something? Then it would be my fault for snitching.

'You all right, son?'

'Yes, Tata.'

'Sure?'

'Yes, Tata.'

He's in a good mood, then. A can of Black Label balances precariously on the armrest.

'The game is going to start, son. Bafana Bafana against France' – pointing to the TV screen – 'we're about to witness history.'

I creep a little closer, giving the TV a cursory glance. 'Oh.' I turn to leave.

'Come watch with me. It will be good.' He takes a sip of beer and wipes froth from his patchy beard.

I can barely keep my eyes on him. I know if I make eye contact and he asks me directly about what I know, I won't be able to lie to him. I know that's crazy; he couldn't possibly know. I don't have an excuse not to chill with him, though. I mean, I don't even have homework.

'It's school holidays now, isn't it?' he says, as if reading my mind. 'Come, boy.' He waves me over with his hand like I'm his buddy or something. He has that sporting look on his face, that excitability he gets when he has something riding on a game.

'Let me change out of these clothes.'

I should have refused, but how could I? He's still my old man.

I go into the kitchen and open the fridge door. I need to know how many beers he's had – that at least might help me know how to deal with him. Years of living with Ernest have taught me what to expect from a one-beer Ernest, a two-beer Ernest and so on. I know what he's like at level-one drunkenness (four beers), moving up the scale to level-five drunkenness (fifteen-plus beers), which is the ultimate. Knowing what to expect at each stage is a necessary means of survival.

Two carry-packs of beer take up space on the top shelf in the fridge. One of them is ripped open, with four remaining long toms. I check the bin and find one can in there. So he's only on his second. At least he made it past his grumpy sobriety into the chilled phase. In some messed-up way, he's more pleasant slightly drunk than sober. He's at his worst at the two extremes: sober and very drunk. There's still plenty of time before he gets to monumental levels of drunkenness, when he becomes a real force of destruction.

I'm in no rush to change out of my clothes; I'm buying time to figure out how not to show Ernest that I know something. A blunt at this moment would be a blessing, but the prospect of being around Ernest half-baked is terrifying.

I put on a second pair of socks over the ones I already got, my long johns and a pair of tracksuit pants over them. I add a hoodie and a beanie for good measure, then remember Ernest doesn't allow them in the house.

Before I leave my room, I stare at the poster of Tupac. *All Eyez on Me*. Give me strength. Tupac looks down on me like the patron saint of street soldiers. I exhale.

'Have you eaten?' the old man asks when I return to the TV room.

'Nah.'

'You should eat. You look hungry.' He chuckles, scratching under his chin. 'Go to the fridge. You'll find some meat. Cut yourself some slices and dish out some of the mashed potato. Eat.'

Ernest being a parent. Wow. That's a nice change.

I go to the kitchen and dish up. Eisbein is his favourite and he hardly ever shares. He must really be in a good mood.

Ernest doesn't need to know anything if I don't tell. But that would mean the old lady gets away with this. It really sucks. I don't know why I have to be the one tiptoeing around these lies and keeping secrets. Should I be the one to call the old lady out on this? She's the one that needs to 'fess up to Ernest. Should I push her to do it?

I didn't realise how hungry I was. The food is good.

On the TV, a panel of experts go through their pre-match commentary. All of them are dressed in suits with colourful ties, and their excitement is nauseating.

'These fools really think Bafana Bafana have a chance,' Ernest says. 'The stupidity of being emotional. Tsk, tsk. You see what it gets you?'

'You don't think they have a chance?'

'There's always a chance. But the occasion will overawe them. The whole country is emotional. Just because we made it to our first World Cup, suddenly we're going to win it. France are the hosts, my boy, seasoned professionals. They'll make quick work of Bafana Bafana.'

'But we have all of the players that won the Africa Cup of Nations a few years ago.'

Ernest turns to me with a sparkle in his eye. He loves nothing more than engaging in debate and deep discussion. The only reason I know what I just said is cos I overheard some boys babbling about it at school.

'The Africa Cup of Nations and the World Cup are two different things. And also, that was two years ago.'

'There's still a chance,' I say, swallowing the last bite on my plate. I consider asking him if I can have more, but think better of it.

'So you think they have a good chance because they have previous experience of winning?'

'Yes.'

'Do you know anything about the French team?' His one knee bounces up and down like it's got a life of its own.

'No.'

'But still you're willing to back Bafana Bafana?'

'Yes.' I don't have the facts, but I know with Ernest, you pick a side and stick to it.

'Okay, boy, do you want to make a wager?'

'A what?'

'A bet, son. Do you want to stand by your statement that Bafana Bafana will beat France today?'

'Sure.'

He rubs his hands together. 'Okay, and what are you willing to put up?' He grins.

'What do you mean?'

'Well, a wager isn't a wager unless you willing to win or lose something. So if I win, you give me something, and if you win, I give you something. Fair?'

'Okay … I guess.'

'Wonderful. So what will it be?'

I'd like to tell him that if Bafana Bafana win, then he has to give up drinking forever. But somehow I know he won't go for that.

He leans towards me expectantly, eyes shiny, nostrils wide and teeth gleaming.

'Hmm, I don't—'

'Tell you what, let's say if you win, that is to say, if Bafana Bafana win, then I'll give you two hundred rand. Okay?' He holds his palms open as if to say this couldn't be easier.

Now that sounds good to me. I could do with the dough. 'Okay.'

'Now, if *I* win, that is to say, if France win, then *you* will spend a few days of your holiday helping me at the business. Fair?'

Hmm, that doesn't sound so good. Not even a little bit.

'Think about your two hundred bucks, son,' he says. 'Think about your Africa Cup of Nations champions.'

'Okay. Fair.'

'Wonderful!'

We shake on it and turn our attention to the TV, on the edge of our seats. The panel of experts is still yapping, and listening to them is getting me excited. If I can get one over Ernest, not only will I have a bit of loot, but it will be a moral victory. And there's plenty I could do with that dough.

'Oh, by the way,' Ernest says casually, 'you do know that when Bafana Bafana won the Africa Cup of Nations, Nigeria was absent from the competition?' He looks at me expectantly, and when I don't respond, he continues. 'No? Well, at least you must know that they're considered the greatest soccer nation on the continent.' This time I nod even though I'm not sure whether he's messing with me. 'Then you'll be interested to know that Nigeria doesn't stand a chance in this World Cup. So, good luck, Bafana Bafana.' He smiles. It isn't a friendly smile. More the kind of crocodile grin that competitors give one another.

'Let's just focus on this game.' I give him a crocodile grin of my own.

Before the game kicks off, the front door rattles. The old lady comes in with Israel close behind her. He tumbles into the TV room. 'Who's playing? Who's playing?'

'Hey, you!' Ernest says, opening his arms for an embrace.

The old lady hesitates by the front door. Our eyes meet and I hold her stare. She's trying to read me and also send a silent message. She steps forward, giving us all a nervous smile. She greets and Ernest greets back jovially. She relaxes a bit and her eyes hold mine.

'We were just dropping off Sizwe at a friend,' she says to nobody in particular. 'She's staying there for the weekend. Then I went to see Sis Pearl. You remember her, Tata?'

Ernest engages her and I see how she watches him, trying to read him. The old lady is not only scandalous, but devious as well. I can't believe it.

Meanwhile the game begins. Israel is supporting Bafana Bafana along with me. The old man loves the extra competition. The old lady stays and watches. She also says Bafana Bafana is going to win, not that anyone cares for her opinion.

When France score their first goal, the old man stands up and does a little jig, clapping his hands and hooting with laughter – he's on beer #5 and still in a good mood. Israel and I both have our hands on our heads. The old man smacks us both on the shoulders while he laughs.

'Bafana Bafana will score, don't worry,' the old lady says in my direction, but I don't acknowledge the comment. Not long after, she leaves.

France score a second goal. Ernest acts the fool. Israel switches allegiance, much to Ernest's delight. I consider going to bed. But I have to see this through.

France score their third and final goal.

It's over. I owe Ernest a week at the firm. He's surprisingly humble in victory. Israel isn't, but that's cool. It's been great shouting and screaming at the hopelessness of Bafana Bafana. This has been a rare moment of father-son time. Israel has enjoyed it too, and I'm glad he's happy.

We stay up longer with the old man, listening to his stories. The old lady has long since gone to bed.

We eventually go to bed, later than usual. It's holidays, after all, so this is okay.

I switch off the lights and lay in bed, staring into the blackness.

'Bobo,' Israel says. 'Do you think Mama and Tata will ever divorce?'

'Why do you ask?'

'My friend Darren's mother and father got divorced. Last year, my other friend Mzwandile's mother and father also got divorced.'

What do I tell him? Why is he asking this tonight of all nights? I want to give him hope, but I don't want to lie to him. 'Nah, Izzy, you don't need to be worrying about all of that.'

He's quiet for a while, but then he speaks again. 'Bobo?'

'Yeah, Izzy?'

'Why do people get divorced?'

'I don't know, Izzy. It's complicated. People change. Things change. Don't worry about it. Go to sleep.'

'Bobo?'

'Yeah?'

'Good night.'

'Good night, Izzy.'

Sixteen

'Wake up, boy.'

The blankets fly off me. Ernest stands at the foot of the bed, looking down at me.

Groaning, I reach for the blankets.

'Come, boy. Up!'

'Why?'

'You've got a debt to settle. Starting today. We leave in thirty minutes.'

Goddamn, I didn't expect him to collect so soon. For a while there, I hoped he was kidding about the whole thing, but clearly not. How is his drinking ass already awake and energetic at this hour?

I get out of bed and look enviously at Israel laying undisturbed in his bed.

It takes me thirty minutes to get dressed and ready. While I'm eating my cornflakes, we hear a double honk from a hooter.

'That's our ride. Let's go.'

I follow Ernest out into the cold morning air. It's heading towards nine o'clock. Tata uMfene's monster bakkie waits for us. Its engine rattles so loudly, it sounds like it might explode. He stands next to it, the door open, smiling like he knows something we don't.

'Heh, Hlathi,' Ernest says, as we climb into the bakkie.

'Radebe.'

'You still know my son, mos?'

'Tshini, of course!' He turns to look at me in the back seat, and sticks out a hand the size of a rotisserie chicken. Everything about the man is huge. His face, its features, his body and its limbs. As I shake his hand, I wonder if the loudness of his voice isn't caused by constantly competing with the rattling of the old diesel engine. 'Molo fondini!' He guffaws as he almost yanks my arm off with a handshake.

'Bokang, I'm sure you still remember Tata uMfene. He's my partner, usaluka wam.' He buckles his seatbelt as the bakkie moves out of our driveway.

Tata uMfene is a hard man to forget, even for the most undeveloped mind. He has a strong smell I remember from my childhood. Now that I'm in his ride, I realise it's the smell of sweat mingled with oil and car parts, probably from the bakkie.

'This one has decided to finally learn the business,' Ernest says.

'Is that so?' Tata uMfene laughs again, adding extra rumbling to the noise of the bakkie.

Ernest and Tata uMfene yak their mouths off nonstop. It's like watching two TV characters working on a limited-budget production.

Traffic flows as there aren't that many cars out at this time. We exit off the North East Expressway into Clermont, joining St Peter's Road.

Hitchhikers stand next to their luggage, lining both sides of the street. Tata uMfene slows the bakkie down to ogle at them. He makes a sucking noise through his teeth. 'Ja, neh, spring chickens.'

Ernest grunts in agreement.

We continue across Oxford Street to the other side of Clermont. We drive down Buffalo Street towards the back end of town, where there's more activity. Taxis everywhere. The streets are crowded. Vendors sell their wares at their stalls. Some of them are still setting up their displays.

We pull up next to an old building that looks like a large house, except it has signs outside with the names of the shops that are inside. There are four marked parking spaces in front. The two on the extreme ends are taken, leaving the two middle ones open. Tata uMfene struggles to get the monster bakkie into one of these. He drives forward with the engine growling, then brakes sharply, almost hitting the car on the left. He battles to get into reverse gear, and when he does, he shoots back, almost hitting a group of women passing by. After shifting gears again, with a screeching metallic sound, he ploughs forward again at the wrong angle.

It's eerily quiet inside the bakkie, considering the amount of yakking that was going on between them earlier. All Tata uMfene's concentration is on what he's doing.

When he eventually parks (skew, basically taking up both parking spaces), he pulls out a handkerchief and wipes a flood from his big forehead. Then he meticulously folds the handkerchief back in small squares. By the time he's done, the sweat drops are back on his forehead.

I cover my mouth to stifle a laugh.

'This is it, umfana,' Ernest says.

'This is what?' The biggest sign on the building reads 'Best Bet' in green lettering.

Ernest climbs out without answering. When Tata uMfene climbs out on the other side – backwards, with one gorilla arm holding onto the roof – the bakkie rocks so much I almost fall out on my side.

Ernest rubs his hands the same way he did last night after France beat Bafana Bafana. The two of them shake hands before we head towards the building. They truly are an odd couple. One is short, scrawny and light-skinned, with long mostly white hair, while the other is tall, bulky and dark-skinned, with short black hair. Tata uMfene is easily three times as big as Ernest.

The glass door, with cracks running through most of its shatterproof surface, stands half open. It's gloomy inside, even though the dim lights are switched on. A few tables occupy the large space that evidently used to be made up of different rooms. At least three people sit inside, two of them at one table and another alone. All three have beers in front of them; it's not even ten in the morning. The one on his own smokes a cigarette with his elbows on the table and his drooping eyes staring at a small TV screen in the corner. At least four other small TV screens take their places around the room, all showing either horse racing or soccer.

Ernest and Tata uMfene swagger in, clearly familiar with the joint. Ernest greets the two men at the table, while Tata uMfene heads over to the far side, which features a counter with a wire-mesh partition running to the ceiling. Behind it, keeping a close eye on the patrons, is an old woman wearing a blue dress. Her blonde hair has a style that should be on someone much younger and prettier. Together with her generously applied makeup, which gives her wrinkled face a plastic quality, the hair has the effect of making her look older.

'Stella, my skat!' Tata uMfene bellows, holding out his colossal arms.

The woman leans forward with her hands on the counter and her hip cocked out to the side. I would hate to be getting the view from behind.

'Moenie my "skat" roep nie,' she says, with a coquettish smile that makes her face look like melting wax reflected in a cracked mirror.

Tata uMfene blows her a kiss with a smacking sound. One of the men sitting at a table glances sideways, his beer suspended close to his gaping mouth.

Ernest joins Tata uMfene and the blonde woman. The three of them exchange words and Ernest pulls out a small piece of paper and hands it to the woman. Her eyebrows lift and she nods. She disappears behind a door and reappears moments later with a wad of cash, which she promptly hands to Ernest, who hands it to Tata uMfene, who stashes it in the pocket of his huge pants.

'See you soon!' Stella calls after us as we walk out. Ernest and Tata uMfene hold up their hands without looking back.

The three of us leave in a rumble of black smoke as the bakkie tumbles back into the traffic. At least two motorists cuss and shake their fists.

We head down Oxford, the main street in town. We pass the City Hall and the buildings occupied by the banks. We turn left into Union Street, where the First National Bank is, and Tata uMfene drives around the island in the middle of the street to get parking. He doesn't make it in a single curve and has to do the reversing-inching-forward thing again just to align his bakkie.

The only available space requires parallel parking. I hold my breath.

After he cocks it up a third time, a car guard in a yellow reflector jacket comes scurrying like a giant stick insect. He stands between the bakkie and the car behind the empty parking bay. Dude looks seriously high off something atomic.

'Tsek, kwedini!' Tata uMfene swears at him.

The car guard stands there unperturbed, waving and directing Tata uMfene into the parking space. Tata uMfene cusses him out some more. The bakkie blocks at least three other cars. Tata uMfene tries again; on his sixth attempt, he's eventually satisfied. The back corner of the bakkie sticks out into traffic, but neither Ernest nor I (nor the skinny car guard) say anything.

We approach the grey building on the opposite side of the road. Although the building looks like it was built in the thirties in terms of style, it has signs of recent renovations.

A cheerful woman vendor sits outside selling fruit, sweets and cigarettes. Ernest greets her and engages in a conversation, while Tata uMfene enters the small café behind her. The glass window behind her has signage: *Damane & Sons Attorneys.*

Whoa. Okay. Didn't know about that one.

I follow Ernest through a narrow wooden door that goes straight up a flight of stairs. Voices echo off the walls, as do our footsteps off the dark grey metal stairs. We pass a hair salon on one floor and what looks like a tailor's working space. Some of the rooms appear to be places where people live.

We stop on the third floor, where Ernest, a lit cigarette in his mouth, searches his pockets for the keys to his office. He's quite the sight with his white hair and the white smoke swirling all around him as he pats down his pockets. He finds the key and fiddles it into the lock, speaking to himself under his breath. 'Come on, come on, come on. Yes, yes, ah-ha!'

The stuffiness is the first thing that assaults me as we enter; it clings to my face, the smell of stale cigarettes and dust strong in the air. An overflowing ashtray filled with the carcasses of dead cigarettes sits on the counter of the reception desk. Boxes filled with files are stacked on the chair behind the reception desk. I bet it's been a minute since there was a secretary here.

'Welcome, son. You remember this place, neh?' He doesn't wait for my answer. He dashes about opening the blinds to let a little light in, a fail since the windows face a wall.

It's been years since I came here, not since primary school and Ernest still had a car. He would sometimes bring me here after scooping me up from school 'to pick up a thing or two', as he'd put it. Ernest had a way even back then of making me feel like a part of what was going on here.

Tata uMfene comes blasting into the office, carrying a plastic in one hand and a two-litre Coca-Cola in the other, looking like a broke man's Father Christmas: all bulk and cheap offerings. 'Breakfast is *served*, madoda!' He places the Coca-Cola bottle on the reception counter next to the ashtray. He holds the plastic open with both hands and peers inside. 'Eggs, chips, russians, namagwinya. The *real* power breakfast!'

He heads out, casting the room into darkness as he does so, and like an eclipse, the sparse light returns after he's exited. *'Bring that Coke!'* he bellows from down the passage. *'And close the door!'*

I do as I'm told, while Ernest stays in his office. Books and files line the floors of the passage. Another office is filled with more books and more files. I give Tata uMfene the Coca-Cola in the kitchenette.

'Bokang!' Ernest calls from his office, and I go back. He points to the wall. 'Look.'

Post it notes and other pages filled with random information cover an old noticeboard; some are on the walls. I guess they aren't random to Ernest. Scattered among the papers are a few photos. I'm in one of them, wearing a blue suit with a white shirt, and holding a piece of paper rolled up like a diploma. I must be five or six in the picture, smiling like I'd never known a day of grief.

'That was taken here,' Ernest says, putting a hand on my shoulder. 'That was the day you told me you wanted to be a lawyer. Just like your old man. That's when I changed the name of the firm to Damane & Sons

Attorneys.' He gives my shoulder a squeeze, then moves his attention to a bookshelf on our right.

The time the photo was taken seems like centuries ago. I didn't even know I could smile like that. It's unnerving.

Tata uMfene comes in, carrying two plates piled with food.

'Hayi, hayi, hayi,' Ernest says. 'Not in here, Hlathi.'

The three of us move into the small boardroom. More files and books are piled on the table. Bookshelves running from ceiling to floor cover three of the walls. Tata uMfene places the food on the table and we dig in.

The dust around us gives the place the quality of a storage room in an old museum. It used to be busy here. 'Are you also a lawyer?' I ask Tata uMfene, noting how casually – and untidily – he's dressed compared to Ernest (on weekends Ernest wears golf shirts with formal pants and shoes instead of suits).

Tata uMfene bursts out laughing, showing us the food in his mouth, then slaps me on the shoulder.

'No, son, Hlathi here is not a lawyer.' Ernest sets his food down. He is generally a slow eater.

'I thought you said he was your partner?'

'He is. My business partner.'

'Friend and associate,' Tata uMfene says, grinning with pride.

'Brother.'

'Usaluka.'

'You see, son, you need someone you can trust in life. Someone you come a long way with. Understand?'

I think of Senzo, moving on without me in more ways than one. I think of Roscoe, who I struggle to keep up with more and more every day. 'Yeah, I think I do.'

'Good. Hold on to that person. You will need them. They will be there for you more than any woman.'

'You can't *trust* a woman' Tata uMfene pipes up. 'You *cannot*, Radebe.'

'Why not?' I ask, thinking of the old lady's eyes when she realised I'd seen her with Pastor Mzoli. How much does the old man trust her?

'Ha! Woman are slippery things, they will *never* tell you anything. You ask *this*, they tell you *that*; you ask *that*, they tell you *this*. Women don't know what truth is; they make it all up!' He nods as he takes another bite from the gwinya in his hands. Egg, russian, chips and crumbs avalanche down his belly, cascading onto the worn linoleum below.

Ernest and Tata uMfene carry on talking, and while they do so, I think about what he said and the situation with the old lady. I hate knowing what I do and not being able to do anything with it. I need to confront the old lady and get her to 'fess up to Ernest.

Ernest gives me my work for the day: searching for books and files on tax law. I work through the bookshelves in the room we ate in while the two of them sit in Ernest's office. I'm not sure what they're doing in there, but one time I go in and see Tata uMfene handing Ernest the wad of cash. Ernest casually puts it in a safe under his desk, all the while maintaining his running commentary.

Some time during the mid-afternoon, Tata uMfene drives us back to Beacon Bay. When we arrive at the crib, Ernest turns to me in the back seat and hands me two crisp hundred-rand notes.

'What's this for?'

'A day's pay for a day's work.' He winks.

'Oh. Thanks. But …'

Tata uMfene laughs, his eyes watching me through the rear-view mirror. 'Don't you *want* it?'

'I do. Thank you.'

'It's a pleasure, son.'

After dropping me, they take off in a rumble of clanging metal and dark smoke.

Nobody is home. A brief nap does me good.

Izzy and the old lady still aren't back when I wake up a couple of hours later. Missioning to JP's spot seems a viable option, but the timing's not good. There's always the cheap weed from this spot called Paradise; it's like an old abandoned house in some bushes, where some of the kids meet to smoke themselves stupid. The weed there is whack and the people aren't much for company — drunks and delinquents. Besides, it's a bit late in the day to be looking for blunts in bushes.

There's a World Cup game on the TV. It grabs my attention for a few minutes before I give up.

There's nothing worthwhile in the fridge, the same as twenty minutes ago when I last checked. Ernest has left one of his long-tom beers, and it stands self-righteously among the lowly food items: a half-bottle of milk, a crumbed bar of butter, some unappetising leftovers, bruised fruit and wilting vegetables.

Back in my room, sketching seems like an option, but my mood doesn't take. I lie on the bed, twirling the notes between my fingers. This money better be real.

I mission to the Caltex garage and buy a phone card, a Coke, a slab of Dairy Milk and some wine gums. Maybe I should call Nokwanda?

The phone rings three times before a woman picks up. What am I doing? I hang up and sprint away from the phone as if the person who answered can see me.

It's dark as I walk home. A half-moon grins sideways, stars wink like flirtatious damsels. On the roof, the view is better. It's cold, though, so I come down.

The old lady returns with Izzy.

Back in my room, the inspiration to sketch finally comes. Israel comes in and tells me all about his afternoon, but I'm listening out for the old lady. She shuffles about in other rooms. What is she doing?

Finally, she comes to our door. 'Izzy, why don't you go watch TV,' she says.

Israel leaves reluctantly. The old lady wants a confrontation.

We take it to the folks' room. She sits on the bed, the same spot she sat when Pastor Mzoli had his meat hooks all over her. Standing works for me.

'Why did you do it?'

'What do you think happened?' She's very composed for somebody who's been lying and cheating.

'You *cheated*!'

'No.'

'Yes, you did! I *saw* you!'

'What did you see?'

She certainly sounds sure of herself. 'I saw you, Ma. You can deny it all you want. I saw you sitting there, with his hands all over you!'

'Pastor Mzoli and I were just talking.'

'Come on! He had his hands all over you. I *saw*!'

'It's not what you think. He was comforting me.'

'I don't believe it. Why were you in Tata's room?'

'Did you not see that I was crying?'

'I saw him with his hands all over you.'

'Come. Sit.' She taps the spot next to her. The same spot the bastard pastor sat in.

'I'm fine here.'

She pats the bed again. Her face is so calm she could be the black Mona Lisa.

I go to the other side and sit on the corner of the bed.

She adjusts her position to look at me. 'Bokang, I have never – and will never – be unfaithful to my husband. Yes, your father and I have problems. Pastor Mzoli was giving me advice. You deserve to know what's happening.'

Her eyes drop to the hands in her lap. I've seen the old lady cry before, many times. The last time at the beach. That time in the kitchen, in the early hours of the morning. The time she picked me up from school, after the suicide essay debacle. Surely she is about to cry now.

She looks up at me with dry eyes. Her stare is determined 'Bokang, I'm going to—'

'Ma?' Israel stands by the door.

'Izzy,' the old lady says.

He runs into her arms. 'Is everything okay?' He looks at me, eyes bulging with innocence.

'Yes, Izzy, everything is fine.'

'Come watch a movie with me, Bobo.' He sounds younger than his twelve years.

Both of them wait for me to respond. My answer will determine what comes next. Not just in the following few minutes, but for the rest of our lives. Israel's eyes plead. The old lady's eyes reveal nothing.

'Yeah, of course, let's do that.'

Seventeen

The old lady has always hated the school holidays. It's just not a good time for her. Kids all up in the crib, eating every damn thing, full of demands and squealing about entertainment.

Today, Sizwe is out at the mall with her friends, while Israel is go-carting with his friends. I'm holding it down at the crib, one man, like I've been doing for most of this holiday. I gave Ernest his days at the office, and an extra without him asking. It pays, and that's something.

I've been good with the loot too. I still have at least two hundred and ninety bucks. The most expensive thing I've bought was a bankie from JP, which cost me fifty bucks. That's what you pay for the good stuff. Otherwise I've bought biscuits and other sweet stuff, and I still have that phone card. This loot will come in handy; it may be a minute before it comes again.

Ernest having money has been a trip. At least he's been spoiling Israel and Sizwe – which is probably the only reason the old lady's been cool with them going out so much.

So, anyways, right now it's me and MaMvundla at the crib. Ma is out in Bisho, working; Ernest is at the office, probably 'working' with Tata uMfene. I'm chilling on my bed, bumping some Naughty by Nature, when MaMvundla pitches up at the door, an overflowing laundry basket against her broad hip, and tells me I have a phone call.

Who the heck, what the heck? I check the time; it's eleven twenty-something.

'Hello?'

'*Heeeeeyyy, yooouuuu!*' Nokwanda. Her voice as syrupy as hell.

'Hey.'

'How are you?'

'I'm good. Chilled.' I wipe non-existent fluff off my shoulder, as if she can see me. 'How are you?'

'I'm *gooood,* man. You've been so scarce. Where have you been?'

'I thought you were touring or whatever. Busy, as you put it.'

'Oh. No, man! So anyway, whatchu doing?'

'Right now?'

'Yeah, silly.' She giggles. Even through the phone it does things to me.

'Nothing. Just chilling.'

'Okay, so why don't you come over?'

'You mean, right *now*?'

'Come in an hour. I miss you, man.'

An hour and fifteen minutes later, I'm standing outside Nokwanda's house for the first time. It's nothing like our house. First off, she lives in a double storey. Secondly, the garden looks like a place where angels come to frolic. Thirdly, it looks like happiness lives here and not some ghosts from the past.

I hesitate before ringing the buzzer. I check the number for the seventh time to make sure it's 14. It is 14, right? I check how I'm dressed and wonder if it's appropriate. My sweat pants are one of the newest items in my wardrobe. My FUBU hoodie is my most prized possession, and I have my Reebok kicks on and a fresh beanie.

I'm about to press the buzzer when I hear kids shouting and screaming. A troop of them appear at the gate. They stare at me with curious eyes.

'Hello!' their leader says. It's a girl, slightly taller than the rest, with braided hair tied in pigtails, and a pair of pink-framed spectacles. She could be the one who answered the phone the time I called.

'Hey, y'all. What's going on?'

'Can we help you?' the little leader asks.

'Yeah. Does Nokwanda live here?'

'Yes, she does!'

'Yes, she does!'

'Yes, yes!'

The other three members of the troop answer out of sync.

'Okay, great. I'm here to see her.'

'Who are you?' one of the little boys says, pointing a water pistol at me. He resembles the older girl, only more feral.

'Bokang.'

'Bokang! Bokang! Bokang!' the little things chant.

'Shush!' says the leader, looking more mature than her single-digit years. 'Open the gate.'

The one who looks like her groans. Then he takes off like a Tasmanian devil, the rest of the troop following.

'Sorry about them,' she says, adjusting her glasses. 'Kids.'

The gate slides open and the little leader welcomes me in with a wave of her hand. 'I'm Fezeka – call me Fez; everyone does. That one is my brother, Xolisa. Those two are his little friends, Luke and Phila.'

The little madam leads me past the growling gang, who keep their water pistols aimed at me all the way to the front door.

The inside of the house is even more impressive than the outside. It's exceptionally clean, considering the savage troop running around the place. Beautiful ornaments, vases, statues and paintings decorate the space. There are all kinds of colours I don't even have names for. Lime-green cushions, deep red and passion-pink carpets, sparkling crystal light fixtures.

'Mom's an interior designer,' Fezeka says, reading my expression.

After passing what looks like a TV room, a lounge, a dining room and other rooms, Fezeka leads me to a second lounge, where Nokwanda waits on a c-shaped couch. Descending stairs lead into the room, which is designed like a small amphitheatre. Nokwanda reclines like royalty on luxurious cushions.

'Heeeey, Bo,' she says, tossing her magazine aside. She doesn't get up, but she reaches her arms out, expecting a hug. 'So glad you could come, hey.' She runs her fingers with their pink fingernail polish over my chest, and my skin ripples in goosebumps.

Fezeka is quietly watching us.

'You can go now,' Nokwanda says.

Fezeka nods like a loyal subject, and gives me a look. I wave, but she doesn't see as she turns to leave.

'Sit,' Nokwanda says. Her leg is elevated on a cushion and she wears a brace around her ankle.

'Yeah – that,' she says, seeing I've noticed. 'Injury during practice. Can you imagine? Messed up my whole freaking tour.'

'I'm sorry to hear that.'

'Are you? Really?'

'Um, yeah. Sorry, but I'm also—'

'Relax, Bo! I'm messing with you.'

I sit and glance around the room. Two of the walls are white. The third is dark facebrick; paintings of many different shapes and sizes hang on it. A sliding door opens out onto a pool and a garden impressive enough to be a feature spread in a glitzy magazine.

'Do you think I'm hot?'

'What?'

'I said, aren't you hot?' She giggles, then points a long pretty finger at my hoodie.

It *is* hot up in here. My armpits and spine are sweating something terrible. A heater stands alongside Nokwanda, who is wearing sky-blue hot pants that expose her really, really, *really* long legs. Her white top doesn't even reach past her belly button – which has a piercing – and it reveals all sorts of curves that I resist putting my hands on. I can't take my hoodie off cos I probably have nasty half-moons under my armpits. 'Nah, I'm cool, yo.'

'So glad you could come, hey. I've been sitting here like seriously *bored*, and I remembered you live nearby.'

Oh, great. So much for being the knight in shining armour.

'I like your hoodie.' Her smile is something else, for real.

'Thanks.'

The room goes quiet. Nokwanda watches me; she's enjoying herself.

'How did your injury happen?'

'Is that really what you wanted to ask?'

'Yeah, I mean. How did it happen?'

'Some stupid bitch tripped me.' She snorts derisively. 'Doesn't matter. I'll get her back.'

I don't say anything.

She picks up the magazine and leafs through it. Many of the photos and paintings on the walls are of flowers; only a few are of people.

'What's with all the flowers?' I ask pointing.

'Hmm?'

'The flowers? On the wall? In the pictures?'

'Oh' – eyes still on the magazine – 'my step-mom is like obsessed with flowers. It's part of her portfolio: flower arrangements, still lifes, all that stuff – what*ever!*'

I try some small talk, but her eyes stay fixed on the damn magazine. Occasionally she looks up, but mostly she gives short answers.

I get up and walk towards the brick wall, to look more closely at the family portraits. They were taken in a studio and certainly with some sort of professional directing.

I stare out at the back yard through the glass door. Not even the grey winter sky can take away from the lushness of this place. It's a garden to be admired, not for kids to play in. 'Can I go out to look at the garden?'

'Did you come here to see me or the garden?' she asks, pouting.

'I came here for you.'

'So then …' She pats the couch.

I hesitate but move closer, standing next to her. She nods towards the couch, but I choose to stand.

'Your nose is sweating,' she says. 'Are you nervous?'

'Me? No! Of course not. Shuuu.'

'Then sit. Unless you too nervous?'

I sit, to prove I'm not nervous. A trickle of sweat runs down from my armpit to my ribcage.

'Take your top off; you won't sweat so much.'

I know she's right, but what colour is my T-shirt again? Grey. No, navy. Do sweat stains show through navy? I take the hoodie off and casually inspect my armpits. Did I put on enough deodorant? You'd need bionic eyesight to see the sweat stains on the navy.

'You see? Isn't that better?'

'Yeah.'

'Damnit!'

'What?'

'My leg is hurting again. Won't you be an angel and massage it for me?' She points to a bottle of oil on the carpet. It's next to a nail-grooming kit, and one blue-and-silver crutch.

'You want me to, um ...?'

She nods.

'First remove the brace. Be gentle.'

I lift up her foot, my heart banging in my chest. My palms are sweaty and I hope to hell she can't tell. I better not hurt her.

When the brace comes off, she points to the oil. I pick it up and she holds out her hand. I give it to her. Then she holds out her other hand indicating that I should do the same. She squeezes some of the amber oil onto my palm. It's warm from being next to the heater.

'Start with the ankle, then move up. Do both legs.' She removes the cushions behind her and lays all the way down. She covers her eyes with the back of one hand.

I stand over her, looking at the oil in my palm and the curvature of her legs. They look so perfect, I'm afraid to ruin them with my monkey-ass hands. The heater behind me is intense, but somehow it seems easier to deal with than what's in front of me.

'Whenever you're ready, Bokang.'

I rub the oil on both hands and get to work on her feet, starting with the injured one. (This sure beats working on Ernest's nasty-ass feet.) I stay on them for a while, not daring to go past her ankles.

'Get some more oil,' she says in a low voice, with her eyes still covered. 'Move higher. All sides of the legs.'

I work a little higher on the first leg, doing the shin, the calf and venturing around the knee for a while.

'Higher.'

I breathe deeply as I work on her thighs. Her mouth is slightly open and I hear her moaning.

'Higher.'

Her hot pants are almost non-existent – if I go any higher I will be inside her. When I reach the highest point I dare go, I swop to the other leg.

She watches me from under the hood of her hand. She doesn't look impressed.

In a broad stroke, I move my hand until it brushes the hot pants, then I move back and work in short strokes closer to her knees.

'That's enough,' she says abruptly. She sits up so fast I almost knock over the heater. 'Getting a little excited there,' she says, pointing at my sweat pants.

'No! What?' I sit down, trying to hide the obvious, but even a sitting position doesn't help. The sweat pants were definitely a bad idea.

'Relax, dude. It's nothing I haven't seen before.' She laughs, a hand over her mouth. 'That's *funny*!'

If there is a God, can He bury me right now? Please?

'I'm sorry. I'm not laughing at you, but that is *funny*!'

'Yeah. Get it out your system. As long as one of us is laughing, right?'

'Sorry, Bo! I'm so sorry!'

I sit there waiting for her laughter, and my erection, to die down, feeling let down by both.

'You shouldn't be so sensitive – you and your, um ...' She points at my crotch.

I look at her.

'Oh, my God! Are you sulking?'

'No.'

'Oh, my word! You are! Oh, Bo!' She reaches out, but can't quite get to me with her leg suspended between us. She puts her hands over her mouth, whether it's to stifle more laughter or to hold back her words I can't tell.

Then the look on her face changes to one of frozen surprise. I turn.

A woman stands behind me. She's tall, slender, dressed in red tights, knee-high boots with heels and a patterned cape-like coat. She holds a tiny dog (as small as JP's, but better groomed) in her arms like a parcel. 'Your father and I are going out tonight,' she says in a stiff voice. 'Reservations at Grazia's. You'll manage?'

'Yes,' Nokwanda says.

'Perfect,' she says, as if addressing an employee. 'Money for takeaways is on the microwave. No meat for Xolisa, he's had his limit for the week. Fez will know what to get herself.' This is the same woman in the pictures on the walls – in fact, most of them. 'Okay, toodles.' She turns to leave but then almost absentmindedly notices me. 'Oh. Who's this? Boyfriend?'

'*No*. This is Bokang.'

'Hi,' I say, lifting a hand.

'Does your father know him?' she asks, ignoring me.

'No.'

'Hmm.'

'Bokang is harmless, Sandy.'

Harmless?

'Sure. You'll tell your father, though?' Then, without waiting for an answer, she turns on her heel and exits like a model on a catwalk.

Nokwanda's face makes me feel sorry for her. Not knowing what else to say, I ask, 'You call your mother by her name?'

'Sandy's not my mother.'

'Oh. My bad.'

Eighteen

The next morning, I'm lying in bed reading a MAD magazine when MaMvundla appears in the doorway, this time carrying a mop and a bucket. 'Phone call. Dining room.' She moves on.

This is becoming a routine, then. I scramble out of bed in my PJs and snatch my gown off the back of the door.

'Hello?'

'Hey, Bo.'

'Hey, Nokwanda.'

'Sleep well?'

'Yeah.'

I had a late night after watching a World Cup game with Ernest. No wager this time, but we still supported opposing sides. It ended in a draw and I stayed up listening to his stories again.

'Did you dream about me?'

'No!'

'*No?* Don't you like me any more?'

'No, I mean, of course I do. But, eish ... How are you?'

'Don't be like that, Bo. You know you can be honest with me. If you like me, just say so. I mean, it's understandable. So?'

'So what?'

'Do you like me or not?'

'Yes, of course I do. I mean, I don't like you like that, or whatever, but yes, I like you.'

'Whatever. That's funny. Anyways, what time can you be here?'

'In an hour?'

'No, Bo. You can't come at an ungodly hour.'

'How about at one o'clock?'

'Make it eleven-thirty.'

'Sure.'

'And Bo? Won't you be a darling and bring me some cigarettes? Pretty please?'

'Sure.'

'Do you still have some of that stuff of yours?'

'What stuff?'

'You know, the weed?' She giggles.

'Oh, yeah. Sure.'

'Okay, cool, bring some of that too. And Bo?'

'Yeah?'

'Maybe wear tight-fitting pants this time.' She hangs up.

After washing up and eating, I head out to the Caltex garage. The sun's warmth is moderated by a chill wind. I'm dressed in black baggy jeans (not because of what she said) and a white NY sweater. I'm also wearing my tan Bronx boots.

I buy Nokwanda's cigarettes and put them in my pocket, tucked in next to the last bit of my blunt stash. I take the initiative by going to the video store to hire us a couple of movies.

This time there is no troop at the gate to meet me at Nokwanda's place. I have to ring the buzzer. As I lift my finger to press it a third time, an irritated woman asks me in isiXhosa who I am and what I want. I have to repeat Nokwanda's name twice before the gate slides open. The irritated woman is the domestic helper, who meets me at the front door.

As I enter, following her in her neat grey-and-white uniform, I hear the sounds of kids coming from one of the rooms. It's the troop. I don't want another encounter with them, although I don't mind Fezeka, the little leader.

Nokwanda meets us in the passage. She's dressed in a pink velvety J-Lo tracksuit with gold trimmings. Her afro is partitioned into two puffs on either side of her head, reminding me of the Lady of Rage. She's using the blue-and-silver crutch to balance as she walks.

'Hey,' she says.

'Hey. What up?'

She exchanges a few words with the domestic, who stalks off, more irritated than before. Is it possible her face is permanently set in that gargoyle scowl?

'What's that?' Nokwanda asks, pointing at the DVDs in my hands.

'Just some movies for us to check out.'

'Oh. Cute. What did you get?'

I hold them up. '*There's Something About Mary* and *Saving Private Ryan*.'

'Oh.' She turns away without comment. 'Come. We sitting out there,' she says, pointing towards the back garden. My eyes stay fixed on the words written on her tracksuit pants in gold across her bum: *Juicy*.

We go through the fancy garden with its perfectly trimmed hedges and flower beds (way more impressive than JP's garden with its koi fish). An old man in grey overalls tends to the flowers, every movement meticulous. He has plenty of energy for an old man.

'Molweni,' he greets with a high hand wave.

'Ewe ke, Tata' – waving back – 'Ninjani namhlanje?'

Nokwanda gives me a look.

'Sikhona, enkosi.'

We keep walking. 'He's just the hired help,' Nokwanda says, without looking at me.

We go to the one-roomed cottage in the back, which might as well be another house. It's spacious, and decorated like the main house, with signs of being newly renovated.

'Who stays back here?' I ask as Nokwanda closes the sliding door behind us.

'Nobody. It's just a place.'

'Wow.'

'Whatever.' She plops herself on the bed, using a couple of cushions to support her injured leg.

The domestic arrives carrying a radio and some CDs. She makes another trip to the main house and back again, this time bringing a spread of eats: fruit, bread, jam, biscuits, chips and cold meats.

Nokwanda doesn't pay any attention to her as she goes about setting up the buffet, just keeps on rapping as if it's only the two of us.

We chill in the cottage, chatting and listening to music.

There are three noteworthy things about Nokwanda. Firstly, she likes to talk. We talk almost exclusively about what she wants to rap about. This is okay, as I'm a good listener. Secondly, she changes topic randomly, jumping back and forth between things we've already discussed and other things we haven't touched on, as if we're having several conversations simultaneously. Thirdly, Nokwanda talks a lot about the popular kids at her school, and my school, which I find kind of superficial, but I suppose as a first-team netball player herself, she moves in those circles.

'So what's up with you and Napoleon?' I ask, feeling brave.

'Nothing. Why?' Her face is a mask.

'I just heard you two were kicking it or whatever.'

'No. Not any more.'

'Oh, cool.' I hope the pleasure at this news doesn't show on my face.

'So what's up with you, since you asking all these personal questions?'

'What do you mean?'

'Who you seeing? Who have you seen?'

'I'm not seeing anybody right now.'

'And before?' Her one eyebrow arches.

'Well ...'

Nokwanda laughs. 'That's *funny!* Sorry, Bo, I'm not laughing at you, but that *is* funny. So what? Are you a virgin?' She squeezes a pillow to her chest, grinning and clearly super-eager for my response.

'Well, I haven't really ... in a while ... you know ...'

'Ha ha! *Reeeaaallly?* So you haven't? *At all?* And you, like, in Grade 11?' She topples over on her side, covering her face with a pillow.

'Hey, yo, I'm not ashamed.'

'Right. Look, I'm not laughing *at* you, but *kwaaaaaaaaaaaaaa!*'

I get up and head for the sliding door.

'Where you going?' she says.

'Come on, Nokwanda. I got better things to do than to sit here whi—'

'But I thought we were playing? I didn't know we were being so serious.'

I put my hand on the door handle.

'I'm sorry. Today's not a good day. Please. Things haven't been easy for me, with missing out on the tour and my step-mom. *Please?* Forgive me?' She holds out a hand.

I'm ready to leave this place. But she looks so sad. 'What's happening with your step-mom?'

Her eyes dart to the sofa, and I sit back down.

'Didn't you notice yesterday? Sandy doesn't like me, dude. She never has.'

'How long has she been married to your dad?'

'Too long. Since before Fez and X were born.'

'What happened to your real moms? If you don't mind me asking?'

She tells me, speaking slowly. This is definitely a story she doesn't tell often, if at all. She tells me about how beautiful her mom was, how close the two of them were, and how different things were then. She was seven when her moms died in a car accident. Her pops remarried and had two new kids. Even though Nokwanda loves them, things haven't been the same since. (Sound familiar?) Her pops is a big-shot doctor, and has always loved his daughter, but he was never able to cope without a partner, and that's why he was quick to remarry. Sandy bullies him, and he takes it, since he's such a good guy. Nokwanda feels sorry for him, but Sandy makes it clear she wants Nokwanda out of the house.

A tear runs down her beautiful face. At first, I'm not sure what to do. She doesn't wipe it away or break down crying. She keeps talking. I offer her a tissue from the box on the bedside table. She makes space for me on the bed next to her. She holds the tissue for a while without using it. She carries on talking about her mother, the things they used to do, and how much she misses her. 'I'm sorry,' she says, wiping the tears at last.

'It's okay, I understand.'

I tell her about my family, how things used to be, and about Ernest and the old lady. I tell her about Izzy and Siz. Hopefully, my words are helpful.

Speaking to her makes me realise I don't really tell anybody these things, not like this. It's dope that we both giving each other this space.

'Ag, enough,' she says. 'I don't ever cry – especially in front of other people. What have you done to me, Bokang?'

'Nothing, I swear.'

She playfully punches me on the shoulder. 'Don't be so hard on your mom, though,' she says, all serious.

'What?'

'I know you mad at her, but she's the only mom you're ever gonna get. Nobody'll ever understand you like your mom. Give her a chance.'

I pull out the blunt and start cleaning it, all the while answering her questions and explaining the mechanisms of smoking. I rib her for her lack of smoking technique, which gets more laughs out of her.

We go into the bathroom and close ourselves off in there, only opening the small window. I load up the pipe and let her take a few hits. I talk her through the actions. She's having a blast, laughing even before she's high. Most people I know don't get high the first few times they smoke. But this stuff JP gave me is not your regular weed. It hits us both pretty quickly.

Nokwanda leans on the basin with her leg up on the bath, puffing smoke into the air. Every time she does it, she laughs like crazy and coughs, which makes me laugh like crazy and cough too.

'Why didn't you tell me this stuff was so good?' she says, with a smile glued to her lips.

'You didn't ask.'

She pokes me in the chest, then giggles uncontrollably. I giggle with her. We sit there in silence, saying nothing, just feeling the buzz. Every now and then, one of us giggles and sets the other off again.

We lie on the bed staring at the ceiling, talking about everything and nothing. We argue about which is better: hip-hop or RNB. We talk about who our worst and best teachers were from primary school until now (Ms Meadows is my favourite, hands down, no doubt). We talk about parents and how lame they are. We talk about which Doc Martens are better: six- or eight-eye black. Yo, there's nothing we don't talk about.

'Hey, I have an idea,' Nokwanda says.

'What?'

'Let's watch a movie. Yes!' She says it like it was her idea from the start, but that's cool.

We start with *There's Something About Mary,* which makes our stomachs sore with laughter. We clean out the buffet left by the domestic. By the time we watch *Saving Private Ryan*, we are nice and mellow. Throughout this one, Nokwanda asks questions about what's happening, almost like a child who is really into something and wants to know more. At the end, I'm surprised to see her wipe away a tear. I'm glad she enjoyed it as much as I did. I don't tell her I've seen both flicks before. I wanted to make sure whatever I took from the video store was a sure bet.

By the time I leave her place, I'm convinced that this has been one of the best days of my life.

Nineteen

Nokwanda becomes a big part of my life over the next couple of weeks. I'm at her place on most days. Most of the time we smoke. Most of my money goes on JP's good stuff and hiring DVDs.

Nokwanda wants to learn everything about smoking: how to clean the weed; how to roll a joint; and how to inhale and hold for maximum effect. I am the perfect teacher.

The cottage becomes our base of operations. A couple of times she even asks me to get some booze. We don't go overboard with the booze, but it's nice to have some. She loves her Hunter's Dry cider.

The one evening, I'm chilling on my bed, going through my Suicide Manifesto. Some of the things in there are insane, for real. Did I really write all of this? Ernest is hanging with Izzy, watching TV, while Siz and the old lady are busy elsewhere in the house.

There's a tapping sound on my bedroom window. At first I don't react. But then it comes again. What the hell? I get up and pull the curtains open enough for me to peek out.

Standing outside in the cold June night is Nokwanda, with her arms wrapped tightly around herself. She flaps a hand, reminding me of those homeless kids waving at motorists for spare change.

I hold up my hand to tell her to wait. What the hell is she doing? Is she still on her crutches? I put on the thickest jacket I can find and throw on my beanie. I wonder about wearing gloves, but decide to leave them.

I use the kitchen door to go out back so nobody hears me. When I get outside she isn't in the spot where I checked her. I look about, feeling like I'm losing my mind. I don't want to call out her name in case somebody hears. Then I see her, standing by the bushes without her crutch, her arms crossed and looking lost. She hasn't noticed me yet.

'Nokwanda.'

Tears run down her cheeks. She leans into me, pulling me into an embrace. She's taller than me by at least half a head, so I feel like the way she's grabbing me might make me fall over. She holds on tight, and through the rustling of the leaves and the whistling of the wind, I hear her crying. This is not like the time when I saw tears running down her face; this is full-on sobbing, like a toddler. I'm not sure what to do, so I put my arms around her and squeeze back, holding on for dear life. I want to ask her what's going on, but something tells me to be quiet.

Her face is on my neck and I can feel her warm tears. Her thick hair brushes against my cheek. The jersey she's wearing is thin, and I want to tell her she's silly for not taking the necessary precautions before coming outside. I want to unzip my jacket and pull her into it and zip it up again.

One of her thighs is between my legs. If we come apart now, will we ever be this close again? I'm quietly shushing her like I'm rocking a baby. We rocking from side to side. Am I doing that?

I can feel a stirring in my tracksuit pants, but thank goodness the jacket is long enough to keep her from feeling it. How sick am I to be getting off from hugging a crying girl? I don't know, but something about this feels right. I don't know what I'm doing, but I know I'm giving her what she needs. Right now, I'm doing something that matters.

Her crying stops but she still holds on, not as tightly as before, but nicely, like we slow jamming or something. I don't know how long we stay like this, but it's for some time. I should be worried about the wind,

I should be worried about somebody in the crib realising I'm missing, but none of that matters while Nokwanda is in my arms.

After a while she giggles.

'Hey.'

'Hey.' She laughs. It's so good to hear her laugh.

'You okay?'

She laughs again. 'Yeah. I'm sorry for—'

'No, don't be sorry, Noks. It's okay.'

'Thanks.' She pulls away, and the cold that sweeps between us is a shock to the system.

'We shouldn't be out here,' I say. 'We'll get sick.' I rub her shoulder. I want to take her inside, but I know Ernest and the old lady would never have that. There's a spot on the other side of the house, between two walls, where there should be less wind. 'Come on.'

I lead her round the house by the hand. Then I sneak back inside to get some blunt, a jacket for her and a small blanket, then meet her back where I left her. When we find the spot where there's less wind, we sit on the ground, huddled together under the blanket like two children. We giggle while we take hits from my pipe.

We barely say a word. Nokwanda hasn't told me why she was crying, and I guess it don't matter right now.

When we finally mellow, she speaks. 'One of these days, I'm going to run away from home, I swear.'

I don't say anything, I just rub her arm.

'Sandy is fucking crazy! My whole life she's been on my case. I should give her what she wants, and leave.'

'It's just half a year left,' I say.

'I guess so. But that might as well be a lifetime.'

'Not really. At least it's something to look forward to. Do you know what you want to do next year?'

'There's an option for me to go to England on a netball scholarship. But it doesn't help if I'm injured. I've also been accepted at UCT on a netball scholarship.'

'Oh, Cape Town. Nice.'

'You think so?'

'Yeah. I hear good things about it. Dope place to be, apparently. Mad-freedom and everything. I can see you out there in Cape Town.'

'Really?' She wraps her arm tighter around mine.

'Yeah. I see you out there doing your thing, just being you, making the world bow to your greatness.'

'Okay, wow.' She laughs. 'Thanks, Bo.'

A moment of silence passes. My bum is numb, but I don't want to move, don't want this to end.

'What are you gonna do after Grade 12?' she asks.

'I don't really know, haven't thought that far.'

'Whatever you do, make sure it's something you good at. I've told myself I'll be playing netball wherever I go. What's the point of doing anything else?'

A light from inside the house comes on above our heads. Someone is in the dining room. We hold each other tighter, trying to stifle our laughter. The light goes out.

'Do you ever think about the future?' she asks.

'How far ahead?'

'I don't know. Like, beyond all of this. Living alone, doing your own thing, working, travelling, whatever.'

Honestly, I never waste time thinking about the future. I mean, I yearn for a time when I won't be in this situation, but I can't imagine what that will look like. Every time I think about the future, all I see is Ernest, standing there like a brick wall. I can't get past that. But now, sitting here with Nokwanda in this moment, I dare to think about what a different future could look like.

'I don't know, but I'd like to live by the sea somewhere. Have a huge yard without a fence, a room upstairs made of glass where I can sketch all day. Yeah, that would be dope.'

'Bokang?'

'Um?'

'You do live by the sea.'

We burst out laughing. I put my finger on her lips to shush her.

When we settle down, she speaks again. 'I want to take annual holidays to Majorca and sit on the beach sipping piña coladas. I missed the Commonwealth Games this year, but I want to be there in 2002, 2006 and even 2010. I want to be in a production on Broadway, a production that tours the world. And in all these things I do, I want to be with friends, friends who understand the journey, friends willing to work hard for the dream. You know what I mean?'

'You got some pretty specific dreams.'

'Your dreams have to be specific, otherwise they're a waste of time. Do you know how long I've been playing netball?'

'Nah.'

'Since I realised I was tall for my age. As soon as I realised my height gave me an advantage, I made an effort to find out what things I could excel at. When I was in primary school, I was already playing high-school netball. It's not an accident that I'm good at it now. This is a stepping stone to where I want to be. So my question to you is: what are you good at? What is your thing?'

'I don't really know about having a thing, I just know that I wish I could get outta here. Be in a different place, and be somebody else.'

The next day, Nokwanda phones me at nine in the morning, telling me she wants to smoke. I tell her the stash is finished. She says we need to make a trip to JP right quick. I tell her I've never been to JP's spot in the morning. She tells me there's a first time for everything. I tell her I don't have any more money. She tells me she doesn't need my money.

We mission through the streets of Beacon Bay, and it's great to see Nokwanda walk comfortably without her crutch.

When we get to JP's spot, his old lady opens for us with a hell of an excited greeting, which I've never received before. The little furry dog, Rasta, seems just as excited as JP's old lady. Even JP himself greets us with unusual enthusiasm, and I realise they all mad-excited because of Nokwanda.

JP and I sit on his bed, while Nokwanda sits on the chair by the desk after JP has removed his clothes from it.

'We just needed to cop some section,' I say.

'Yeah, of course, bro.' He pulls out a small bankie from his wardrobe. He hands it to me and I signal for Nokwanda to pay him.

'So Bokang told me about the koi,' she says, ignoring my signal.

JP smiles. 'What did he tell you?'

'He said something about the fish helping him find his centre or something.'

'Would you like to see them?'

We stroll down to the pond at the far end of the garden and stand on the bridge while Nokwanda laughs and coos with excitement. I'm surprised JP is cool with all of this – I guess it's the Nokwanda effect.

When we get back inside, Nokwanda finally gives him the money.

I'm even more surprised by what JP says to us at the gate as we leaving. 'Yo, a few people I know are getting together at Bonza Bay Beach on Saturday afternoon. You should come, both of you.'

'Oh, yeah?' Nokwanda says. 'Of course we'll be there.'

'Rad.'

When I get home later, I find Ernest sitting with Israel in the dining room. The table is covered with books, and Ernest is explaining something from an encyclopaedia.

After exchanging greetings, Ernest says, 'What did I tell you about France and the World Cup?'

'What?'

'They made it to the final.'

'Oh, sure.'

'As for Bafana Bafana …'

'Yeah, I know, Tata, they lost all three games.'

He holds up his hands in a *what did you expect?* gesture. 'So are you going to watch with us?'

'When is it?'

'Sunday.'

'Sure.'

The old lady sits with Sizwe in the TV room. I greet them too.

'Back to school next week,' the old lady says.

'Yeah.'

'Have you had a good holiday?'

'Sure.'

'Good. I'm so glad.'

I turn to leave.

'By the way, you had a phone call. Lulama called – Senzo's sister? She invited you to his umgidi.'

Oh, snap, I forgot about that. 'When is it?'

'Saturday. She said Senzo can't wait to see you.'

Twenty

As soon as the old lady tells me about Lulama's invite to Senzo's umgidi, I know I'm not going. Maybe I knew back when I last saw
Senzo, when he told me he's leaving East London. Maybe the decision
was made for me when I met Nokwanda, or when JP invited us to the
party: I don't know. Whatever the case, the decision is beyond me. I
don't feel bad about it, I'm just getting on with it. Senzo moved on a
long time ago and I guess I have to do the same. He's clearly not going
to be part of my immediate future, but Nokwanda is.

I meet up with her at about five on Saturday. She's wearing white
jeans, a white bomber jacket, tan boots and a beanie. Every time I see
her, she looks more fly than the last time.

We make our way to the bottle store. We have to ask the dudes
begging for change in the parking lot to buy the booze for us. Today,
Nokwanda wants to try something different so she suggests Absolut
vodka. We smoke a joint behind Spargs supermarket and take a few
raw hits of the vodka. It doesn't take long for us to feel on top of the
world with our middle fingers facing skywards.

We hook up with JP at his spot. He gives us a ride to the beach in his
little Ford bakkie. A friend of his, Gerhard – who says we should call
him G – sits in the passenger seat, while Dewaldt, a short blond kid
with mad-acne, and Yolandi, a girl who doesn't stop giggling, sit in the

back with us. Everybody in the ride is mad-high and in the mood for an even greater time.

We approach an area by the beachfront that is open grass with tables and benches and places to braai. We stop next to four other cars, where a bunch more of JP's friends hang out. Happy greetings. Friendly smiles. Hugs and cheeks rubbing together. Nokwanda fits in with everyone, and the mad-attention we getting is all because of her.

'Yo, everybody!' JP shouts above the chatter. 'Check this out. This is my man, the Supreme Khon, right here.' He turns up the volume from his bakkie and one of my songs, recorded on his beat, comes on.

Everyone goes wild. Some of them know the song; they sing along to the hook.

'Is this really you?' Nokwanda asks, elbowing me in the ribs.

I nod.

'Wow. I didn't know you rhyme.'

'No way!' says some random girl, with red-streaked blonde hair and thick mascara.

'It *is* him!' Dewaldt says. I don't even know how he knows it's me.

'If it's you, why don't you do it right now?'

The crowd gets excited, expecting me to rise to the challenge.

'Come on, Khon, bro,' JP says. 'Show them.' He turns the music off and comes towards me. Before I know it, we're surrounded: in the centre JP, me and this other kid, Sanele, who I've rhymed with before. JP drops a beat-box and Sanele and I start ripping it. Flows come easily when I'm this blunted (and drunk), so I straight-up kill it. This has got to be the dopest cipher I've ever been in with people watching. It's extra dope that Nokwanda is here, checking me out.

Afterwards, everybody wants to say something to me, asking where I learned to do that, if I'm American, where I hang out. The attention is a trip.

This one girl comes up to me and says, 'That was dope.'

'Thanks.'

We standing to the side, next to one of the rides. Everybody else is by the tables and benches and the other rides, having their own conversations.

'Do you think you could teach me to do that?' She has long black hair and a nose ring. She's dressed all in black.

'I don't know. I mean, you have to really want it, and put in the work.'

'I bet you could teach me lots of things.' She pulls on the drawstring of my hoodie. 'Is that your girlfriend?'

'Who, Nokwanda? Well, no, not exactly.'

'I think you really cool.' She rubs her hand on my chest.

'Hey, Bokang.' Nokwanda approaches. 'There you are.' She leans in really close to me. 'Who's this?'

'Oh, this is … um … Actually, we haven't met yet.'

The girl laughs. 'I'm Carla.'

'Oh, nice, *Carla*,' Nokwanda says. 'Won't you excuse us?'

We walk away from everybody. Other people are enjoying the park in their own groups, the cold weather not enough to stop them having fun. Some of them have fires blazing to keep them warm.

Nokwanda and I find a quiet place to sit. It's dark and the breeze feels good on my face.

'What a night,' Nokwanda says, putting her head on my shoulder.

'Yeah, it's pretty dope.'

'Thanks for this.'

'Yo, thanks to you. You make it so much doper.'

'Ncaah, you say the sweetest things sometimes.'

Could there ever be a better moment to kiss Nokwanda?

'You know, Nokwanda, these past few weeks have really been special to me.'

'Oh, Bo, they've been special to me too.'

'I've been meaning to um … you know …'

'Your face looks like Mickey Mouse right now!' She bursts out laughing.

I hold her, to stop her from falling over. 'Nokwanda, what I want to say—'

'Yo, Supreme!' JP shouts. 'This where you two disappeared to.'

JP stands there with two other dudes – one of them is Dewaldt – and two girls. Everybody is laughing and leaning all over each other.

Nokwanda jumps up and grabs one of the girls. She says something to her and the two of them screech with laughter.

'We going down to the beach,' Dewaldt says. 'Come with us.'

'Yes!' Nokwanda says.

'We'll catch up to you,' JP says. 'Sit with me a moment, bro.' He places a gentle hand on my arm.

We watch Nokwanda and the rest of the small group go down the grass embankment towards the parking lot leading to the beach.

'You having a rad time?'

'I am, man. What about you?'

'Yeah, I'm always good, bro. So glad you and your woman could come.'

'Yeah, big up for that.'

He silently checks me out with his eyes half-closed; he smiles like a chimp.

'What, man?'

He doesn't say anything.

'Come on, man.' I punch him on the shoulder.

'*Is* she your woman?'

'I don't know.'

'You do like her, though. That much is obvious.'

'You think she likes me back?'

'Hmm, now, that's not such an easy one.'

That's not what I want to hear. But JP is usually on point with how he sees things.

'No doubt she's happy around you, bro, but sometimes that don't mean anything if you expecting a lot. Catch my drift? But all's not lost. Only one way to find out, for sure.'

'How?'

He takes a joint from behind his ear and licks it along the side. 'Ask her, man.'

'*Ask her*? I can't just ask her.'

'How else you gonna know, bro?' He pats his pockets, swaying like he's about to fall over. When he finds his lighter, he sparks the joint. He waves the smoke away, scrunching up his face. 'I've been watching you all night – hope you don't mind – how you are with people. Like I said to you before, you got dope energy, bro.' He passes the joint to me after taking a couple of puffs. 'The people you attract are interesting.'

'What do you mean?' I take a long pull on the joint.

'I see you met Carla.'

'Yeah, I did.' I wonder if he saw us when she had her hand all over my chest.

'Carla's the one I was telling you about. Gert's ex? The one I said had that negative energy or whatever? Tried to kill herself?'

'What?'

He nods. 'Destructive girl. Sucks the life outta everything. You wouldn't say it, though. She has this beauty, you know?'

I know exactly what he means.

'This Nokwanda seems to be quite the same.'

'What do you mean?'

He smiles. Looks at the joint. I hand it back to him. He takes a pull, holds it in and exhales in a coughing fit. I wait for him to finish. 'Nokwanda seems to have something about her too, something very likable, kinda sucks you in.' He gives me a smirk.

'Yeah, she does.'

'Also seems to be running from something.'

'What do you mean?'

He stands up and places a hand on my shoulder. 'They all seem to come to you, bro, with whatever they running from. Either you some kind of saviour, or misery just loves company.'

'What?'

'Let's go, dude.'

Under other circumstances I would say the short walk down to the beach is a bad idea. Not only is it dark beyond the parking lot where the sand starts, but it's also windy and the salty air creeps beneath my layers of clothing. But tonight is no ordinary night. Tonight is too awesome for me to be stressing about what I can't control.

JP and I find the others standing at the edge of where the light ends, daring each other to go into the darkness towards the raging waters.

'You go first!' one of the girls screeches.

'No! You!' another screams.

One of the dudes picks up the first girl and carries her towards the darkness. She shrieks with laughter and he puts her down and they both come running back into the light.

'Come on, let's do this,' I say, taking Nokwanda by the hand.

She doesn't say anything, just lets me lead.

'Oooooooooh!' The others crow.

'Go, Supreme!' JP shouts. He grabs the hand of one of the other girls and follows. The others chase behind them, laughing like crazy.

Walking into the darkness towards the water with Nokwanda by my side is something I was made for. It helps that I know this beach intimately, even though I've never been here in the dark. I see clearly in my mind exactly where we going.

Nokwanda tightens her grip around my hand and arm. I can tell she's loving this. It reminds me of the night I held her crying in my arms, when we rocked to the sound of the wind between the leaves. The moon is out tonight, its shiny forehead protruding from behind the clouds.

We walk all the way until we're close to the water's edge. It's low tide, so we pretty far out. One of the other girls freaks out and says we should all head back.

I don't want to leave this place. I wish they would all leave me alone here with Nokwanda. She isn't saying much, which is cool. The sound of the waves and the wind are too loud anyways.

Nokwanda's lips touch my neck. She kisses me on the ear lobe and whispers something into my ear. My body buzzes.

'What?'

She keeps on kissing. Her heavy breathing deepens my own.

'Yo! We going back, bro,' JP says.

'Come on, I'll race you!' Nokwanda says.

The others catch on and we all run, laughing, shouting, not giving a damn. Nokwanda beats us all, and jumps up and down celebrating her victory.

When we decide the evening is over, Nokwanda and I catch a ride in JP's bakkie. This time G drives while JP sits semi-conscious in the passenger seat. Nokwanda sits next to me in the back. We drop off the other two people in the back first. Then we head to Nokwanda's place.

I climb out with her to give her a hug. 'You should come to the matric dance with me,' Nokwanda says.

'Really?' I can't believe what I'm hearing.

'Yeah, next month.'

'Wow.'

'It's no biggie. Think about it.'

There's nothing to think about. 'Yeah, of course I'll go with you.'

'Cool.'

I stand there in the middle of the street, some time in the early hours of the morning, swaying from side to side, watching her enter the gate. The street lights appear brighter than I've ever seen them.

When she turns back, smiles and waves before entering the house, the moment is perfect. I'm floating and I can't tell if it's the blunt, the booze, or this feeling I can't describe flowing through me.

Twenty-one

Back to school. Everything is different. Senzo's no longer here. Roscoe's unrelatable. I'm on a new planet. This is just the way it is.

During my break times, I hang with Randall Leonard (Delinquents R US), Dylan McFarland, Warren Scheepers and Paul Fisher – the stoner crowd. It ain't like I purposely set out to hang with them; it just kind of happened. Dylan lives down the road from St Stephen's College, so during second break we usually mission to his spot to hit a few bongs. They actually not such a bad bunch of dudes; they remind me of JP's crowd – rich white kids, mad at their parents, in love with weed, rock bands and surfing, and somewhat fascinated by black street culture.

Ernest and I come to an agreement that I can work two afternoons a week at his office. I usually make time when I don't have rugby practice. I take a taxi from Clermont to town, then, when I'm done, a taxi back to Beacon Bay. Then I go on Saturdays when we can leave together from the crib, with Tata uMfene. The only reason I do it is for the money. With my smoking habit becoming regular, and Nokwanda being a part of my life, I need the dosh.

I don't see as much of Nokwanda now that school is open. She told me straight-up on that last Sunday of the holiday (she called while Ernest, Israel and I were watching the Soccer World Cup final) that she needs to focus on getting her fitness back. I dig how she takes her netball so seriously. So most days she's practising and getting back to full fitness. Of course, I miss her, even our chats on the phone, but I understand. At least I know we going to the matric dance together, and that's good enough.

During the third week of term, I'm chilling with Randall, Warren and Paul at Dylan's spot. We hitting one bong after another. These dudes don't do rolled joints, they strictly do bongs. I suppose it's more convenient when you want a quick fix. I find the bong gets us really high, really quickly; these dudes love being high to the point where we all laughing like idiots. It's second break on a Thursday and we got about twenty-five minutes before we have to return to class.

'I don't know what I'm gonna do, bra,' Randall says. 'If I don't do something, I'm gonna fail.'

The others laugh.

'It isn't funny!' He grabs Dylan and wrestles his skinny ass to the ground. The others laugh some more.

We standing in the back garden, behind the shed. The only person home is the domestic, who already knows Dylan and his friends are crazy.

'Hey, man, why don't you ask Bokang to help?' Paul says. 'He's fucking clever, don't you know that?'

'What?' Randall says, getting up. 'Really?'

'Yeah, man,' Paul continues. 'Bokang is like some sort of black genius – no offence, bra. He creams every subject.'

'What do you need help with?' I ask.

'Fucking everything!' Warren says, to a chorus of laughter.

Randall is in Grade 9 and Warren in Grade 10, while Dylan and Paul are in Grade 11 with me.

'I can't afford to fail, bra. My mom will kill me!'

'Let's meet up, see what you struggling with.'

'He's a lost cause, bru,' Warren says.

'Give him a chance,' Paul says. 'Bokang will get him right.'

'Why don't you just stick to rugby, bru?' Warren asks.

Randall Leonard is a big kid and one of the recognised rugby heroes at junior level.

'Yeah! Maybe I should.' Randall flexes his arms like the Hulk. 'I swear I'm better than that loser Napoleon! I should be in the first team!'

'Of course you are, bru. You could take him out any day.'

'Hey, I checked Napoleon yesterday,' Paul says. 'He was losing his shit, arguing with some chick. He was ready to hit her or something, but she was shouting back at him.'

'No way!' Dylan says. 'Where was this?'

'By the park, bra. I swear the dude was about to klap her a good one, but she was ready to klap him a good one, too.'

Randall laughs, sounding like a sick-ass donkey.

'Who was this chick?' I ask.

'Don't know, bru, some black chick – no offence.'

'It must have been that chick of his,' Dylan says. 'I hear they like a celebrity couple or something. She's a netball star at Meredith House, apparently.'

'Nah, they broke up a while ago,' I say.

'Can't be,' Dylan says. 'I check them together all the time. Saw them together at least twice last week, sometimes walking past my place, probably on their way to Westwood or something.'

'Or on their way to have some fun time!' Randall says, thrusting his hips to a chorus of laughter.

It can't be. Nokwanda and Napoleon?

Two days later, my mind is put to rest when I hear from her. It's Thursday evening and I'm studying for a test the next day when I hear the familiar tapping on the window. I go out back to meet her.

As soon as I appear, she gives me a hug. I didn't realise how much I missed that.

'Hey, what up, girl?'

'You got a joint?'

'Whoa! Take it easy. Nah, actually I don't.' I need answers from her. The past few days have been madness, with me second-guessing myself and wondering if what Dylan said was true.

She pulls away from me, crossing her arms and clicking her tongue.

'You okay?'

'Yeah. Where can we score some?'

'Some what?'

'Weed, Bokang! Are you retarded?'

I don't say anything.

She sees the look on my face and leans in again for a hug. 'I'm sorry, babe. I'm not having a great day.'

'Fight with Sandy?'

'No. Can we please find a joint somewhere?'

I need to pass this English test tomorrow. I need to get my English mark up to prove a point to Ms Hargreaves, to prove a point to Roscoe, and to prove a point to myself. I haven't studied enough, and there's a lot to get through.

'*Please.*' She looks me in the eye, gives me another squeeze, rubbing her cheek against mine and touching her lips to my ear lobe. God, I've missed her these past few weeks.

'I'm not sure where we can get at this time.' I put my hands around her, feeling the dip of her spine through her top.

'What about JP?'

'Come on, you know how he is. I can't just rock up at his spot at this hour.'

'My mother died today.'

'What?'

She pulls away. 'Ten years ago today.'

I should hug her again, but she's so guarded. 'Okay, wait here, I'll be right back.'

There's nowhere we can get blunt at this hour, but at least we can get something to drink. I go into the house to get the hundred bucks Ernest paid me for the work I did this week. We still have time to get to a bottle store before they close.

We mission to one by Sherwood Place, next to the video store. I buy the bottle myself, ignoring the frown from the cashier. I put it in my backpack and we walk.

'Where we going?' Nokwanda asks, visibly happier, if only a little.
'Chill, you'll see.'

We walk down Edge Road where some of the street lights are not working.

Nokwanda tells me she's been suspended from her school netball team for fighting. Some girl tried to pull a bitch-ass move on her and she reacted harshly. She's been suspended for the next three games.

She tells me this time of the year is never easy for her. Something always happens when she starts thinking about her mom's death. What makes it worse is her pops is never willing to talk about it. It's like the dude decided that part of his life don't exist no more, even though Nokwanda is living proof of a life that once was.

At the point of the curve on Edge Road, there's a small grass area for a few cars to park. Lucky for us, nobody is here now. It's one of those nice quiet places to come to, just to clear the head. A little way from the road, a narrow path leads to a cliff that looks down on the Nahoon River and Batting Bridge.

Nokwanda and I sit on the bench, taking in the view. We can see the lights of Beacon Bay, Nahoon Valley, Vincent Heights and Dorchester Heights. Cars light up the streets in red and yellow, going back and forth, people on their way to and from wherever they spend their time.

We share the bottle of Absolut between us. We don't have dash, so we hit it raw from the bottle. It's nice in this weather: the burn in the chest goes all the way through the body. We don't talk much. It feels sacrilegious to utter unnecessary words out here.

Nokwanda moves from the bench, standing really close to the edge of the cliff. She sits down with her legs dangling over. For a moment I think she might take a leap over the edge. I hope she doesn't. There's a lot I hope for her; for me.

I move closer to her and sit exactly like she is. She smiles at me. I can't look straight down: with the vodka in my system, it makes me dizzy. It's easier to stare out ahead into the distance.

When the bottle is half-empty, Nokwanda gets up without saying anything and walks back up the path. I follow with wobbly steps.

When we get to the top, she turns suddenly, grabs me by the front of my hoodie, and pulls me in for a kiss. Our teeth clatter together; her tongue thrusts deep into my mouth. With no time to react, my arms freeze to my sides, my dizziness intensifies, and it isn't until she releases me that I open my eyes.

Everything is fuzzy. My head is light. Nokwanda's face is unreadable.

'Let's go,' she says, turning to leave.

We walk back in silence, but unlike the comfortable silence we shared at the edge of the cliff, this one feels like it should be filled with words.

Twenty-two

When it comes to planning for the matric dance, Ernest is the only person I can speak to. Not only will he make a big deal about it, but he's the only person I can ask for the money for the suit and shoes and whatever else I need for the big day. I ask him one day when we in the office, and Tata uMfene is there too. The two of them love the idea of helping me find a suit for the dance.

So on Saturday, I'm in the monster bakkie with Ernest and Tata uMfene, on our way to see Habib the Indian (that's what they keep calling him).

'I can see it already!' Tata uMfene says. 'Navy shirt, mustard pants, white fedora, white jacket, gold chain. Aneh, Radebe?'

'Hayi, hayi, hayi, Hlathi. My son is not some cheap pimp.'

'But that is a classic look, maan. Imagine it complete with a lime-green cane! Yes! And a lime-green pocket square? Yes! Finish it with a gold tooth! To go with the gold chain! Tshisa!' He laughs again, taking a corner at such high speed I'm pressed against the door in the back seat.

'There's nothing classic about that, Hlathi. We show him the options, and allow Habib to give his professional judgements.'

'Eish, wena! You always so fussy, maan! We want this to be a special night for the boy. Is this your first dance?' he asks, catching my eye in the rear-view mirror.

'Yes,' I say, with a balancing hand on the inside roof.

'So who's this lucky gal?'

What is Nokwanda to me, really? 'She's a girl I know.'

Still watching in the rear-view mirror, Tata uMfene's smile drops so hard it's almost like his cheeks are about to avalanche down his big face. 'Hayi, umfana, is she not your woo-man?'

Ernest turns back to regard me.

'Well, she is … but …'

They wait for me to finish. The rumbling of the diesel engine also seems to quieten in anticipation of my answer.

'Did you ask her to the dance?' Ernest asks.

'No, it's her dance.'

'So she's older than you?'

'Yeah.'

Ernest and Tata uMfene grin at each other.

'So she asked you, *and* she's older?'

'Yes, Tata.'

'Heh, Radebe, this boy of yours is dangerous, neh!'

'Have you kissed this girl, son?'

How can I ever forget that kiss? 'Yes, Tata.'

'Ha! Ha! Ha!' Tata uMfene grabs Ernest's hand and the two of them laugh like a couple of crooks.

'Good son, good. So she's yours, mos … ja.'

'So have you …?' Tata uMfene motions his index and middle fingers forwards twice.

The silence in the ride is hectic, both of them expectant. Ernest turns back and Tata uMfene stares at me in the rear-view mirror.

'Er … no.'

'Have you ever?' Ernest makes the same two-stroke motion with his two fingers.

'No.'

They both sigh heavily, the way I often hear them do when watching soccer and someone misses a scoring opportunity.

'Eish, ja,' Tata uMfene says. 'I guess you still a boy. But when I was your age, I was busy, maan.'

'These kids today are not the same as us, Hlathi. We became men sooner. By twenty we were moving out of home, working and standing on our own two feet. It's okay, umfana.'

He doesn't make it sound okay. He can't even look at me.

'But you know she's older than you, and she invited *you* to *her* dance, then she *wants it*, Radebe!'

I don't say anything.

'You need to make it happen! You don't want to wait until after uwolukile! I mean, after that, when you are properly a Xhosa man, you will have plenty of women, plenty, umfana wam! But still now is a time to know! Does your boy have condoms, Radebe?'

I can't believe they talking like I'm not even here.

'If he does, then not from me.'

'Well, he needs them, and he needs a talk! We can't have this!' Tata uMfene shakes his cratered cannonball of a head.

They have their own conversation for the rest of the ride to our destination. Habib's shop is at the Oriental Plaza. I've never been out here before, and the place is a trip. People everywhere. Habib's store is in a corner, the meeting point between two long rows of shops. He stands outside the store with his wrists on his hips and his fists pointing downwards. With his thinning grey hair, he looks like a sage guarding the entrance to a cave of enlightenment.

'Habib!' Tata uMfene greets in his typical way.

'Yes, Sir,' Ernest says, lifting a hand.

Habib acknowledges us with a nod. The store smells of incense: something like roots burning, with a hint of earth. Different coloured and patterned cloths hang in rows all over the place, going up towards the ceiling. Low music comes from somewhere.

'Where-you-been-Damane?' Habib says. He speaks in rapid-fire staccato like an AK-47 going off.

'Around, my good man.'

'No, no, no, no, no, no. I-don't-see-you-you-don't-come-you-find-new-tailor-huh? Where-you-been-Damane? Huh?' He gestures at Ernest's face with an open palm. 'Huh?'

Smiling, Ernest says, 'Ah, Habib, you know I'm a busy man. But I always come back.' He laughs.

Tata uMfene joins him, throwing himself into a chair uninvited.

'Ja, ja, ja. You-come-back-my-business-wait-for-you. What-I-do-for-you-today? Huh?'

'I'm here for the boy.' Ernest holds his hand out towards me like he's presenting a show pony.

Habib frowns. He eyeballs me from head to toe, all the while standing with his fists against his hips. His shirt sleeves are rolled up to the elbows, revealing his hairy forearms. He has a pencil behind one ear, a measuring tape draped around his neck like a flattened snake, and folded glasses poking from his breast pocket.

Pointing at me with his whole hand, he says, 'What-we-do-for-the-young-master? Huh? Full suit, no? Maybe two? Huh? I-give-you-three-for-nice-deal. Very-nice-deal.' He kisses the tips of his fingers. 'How-much-you-got?'

'This is what I like about you, Habib,' Ernest says. 'You always know what I want. This boy has a dance to attend.'

'Oh, I see.' Habib ushers me onto a small platform, where I stand with my arms out. He takes my measurements while Ernest and Tata uMfene argue again about which colours and material will work best.

Habib moves like a man who knows what he's doing. He keeps moving my limbs every time I try rest an arm or a leg. Every time he adjusts one of them, he makes a low one-syllable grunt. He stands upright, takes off his glasses and shouts something in a language I've never heard before to someone in the back.

A woman dressed in a purple-and-gold sari comes out. Habib shouts some more at her as if she's deaf. The woman greets Ernest and Tata uMfene – ignoring Habib – by taking their hands and touching them to her forehead. Habib carries on shouting his instructions and the woman waves him away with her hand. Tata uMfene finds all of this hilarious.

The woman disappears into the back and returns carrying folded material. She displays it on a little table in front of Ernest and Tata uMfene. Habib talks about each of the cloths, giving a detailed history. He tells us these cloths are better than the ones hanging up everywhere, and he only shows them to his supreme clientele. Ernest and Tata uMfene love the royal treatment, and Habib and his wife play right along.

I don't understand what they're yakking about, what they comparing, or even what they eventually decide. All I know is, they shake hands and come to an agreement.

Afterwards Ernest and Tata uMfene take me on a joy ride to one of their spots in Mdantsane NU 15. The place we come to is an old house converted into a hangout place. Lots of people sit outside, while others go in and out. It reminds me of the Best Bet spot they took me to in Clermont, except this place looks dodgier.

Ernest and Tata uMfene tell me to stay in the ride while they do their thing. They come out after fifteen minutes, with the old man carrying four Black Label quarts.

As we drive back to Beacon Bay, they share a beer, getting more animated with every sip. Tata uMfene tells me about how much sex he had when he was my age. He tells me what a player Ernest is. (I note with interest that he speaks about him being a player in the present tense.) They both preach about the need to always use protection, and go on and on about how HIV/Aids is killing 'our people'.

When they finally drop me back home, I sit on my bed, staring up at the ceiling, contemplating the events of the day and those still to come. For the first time in a while, I miss Senzo. He'd be pretty cool to chat with right now.

Twenty-three

On the Friday eight days before Nokwanda's matric dance, I sit in the school grandstand during sing-song. Tomorrow is a derby day against Crosby College, our biggest rivals. We always have sing-song the day before matches against a rival school. On days like this, the singing and cheering is louder, the hunger to destroy the enemy deeper and the sense of 'togetherness' heightened.

These are my worst days out here. I don't get all the hype. Everybody is out here preaching about brotherly bonding, which will help us overcome the old enemy, but all I see are more reasons to justify bullying. Anybody who isn't rugby-mad is an easy target. All juniors are cannon fodder. If you fall into these categories, arriving too early or late to sing-song puts you in the firing line. Getting away afterwards is just as hazardous, and basically as soon as sing-song ends, all potential victims have to run across the fields, away from the grandstand, towards the relative safety of the buildings.

As sing-song (and second break) ends, everybody runs towards the buildings, either in fear or with bloodthirsty eagerness. The Batter and Brawl Twins rush past me, on the hunt for easy prey. This is happy hour for oafs like them.

My status as a member of the stoner crowd has kept me off the radar of the Batter and Brawl Twins in this third term. Spending time at

Dylan's place with those cats has changed plenty for me, mostly in a good way, although Ms Meadows and Mr Knowles don't think so. Nobody really messes with the stoner crowd.

That's how it is here: you drift with certain people and next thing, everybody puts you in a box.

Even Humphrey Thorpe, the exchange kid from England, has found his box. He hangs with Rory Beard and all the other kids pushing hard to be prefects next year. Good for him. Everybody keeps their distance from them – they too close to the teachers. The Batter and Brawl Twins breeze right past them.

Chad tackles somebody from the back and Duncan piles on. Chad then sits on top of the prone victim. I'm not sure what they're doing, but it involves messing with the victim's hair and smacking him across the face, much to the delight of the boys in the vicinity, who are grateful it ain't one of them catching a beatdown.

It's only when I'm real close that I see the person they beating on is Roscoe. He lays there trapped and damn sure shedding a few tears. Everybody else is laughing and walking on. My eyes meet his, and I keep on walking by with everybody else. I guess we really are worlds apart now.

After school, I rush out of the gate to a nearby park to meet Nokwanda – she left a message last night saying she wants to see me today. When I get to the spot, I sit on a bench and wait. I've never met her, or any girl, here before. This is the neutral zone where boys and girls from our respective schools find time to be together. Only the players come out here with the ladies, though, so I feel great knowing I'm here to see Nokwanda.

I wait for almost two hours before I decide she's not coming. On the taxi ride home, all I can think about is how messed up it is that she didn't show. A part of me reasons that maybe she was caught up with something important. But then another part of me remembers that the meeting was supposed to be important.

When I take a walk to the payphone to call her that evening, Fezeka answers and tells me Nokwanda isn't home.

Back at the crib, the old lady stops me in the passage. 'What's wrong?'

'Nothing.'

'I know when something's wrong with my baby.'

I don't respond, just head on to my room. I wish she'd stop thinking of me as her baby.

A while later I'm chilling, doing homework, when I hear a freaking ruction coming from somewhere in the house: Ernest's voice and the familiar laughter of Tata uMfene. This can't be good.

I get up off the bed and open the door into the passage. The old man calls my name from the TV room. Israel and Sizwe are busy with their homework while the old lady catches up on her soap operas. Now everybody stops what they're doing to watch Ernest. He's standing in the middle of the room, dancing around with some huge plastic in his hands.

'Come here, boy.' Ernest smiles and Tata uMfene can't help grinning. The two of them are properly soused, and I'm trying to figure out why the old lady isn't having a fit over it. I'm also stunned she allowed Tata uMfene inside the house, especially on a week night.

'What is it, Tata?'

'This is for you, my boy.' He holds out the plastic thing, and I take it from his hands.

It's a coat hanger with a suit covered by a huge white plastic. I take the plastic off and admire the suit made by Habib the Indian. I don't know anything about suits, but I can tell right off that this one is a thing of beauty. It's a dark-brown colour that shimmers gold under a certain angle of the light. The trimming has a lime-green pattern that shows at the cuffs and along the edges. The shirt is white, with the same pattern along the edges. The tie is a darker shade of the same brownish gold, except it has a fine red pattern.

I'm standing with my mouth open like a freak.

'What do you say, son?'

'Put it on!' Tata uMfene says. His eyes dart quickly to the old lady.

'Yes, put it on, Bobo,' she says, smiling.

'These are yours too,' Ernest says, handing me a shoebox.

I take it from him, but I still stand like a fool, too stunned to know what to do.

'Put them on, son.'

I go back to my room to try everything on. I can't believe how perfectly everything fits. I do look kind of slick. The shoes are amazing too, and I'm surprised Ernest and Tata uMfene chose such a nice pair without me there. Maybe I shouldn't be so surprised – I always knew the old man can throw down when it comes to threads.

When I walk back into the TV room, Ernest and Tata uMfene shout and cheer. Israel and Sizwe abandon their homework to watch the spectacle.

'Wow,' the old lady says. I haven't seen her look at me like that in ages. Dare I say, she might be proud?

I can't believe the effect me-in-a-suit is having on everybody. Ernest and Ma are happy. Israel and Sizwe are happy. Everybody is hugging. Ma has allowed Tata uMfene into the house and is treating him kindly. It's a trip. I can't even believe how excited I feel in this damn suit. The feeling is so dope, I forget Nokwanda standing me up earlier in the day. I also forget that this suit is needed for a dance I'm supposed to be going to with her.

Twenty-four

The first time I ever thought about a matric dance as something I would be part of was four years ago, when Senzo's sister, Lulama, was planning for hers. It was one of the most painful times of my life, probably the first time I had my heart broken.

See, I'd been into Lulama for as long as I'd been friends with Senzo. She knew it too, cos she led me on, pretending she wanted me as much as I wanted her. I remember times when I would visit Senzo and see her in another room, and she would call me and chat me up, laughing at things I had to say. That year she went as far as saying I could be her date for her matric dance. Imagine that – thirteen at a matric dance!

Of course, then I was too naïve to know she was playing me. But I believed it when she first said it. I really thought I had a shot with her cos that's the year I grew much taller than Senzo, and I thought I was maturing. She was the one who kept noticing my growth every time I was visiting Senzo. Right up until a month before the dance, I thought we were going together. Then Senzo's punk ass told me she had a boy-friend and everybody was laughing at me. Even Roscoe had a good laugh.

For the four weeks building up to the dance, I pretended I was over the whole damn thing, but when I saw her on the night, in her maroon dress, cleavage all out, lips all shiny, hair all done in my favourite style,

I damn near died. My heart broke all over again. And then this dude, Vumile Somebody-or-other, showed up in his mom's Benzo and took the woman of my dreams to the dance of a lifetime. It was ugly.

From that day, though, Senzo and I started planning our matric dance. Senzo said he'd have his licence by then and he would drive us in his mom's SUV – it was a BMW x5 back then, but now it's an Audi Q7. We'd be rolling like pimps.

But that's never going to happen now. Senzo's gone for good. Here I am, going to my first matric dance, and I'm not even in matric yet. I'm over my feelings for Lulama, and that's mostly thanks to Nokwanda.

My new threads are slamming, and the biggest surprise is that Tata uMfene arranged a ride for me. This nigga really came through for me, with a royal-blue 1988 Toyota Cressida 2.8 RSi. This is a true pimp-mobile and I couldn't have thought of a better ride to roll up in. Of course, I can't drive it cos I don't have a licence yet, and Tata uMfene is protective of the damn thing. So he got some nephew of his, who's in his twenties, to be my chauffeur. He even ordered the dude to dress the part to make my night proper.

Dude scoops me up right on time at 4.45 p.m. He's bumping RNB in the ride, some Johnny Gill, which under different circumstances I would have issues with. I've been practising my dance moves to RNB, preparing for this night. The dance starts at 6.00 p.m. so my plan is to show up at Nokwanda's at 5.15 p.m. We haven't spoken all week and we never really discussed a pick-up time, or what time the dance starts. I took the initiative and found that out from some of the matrics at our school who are going to the dance. This is probably Nokwanda's test to see if I can plan and execute successfully. Well, she better be ready, cos she's in for a surprise.

I say bye to the fam – old lady and the kids – standing there waving like I'm leaving the planet or something. Ernest isn't here to see me off, which is a pity, but I guess he's already done enough with the suit and everything.

'Where are your clothes for the after-party?' my chauffeur asks. His name is Daniel.

'Oh, yeah. Good looking.' I run back and pack a bag with some fresh clothing.

I sit in the back seat of the ride to get the real feeling of being chauffeured. The drive over to Nokwanda's is quick. My chauffeur gets out and opens the door for me. Imagine that?

While I ring the buzzer, he leans against the ride, looking slick. He gives me a double thumbs-up. I fix my collar and straighten my tie.

'Can I help you?' The voice over the intercom is stiff and formal – Sandy.

I clear my throat. 'Yeah, I'm here for Nokwanda.'

'She isn't here.'

'Oh. But I'm here to pick her up.'

'Well, she isn't here.'

The click is loud. I clear my ear with my index finger. Daniel looks at me, holding up his hands in a *what's going on?* gesture. I wish I knew.

While I'm still trying to figure it out, the front door opens. A little person comes sneaking out and runs towards the gate.

'Hey.'

'Hey, Fez. What up?'

'I'm good, thanks. You looking for Nokwanda?' She pushes her glasses up on the bridge of her nose.

'Your mom said she's not here?'

Fezeka looks back over her shoulder. 'Mom's not in a good mood. She's never in a good mood these days.' I'm reminded how mature this little thing is. 'Nokwanda already left for the dance.'

'So she wants to meet there? Cool.' The girl stares at me until I feel foolish under her gaze. 'What?'

'She left with her date.'

'No, no. That can't be right, see. *I'm* her date.' I hit my hands on my chest to make my point.

The little girl wraps her jacket tighter around herself and gives me that same patient look, pity brimming in her little eyes.

'You mean she went with somebody else?'

'I have to go now. Mom will be looking for me. Good luck.'

The little thing runs back into the house.

Gone with somebody else? What April-Fool's-Day-Halloween-Sucker-Hour-Joke's-On-You-Nonsense is this?

'So what's happening, brother?' Daniel asks.

'She's already at the dance.'

'So you meeting her there?'

'She's with somebody else.'

'Eish, no, baba!' He rubs a hand over his head. 'Forget it.'

'Drive.'

'Are you sure?'

'*Drive.*'

Daniel talks as we move – I'm sitting up front now, forget the chauffeur experience. He drives with little urgency, as if he's stalling for time. He asks for my opinion on random things, a nervous edge to his voice. I don't listen to what he says or respond either. He doesn't do well in silence, so he puts the music up. Keith Sweat croons about a girl that's got him twisted. Then he asks some girl who can love her like he does, who can sex her like he does, and who can treat her like he does. Nobody, apparently. I switch off the sound without asking Daniel's permission. He doesn't argue.

A line of cars is pulling into the main gate of Meredith House. All of them are fancy; there's even a horse-drawn carriage. They pass a gauntlet of fascinated onlookers crowded outside the school hall. It looks like a night at the Oscars. Huge lights brighten the area outside the hall, pointing upwards like a Batman signal. A red carpet flows from the double doors of the main entrance to the hall, down the steps and into the path the cars drive past. Each car (and the horse-drawn carriage) stops on the red carpet and the partner to each lady steps out, opens the door for their date, and then waves to cheers and flashes from cameras. A professional photographer asks each couple to pose before moving on to greet the head of the school and her spouse, after which they enter the colourfully decorated hall.

All of this I watch from the passenger seat of the Cressida. A security guard leans in Daniel's window, asking him what we're doing here.

Can't he tell we're here for the goddamn dance? While the two of them discuss the obvious, I open the door and rush into the crowd. I hear the security guard holler, but I'm not listening. I have to find Nokwanda.

Everybody is mad-excited, cheering while the ladies pose in their fancy dresses. I'm straining my neck, wondering where the hell Nokwanda is. I figure she must be inside already, with this mystery date. I'd love nothing more than to race up the red carpet, push over the foolishly grinning chick with her muppet-faced partner, kick the photographer in the groin, backhand the head of the school and her spouse, and enter the building like Chuck Norris on uppers. But that wouldn't work; everybody is staring directly at the double-door main entrance.

The security guard cuts a swathe through the crowd, coming towards me. I scoot away towards one of the side entrances. Two girls dressed like forest nymphs stand on either side on the doors. I move past them into the hall. One of them says something with a smile, but I ignore her.

The theme for the dance is an enchanted forest. Fake trees line the walls of the hall. Blue, white and green streamers hang from the ceiling. More of the little nymph girls flitter about the place. They must be Grade 8s playing waitresses tonight. Excited girls in pretty dresses and garish makeup stand talking; others are already seated and all teeth, eagerly waiting for proceedings to begin. Their partners smile stiffly, playing their parts.

I scan the hall, searching for Nokwanda. Two security guards enter the hall from the main entrance. I have to find her before those fools get to me. I move through the crowd. More ladies and their dates come in through the main entrance.

A lady up on stage at the front fiddles with the mic. A technician dressed in jeans and a jersey, out of place in this enchanted world, holds the mic stand, helping her. I head towards them and climb onto the stage. The lady gives me a plastic smile while the technician looks bewildered. I ignore both of them, using my elevated position to scan the hall.

Nokwanda's afro is easy to spot, to my far left. She's standing, taller than everybody around her, by a table chatting with a group of girls, her emerald-green dress sparkling in the light. Even from up here, I can see the tiara she's wearing; it gleams like metal from a distant solar system. Next to her, I see Napoleon's ugly face absorbing all the light in the room like a black hole.

I jump off the stage and cut through the people. My heart pumps diesel and I'm sweating like a man living on borrowed time. I elbow my way through the crowd, not stopping to apologise.

'Nokwanda!'

She turns to me. '*Bokang*? What are you doing here?'

'What do you mean, what am I doing here? I'm your *date*!'

Heads turn. Eyes widen. Mouths gape. Doesn't everybody love a good show?

'You must be confused.'

'Nah, don't give me that!'

Napoleon snatches at my arm, and I smack his with my other arm.

Somebody puts a hand on my shoulder. Another seizes my arm. Napoleon grabs the front of my suit, and a couple of my shirt buttons pop like corn kernels in a hot pan.

'You're not supposed to be here,' one of the security guards says.

'Of course I am! I'm here with her!'

'You crazy, Damane!' Napoleon says.

A teacher approaches. 'Excuse me, what is happening here?'

'This boy is not supposed to be here, Ma'am.'

'Of course I am! I'm her *date*!'

Napoleon shoves me in the chest and a scuffle breaks out, but the security guards hold me back. I have to catch my breath when they pull us apart.

'Hey! Hey!' the teacher says. '*You*, back!' – pointing at Napoleon. 'Nokwanda? Is this your date?' – pointing at me.

'No, Ma'am.'

'Then I think you need to leave, young man.' She nods to the security guards.

They haul me out like I'm some sort of criminal. I shout Nokwanda's name, but they have me out of there so fast, nobody's listening. They toss me like garbage onto the pavement.

I get up and rush one of them.

He puts his hands on my chest and says, 'Hey! Stop it! You'll get hurt.'

I want to fight him, I want to fight them all. They grab my fists as I wriggle my arms. They wait for the fight to deflate from my body.

Falling to the ground. Staring at the concrete. Gagging.

'Go home.'

They go back inside, leaving me with nothing.

Twenty-five

One time, when I was ten years old, Israel was four and Sizwe was a few months, we were coming back from somewhere as a family at night. I don't remember where we had been, but Ernest was driving, and the old lady was in the passenger seat, holding Sizwe. Israel and I were arguing in the back seat and Ernest kept telling us to hush up.

Eventually Ernest lost his temper when something I did made Israel cry. He pulled the car over to the side of the road and told me to get out. At first I thought I didn't hear him right, but when he said it again, I thought he must be joking. Well, he wasn't, and I stepped out into the night and watched them drive off.

That was the first time I realised how cold and lonely the world can be. I don't know where it was they left me, by some bridge on a curving road. There I was, standing under the bridge, listening to echoing sounds, water dripping from somewhere, stones crunching under my feet, my ears clogged with the sounds of my own sobbing. Voices carried through the night air but I couldn't see anybody.

For the longest while no car passed, and I remember feeling like something was coming for me. My child's mind made me believe a troll living under the bridge would find me. It felt like everything was plotting against me: the darkness of the night threatening to fall on me; the cold wind laughing at me; my crying giving away my position; the voices in my damn head telling me terrible things; and the distant sounds of people living their lives, mocking me in my situation.

The folks eventually came back. It probably wasn't long after leaving me, but it was long enough to open up a gap in my subconscious. That gap has been tearing wider over the years, filling with all sorts of things I have no control over. I remember nightmares I had from that time onwards, where I'd wake up in the middle of the night, feeling like I did under that bridge with the dirty-ass water dripping from somewhere I was too scared to look. During those days at the facility with Dr Schultz, that same feeling of something inside me splitting open, and something horrible and sludgy pouring in, consumed me beyond agony.

That feeling has never really left me. It comes and goes. For the most part, I keep it buried. When it returns, though, I sometimes can't fight it off. I can't stop the gap tearing wider, the grime pouring in, mixing with whatever is within, so that only vileness spews back out.

Walking through the night, from Meredith House to Beacon Bay, this is how it feels. Raindrops fall all around me, inside me. My eyes are raw, but I have no more tears. Tears for what? Am I angry? Embarrassed? Sad? Crazy? Who knows? All I know is that this right here is the walk of the dead. I don't feel like reaching where I'm going. I know I can't go back. I'm wandering aimlessly. All I have is the same questions and an emptiness.

Outside the crib, blue lights flash, cars block the driveway. The Cressida is there. Two police vans. The old lady comes running, screaming my name. Daniel screams with her, holding his hands over his head.

'Bokang! Oh, my baby!' She wraps me in a hug.

The police aren't impressed.

Apparently Daniel told everybody I went missing.

Missing from what?

It's almost two in the morning.

Oh. I guess I have been missing.

Bokang Damane: Tell me, what is the true nature of the thing?

The Supreme Khon: The thing is unbound. It can manifest in any way it so pleases, in different moments.

Bokang Damane: Why must this thing be? Why does it always come for me? Why me?

The Supreme Khon: You created the thing, young apprentice.

Bokang Damane: No, no, that cannot be. Why would I create something that would destroy me?

The Supreme Khon: It is in your nature. It is in the nature of all of your kind

Bokang Damane: I don't believe you. How don't I know you are not the thing itself?

The Supreme Khon: …

Bokang Damane: Khon? Talk to me. Don't leave me alone!

Twenty-six

I'm absent the first two days of school the following week. I don't know what's ailing me, but whatever it is, it keeps me in bed right through the weekend. The old lady takes half a day off work to take me to the doctor. He books me off for those two days and gives me a prescription, which we collect from the pharmacy. It's a mountain of medication and I'm only too happy to take the pills. They knock me out enough to pretend I'm sleeping.

On Wednesday morning, I walk through the main school gate. I'm watching all the boys to see who is checking me out. Nobody seems interested, so I figure most of them don't know about the dance. Why would they know? It's not like I'm famous around here.

First period is Science class. Outside the classroom, I check Roscoe. He's eyeballing me hard. He's still got a bit of bruising under one eye. He doesn't come close, though. He's not the confrontational type. He wants me to know what he's going through by staring me down. I don't have time for that, not today.

Throughout the class Roscoe keeps turning around to eyeball me. He does it again in the next class and the one after that. I ignore him. I got my own problems.

I didn't bring lunch today, so at first break I head on down to the cafeteria to get something to eat. I push to the front to buy a cheese-andham pie. As I push my way back through the queue, I come face to face with Napoleon Dikembe and his monkey-ass sidekicks, Siyabulela Mthembu and Lonwabo Dyini.

'What's up, Damane?' Lonwabo says, grinning.

Siyabulela laughs his irritating laugh: *ahaw, ahaw, ahaw, ahaaaw.*

I don't say anything.

Napoleon also remains silent. The tip of his tongue is visible as he rubs his left hand over his right fist.

'Don't be rude,' Lonwabo says. 'Say hello. Damn, nigga.'

'Maybe he's too much of a celebrity to say hello,' Siyabulela says.

'Maybe he's too much of a *ladies' man.*'

I don't have time for this shit.

'Where you think you going?' Lonwabo says, placing his hand on my chest.

I swipe Lonwabo's hand away, then throw the pie in the direction of Siyabulela's face. The pie misses its target and strikes some other boy in the back of the head.

Napoleon lunges forward, grabbing me by the blazer. He pulls me so close, our foreheads touch. 'What the fuck you think you doing, Damane?' His breath is empty-stomach sour.

'Ah, you dead now, sani,' Siyabulela says, clapping his hands. *Ahaw, ahaw, ahaw, ahaaaw.*

Napoleon breathes heavily and white spit bubbles form at the sides of his mouth. He's like a bull about to charge. He pulls my blazer so tight it pinches me in the armpits. 'Say something!'

What is there to say? I wriggle hard, trying to get free.

He grabs me tighter and drags me out of the cafeteria into the tarred area outside the buildings. Everybody watches. Nothing like a first-break cafeteria brawl to get tongues wagging.

Napoleon puts me in a headlock. From my bent position, I see the Batter and Brawl Twins watching.

'Oh, you so fucked, Dama-nee bru,' Chad says, clapping his hands.

Others clap too. Roscoe also watches. He isn't grinning like the rest of them. He watches with the same intense stare he's been giving me all morning.

Napoleon squeezes me in the headlock, forcing me to my knees and damn near causing me to pass out.

I sink my teeth into his thigh.

'What the fuck! Nigga, did you just bite me?'

Everybody laughs. At least I'm no longer in the headlock. I'm down on all fours, trying to catch my breath.

A bloodthirsty circle forms around us.

Ahaw, ahaw, ahaw, ahaaaw. Siyabulela is clapping.

'What were you doing with my woman?' Napoleon says. He's playing to the crowd; we gladiators in an arena.

'Go to hell!'

The crowd lets out a loud 'oooh'. They laugh at Napoleon. He doesn't like that. Not at all. He grabs me again by the blazer and uses me as a battering ram, busting through the circle of boys and banging me against the wall head first. White stars. Purple moons. Nausea.

'You think you hard, huh? I'm gonna teach you a lesson.'

He gorilla-punches me in the gut. Falling forever. On all fours. Choking for breath. Spitting out whatever I'm gagging on.

'This loser,' he says, walking around the circle of onlookers, 'really, really, *really* thinks he can take my woman!'

'*Nooooo*!' the crowd roars.

'He thinks he's a *player*!'

The crowd laughs.

'What should I do to this *punk*?'

'Fuck him up!'

'Kill him!'

'Kick his ass!'

Napoleon turns towards me, right at the second I rise up, launching myself at him for an attack, grabbing him around the midriff, trying to knock him backwards. It doesn't work: he's built like a tree trunk. He plants two elbows in my back, sending me to the ground. Then he lifts me up and holds me by the shoulder while he drives, one, two, three punches into my gut, which results in me firstly throwing up my break-fast, and secondly landing in the vomit, where I lie, convinced I must be dead.

Ahaw, ahaw, ahaw, ahaaaw.

'Stay the fuck away from my woman!'

Feet move away. Muffled echoes become fading voices. The world is fuzzy. I drag my face off the tarred surface. Everything spins for a while so I have to sit. I lean against the wall, my head between my legs.

Eventually I go to the toilets to clean up. I throw up again. It feels like Napoleon's fist is still lodged in my gut. The bell signals the end of break while I'm leaning over the basin holding back another surge of vomit. I take my time. I let water run over my head and face.

I can't go back to class. There's no one to talk to here, no Roscoe and no Senzo. Out the school gate. Across Main Road by Meredith House, Nokwanda's school. The memory of being tossed out like a sack of garbage still stings. Westwood train station. I go through the hole in the fence. The place is deserted.

The track is open, long and wide. I move to cross but stop, standing in the middle. I stare in the direction of the tracks. I turn back the other way. I have nowhere to go. I can't go back to school and I can't go home. I toss my school bag aside. I lie down on the metal rails. I was always headed here. This is it.

Does it hurt when metal wheels crush bones? When organs pop and liquids soak into the ground? Probably not. When it happens, it will be as perfect as can be: splattered, battered and shattered. That will be me. If the train comes from the front, from the direction of my legs, there will be an extra split second of hurt before it hits me. But if the train comes from behind, from the direction of my head, it'll be all over before I know what hit me.

Lord, give me this.

Just this.

Please.

I've never really asked for much. There should be a discount on the things you don't get in life, like afterlife bonus points for unanswered prayers or something. I don't have much more to ask for, except a simple death.

Death by Train, Suicide #23.

There's something poetic about that.

The coarse gravel is hard against my back. The sun is intense today, defiant and raging in these last cold winter days when things have been dying. A time to die. What a time to die.

My hip bone aches.

A gust of wind, like the hand of something withered and mean, makes its way under my collar. Goosebumps ripple their way across my flesh. I pull my school blazer closer around me. (Ha, ha, ha. What's the point?) The best part about all this is that I'm in my school uniform: the proud maroon-and-navy stripes of St Stephen's College. It couldn't be more fitting: 'Boy from College with Proud Tradition Found on Railway Line, Mangled by Metrorail Passenger Train; City Crushed by Incident.' The irony. I hope they get the principal, Mr Summers, to personally come scrape my remains off the tracks. Knowing him, he would find a way to spin this into something that had nothing to do with the school.

The rusty railway tracks vibrate. The rim of my ear touches the cold rail. The gravel dances above the ground. Something heavy is coming. It has my name on it.

Is this what I want?

Yes.

No.

What does it matter what I want?

The train is coming. It's time to go. Whatever comes next is waiting for me. The train hoots; the sound bellows through the late-morning air.

My heart beats double-time. *Oh, God, this is gonna hurt!* I squeeze my eyes shut; tears run down my temples into my ears. The train hoots again, this time louder, a pleading wail. The railway tracks quiver so much it feels like a demon is digging itself up out of the ground.

'Hey, wena!' someone yells. *'Hey! Get out of the way!'*

The train hoots, louder this time.

The front of the train has death written all over it, the invitation I've been waiting for. Its head is an angry orange, the rest of its snaking body grey and yellow. It's hungry for me. Its grinding wheels chomping down; oily saliva slicks the sides of its face, dripping from its metal gums. Smoke billows from its machinery.

I shut my eyes and hold my arms out to the sides, beckoning for death to take me.

My story ends here.

'Hey!'

Somebody stands over me. Two of them. Hands yank me up roughly. Two security guards pull me off the tracks.

I fight them off, like I fought those bastards who threw me out of the dance, catching one of them with a punch to the ear. They tag-team me and the three of us tumble onto the grass. A rush of wind blasts us as we hit the ground, rolling down the small embankment, arms and legs flailing, heads colliding.

The hoot of the train is a deep blast of fury. The train rattles past, carriage by carriage, like a lifetime of bad memories. It's so loud, a weight presses down on my chest. I'm on my back and I can't breathe.

I'm dying.

From what?

Silence.

The noise of the train stops with a jarring suddenness as the last carriage whizzes by.

The weight on my chest is lifted. A security guard stands over me.

'Hey, wena! What's wrong with you?' He slaps me across the face, then shakes me like a rag doll. His partner tries to stop him, but not before his palm swishes across my face twice more.

I don't resist. I'm limp in his arms.

I've got nothing left.

I can't even get dying right.

Book III
September 1998

Book III
September 1998

Twenty-seven

Seconds, minutes, hours, days, weeks and months. Everything is a mess.

I'm twelve years old again, back at Milton Mental Health Centre in Clermont with Dr Schultz – except he's no longer here, there's a Dr Mbatha instead. She's a short, serious woman with an afro – not like Nokwanda's, more compact, closer to the skull. Her glasses have thick black frames. A silver crucifix hangs around her neck.

I'm in Mr Summers' office, sitting with my head hanging between my legs; I taste the vomit brought up from my gut by Napoleon's fist. *Ahaw, ahaw, ahaw, ahaaw.* Mr Summers speaks to the old lady in a grave voice, the voice of a man juggling the need to care for the erratic scholar and the need to preserve the reputation of the great college. Ma bends down to say something. She's scared to come close and put a hand on me, as if I'm a circus lion no longer interested in doing tricks. Mr Knowles is here, too. In his shitty brown suit. He doesn't say much. He doesn't look surprised.

A crowd of people gathers. Some shout. Others argue. Someone is trying to hit me. It's that same security guard. He's still mad as hell. (Why is he mad?) I'm in handcuffs. (Why?) Someone is telling them to release me. I'm sitting against a brick wall. (It's so cold.) This is Westwood train station. The security guard won't let me sit. He says I don't deserve to sit. He says I'm a cheese boy. Someone says they should take me to school. Why am I not at school?

Ahaw, ahaw, ahaw, ahaaw.

The security guard holds his hat in his hands, explaining to Mr Summers – no, it's not a security guard, it's a police officer. Mr Summers asks if I really was on the train tracks. He watches me, his perfect face masking nothing – he's scared, scared of *me*.

Ma has her white shoes on. She usually wears those to church. I remember the day she bought them; it was a Sunday, and the two of us had been at Bonza Bay Beach that morning. I wonder if Pastor Mzoli digs these shoes – *bastard Pastor Mzoli*, with his nasty-ass overgrown pinkie fingernails.

Ma doesn't talk to me in the ride. She doesn't talk to me in the reception area of Milton Mental Health Centre. Am I back here again? Just like when I was twelve years old, when she last brought me here, she leaves it up to me to figure out what's going on. She only talks to me when she says she has to go, and she will see me.

See me when?

> I'm back on the highway, in the black car, with a dude in a black hoodie driving. We speeding. 'Where we going?' Dude ignores me. He's struggling to keep the car under control as we swerve on the wet road. He almost hits a car driving in the opposite direction. The other car hoots. 'You must find it, Bokang,' he says. *'What must I find?'*
>
> He turns around. He has no eyes in his sockets. I want to tell him to keep his eyes on the road, but he has no damn eyes. Loud hooting. It's the train! Behind us, through the rain, the orange snarling metallic face of the train, slick with black oil (insane), bashing its way through traffic (it's not a game! It's not a game! It's not a game!). It crushes cars beneath it and sends others flying in all directions. It hoots again, catching up fast. *'You must find it!'*
>
> The train smashes into us.

'Did you f-f-find it?'

A pale creature with big eyes stares, tilting its head – no, wait, I'm the one lying down.

Get up slowly. The creature sits on the bed on the other side of the room, its feet on the bed and its knees drawn to its chest. The creature is impossibly thin, with big feet and sunken hollows for eyes. Shaved head. Bandaging covers half of it. Both wrists also wrapped in filthy bandages.

'S-s-so?'

'So what?' Throat hurts. The water on the bedside table tastes stale and dusty.

'So did you find it – *find it*?'

'What?'

Big smile; the creature has triangular teeth. 'The p-present I left you?'

'What present?'

The door opens, sending the creature flinching into a corner on the other bed. It draws the sheet over itself as a shield.

'Morning,' a short woman in a white coat says. She's wearing thick black-framed glasses. A bigger woman in a nurse's outfit follows behind, carrying a small tray with authority. 'How are you this morning?'

I don't respond, but I sit up straighter.

'How did you sleep?' She has a silver crucifix around her neck.

'Fine. Where am I?'

She looks at me quizzically. 'You don't remember?'

The creature stares at me, horrified, from the corner of its bed, slow-ly shaking its head.

I do know where I am. Dr Schultz is no longer here. (Right.) Dr Mbatha is my new doctor. (Right.)

'I do.'

She looks at me expectantly.

'Clermont. Milton.'

'Great. How long have you been here?'

Shit. 'Er ... two days?'

She watches me like a hungry cat. 'So how did you sleep?'

'Great.' *How long have I been here?*

She turns to the creature. 'And you? How are we this morning?'

'F-fine, Doctor,' the creature responds in a surprisingly deep voice I didn't notice before. I see how big its Adam's apple is, despite its slight frame.

'Good. So I'll be seeing both of you later this afternoon.'

'Yes, Doctor.' The creature smiles, revealing its sharp teeth.

The nurse steps forward, holding a tray with an assortment of medication. The creature comes forward gleefully, like a child offered sweets. It grabs some pills, tosses them in its mouth and washes them down with a green liquid.

The nurse turns the tray to me. All eyes watch me closely: Dr Mbatha, the nurse whose name I don't know (or can't remember) and the creature. I take the pills and wash them down without fuss.

'Good,' Dr Mbatha says, turning on her heel. The nurse follows, closing the door behind her, and something about her demeanour tells me she thinks she runs this place.

The creature moves to the edge of my bed, smiling and rubbing its hands together. 'I thought – *thought* – you were going to defy.'

'Going to what?'

'Defy Nurse Swaartbooi. Not take your p-pills – *pills*.' Every time it repeats a word, it blinks twice, but one eye blinks before the other.

'Why would I do that?'

'It's what you did when you got here. You kicked and p-punched!'

'When was this?'

'F-four days ago! That's why I left you a p-p-p … p-present! I p-put p-p-pills there for you!' The creature points at my side table. 'You s-swallowed them at night.'

The side table is bare. I must have taken the pills. Maybe they helped me sleep. *Four days?*

'S-s-so what did you do?'

'Huh?'

'Yass! There was p-police with you when you came here. They wanted to arrest you. But your mother, and this white toppie in a suit, and a white sister, told them no. *No*! S-so the police left! What did you do?'

Train station. Train tracks. Angry orange-faced train. Security guards. They must have called the police on me. Mr Summers' office, the old lady, Mr Knowles and Ms Meadows. The police must have wanted to arrest me, and somehow the old lady, Mr Summers or Mr Knowles (probably him, as a psychologist), convinced them to bring me here instead. It's just down the road from St Stephen's College.

'I didn't do anything.'

'Everyone's talking about you. Yass! They want to know you.'

'What's your name?'

'Sheldon – *Sheldon*.'

'How long have you been here?'

'Over three weeks. Nobody stays more than two months. It's not my first time here – *here*. Doctor Mb-batha says I'm getting better. B-b-but my mother ...'

'What about your mother?'

'She says it's b-better I stay here a b-bit.' He looks down, biting the side of his thumb. All his nails are bitten down to the stubs. It looks painful.

The medication is starting to work. Heavy eyelids. Thick tongue. I sink back down in my bed, pulling up the covers while Sheldon looks down at me, his teeth glistening.

Later that day, I shower before eating a lunch that tastes like cardboard. The shower hasn't freshened me up as I expected, and the food hasn't helped; I feel sluggish. I don't know what medication I'm taking.

We sit in a grey room with a grey ceiling and a grey floor. These colours surely aren't the best for lifting people's moods. The fluorescent lights above are low-hanging and bright. We sit in a semi-circle. Next to me, Sheldon gnaws at what's left of his thumb.

'I mean, I'm not complaining or anything,' the girl sitting across from me says in a complaining voice. 'If it's the best they can do, then it's the best they can do.' She shrugs, her hands on her elbows.

'Okay, Pinky. Your request is noted,' Dr Mbatha says. 'Anybody else want to share how they feel about lunch?'

Sheldon shakes his head while scratching at the bandages on his wrists; the others (including me) look at the floor.

'Maybe you've had budget cuts,' Pinky says, taking advantage of the silence. 'Cheap is what you are.'

Dr Mbatha gives her a benevolent smile, allowing her to ramble on.

When Pinky stops talking (an impressive two minutes and thirty-nine seconds later), Dr Mbatha turns her gaze on me. 'Who here would you say you know?'

Around the circle, faces gawk at me. Pinky gives me a look that could peel skin. Next to her is Solomzi, a dude built like a penguin that's let itself go. His eyes move back and forth between Pinky's exposed legs and her neck.

'Sheldon,' I say.

They all wait. Sheldon bites on his bottom lip. I'm not sure if that's an intended smile.

'And?' Dr Mbatha motions with her hand.

'And he's been great.'

'What do you know about him?'

'He's thoughtful.'

'Oh? Really? Explain.'

'He gave me a present.'

'That's nice of you, Sheldon.' Dr Mbatha does a silent clap.

'You better be careful,' Solomzi says, with a chuckle.

'Solomzi, you'll get your turn. Sheldon, what made you give him the present?'

Sheldon crosses his legs, one way and then the other. He folds his arms. His elasticity is grotesque. 'I was just b-being nice – *nice*.'

'Because you want him,' Solomzi says.

Pinky laughs with Solomzi.

Sheldon shakes his head. 'What nice thing have you done for any-b-body in here?'

'I don't need to do anything nice for anybody. I don't belong here.'

'Why not?' Dr Mbatha asks.

'I don't know what's up with this place. I don't know why we have to sit here talking about our feelings.'

'You haven't said anything about your feelings, Solomzi,' Dr Mbatha says. 'Want to share something? Anything?'

'I don't want to be here. How's that for sharing?'

'What is it about this place you don't like?'

'The food, for one.'

'Yes! Thank you,' Pinky says, clearly feeling vindicated. She pats Solomzi's thigh in a gesture that seems overly intimate.

Sheldon scoffs, shaking his head.

'What?' Pinky says, pointing a finger at Sheldon. 'You think something's funny?'

Sheldon covers his mouth.

'Ja, exactly! Say nothing.'

'Okay, easy, Pinky,' Dr Mbatha says. 'We all get along here. Nobody's fighting. Everybody gets heard.'

'Well, *she* doesn't say anything,' Pinky says, pointing at the girl on the other side of Sheldon.

The girl Pinky is referring to gazes fixedly at the floor. Can she hear us? The spot she's looking at is blank. I'd love to be on whatever meds she's on.

'Don't worry about Noxy,' Dr Mbatha says. 'Focus on what you'd like to share.'

'I agree with Solly,' Pinky says. 'Something is very wrong in this place.'

'You *would* agree with him,' Sheldon says under his breath.

'The standards have gone down. I mean, we don't even know your qualifications, *Doctor*. You can't be much older than me.'

Dr Mbatha smiles but doesn't say anything.

Pinky goes on another rant, sounding like a power drill working through a sheet of corrugated iron. She complains about everything. Nothing she says makes sense and she keeps repeating herself. Why isn't Dr Mbatha cutting her off?

'Okay, thanks, Pinky,' Dr Mbatha says eventually. 'Nox? What do you have to say today?'

'About what, Doc?' She slouches so much that the back of her head is almost on the headrest of the chair.

'How you're feeling?'

Solomzi makes a hissing sound. Pinky shakes her head.

'I … I'm okay, Doc.'

'Is the Holy Spirit still visiting you?' Pinky says. Solomzi gives her a high-five.

'Leave her alone!' Sheldon says. 'At least she's not sleeping around!'

'You just jealous because he won't give you any!' Pinky says, pointing at me.

Why isn't Dr Mbatha intervening?

Sheldon stands up and covers his ears.

'You see, Doc,' Solomzi says. 'I don't belong in here, with this.'

'So what exactly makes you better than him?' I ask.

Everyone turns to me, including Sheldon, who opens his eyes. One of them won't stop blinking.

'Well, for one, I'm not a *freak*!'

'Something must be wrong with you, otherwise you wouldn't be here.'

Sheldon sits down. Noxy sits up in her chair, marginally more attentive. Pinky's knee bounces up and down.

'Yeah, you one to talk,' Solomzi says. 'What's your story, jo?'

'I don't have a story.'

'Yeah, of course you don't. You show up here with the police. What did you do?'

'I bet he tried to kill his parents!' Pinky says.

'Yeah, the devil probably paid him a visit, like he does this one!' Solomzi says, pointing at Noxy.

'Yeah, and you just a fat bastard, lusting over this depressed skank,' I say.

Sheldon laughs hysterically, clapping his hands. Noxy holds her hands above her head and applauds too.

'Excuse me!' Pinky says. 'Are you just going to let him call me a skank?' She stands up.

'You suggested he might have killed his parents,' Dr Mbatha says in a matter-of-fact voice.

'Ah, jo, is this even therapy?' Solomzi says.

'You're having a conversation with Bokang. You said some horrible things to him. He retaliated. Now you question *me*? If Bokang is right about one thing, it's this: all of you are here for a reason. What's important is what each of you *thinks* of that reason. Bokang. Do you know why you're here?'

Suicide attempt. Nokwanda's rejection. Napoleon's fists. St Stephen's College. Ernest's drinking. Ma's cheating. Israel and Sizwe. Roscoe's judgement. Senzo leaving. (Ernest. Ernest. Ernest.) The *thing*. I could say any one of these things.

'Because I messed up. Really badly.'

Two nights later I'm sitting outside in the garden, huddled next to an outbuilding, trying my best to keep warm. This is the first time I've been outside since I've been here. It's not that cold, but I don't have warm clothing here at Milton.

The roof would be perfect to sit on to watch the sky tonight. The constellations are clearly visible. It's been a while since I gazed up at the sky.

Someone comes out of the main building. It's Solomzi, trying his best to go unnoticed. He shuffles his sagging frame over to where I stand. He's surprised to see me in a place he thought he could have all to himself. But now that he's here, he can't go back.

'Hey, jo.'

'Hey.'

In the six days I've been here, I've never been alone with Solomzi. He's one of those guys I'd never get along with (like so many at St Stephen's), even if we were stranded together on a desert island.

He pulls out a lighter and sparks the cigarette dangling from his lips. When he coughs, I smell the smoke and realise it's not a cigarette.

He pulls long and hard, flaring up the ash so it glows a volcanic red. He exhales again, coughing uncontrollably, and offers me the joint.

I haven't smoked since I've been here. That's my longest clean streak in months. I decline the joint with a shake of my head. It doesn't seem like a great idea with all the meds.

'What's your story?' Solomzi asks.

'What do you mean?'

'I can't figure you out. You not a smoker, but the police want to arrest you. You not gay, but you defend a fag. Everyone wants to talk to you, but you keep to yourself. You pretend to follow the rules, but you break them all the time.'

I shrug. It's best to leave him to his own conclusions (or delusions).

'This place is fucked up, jo.' He holds the last part of the joint between his index finger and thumb, pulling on it for all he's worth. 'You know those pills they give us are making us worse, right? They don't want us to leave here.'

'I thought nobody stays here longer than eight weeks?'

He shakes his head. 'Man, they tricking us. Some people have been here longer than that. They think we don't know what they up to.' He tosses the stump of the finished joint into the bushes. He dry-spits, trying to get something off his tongue.

'Do you take the medication?'

'Yeah, jo! What choice do I have? I'm in here, right?' He stomps a foot, kicking up a clump of grass.

'Why're you in here, Solomzi?'

'I told you I don't know, jo. Everybody's crazy. They want to make me crazy too.'

'Who brought you here?'

'My parents.'

'Why?'

He shakes his head.

'How old are you?'

'Twenty-two.'

'Nobody can force you to stay here if you're an adult. Not unless you're a danger to yourself. Not even then. This is not that kind of place.'

He glares at me, trying to comprehend what I just said. 'What are you saying, jo?'

'I'm not saying anything other than you're not forced to be here, and you wouldn't be here if you didn't need to be.'

'You see? They already have you fooled. It's that medicine, jo! It messes with the brain!'

'The same medication you taking?'

'Yeah!'

'Good night, Solomzi.'

Twenty-eight

The biggest mistake parents make with their kids is withholding the truth from them. It's always worse when the withholding is supposedly for the kid's own good. Where do parents get this logic? Were they not children themselves once upon a time?

When the folks first brought me to Milton as a twelve-year-old, they not only neglected to tell me why I was coming here; they also failed to tell me how long I'd be staying. Sure, I was having problems at school and at home, but which kid wasn't? None of the other kids had to stay overnight at a place like this. What was so bad about me?

It was only three days and three nights but a lot can happen in a child's mind in this time. It was after that outburst I had that led to Gareth Fisher getting a bloody nose. The old lady came to pick me up and brought me out here. I thought she was going to take me for ice cream to make me feel better or something. Next thing I know, I was in Dr Schultz's office drawing and playing with toys. I don't even know why I had to play with toys, as I'd stopped playing with them at home. I didn't mind the drawing, though. Dr Schultz asked me a whole bunch of questions about them. Next thing, he's telling me to say goodbye to the old lady. When I asked her why I had to stay, she didn't answer, she just told me she would be back to fetch me.

I thought that would be the next day, but it wasn't. Was I being punished? Dr Schultz was just as cryptic as the old lady. I never knew why he was asking me the things he was asking or telling me to do the things he said.

At night, he would be 'running tests', as he put it. He was supposedly trying to help me sleep better. Back then, the medication kept me awake at night, which wasn't so bad since it meant I could avoid the frequent nightmares. It did mean I was always tired, though.

I spent time with the other kids in the ward, but I actually don't remember their faces or their names, which is kind of funny. What I do remember is Senzo and Roscoe coming to visit on one of the days. That made me feel really good. It made me feel normal. It was only once they were gone that I wondered what about me was so different that I had to be in here while they were out there.

Some kids are labelled different from a young age, hardly given a chance to deal with life, and that makes them believe what is said about them until they find themselves adrift of everybody. Standing here now, in the children's ward of Milton, I watch one of the kids. I can see he is on that same trajectory. He sits with the others but doesn't interact the way they do. He's younger than I was when I first came here.

I'm not supposed to be in this side of the clinic; they keep the children away from the adolescents and adults, which is probably a good thing.

I return to my room to find Sheldon curled up in a ball on his bed, his eyes staring off to the side. He gets like this at times when he has terrible stomach cramps, among a myriad other physical complaints. He moans like a sick puppy. I'd love to slam my fist into his head to make him stop, but that probably wouldn't be cool. 'Sheldon, buddy.'

His eyes turn slowly to me.

'How's it going?'

He moans.

I put a reluctant hand on his shoulder. 'You'll be okay.'

Nurse Swartbooi shows up at the door, standing there like The Great Authority. 'Bokang. Time to wash and pack your things. You're leaving.'

'I'm what?'

'Your mother's coming to fetch you.'

The old lady arrives after breakfast. I haven't yet processed how I feel about leaving. I mean, this place sucks, for sure, but I don't know what lies out there for me. I don't want to face what's out there. Maybe I'd get better if I stay, although I don't know what better would be like. Inside here, I haven't had to think about anything. Out there, I'll have to think and feel and make sense of what people expect of me.

'Hey, Bobo.'

'Hey, Ma.'

I haven't seen her in six days (she tells me later that she came twice in the first few days while I was zonked out).

She gives me the car keys. Pinky sits in a chair, watching us like a caged zoo animal, both miserable and envious. I carry my bags to the ride while the old lady speaks with the nurses.

'How're you?' the old lady asks as we drive out the gate.

'I'm fine.'

'That's good.'

'Why do I have to leave?'

'We miss you.'

I don't say anything.

'Really, we do. But …' She waits for oncoming traffic before she makes a right turn. 'This place is not cheap. My medical aid won't cover it. Your father paid for these past few days but now …'

She doesn't have to finish her sentence. This is a financial inconvenience. I'm an inconvenience. As if it was ever any other way.

We drive in silence for a while. So much is happening in the world: people walking, cars driving by, birds flying, and a plane overhead. Life going on. Mine has been standing still, which hasn't necessarily been a bad thing.

'So I spoke to the school about your exams.'

Exams. I forget it's that time of the year.

'Since you've missed the first week, with everything that's happened, you don't have to write this last week. It wasn't easy to convince them.

Some of them wanted you out. I'm still speaking to Mr Summers.'

If I don't write exams, it means I fail. These are only preliminary exams but they still count. Will I have to repeat Grade 11?

'I told him you can't go back to school. Not now. They can't make a big deal about this. You still have exams at the end of the year. You also have a strong track record. Leave it to me – I'll make sure you pass.'

'Thanks.' I feel tired. These past few days, I've been napping after breakfast and my morning medication. Dr Mbatha gave me a prescription to last me at least a month.

'I don't think you should be home right now. You need time away. The holiday is only in two weeks, but I think you should go away, take a longer holiday. I've arranged for you to stay with my family in Sebokeng. You still remember the place?'

I nod.

'My family will look after you. They miss you.'

'Yes, Ma.'

I don't know what else to say. Anywhere different will be better than here.

Twenty-nine

The following day, Ma books me on a 5.00 p.m. TransLux bus departing from the Windmill at the beach front. She dumps me and leaves before I even climb onto the bus.

I score a window seat. It's an overcast day, and it's been drizzling steadily since morning. Little raindrops trickle down the outside of the bus windows, while on the inside condensation creates ghostly shadows. The waves on the ocean surface froth listlessly. The beach is empty and uninviting.

As the bus moves off, families and friends call out their goodbyes. The girl in the seat in front of me wipes tears from her face. A guy who must be her boyfriend stands with her parents, waving enthusiastically. (Shame.)

Next to me, an old lady offers me some of her sandwich. The smell of boiled egg is enough to dissuade me. I lean my head against the window, taking in East London sideways, which seems fitting since my world has tilted on its axis.

This is my first time travelling long distance on a bus. It's also my first time travelling alone to Gauteng (my one and only other trip was a long time ago). I'm meeting my uncle at Park Station in Joburg.

It's a twelve-hour journey, and I try sleeping, without much success. I spend most of the time shifting positions in the cramped seat.

The old lady next to me speaks to me as if I'm her son and we're travelling together. Some time late that night, she gets off the bus and is surprised I'm not disembarking with her. The old lady's seat is taken by a young woman who spends most of the journey feeding a baby, which is so silent I keep checking if the little thing is alive.

Throughout the long night, it's hot and stuffy in the bus. The heater system is cranked up ridiculously high. Everyone else on the bus sleeps just fine, including the silent baby next to me. At least two people lay down on the floor, using the aisle as a bed. They don't seem mindful of anybody else who might need to walk up and down. I wish I had that kind of indifference. Every time it feels like I'm about to sleep, the bus stops and passengers disembark while new ones climb on. It seems like a deliberate plot on the bus driver's part to foil any attempts of mine to sleep.

I arrive at Park Station at quarter past six in the morning. My body is stiff from sitting for so long. I don't have much luggage, only one backpack, contents tossed in absentmindedly.

Joburg looks nothing like I expected. I don't know what exactly I expected, but I know this is not it. People move everywhere, people sit, people talk. There's *a lot* of talking at Park Station. I could stand here all day watching people.

I remember that Senzo is out here now; I wonder where exactly he is and what he's up to. I wonder how much he's changed since moving up here.

I'm not sure which direction to go, so I wait by the TransLux kiosk. People all around me move like they know where they're going. I don't know what to do. I don't even remember what my uncle looks like. How will I find him?

A man approaches. He's vaguely familiar. I'm relieved when he calls my name. It's Uncle Katlego, Ma's youngest brother. He greets me with so much enthusiasm, he makes me feel like a celebrity. He's an energetic man. Short and skinny, with a fat stomach. He has a gold tooth and a ratty moustache populates the edge of his mouth. He speaks fast and constantly chews gum.

'Bokang! Eish, you've grown so much, my man.' He hugs me, pats me on the back, hugs me again, then slaps me on the arm for good measure. 'Eish wena, where have you been, maan?' He laughs as he offers to carry my backpack. I choose to hold onto it.

'This is Thato.' He points to a bearded friend in the passenger seat of his car. 'And this is Tshidi.' He points to a woman in the back seat. She sports a thick weave that looks like a dozing skunk. 'Guys, ke Bokang.' The two of them also greet me enthusiastically. It must be a thing out here.

We drive out of Park Station in Uncle Katlego's sky-blue Ford Escort. The ride is old but in immaculate condition. The inside is clean and well looked after. The power of its engine vibrates through my seat, reminding me of something I once heard someone (Tata uMfene?) say: Once upon a time, cars were built to last.

It's still dark out but the roads are busy. I can't believe how alive Joburg is with cars. The highways stretch, going over and under each other. We take off-ramps from one highway to another, all filled with cars with bright shining headlights.

Katlego sees me staring out the window. 'Eish ja, jo, this is Jozi morning rush.'

'Is it like this every day?'

'Every day, Ntate,' Thato says. 'And it gets worse.'

'It gets worse?' The thought is insane.

The three of them laugh.

We drive out of the city towards the rising sun. Katlego, Thato and Tshidi ramble on in Sesotho, a language I don't speak at all. I forget Ma is Sotho; she never speaks the language unless her family is around, which is hardly ever. I don't mind the three of them rapping without me. I enjoy listening to them. They speak so fast, they sound like chirping birds. They speak to me in English and isiZulu. I can tell they're happy to explain things to me like I'm a tourist.

Close to an hour later, we enter the township of Sebokeng. Again, I'm staring out the window like a kid on a trip to a theme park.

Sebokeng is really flat. Large expanses of red sand take up the spaces in and around the houses, buildings and streets. I can't tell if the sand has covered some of the roads and paved areas, or if development has yet to get to those areas. The streets are narrow and cramped, and navigating them with traffic in both directions and people walking requires patience and a bit of give-and-take. Katlego makes a lot of turns as he drives through the neighbourhood, greeting and hooting at people as he goes. His head and elbow hang out the car, and he chats with people as if these were unfinished conversations from yesterday.

'They love Xhosa men out here,' Katlego says, sticking another piece of gum in his mouth. 'You going to be a busy guy.' The smell of spearmint wafts from him.

'I hope you not a liar and cheat?' Tshidi says.

'No, I'm not.'

Katlego and Thato laugh.

'Do you have a girlfriend, Ntate Bokang?' Thato asks, scratching his beard so it makes a crackling sound.

'No,' I respond quickly. 'I don't.'

'Ska'wara. We'll have you sorted, impintsh'yaka.'

Katlego and Thato nod at each other.

'Do you remember this place?' Katlego asks, as we turn into another street.

I want to say yes. The place is familiar in a distant kind of way. Maybe I want it to be familiar. 'Some of it.'

'Your grandparents lived in that house.' He points down the street as we approach at a crawl. 'I live here now.'

'Didn't they live on a farm?' I ask.

'Eish, ja, you're right. They have two houses. First they lived here, before moving to the farm. Oupa is no longer with us but Ouma is still there. Your other uncles, Papi and Molefi, stay with her, with your aunts Miriam and Karabo and their families. Do you remember them?'

'Yes,' I say, with only a vague recollection.

'I'll take you there.'

We stop outside a facebrick house with red tiles, a red veranda and a red garage. The house has a neat garden around it, complete with a painted black fence. The house is neat and well cared for – like the Ford Escort, it has Katlego's touch all over it.

'This is home,' he says with pride, pointing at the house as we all climb out. A sparkle of morning sun glimmers off his gold tooth.

The sunlight feels good on my face and forearms. The air is crisp and thin, and I'm reminded that I'm no longer by the coast.

A group of kids play outside the house. Katlego says something to them in Sesotho that makes them all laugh. A few other peeps come out of the house, and once again I feel like a celebrity as Katlego takes pride in introducing me to all my extended family members. A small crowd of about nine people gathers.

'You remember your cousin Dikeledi?' Katlego says.

'Bokang!' Dikeledi rushes through the crowd and embraces me. She's wearing a thin gown and a nightie with no bra, and her hug feels like heaven.

I do remember Dikeledi. She's about my age, and as a child I had a crush on her. We used to play house together and she was my first (and only) experience of dry humping. Looking at her now, I think I might still have a crush on her; she's an absolute belter.

'Hey, Dikeledi. How are you?'

'I'm good. Wow! Look at you!'

'Look at *you*.'

'O kae?'

'Er ...'

'I mean, how are you? Sorry, I forget you not from here, and ha o bue Sotho.'

'I'm good, thanks.'

Two of the smaller kids pull at my hands. 'Bokang! Bokang!' They speak in Sesotho. I smile like someone lost in translation.

'Give him a chance, you guys,' Dikeledi says. 'Come inside. You'll have plenty of time to play with these little ones.'

Dikeledi shows me a room to put my bag down. She drags me back to the dining room, where we sit at the table and spend a long time catching up, while other family members and neighbours come in and out.

I'm not used to having so many people around me. Things are way different here, compared to home. Back home, family time means everybody is in the crib but in different rooms, doing their own thing. We don't need to be *sitting* together to *be* together. Here in Sebokeng, nobody has a room of their own, and when everybody is home they're all in the same room.

I would love to be left alone, but for now I don't mind all of this. Being in a strange place where nobody knows me and not speaking the local language gives me a desirable anonymity.

In the late afternoon, Dikeledi and I walk through the streets of Zone Six. Some of the houses have nice gardens; it's like a competition to see who can keep their little garden looking the most beautiful. We seem to pass a school, daycare centre or church around every corner.

The house we're staying in is in Maseru Street. Right now we walk along Moshoeshoe Street.

'This is the main street of Sebokeng,' Dikeledi says.

Traffic everywhere. People. Cars. Minibus taxis infest the roads like cockroaches. They hoot, blast music, and do as they please. The road has endless speed bumps; one has to be patient driving here.

Dikeledi, like Katlego, takes pride in showing me the neighbourhood. She also knows a lot of people, and every man, young and old, takes an opportunity to greet her. I don't blame them. It's a privilege just walking with her. She's wearing a white crop top beneath a jean jacket and low-cut jeans. Her hair is done up in thin braids tied in a high ponytail hanging long down her back – my favourite hairstyle.

'Have you always stayed here?' I ask.

'No, not always. I stayed in Zone Thirteen with my parents. But later, I moved in with Uncle Katlego.'

'What happened? I mean, if you don't mind me asking.'

'Do you still remember my mother?'

'Yes. Auntie Tumi.'

'Well, I don't know if you heard, but my father – he was a policeman – shot my mother and killed himself when I young.'

'Oh, Dikeledi … I'm so sorry.'

'It's okay. I miss her. But living with Katlego and the rest of the family isn't bad.'

I do vaguely remember hearing stories of my aunt passing away, but I didn't know the details. Talk about a rough childhood: mine suddenly seems like child's play.

'You remind me so much of her,' I say. 'I mean, she was kind and beautiful, from what I remember, and she always made me feel special. I can see you take after her.'

Dikeledi doesn't say anything but she does smile. I'm glad to see that.

It's true what I say about her mother. She had such an energy about her. Whenever she visited, the old lady would become bubbly, and their joy at being together would be evident. Even Ernest had a good relationship with her.

We spend the rest of the afternoon at Dikeledi's friend's house. I'm the only dude among four girls, but it doesn't feel weird. Dikeledi's friends are pretty cool. They're also fascinated by me being Xhosa. They ask me all sorts of ridiculous questions that make me laugh (it's good to laugh). I enjoy the attention, I have to admit. I didn't know being Xhosa could work out like this for me. For once, being different feels great.

Dikeledi and I walk back after dark. The streets are alive with activity, and it makes me think of how different this is from my life in the suburb of Beacon Bay. There, life stands still as soon as the sun sets. The streets are quiet. In fact, even during the day the streets are quiet. We've been living in the same house for more than ten years, and I've never had any conversations with my neighbours. We greet with tight smiles or a raised hand, and that's it.

'So, Bokang,' Dikeledi says as we sit on the veranda of the house, 'why did you take so long to visit?'

'I really don't know. Life has kept me busy, I guess.'

'I'm so glad you here.'

'Yeah, me too.'

A moment later, she speaks again. 'Is everything okay with you?'

'Yeah, I'm good.'

'You sure? You just seem … I don't know … like something is up.'

'No. I'm okay. Maybe tired, from the bus ride and all.'

After a long and interesting day, I finally end my conversation with Dikeledi and go to bed just before midnight. Dikeledi tells me that I can sleep in my cousin Rantsi's small dwelling at the back of the main house. There are two beds in the room. Rantsi isn't home; I haven't seen him since arriving this morning.

I lie, fatigued, in the double bed. The long bus ride has finally caught up with me, as has the walking with Dikeledi. It feels like I'm dreaming, but I know I'm not since I'm not quite asleep; I'm in that place between extreme tiredness and semi-consciousness. The room is strange to me, and the sounds of the township are fascinating. Life carries on outside as if it's not night-time. I hear muffled voices in conversation, the occasional shout or laugh, music in the distance, and the barking of lonely dogs. All these sounds mingle in my head with flashbacks of some of the sights I've seen and heard throughout the day.

Eventually I pass out into a deep dreamless sleep.

Thirty

The next morning, I get out of bed after ten o'clock. Dikeledi won't let me snooze any longer. We eat a breakfast of porridge at the kitchen table.

'Do you still live in that house with a swimming pool?' she asks.

'Yes.' I don't mention that the pool is more of a swamp these days since the pool service stopped coming.

She smiles. 'We spent every day in the pool the last time I visited. You remember?'

'You had that yellow costume your mother bought for you in East London.'

'Yes! You know, I still have it. It doesn't fit, but I still keep it.'

'Wow.'

'Yeah. It's nice. It was nice at your house.' She twirls her spoon through her porridge.

I remember Dikeledi being a shy girl, or maybe I was just forward. We used to always do the things I wanted to do – including the dry humping. (I wonder if she still remembers that.)

'It was nice when you visited,' I say. 'I wasn't always the best host. I know I was kinda spoilt.'

'No, you were just a kid.'

'Yeah, but some of the things I did. I'm really sorry.'

'Ag, Bokang, we were kids.' She briefly touches my hand. She's so free, it's as if we've been in each other's lives all this time. Is there a special place in hell for people who find their cousins attractive?

'Your father was so funny – he used to make me laugh. How is he?'

'Are you sure we talking about the same man?'

'Yes! He would tickle us. He even tickled my mother, and your mother. Don't you remember?'

'Hmm, maybe I've forgotten.'

'If it wasn't for your father, I wouldn't speak English so well. He taught me how to listen when watching TV. Remember that?'

'Hmm …'

'Hawu, Bokang!' She playfully smacks my hand. 'Your father is amazing. Like you. He used to tell us to read. Speaking English with you helped me a lot. I really loved coming to your house.'

We take our coffee outside into the sun. The street is full of people walking up and down, going about their day. Several people greet us as they pass.

'Dumelang,' an old man greets, stopping by the veranda.

'Dumelang, Ntate,' Dikeledi greets back.

They have a brief exchange in Sesotho, then Dikeledi says, 'This is Bokang. Aus Khensani's boy.'

'Aus Khensani!' The man puts his hands on his cheeks in comical surprise. 'Oh, wonderful to meet you, Sir. You are welcome here. We miss your mother. Very good woman.'

After a few more words, the man says goodbye. The same thing happens again not long after, this time with a woman who tells me stories about my mother.

'How do all these people know so much about my mother?' I ask when we're alone again.

'Your mother was popular.'

'How come?'

'Wait.' Dikeledi goes into the house and comes back carrying a photo album. Before she opens it she says, 'Our grandparents are famous here. They had a shop where they sold vegetables and other things. Everyone bought from there. Oupa was also a serious member of the church; he expected all his children to go with him.'

She opens the album and shows me photos of Ma's family. She explains who everyone is as she goes along. There are photos of Ma when she was younger, before I was born. Ma was a competing beauty queen; there are shots of her posing in shiny stockings, a white bathing suit, red first-prize sash and a bouquet of flowers. There are also photos of Ma competing in track and field athletics, wearing graduation gowns, and attending community events. Her liveliness in these photos is something I've never known. In pictures where she poses with Auntie Tumi, Dikeledi's moms, the resemblance is stark. The young Ma looks almost identical to Dikeledi next to me.

'Wow, what's this?' I say, pointing at a black-and-white photo.

'This was the community centre. It was like a non-profit our grand-parents built for the community. They used to have a feeding scheme there, giving food to people that couldn't afford it. They took in women and children who were victims of domestic violence. There was even a sewing group for the older mamas. It was quite big.'

'What happened to it? Is it still here?'

'No. It was burned down, not long after your mother left. She played a big role in running the place. There was a lot of respect for the place when she was still here, but then people just didn't take care of it.'

'Who burned it?'

'There are different stories. Some say the apartheid police, others say the gangsters. Eish, I don't know. I think it was jealous people. People around here don't like to see a good thing. People were not happy for our family's success. I see it still now, when they talk badly about our family. I even think someone burned down the centre because they were angry your mother left. You know, people have a funny way of showing what you mean to them. It wasn't only your mother who left. Our other aunts and uncles left too. This is not a place to stay.'

I wish I had come here more often in my childhood. The only times I ever saw Ma's family was when they visited East London, which was once a year at most. It's Ernest's family we've grown up with, but even with them, we see them only when we must. Family is a strange thing. It's funny how knowing a little more about people you are related to suddenly makes you feel connected, part of something.

'Hey, hey. What're you two up to?' Dikeledi's friend Mashoto joins us on the veranda. She's one of the friends I met yesterday.

'Hey, friend,' Dikeledi says. 'We just catching up. Wena, what's up with you?'

'I'm fresh, my friend.'

'I see that, dressed like you going to a party. So early in the morning?'

'Can't I just look beautiful?'

Dikeledi covers her mouth, laughing. She elbows me in the ribs, but I'm not sure what's so funny.

Mashoto smiles. 'Hey, Bokang.' She leans in for a hug before I have a chance to return her greeting. She smells like a bowl of sweet fruits. Dikeledi laughs so much she almost falls off her chair.

We spend most of the day on the veranda. People come and go. Conversation is a big thing around here and even though I don't catch most of what is said, I'm okay around the people.

After another long day, I go to bed after midnight, close to one in the morning; I'm drifting off to sleep when I hear two voices outside. One belongs to a man, the other a woman. Kissing. Giggling. The door flies open. Two intertwined bodies fall on top of me. The woman screams and the man gets off her in a flash, cussing.

The lights come on. A man with a big-ass scar running down his face stands over me, pointing a gun. 'Who are you?' The scar runs from his forehead, down over his left eye and cheek.

'It's me, Bokang!' I hold my hands up in surrender.

'Bokang?' The man asks, squinting his eyes.

'Yes, it's me. Rantsi?'

'Heh? *Bokang*? Ngwana ka Aus Khensani?'

'Yes,' I say, hearing the old lady's name.

'Ah! Cuzzie!' He pulls me up with one hand to give me a hug, the gun still in the other hand. 'Heh, this is my cousin, Bokang!' he says to his female companion, using the gun to point at me. 'How are you, ntwana?'

'I'm fine. H-h-how are you?' My eyes dart from his scarred face to the gun in his hand and back to his face.

'This cheese boy with fancy English, he is your cousin?' his companion asks. Her lips are a smudged pink and her cleavage speaks louder than any words coming out of her mouth.

'Ja, Bokang ke president, he's educated. Not like you.' He laughs. His female companion pouts. He tickles her with the hand not holding the gun. 'It's good to have you here, ntwana. If I knew you were here, I would have come to fetch you. How long you been here?'

'Two days.'

'*Two days*? No, no, no, maan. And what have you been doing?'

'Dikeledi has been showing me around.'

'Dikeledi? And her loud friends? No, maan. Tomorrow you come with me, ntwana. I show you Sebokeng, proper. Okay?'

'Yeah, okay.'

He gives me a complicated handshake, the sequence of which I mess up. He puts the gun under the other bed, much to my relief. He takes his companion in his arms; she giggles while pretending not to want his attention. They kiss noisily as he gropes her. His lady friend takes off her top and bra, and her breasts bounce as if they have springs in them. She makes eye contact with me, and I look away. She can't be much older than me. Rantsi, who is easily in his late thirties, if not forties, winks at me as he helps her take off her jeans. She's wearing a G-string and her substantial backside shows me a whole new perspective on life.

Rantsi switches off the lights and the two of them climb onto the other bed as if I'm not in the room. I turn my back and draw the covers over my head. The noises coming from the other bed are amplified: heavy breathing, slurping, and squealing bedsprings.

'Bokang … do you … want some?' Rantsi says, in between wet kisses.

I pull the covers off my head. 'Er … some what?'

The girl giggles.

'Some of this … beautiful woman. Hawu, Bokang.'

'No, I'm fine. Thanks.'

'Come on,' he says sportingly. 'Join us.'

'Hayi, Rantsi, he's just a boy,' the girl says.

Rantsi laughs. 'A boy? He's probably older than *you*, Lerato. And don't forget this is a Xhosa man. You know they still go to the mountains for circumcision? When they come back, their dicks are three times bigger.'

'*Really?*' The kissing stops. 'Let me see.'

'Come on, show her.'

'Er … no … I … I can't … I have a girlfriend.'

They both laugh, loud enough to make me cringe under my blanket. Rantsi claps his hands. I'm not sure why I said that.

'I have *lots* of girlfriends. Lerato has a boyfriend – some mampara from her school. But it's okay. Do whatever you want.'

The kissing resumes. The slapping of flesh is torture to my ears. I wonder if the bed will break. They go on forever. I cover my ears and clench my teeth. Sleep doesn't come.

Thirty-one

The next day begins at eleven o'clock, when Rantsi wakes me up. He stands just outside the door, topless, in only a pair of jeans; his torso is covered in tattoos that look like they were scrawled by a four-year-old. He sips something steaming from a tin cup.

'Tsoha, Bokang.' He takes a drag from a cigarette and blows a huge cloud of smoke into the morning air. 'It's time to get up. Today's a big day.' He takes one last sip before pouring the remainder of his hot beverage onto the red earth.

'What's going on?'

'Get out of bed. Dress. You'll see.'

Washed and dressed; quick breakfast of eggs, fried polony and thickly buttered bread. Driving down the street with Rantsi. (Lerato left before I woke up, and I don't ask Rantsi anything about her.) We driving in a white BMW 325i, better known as iGusheshe. Rantsi, dressed in all white, including new Converse All Star sneakers and a matching hat, sits so comfortably in the driver's seat it's as if the car is an extension of him. Every time he changes gears, turns the steering wheel or accelerates, he exclaims in approval or whistles.

He pats the wheel as if the car is a living thing. 'This is my baby; she knows how to treat me. She's like Lerato – that one also knows how to treat me right. Yho, the things she did to me last night, ntwana. Ha!

I'm telling you. She rides like a pro. I don't know where these girls learn these things. And inside she was so … hmm … you know what I mean, lightie?'

'Er, yeah. Sure.'

He laughs, the scar on his face curving like a Nike sign. Even though the windows and sun roof are all open, his cologne funks up the interior of the ride.

He accelerates the Gusheshe down the narrow street, swerving past cars and potholes. A few streets later, we pull into a back yard filled with the rusty carcasses of cars in varying stages of decay.

'Bra Sello needs to get my baby right for the weekend.'

'What's happening on the weekend?' I ask.

'You'll see.'

The man introduced as Bra Sello comes out and tinkers under the hood of the BMW. Rantsi and Bra Sello have a long conversation about the car and whatever this big weekend entails. I don't catch most of it. Two young boys come out to wash the car while Rantsi and Bra Sello continue their chat. As always, I don't mind being silent, especially in this context, where I can observe without having to engage anybody.

Bra Sello offers me some of the Black Label they're drinking but I decline. There's something unsettling about being presented with Ernest's beer of choice.

It's two days later, when the weekend comes, that I finally understand what the 'big day' is, and what the visit to Bra Sello's place was about. It's early afternoon and I'm driving with Rantsi in the Gusheshe. Today he's dressed in red shoes, yellow pants, a multicoloured shirt and a blue hat.

We head to KwaMazisa Stadium in Vanderbijlpark, which is part of Sebokeng and the Vaal Triangle. Heavy traffic moves in the same direction as us. Other Gusheshes of different colours drive towards the stadium.

We leave the car in a parking area reserved for the Gusheshes. Rantsi tucks his gun in the front of his pants and covers it with his multi-coloured shirt as we walk away from the car. He puts an arm around me and starts explaining what the Spinfest is all about.

The stadium reminds me of the Colosseum. We learned about that in school back when I still did History as a subject. KwaMasiza Stadium is significantly smaller than what the Romans built, but I'm still impressed. The middle of the arena is filled with sand disturbed by tyre treads. As we walk into the stadium, a silver Gusheshe burns rubber doing spins in interweaving movements that leave distinct shapes in the sand.

'Beginners,' Rantsi says. 'Wasting our time.'

Two men approach and greet with handshakes. A few others nod their heads as we walk by. In this place – and everywhere else I've been with him – Rantsi commands respect.

We head for a group of men in the stands who resemble characters from an SABC prime-time TV show. They are dressed to the nines, like Rantsi, in outfits that show a lot of planning went into them. They have shiny accessories to complete their colourful outfits, and the way they talk and interact seems scripted. There's a lot of respect between the members of this circle, and being part of it demands a certain measure of decorum.

'Hey, Bokang.' Dikeledi and her friends Mashoto, Maria, Boitumelo and Thembi appear from behind me.

'Hey, how you guys doing?'

'Good thanks,' Dikeledi says. 'I see you've met the Spin Kings.'

'Spin Kings?'

'Those men with Rantsi. Some of them are the best spinners in this whole area.'

'Others have other reputations that you must respect,' Mashoto says, stepping closer to me.

I sit with Dikeledi and her friends close to Rantsi and the Spin Kings. Rantsi pulls out a wad of cash and gives me a few notes to buy myself beer and 'entertain the ladies', as he puts it. A few beers might not be so bad today. Why not? It's not like I'm locked up any more.

We watch the various rounds of spinners doing their thing. Rantsi's friends also get their chance: they're clearly much better than the ones we've been watching since we arrived.

Rantsi's turn comes. He drives into the arena with a friend in the passenger seat. The crowd goes bonkers as soon as they drive out. Dikeledi and her friends scream the loudest. We're on our feet, cheering them on.

It doesn't take long for Rantsi to get the crowd going. He revs up the ride until the engine threatens to explode. He takes the Gusheshe through donuts and suicidal turns – the entire arena fills with grey smoke. The smell of burning rubber is enough to make me choke, but instead I cheer even louder, along with the rest of the crowd. At some point, Rantsi gets out of the car while it's spinning in circles and dances alongside it. The audience goes ballistic. He hops back in and speeds off out of the arena in a cloud of smoke, to the sound of high-pitched whistles.

After the drivers are done doing their thing, and the sun has set, a party breaks out in the parking lot. Loud music thumps from the speakers, and blue lights flash from the makeshift DJ's booth. The air is thick with smoke and the smell of braai meat. Ghetto petrolheads rev their engines, much to the party people's delight.

Dikeledi and her friends are pretty good dancers, and I take my chances with them. Thank goodness it's night-time so nobody can check my dance moves, or lack thereof (thank goodness for the beer too). Later on, nauseous from the beer, I throw up in the toilets. It helps a whole bunch. After washing up in the basin, I return to the throng of people dancing among the parked cars.

Dikeledi's friend Mashoto won't stop looking at me. Her stare intensifies while she's dancing, as if she's dancing only for me. She comes close and puts her hands on my shoulders. The back of my neck tingles. 'So what do you think of the vibe in Sebokeng?'

'It's great,' I shout over the loud music. 'It feels like home.'

She laughs, her face almost touching mine. She has dimples and her lips glisten in the flashing lights. 'I want to show you something.'

'Okay,' I say, not really sure if it's okay.

'Come with me.' She takes me by the hand and leads me away from the mass of dancing people. We move to a more secluded part of the parking lot. I'm floating as I walk behind her, watching her hips sway. She keeps looking back with eyes that say so many things. At last she pushes me up against the bonnet of a car and stands between my legs. 'So what have you enjoyed the most since you've been here?' Her hands rub my arms. At least three other couples are getting intimate around us.

'It's all been amazing.'

'You haven't seen amazing yet …' She tastes sweet like a berry. Her tongue moves slowly over the surface of my bottom lip; she gently sucks my top lip. She pulls away to look at me. Goosebumps ripple along my arms and neck. 'You should come visit me,' she says. 'We can spend time alone.'

I don't say anything. My head is spinning. It could be from the kiss, the booze, or the medication I shouldn't be mixing with the booze.

I don't take Mashoto up on her offer to spend any more alone time together, either on that night or for the rest of my stay in Sebokeng. She is an unbelievably attractive girl, and I feel lucky to be getting this kind of attention from her. But it's difficult for me to allow her any closer. It's been great being here in Sebokeng where nobody really knows me. Connecting with relatives like Dikeledi has been easy and stress-free. This kind of connecting doesn't delve beneath the surface, so I've been able to handle it. Mashoto wanting to get closer to me is too overwhelming. It was easy when we were drunk, but now I just can't deal.

She comes to Katlego's family crib more often, which is okay, as there are always other people around. I just make sure we're never alone. Dikeledi finds our interactions amusing as Mashoto tries to make excuses for us to be alone.

One day, when she's leaving the house, she asks me to walk her to the corner. She comes right out with it: 'Is there something wrong with me?'

'No, of course not. Why would you ask that?'

'I'm sure you know how much I like you. But I can see you running away from me.'

'It's not you. It's me. I'm not in a good place.'

'Do you have a girlfriend?'

'No.'

'Is there someone you love?'

'No. Yes, but … I don't know how to really put it. There was someone, but things didn't work out.'

'Tell me about it.'

So I tell her. Only about Nokwanda and the dance – I leave out the suicide attempt and everything at Milton. It's the first time I'm speaking about it since it all went down.

'What kind of girl is this?' Mashoto says angrily. 'How did you not see what kind of person she is? I'm sorry, but only a person with serious problems could do something like that.'

I don't know what to say.

'You shouldn't let someone who is clearly sick get you down like this.' She grabs my hand and stops us from walking. We've reached the end of the street where she usually catches the taxi. 'You need to move on. If you think about this any more, it will keep you down.'

'I can't just forget it all, like it never happened. When I'm not thinking about it, it's there. When I think about it, like now, it's there. It just won't go away. I'm tired, and I don't have the strength.'

'You need to find it, Bokang.' She gives me a hug that won't end.

Tears sting the corners of my eyes, and I bury my face in her sweater.

'Come with me,' she says. 'Let me put a smile on your face.'

'I can't.'

Those simple words are like a punch in the face. Standing so close to her, looking into her eyes, I see the pain of rejection, then sadness, then anger, all in less than three seconds. I want to take my words back, but I can't. Find strength, she said. How?

Eventually, I spend less time with Dikeledi and her friends. That's cool, though, cos it's only in my last few days in Sebokeng that this happens. I sleep a lot during the day, a habit that started at Milton. Still, I feel tired all the time. Sometimes I cry during these day naps, but I couldn't tell you what all the crying is about. I don't drink again after the night of the Spinfest; the hangover the next day was too much.

When the day comes for me to leave, after three weeks in Sebokeng, I'm filled with uncertainty. Things are very different from when I came out of Milton. Then I didn't feel ready to face the world; I wanted to hide and be left alone. I'm probably still not ready to face my world, but at least now I accept that life must go on.

It's a Saturday when I leave. Everything happens so fast that morning. Before I know it, I'm washed, dressed, and saying goodbye. The goodbyes are miserable. Dikeledi is so sad she cries as she hugs me repeatedly, urging me to call from time to time. Rantsi's way of saying goodbye is to hand me a wad of cash (a whopping R450), which he tells me to spend wisely.

The drive to Joburg with Katlego is miserable. He doesn't seem happy for reasons that have nothing to do with me leaving. He's quiet in the car, so we listen to the radio. He chews his gum, his jaw working furiously.

Katlego walks me into Park Station and waits over thirty minutes with me until it's time to board the bus back to East London. He gives me a hug and says, 'Eish. Go well, ntwana.'

As the bus pulls out of Park Station, I wipe a tear from my face.

Thirty-two

Back home in East London, aka Slummies, the fam treats me like a patient. Everyone tiptoes around me, cooped up in my room like I have an infectious disease, quarantined from the gen pop. Poor Izzy has to share the space with me. He's all twitchy – probably been given a talking-to (beware the contagious freak). Siz doesn't come close, unless it's to call me to come eat, following the old lady's instructions. She's also restrained around me; it's killing the little thing.

The loneliness is good. Most of the time I'm sleeping or doing school work; there's plenty of catching up to do on both. The old lady did good by putting in a word for me at school, and I'm grateful to her. They won't fail me if I do well in my end-of-year exams, so all my focus is on trying to make that happen.

School sucks, but then again, when did it ever not? This is a different kind of sucking, though. The first few weeks are tough, dealing with all the stares and the whispers. I stay away from everybody. I don't hang with Randall Leonard and the rest of the stoners. By the third week, I don't care any more, and apparently neither does anybody else. Life goes on, as it must.

I get used to being a loner. No more trips to JP's, only trips to Dr Mbatha. She gives me a new prescription (higher dosage), and I attend a once-off group session (Pinky and Noxy are the only ones I recognise from before).

I have to admit something about the meds I'm on: they intensify this loner world, but in a good way. My concentration is better, so I can focus on my school work, and my emotions are flat most of the time, so I don't have to deal with other people's expectations of me. Sure, the meds affect my sleeping and my appetite too, not to mention the mad-constipation, but with everything that's happened, I really don't mind. I'd take this calm over the boost to the imagination the blunt gives me, and the sense of freedom from the booze.

I pretty much stop existing in Ernest's world. He only speaks to me when giving instructions like clean the garage, cut the grass, cut my toenails, bring me a beer, wash the dishes, take out the garbage. He's always grumpy. He doesn't ask me to help out at the office either, and I don't offer. There's a stand-off there. Like everybody else, he has no idea how to handle me. He must think he's the only person in the world with problems, the only one allowed to act out. His treatment of me is a punishment of sorts, I can tell. Maybe in his head he thinks I need to toughen up, that I don't have what it takes to be a stupid lawyer like he is (or a bloody Xhosa man).

One day in early October, I'm chilling in my room when the old lady appears at the door. She sits on the corner of my bed while I sit at my desk.

'How are things?'

'Fine.'

'Studying?'

'Fine.'

'School?'

'Fine.'

She picks at her fingernails. I look back at the book in front of me. After a while she stands up. 'Okay. I'm glad you're fine.'

'Ma ...'

She stops by the doorway.

'Do you miss Sebokeng?'

She sits back down. 'No, not really. I mean, it will always be my home-town. My family is there. I will always visit, but ... Why do you ask?'

'It's a great place. Your family is great. Don't you miss them?'

'I do. Of course I do.'

'Why did you leave?'

'I wanted to study. I met your father at Fort Hare, and we started a life together.'

'But don't you miss it? The life you had back there?'

'I have you guys now.'

Neither of us says anything. The microwave hums in the background (probably Israel), and a car hoots a few streets away. 'Are you happy?' I ask.

'What? Why would you ask?'

'You looked happier, then. I saw the photos.'

She looks down at her hands in her lap for a while without saying anything.

When she looks up at me again, I speak. 'Uncle Katlego took me to see your mother, on the farm. I saw your brothers and sisters, and listened to their stories. There's so much I didn't know. I almost feel like we've taken something away from you.'

'No, Bokang. I choose to be here, with *my* family.'

'But it can't be easy. Surely you'd rather be doing something else other than taking care of a depressed son?'

There it is – out there in word form. We've never called what I'm going through by its true name. Now that it's out there, what more is there to say?

'This is where I belong. We are a family. We stick together. Your father …'

I turn away, shaking my head.

'Your father cares about you too. It's just—'

'Just what? Why defend him? He doesn't care about anything. Why must we live like we're poor, just because of him? Why do you pretend you're fine with it, Ma?'

'Some things you'll never understand, my child. We protect you as parents.'

Really? Some things are just tiring, especially when you deal with them over and over again. Maybe this is why people disappear into their own heads. The old lady certainly lives in her own space, as does Ernest. I don't know why I bother coming out of mine to engage with people who won't see the reality before them.

The old lady gets up and leaves after saying a few more pacifying things, none of which make an impression.

Outside, I can breathe again. Senzo is on my mind; I used to share everything with him. The drizzle paints me silver on my way to the payphone by the Caltex garage. This is where I first met Nokwanda. So much has happened since then.

Why have I waited this long to speak to Senzo?

He answers on the third ring.

'Hey, Enzo.'

The line cuts off. I dial again, but this time it rings and nobody answers. I phone a third time – and a fourth. The phone rings on, but nobody picks up.

I don't want to believe Senzo wouldn't want to holler at me when he knows it's me. It's been four months; why wouldn't he answer?

I'm walking through a desert of charcoal-coloured sand. A sandstorm is brewing, and all around me the particles dance violently in wisps that reach up to a sagging sky of bubbling black ink. A red shawl covers my shoulders, wraps around my head in a turban, and masks my face. It billows in the wind about me like Superman's cape. My bare feet crush the skulls and bones of dead things as I walk. The sand tries hungrily to get under my skin. I trudge on, my right forearm over the mask covering my face. A huge black face forms in the folds of the lowering sky, an endlessly moving three-dimensional Rorschach test. The fierce wind blowing comes from the face's mouth; it opens wide, revealing more blackness among its black teeth.

'Find it, Bokang!' It screams at me. 'You must find it!'

'What must I find?' My voice disappears in the whirling wind. My eyes burn and tears stream down my face. The sand particles stick to me, blackening my skin. My palms are as black as the face-thing in the sky.

'No!'

The face-thing in the sky laughs, its obsidian face looming like a volcanic mountain turned on its side.

'Find it, Bokang!'

'He can't find anything,' a girl's voice says.

'Hello?' I call, looking around frantically until the sand forces me to shut my eyes. I sit down on the skulls and bones and cover my head.

'He can't find *anything*!'

I know that voice. It's coming from underneath me. I dig my hands into the skulls and bones. I can't see what I'm doing, but I dig. Skulls and bones shift, and I fall into a hole. I open my eyes inside the hole, and the surface is glass. I'm in a container like an hourglass, with the charcoal sandstorm raging inside. The hourglass is held by a giant girl. It's Mashoto, Dikeledi's friend.

'Mashoto! Help me!'

'Oh, now you see me?' She's naked as she holds the hourglass up above her. She's striking poses and showing off her curves. 'I thought you didn't want this?'

'I want it, Mashoto! I want you! *Please*! Help me!'

Her high-pitched laugh echoes through the hourglass. I reach out to her, but the glass keeps me trapped. The skulls around me laugh with their gaping grins. Their jaws unhinge and teeth tumble out as they fly into the whirlwind heading into the mouth of the giant face-thing in the sky. Everything is sucked up into its mouth. My resistance is giving in. I don't have anything to hold onto. I'm flying into the sky.

'Mashoto! Please! I love you!'

Mashoto's laugh makes the sides of the hourglass shimmer and my ears ache. I fall upwards and the face-thing in the sky closes its giant mouth over me.

I sit up in the darkness of my room, sleep having left me for good. I don't know what these dreams – nightmares – mean. Sometimes I'll go weeks without them, and then they come back suddenly, making no sense at all.

Thunk. Thunk. Thunk. Thunk. Something (someone) is knocking on the door.

I switch on my bedside lamp. On the other side of the room, Israel's bed is a mess of abandoned linen. He stands by the door with his eyes closed, his hands hanging limply by his sides. He bangs his head against the door in a slow rhythm. *Thunk. Thunk. Thunk. Thunk.*

I climb out of bed and move cautiously towards him. I put my hands on his shoulders. As soon as I touch him, his head snaps up and his eyes open wide as if he's about to cry.

'Israel, you were jus—'

His body tenses. His eyes roll back into his skull; pure white orbs vibrate in their sockets.

'Israel!'

He loses his balance and I catch him. Froth comes out of his mouth while his eyes do the rolling thing. His body shakes so much I have to push him down on my bed.

'Maaaa!' I scream. 'Tataaaa!'

Israel shakes uncontrollably. I put my weight on him to stop the shaking. '*Ma! Tata! Help!*'

The froth coming out of his mouth is tinted red; he must be bleeding inside his mouth. I feel warmth as he releases urine on both of us. I don't move from my position even though holding him seems useless against the violent movements of his body.

Ma bursts into the room and rushes to Israel's side, fear all over her face. '*Israel!* What happened?'

'I don't know. We need to get him to a hospital! Where's Tata?'

Ma doesn't respond, all her attention on Israel. Ernest needs to drive us to the hospital. I'm hoping he's not passed out in a drunken stupor. He's not in the folks' room, though.

The old lady speaks to Israel in pleading tones. Sizwe stands in the passage, rubbing her eyes.

'Siz, hey.' I go down on my knees and place my hands on her shoulders. 'Listen to me. I need you to go to your room and put on your pink jacket and your boots. Okay?'

'What's going on?'

It's no use lying to her. 'We need to take Izzy to the hospital. Can you get yourself dressed while I help Izzy?'

'Yes.'

'Good girl.' I give her tummy a quick rub.

I rush back into the folks' room to grab the old lady's handbag and her gown from where it hangs behind the door.

'Ma, we need to take him to the hospital, now,' I say standing in the doorway to my room.

'Okay.'

Sizwe unlocks the car, and the old lady and I load Israel into the back seat. His shaking is not as violent as before, but he's twitching, and I can tell he's far from cool.

'Siz, you gonna have to sit in front with Ma.'

'But Tata said I must never sit in front.'

'I know, Siz. But this is an emergency. Izzy needs your help.'

Her eyes dart to her brother lying prone in the back seat.

The old lady climbs into the driver's side and starts the car.

I sit in the back with Israel's head on my lap. The car pulls out of the garage. The old lady grips the steering wheel with both hands, and sits so far forward her head might as well be touching the windscreen.

'Siz.'

'Yes, Bobo.'

'Ma needs you to keep an eye on the left and right sides of the road. Every time we pass a traffic light, you need to check for other cars. You understand?'

'Yes.'

'Ma can't stop at the red lights, she needs to go without stopping. You must make sure there are no other cars. Got it?'

'Yes.'

'Good girl!'

The old lady looks back at Israel. Our eyes meet, and she knows she needs to step on it. Fortunately, at almost three in the morning, the roads are empty. We scream through traffic lights. Israel's head lies limp in my lap. I lift his eyelids and all I see is white.

'Hurry, Ma.'

It takes us just under fifteen minutes to reach Wallace Hospital in Clermont. Ma helps me carry Israel inside while Sizwe sticks close behind us. Hospital staff rush towards us, then disappear down a brightly lit passage with Israel on a gurney and the old lady following after.

In the waiting area, Sizwe sits on my lap, our arms tightly wrapped around each other. One of the nurses offers to take Sizwe, but I refuse.

'You did good, Siz.'

'Will Izzy be okay?'

'I hope so, Siz. I'm sure the doctors will do what they can.'

Sizwe falls asleep in my arms.

Natural light breaks through the windows. Hospital staff change shifts. We are the only ones in the waiting area. Ma eventually returns, looking two hundred years older.

'Is he all right?'

'Yes, he's better. He's sleeping now. The doctors are with him.' She collapses in the seat besides me, no doubt wanting nothing more than to pass out and perhaps never wake up. But there is a fear in her eyes that if she closes them, something bad might happen – again.

'It's okay,' I say. 'Everything will be fine. I'm here.' I give her a reassuring smile. Within ten seconds, she's asleep.

The old lady arranges for one of her friends to take me and Sizwe home while she stays at the hospital with Israel. The doctors need to do more tests. No school for me and Sizwe for the next day or two. MaMvundla will stay with us.

Epileptic seizure, the doctors say. Ma tells us the next day when she finally comes home with Izzy. He must get regular sleep, he must watch his stress levels (which Ma immediately interprets as 'no more rugby'), he must take his medication, and the doctors will monitor his progress.

Israel himself doesn't seem half as bothered by all of this as the rest of us. He chatters as if nothing's happened. I sit on my bed, with Sizwe, while the old lady sits next to Israel.

'What did they say at school?' Israel asks.

'They know you're booked off sick,' Ma says. 'Don't worry about it. Worry about getting better.'

'I am better.' He flexes his biceps. 'I can go back tomorrow.'

'No. The doctor said only next week.'

'Aaah, Maaaaa.'

'Can I also stay home?' Sizwe asks optimistically.

'No, young lady, you go back tomorrow.'

'Will you be going back to work?' Sizwe asks.

'Only next week.'

'That's unfair!'

'But you like school, Siz,' I say.

'Yes, I do!'

'But then why don't you want to go back?'

She thinks about it and when nothing comes to mind, she giggles uncontrollably.

'Okay, only Bobo will go back tomorrow.' Ma gives me a smile that I take as some kind of thank-you.

Thirty-three

Ernest first learns of Israel's episode and the dash to the hospital the day after Israel comes home. By then, Ernest has been missing for five days – a record for him.

I'm not sure what he tells the old lady upon his return. All I know is it involves a lot of shouting, probably more than I've ever heard between the two of them. I'm impressed with the heart the old lady has in the arguments: standing up not only for herself, but for us kids as well.

Ernest doesn't respond to Israel's episode like a concerned parent. Instead, he goes into a monumental sulk. The rest of us pretty much continue with our lives as if he doesn't exist. I'm glad to see the old lady fighting for her happiness – or what's left of it.

Two weeks later, though, that all melts away like an ice cream dropped on a hot pavement. And, as you can guess, it's Ernest who plays a starring role in the drama.

It's early on a Saturday evening and I'm cooped up in my room trying to sketch. Ma stands at the door and the expression on her face tells a story before she's even spoken.

'I need you to come with me. Israel and Sizwe will stay here.'

I don't argue or ask questions. Apart from the look on her face, I know this must be serious because we've never left Israel and Sizwe home alone.

We drive out into the street as the lamps start lighting up.

'We need to fetch your father,' she says, without looking at me. 'He's in some trouble. I don't know exactly where he is, somewhere in Mdantsane. Do you know where exactly in Amalinda Albert stays?'

'Albert?'

'His friend. That man he's always with.'

'You mean Tata uMfene?'

'Yes.'

'Oh. Yes, I've been there.'

We fall back into silence. Only when we are in Amalinda does Ma ask me for directions, which I give from memory.

As we pull up outside the house, Ma says, 'Wait in the car.'

Tata uMfene's house is a small square structure surrounded by a wire fence and a balding lawn. The front door stands open; there's movement inside. Two guys stand smoking outside, holding beer bottles. I bet the ones inside are also holding beer bottles and glasses filled with hard liquor. Ma shouts something to one of the men standing outside the house, and the man next to him calls into the house.

Music comes from the house through my rolled-down window. Tata uMfene's large frame comes bouncing out the house, his arm around a young woman. He says something jovial to one of his friends outside, but stops mid-sentence when he sees the old lady standing with her hands on her hips by the gate.

Tata uMfene immediately removes the cap sitting tilted on his head, says something to the young lady that sends her scampering back inside the house, and moves towards the old lady like a naughty child who recognises they are in a heap of trouble.

The words exchanged between the two of them don't travel all the way to the car, but I can tell the old lady is asking him where Ernest is. What I do catch is her asking him how he could let this happen, what kind of man he is, and what kind of friend he is. I also hear her telling him she never wants to see him in her house or near her children ever again.

We drive on the highway towards Mdantsane. The old lady hasn't elaborated on what Ernest has done, and where we are going to find him. I wonder if it isn't the place where he and Tata uMfene took me before. I suppose I don't need to know exactly what's happened. All I know is there's a finality about everything. No turning back from here. One way or another, the old lady has made a decision.

The off-ramp we take confirms where we're going. We arrive at the old house where I've been with Ernest and Tata uMfene before. Every time they tell me to wait in the car while they go in for 'business'. They always come out slapping hands with big smiles. I've never been here at night, though, and what I see is quite something. Loud music thumps from inside. People stand about outside among the haphazardly parked cars. Other cars block the road.

Ma hoots at the ride in front of us, where the driver is hollering at another man leaning into the window. The car moves forward and the man who was leaning into it stares at the old lady with bleary eyes.

We park outside a neighbour's house. 'Wait here,' Ma says.

'Let me come with you.'

'Okay.'

I actually feel proud of her. Whatever mess awaits us inside, I know something in the old lady has shifted forever.

We shove our way through a mess of people by the doorway. Inside it's dark and the ceiling is too low. Ma holds a tightly wrapped plastic bag, which she clutches close to her chest. Drunk people stagger all over the place like zombies drawn to a feed. Ma and I make our way through the swarm, searching for Ernest. A drunk woman throws her arms around me, saying something as if she knows me. A spray of something sour hits my face. I peel her off while Ma curses. The woman moves on, undeterred, taking a swig from a beer quart.

We find Ernest slumped in a chair at the back of the room. His white hair, even in the gloomy light, is hard to miss. We can't see his face because it's buried in his chest. He has blood all over the front of his shirt and waistcoat. One hand is crudely bandaged. A group of men sit at a table next to him, and as we approach them, they turn, blocking us from him, like bodyguards.

Ma exchanges words with one of the men. She hands over the plastic bag. He unwraps it and pulls out a stack of money. Of course. It had to be about money. He counts it in front of us, and gives us the nod to take Ernest.

With the two of us on either side of him, we lift Ernest by putting his arms behind our necks. He's barely aware of us. Only when his bandaged hand brushes against the wall does he grimace. The dry blood all over him makes me wonder how long he's been sitting here.

We make our way through the crowd. Nobody takes much notice. Everybody is drunk beyond any reasonable state. Ernest wasn't the only person passed out in the establishment, and he certainly won't be the last.

It's a relief to exit into the night air. Ma unlocks the car, and I open the back door and bundle Ernest in. Ma pulls his arms from the other end so he's lying on his back. I close the door and Ma climbs into the driver's seat.

Ernest stays passed out for the entire trip back to Beacon Bay. Ma and I don't speak. I keep glancing back at Ernest as he lies there, his skinny knees pointing upwards. Only a few days ago, I was in that back seat cradling Israel as the old lady rushed to the hospital. Then, there was urgency. Now we're in a similar situation, but there is no urgency here. What help is there for the hopeless?

Ernest doesn't wake up when we drag him out of the car and into the house. I leave Ma with her husband in their bedroom. We don't speak. What is there to say? The look we exchange as I leave the room says enough.

I don't know how much money trouble Ernest got himself into. All I know is that the old lady literally had to bail him out, and that's put us in a worse financial hole than we've ever been in before.

The old lady files for divorce, and Ernest moves out within two weeks (with one broken finger and a fractured wrist). I'm not sure of the conversation the folks have with Israel and Sizwe to explain things to them – or even if they do. They do both talk to me, though, separately, because of the way all this affects me.

The old lady sits me down and speaks in that determined voice I've come to hear from her these days. 'I don't have to explain to you what has happened between your father and me. You have seen it over the years, how things have changed. I told you this is my decision.'

'Yes, Ma.'

'Your father has put us in serious financial trouble and I can't afford to keep all of us in this house. I have a buyer who will let me pay rent and go on living here. But the only way we can stay here is if you go live with your father. He has asked for that, and we have discussed it. I'm sorry, my child. It won't be forever, but for now it's the only way the Lord has shown me.'

Ernest gives me his shorter version the same day. 'Did you talk to your mother?'

'Yes, Tata.'

'All right, then. So you know, we'll be staying together. It's for the best, son. We'll survive this. I love you, son.'

At first, it comes as a numbing shock. But the more I think about it, the less surprising it becomes.

The day Ernest leaves is in mid-November. He uses Tata uMfene's bakkie to move his things, which consist almost exclusively of his clothes and his books. There's no sign of the big guy, but his nephew, Daniel, the guy who drove me to the matric dance, helps. It takes only one trip on that Saturday to move everything. The crib looks like it's been robbed after his books are removed from all the shelves, and the emptiness they create hangs like uncertainty.

My day to leave comes in the first week of December, after exams (thank God). It's also a Saturday, a soggy drizzling day after a week of rain. Fortunately, there's no need for a bakkie to move all of my stuff; all I have are clothes, really. There's also all the stuff from under my bed: sketchpads, the Suicide Manifesto, pencils, and other odd bits (I throw away the filthy rag). There's nothing like a move to another place to put your life into perspective. I thought I took up more space in the world than these few things, but now I'm realising otherwise. I don't take my hip-hop posters from the walls; I tell Izzy they belong to him now; that's enough to make him teary.

The other thing of significance I have is a letter – unopened – that was put in our letterbox two days ago. I know who the letter is from, but I don't have the heart to read it.

Three nights ago, Israel called me to come to the phone. When I asked him who it was, he said it was a girl. I told him to say I wasn't home. Then the next day this letter turned up. I recognised the writing on the envelope immediately, but couldn't open it or throw it away. So instead I stashed it in the shoebox under my bed.

Ma gives me a ride to Ernest's new spot (*our* new spot). Izzy and Siz are with us. Siz asks all sorts of questions she knows the answers to. Izzy imitates my slient behaviour, something he does when he's uncertain. I don't think any of us know much about what's happening right now. What do you call this? What do you compare it to? Older brother going away. To where? To his father's place? I'm not sure I understand the reasoning for me having to go stay with Ernest.

I don't say much in the ride; neither does the old lady.

When we arrive outside the block of flats in Clermont, Ernest comes out, but says barely a word. Nobody but me gets out of the ride. Ma, Israel and Sizwe watch from behind misty windows as I stand in the rain.

Ernest helps me with my bags. 'Is this everything?' he asks.

'Yes, Tata.'

'Good. Welcome home, son.'

Book IV
February 1999

Thirty-four

Privilege. Never thought I'd ever be basking in it. But here I am, among my peers, outside the school cafeteria, on the side that overlooks the first-team cricket field.

Only Grade 12s are allowed here. We've finally made it. Everything is better this side of life: the grass is greener, the sky bluer, the wind cooler, and even my sandwich tastes better. I can now walk on the grass in the quad areas. I can walk with my hands in my pockets. I can wear my blazer with both buttons undone.

Privilege. This is what heaven must be like, if there is such a place. I bet everyone in heaven right now is looking at the next person, smiling and asking, 'How's your sandwich?'

Three weeks into it and I can tell the difference. No matter what you were before, sports god (water-polo, swimming, rugby, cricket, hockey — in that order), popular kid, academic nerd or big-time loser, once you're in matric, you're absolved of your former identity and accepted as someone to be given some modicum of respect. Grade 8s trip over themselves to greet you by your surname, or the title of Sir. Even those you had issues with in your own grade now see you as an equal. The Batter and Brawl Twins are a case in point: Duncan and Chad smile at me every time we meet here with the rest of the high and mighty.

I never thought all this privilege would mean anything to me, but the way last year went, I had plenty of ground to make up. I damn near failed Grade 11, and making it through is worth celebrating.

Even Roscoe is out here making the most of our newfound status. Every day that I've checked him in class, these first few weeks, I've made a conscious effort to greet him. But he isn't making it easy; he's a tough bastard to crack.

Today is yet another day to try, though.

'Hey, Big Ros, what up?'

Roscoe doesn't bite; his face remains still.

'Ishmael. Warren. Richard.' I acknowledge his three companions.

'Hey, Bokang.'

'Bokang.'

'Hey.'

I stand there for a moment, smiling benevolently at Roscoe. He turns away. I guess today's not the day.

On the other side of the cafeteria, Ms Meadows waddles along, carrying a box of files. It's the first time I'm seeing her this year, and I didn't realise she's pregnant (so pregnant I'm wondering how I've missed it). 'Hi, Ma'am. Can I give you a hand?'

'Bokang! Thank you. Wow! How are you?'

'I'm well, thanks. How are you?'

'Wonderful. Gosh, it's been forever. I didn't think you were back. Goodness me!'

'I made it, thanks to your support'

'That's what teachers do. We're not all bad, you know.' She honks with laughter as we walk down the corridor towards her classroom.

'You're looking really great. How's Ms Prangley's class?' she asks, rattling the key in the lock.

'Hmm, it's okay, I guess.'

She gives me a big smile as I put the box down on one of the desks. She indicates I should sit, and takes a seat next to me.

'So I didn't know you were, um, expecting.'

'Oh, this!' – rubbing her tummy – 'Yeah. Wish the baby would bloody come already. Sorry! But it's such hard work!'

I can imagine. Ms Meadows has such a tiny frame.

'Ken and I just moved into a new place in Cambridge, so it's been extra madness.'

'Congrats.' I'm really happy for her. She deserves it.

'So, tell me, how have you been?'

'Okay, Ma'am. Better.'

'Good. And the family?'

How do I answer that? Seems these days Ernest is my only family, but that's awkward even to contemplate. I still see Izzy, Siz and the old lady, but not living with them has changed things. 'Good, Ma'am. They all good.'

'Great. And what are your plans for the year?'

'What do you mean, Ma'am?'

'Preparations for next year? Applications? What will you be doing next year?'

'Law. Probably here in East London, at Rhodes.'

'*Really?* Wow, Bokang. I never would have thought. Good for you, if that's what you want.'

'Yeah.'

'Is it *really* what you want to do?'

'Well, yeah, I guess. There's an opportunity there. My dad's a lawyer, and I've been working with him, especially during the holidays.'

'Oh, I see. Okay, then.'

If privilege at school is something I'm enjoying, then the change of home is something that's gone in the opposite direction. It's not all bad, though. First off, let me say the greatest thing is that I now live down the road from school. I think about this every time I walk to and from school. It takes me less than twenty minutes to walk at a chilled pace. The other great thing is that Ernest is no longer drinking (I know, right?), which is like a new trippy reality. I'm still trying to get used to it but I guess it's all good. It just kind of happened, without any kind of explanation or discussion. As I say, I'll gladly take it.

But Clermont itself, in comparison to Beacon Bay, is a hell hole.

Me and Ernest stay in a three-bedroom flat, on the third floor of an eight-flat building. It's tough getting used to living in such a small place with so many neighbours all around. I have to be grateful that by Clermont standards, this is the quiet side.

Norden Place is an old building that used to be yellow, but now looks grey, white and green where the paint has faded, chipped and grown dirty over the years. On the one side is an abandoned house, parts of it reduced to rubble. The standing walls are covered in graffiti, and some of the neighbourhood kids play there when the adults aren't watching, which is most of the time. A few tall trees stand on the other side of the building, rising as high as the roof and creating darkness on that side of the building. Some of the trees are on the other side of the fence on the neighbour's property, which is a house.

One of the positive differences between Clermont and Beacon Bay (or at least our street) is that I know most of my neighbours, and we've only been here two months. The ground floor of our building is occupied by Mr Magadla (who is the building representative or something) and his wife and son. The other flat on that floor is occupied by Mrs Thuso and her two teenage children. On the second floor are the Grootbooms and the Naidoos. The third floor is where we stay, and across the hall is Mrs Mafanya, a lady who works as a nurse at the clinic down the street. The top floor is occupied by Mr and Mrs Mentoor in one flat, and Dr Stanley and Sally Abedu and their children in the other.

Word has got out that Ernest is a lawyer, and now everybody and their damn cat is always coming over for legal advice. Who knew lawyers were such revered people in the world? This is one of the things that's made me reconsider my decision about law (and Ernest's sober ways). I've never seen Ernest as a person that helps people, but now I get to see it every day. He sits one-on-one, or sometimes with couples, giving advice and helping people make better decisions about their lives. I know he's not getting paid for most of the people he sees at home, but the love of what he does is obvious.

When I moved in with Ernest, he made it clear that we didn't need a helper around the house. He also made it clear that he wasn't going

to be my maid. So he gave me a crash course in cooking, laundry, iron-
ing and cleaning. I learned pretty fast, and I've taken a liking to the
cooking. We share the duties, but on most days if I'm home first, then
I get to it. I don't cook anything fancy, but the standard meal for supper
is rice, veggies and meat.

Our place isn't that big (none of them are in this building), but it
does have three bedrooms, one of which is full of boxes and books.
There aren't enough shelves in the place, so books are piled up everywhere, and almost every day we have to rummage through boxes and
stacks of books searching for a specific one. It's become almost like an
adventure. The only time I ever see any joy in Ernest is when he's
searching for a book (usually with a smouldering cigarette hanging
from the corner of his mouth), reading a book, or giving somebody
legal advice.

When I think about it, this flat might as well be another office space
for Ernest. We don't have much conventional furniture – no couches,
coffee tables, room dividers or appliances. Only the bare necessities,
like a table to eat at, chairs for sitting, a fridge and stove in the kitchen,
and beds in the two bedrooms. The only 'luxury' item is a small radio
that Ernest uses to listen to the news. Fortunately, there are built-in
cupboards, because I don't think Ernest would bother getting those. It's
dope to have my own room, though; it's where I spend most of my
time, if I'm not doing chores. Ernest was kind enough to get me a desk
to work at, since he's always working at the dining table.

Independence is something I'm learning fast, living with Ernest. He
wasn't even there when I needed to complete my school registration
process. All he did was ask how much money I needed and make the
payment. He does the same with groceries and items for the house. He
asks how much is needed, and gives it to me to sort out.

Ernest comes home just before six, as I'm finishing preparing supper.

'Bokang,' he greets in a serious voice.

'Tata.'

'Come with me.'

'But the pots—'

'Switch them off. Come.'

This is not his usual routine. I follow him outside onto the street, where the light is draining away.

'Look,' Ernest says, holding out his hands.

'What is it?'

'Hawu, Bokang. The car.'

In front of us, parked next to all the other cars lining the street, is a vw Jetta. Hardly new, but still nice.

'Is this yours?'

'*Ours.*'

'Oh. Nice.'

'Hard work pays off, son,' Ernest says, as if reading the scepticism on my face. 'We deserve this. Get in. Let's go for a spin.'

Ernest takes me for a brief whirl around the neighbourhood. The entire time he's chatting about the opportunities this will bring, what it means for us. I guess he's right, in a sense. However, all I can think about is how ironic it is that he finally has a ride when we live within walking distance of my school and barely a ten-minute taxi ride from his office.

Thirty-five

The next day, Saturday, Ernest drives us down to the office on Union Street in town. It's not far, but we drive with the windows down, enjoying this new experience. It's a hot morning already, and the breeze is more than welcome.

We buy breakfast at the café on the ground floor of the building and sit inside the office, eating.

'You know,' Ernest says, wiping his mouth with a serviette, 'we need to start thinking about a receptionist. Put out an advert, hold interviews, you know?'

'Yeah, well, I already cleaned out the space over there, and we've been getting more queries since the phone line's been working.'

'Yes. I'll ask Titus when we go down to the university today. He should have some ideas.'

'You want someone with a legal background?'

'Makes sense, son. That way the person is hungry to learn, and comes cheap, since they not fully qualified. It's a win-win situation.'

'Ah.'

The first client by appointment arrives at 8.15 a.m. by my watch. It's an elderly woman who walks with a limp, accompanied by her two small grandchildren.

Ernest takes them into the boardroom, while I make a run to the stationery shop.

I never thought I'd get used to the hustle and bustle of town, but I've come to find it quite fascinating. I stop by a street vendor and cop a loosie (a bad habit I've picked up since quitting booze and weed). I also cop an orange and some sweets to mask the smell afterwards. I stand on the corner of Union and Cambridge, smoking, with my hand covering the cigarette. The sun on my skin feels as good as the smoke blowing through my nostrils. I don't smoke that much, maybe two or three times a week.

I return to the office with the box of paper. Ernest sees three more clients before we lock up to go to the Rhodes University campus, down the street at the end of Oxford. We walk down the stairs and exit the building.

'Radebe!' Tata uMfene greets us in his booming voice, right at the entrance of the building. 'Tshini! Ninjani?'

'Hlathi,' Ernest says.

Tata uMfene grabs him in an embrace. This is the first time I'm seeing Tata uMfene since that night last year when the old lady and I went to his place in Amalinda. Seeing him now brings back too many unpleasant memories. I don't think the old man has seen much of him either, which is great. (It certainly contributes towards Ernest's sobriety.)

'Hey, Bokang! What's happening, little man?' Tata uMfene also grabs me in a bear hug.

'I'm good, thanks.'

'Are you going out?' he asks, turning to Ernest. 'I came to see you, nje.'

Ernest doesn't say anything, but he's suddenly irritable.

'How have you been, maan?'

'We have to go, Hlathi.' Ernest moves towards the ride standing two parking spaces away.

'Are these your wheels? He he heeee!' He tries to open a door before Ernest presses the key fob.

'Hlathi, we have to go.'

'Let's go, then.'

'No. Me and my son.'

Tata uMfene doesn't even have the decency to look surprised. 'We need to talk business, Radebe,' he says. 'I've received a good tip-off.'

Ernest hesitates for a moment, then unlocks his door. 'Bokang, get in. We have to go.'

We climb into the ride.

'We'll talk, saluka,' Tata uMfene says, still smiling affably. Only when we drive off does his smile drop with a suddenness that makes me wonder about his sincerity.

The drive to the Rhodes campus takes literally two minutes. We navigate the law department, looking for the office of Professor Titus Manqina, an old classmate of Ernest's from the University of Fort Hare. He's now the head of department here, and we find him in his office. Ernest and the professor exchange happy greetings, and Ernest introduces me to him. The man has greying-to-white hair and a happy face with serious eyes.

After catching up on news and sharing stories, Prof Manqina says, 'So, Radebe, what can I do for you?'

'This boy will be studying here next year. He's already working with me at the firm. It's in the blood.' He laughs. 'We need to know about bursaries.'

'Ah, yes, yes. I know who we should talk to.'

Prof Manqina takes us on a brief tour of the department and the building on our way to the person who can assist us. She gives us the forms and tells us to bring them directly back to her, not to follow the normal process for everybody else. Prof Manqina also gives Ernest the names of his students who would make good receptionists.

Apart from the surprising visit from Tata uMfene, it has been a great morning.

The next day is the old lady's birthday. I haven't seen her in about three weeks. She phones sometimes, but our conversations are brief. She phoned almost every day in December, and I saw more of her then than I do now. We've probably spoken on the phone about twice this month. If it wasn't her birthday, I wouldn't be considering going to see her, but she's insisting. Ernest also seems surprisingly keen to go. She's invited both of us for a Sunday lunch, like the good old days (yeah, right).

That morning, Ernest has an intensity about him. He doesn't speak much, and when he does, it's in short sentences. His steps are louder, and he keeps mumbling as if he's having an ongoing dialogue with himself. He usually gets like this when he's in a confrontational mood. He dresses in a three-piece suit, which is normal during the week, but odd for a Sunday.

Late yesterday afternoon, he made me wash the car out in the street, and now when we step into it, it's all clean and shiny.

All I can do is keep sighing. I don't know how I feel about this lunch. At the time when Ma made the decision to divorce the old man, I was all for it. I truly understood where she was coming from. But that was before I knew I would have to contend with the reality of living alone with Ernest in Clermont.

We drive in silence with the windows down. Ernest has a cigarette burning between his fingers. He smokes slowly, only dragging when the ash is about to fall. I've noticed both of us enjoy these silent moments. When I was a kid, he used to tell me not to talk in the ride. He'd switch the radio off and encourage me to listen to the quiet. Now that he has a ride again, after all these years, he's gone back to those ways. I guess it's the same in the flat, too. Unless we're working on something or having a constructive conversation, the place is usually quiet, with only the sounds from outside filtering in.

When we arrive at the house in Beacon Bay, Ernest blasts the hooter a number of times instead of ringing the buzzer. Sizwe comes running out as the gate slides open. Ernest keeps on hooting to announce our arrival.

The old lady stands in the doorway in a church dress, her hands holding her elbows. Israel stands behind her.

Ernest opens his door wide and makes a show of hugging Sizwe. He lifts her up in his knotted hands and twirls her around.

Israel is significantly bigger since I last saw him. Both he and Sizwe are dressed smartly, like Ma and Ernest. I'm the only one dressed casually.

'How are my little ones?' Ernest growls.

'Great!' Sizwe says.

The two of them laugh. The rest of us watch them, unsure what to do.

'Is this your car, Tata?' Sizwe asks.

'Yes, my girl,' Ernest says, opening the driver's door for Sizwe to climb in.

'Can we go for a ride?' Sizwe plays with the steering wheel.

'Sure, why not?'

'No, Sizwekazi,' Ma says. 'It's time for lunch.'

'Come on!' Sizwe pouts.

'You haven't even greeted your brother yet.'

Neither has she, as a matter of fact, but I don't say anything. I stand next to the car watching the big smiles on Ernest and Sizwe's faces.

Israel comes over and gives me a tight hug.

'Hey, Bobo.' Ma gives me a clumsy wave and then leans in for a hug. 'How are you, my child?' She puts a hand on my cheek.

'I'm fine, thanks. How are you?'

'Good, thanks.'

The folks aren't really acknowledging each other. Ma is using me as a distraction while Ernest fools around with Sizwe.

'*Please* can we go for a ride?' Sizwe pleads.

'No, Sizwe.'

'Ag, Khensani, relax,' Ernest says, climbing back into the ride. 'We'll only be a few minutes. Come on, Izzy.'

'No, thanks,' Israel says.

Ernest starts up the ride without waiting for Ma's response, and backs down the driveway. Ma reluctantly opens the gate. The three of us stand there after they've left.

'Come inside,' she says.

It's strange being back inside this house. It feels familiar, but it certainly don't feel like home no more (maybe I'm just telling myself it ain't home). Everything is still the same, except the places that used to be occupied by books are now filled with ornaments, vases and pictures.

Those things don't quite fill the shelves, but the absence of the books is enough to make the place different.

'Is everything going well at school?'

The two of us sit in the lounge while Israel disappears into his room.

'Yes, Ma.'

'The teachers being good to you?'

'Yes, Ma.'

Through the sliding door, I notice the pool is clean. The garden all around the house is also trimmed and neat.

'Has Mr Summers said anything to you?'

'He asked to see me in my first week. Wanted to know how I'm doing and everything.'

'Good. I also spoke to him. He's a good man. Tries to do the right thing.'

I give her a smile. I can't forget what she did for me to pass last year, regardless of everything else.

'I was at the beach on Sunday morning last week,' she says. 'With Izzy and Sizwe. We took a walk.'

'How did you manage to get them out of bed so early?'

She laughs. 'It was tough, yho! But it was nice. I wish you had been there.'

I avoid her eyes.

'How's Clermont?'

She shouldn't ask. Not yet.

'I know it's not easy, my child. Just remember it's not forever.'

She changes the subject, talking about the improvements in the house. She tells me what's happening at Israel's and Sizwe's school.

Not long after, we hear Ernest returning with Sizwe. Before the old lady lets them in, she says one more thing. 'Oh, by the way, there was a young lady here looking for you earlier this week. Noxolo, she said her name was – no, Nokwanda. Yes, that's her name. Beautiful girl. She said you should call her.'

Sunday lunch is as good as I remember. I wonder if this has become a weekly tradition again now that Ernest and I no longer live here (like a celebration that the monsters are finally gone). It's been ages since the old lady's cooking tasted this good.

Ernest, as always, sits at the head of the table. I sit next to Sizwe on one side, while Ma and Israel sit on the other side. (Ma had to call Israel a couple of times before he came to join us.)

'It's a nice car you have,' Ma says.

Ernest smiles at Sizwe. He rubs his hand over her head.

'When did you get it?'

'You think we can't afford a car?'

'I'm just saying it's a nice car.'

'We went to Rhodes yesterday,' I say. 'Had a look at the law department.'

'Oh, that's wonderful. And what do you think?'

'It's nice. I'm looking forward to studying there.'

Ernest gives the old lady a triumphant smile.

'Are you still drawing?' the old lady asks.

'No. Not so much these days.'

'His mind is focused on serious things now, Khensani. Staying with me is giving him focus.' He grins at the old lady. 'I see you putting my shelves to good use.'

'Yes, we've decorated,' Ma says.

'That's not what bookshelves are for.'

'We couldn't just leave them empty.'

'Maybe you should have.'

'Some of my books are on the shelf, Tata,' Sizwe says. Her timing is perfect – I'm not even sure if she knows it.

'Oh, wonderful,' Ernest says, still watching the old lady. The look he had this morning is back; a predatory look. 'And did your mother tell you to put your books there?'

'Yes!'

'Oh. So shelves are still for books in this house.' He laughs unpleasantly.

'Yes, Tata.'

'Have some more vegetables, Izzy,' Ma says.

The boy has barely touched his plate. 'I'm okay.'

Ernest pushes his half-finished plate forward so it clangs against a serving bowl. Everyone looks in his direction as he pulls out a cigarette and holds up a lighter in his other hand. 'So I saw a nice pair of rugby boots.' Israel, to whom the comment is directed, doesn't move his eyes from his plate. 'The salesperson told me they're the best on the market. But your old man will get you a deal, don't you worry.' He winks.

'It's not rugby season,' Israel says.

'Ha! So what? We get them early and beat all the other fools to the punch. Heh?' He laughs.

Israel also pushes his plate against a serving bowl, the sound making all of us (except Ernest) jump. 'I don't play rugby any more, since my fits.'

Ernest puts the cigarette in his mouth and sparks the lighter.

'We don't smoke in this house,' Ma says.

Ernest gives her an incredulous look, the cigarette still dangling from his mouth. 'Seriously?'

'Yes.'

'This is my house.'

'No, it is not.'

The folks are deadlocked in a stare. Sizwe's pretty eyes are confused. Israel is a bull about to charge.

Ernest lets out a laugh. 'What is this? Since when can't I smoke here?'

'Since you don't live here,' Israel says. He stands up.

'Tata,' I say. 'Let it go.'

'Let what go?'

'Don't spoil this,' Ma says.

'*You* the one who wanted a divorce! You spoilt *everything*!'

Israel pushes his chair back and turns towards the old man.

'Izzy, no,' I say.

He turns his bull face to me, and I can tell he's not interested in my words either.

'Tata, let's just go,' I say.

Ernest gets up so fast he knocks his chair over backwards. The sound is enough to get Israel moving forward, but the old lady grabs his wrist. I'm also on my feet, even though I don't know what my next move is. I look at the old lady, and she gives an almost imperceptible nod. Ernest drags his feet towards the front door, sparking the cigarette just inside the house to let everyone know how he really feels. Sizwe climbs onto the old lady's lap.

If Ernest leaves, I guess it means I also have to leave; the sides have been chosen. I say my goodbyes.

Ernest smokes two cigarettes on the fifteen-minute ride home. This time, there's no sense of quiet in the ride. He rants about the old lady, telling me the divorce is her fault. He tells me all the selfish things she's done in their marriage, how he's sacrificed for her, but she's been the one who's taken everything from him. He tells me what a useless mother she is, and that I shouldn't be surprised I've turned out the way I have.

I don't say anything. I barely listen to what he's saying. It's all poison; his words are a buzzing sound and I tune out. All I'm wondering is how it is that Ernest never seems to blame himself for anything. Can he seriously not see what role he's played all these years in making our home life miserable?

He drops me off outside Norden Place, and drives off without telling me where he's going.

Inside the flat, I take out the shoebox from under my bed. I rummage through the things in it and find the letter I've had for more than two months but still haven't read. I know it's from Nokwanda. Why did she write this letter? Why did she come to the house in Beacon Bay? What does she want from me? I want to open the letter, but at the same time I want to throw it away without ever reading it. Maybe the letter is her final insult. But after all this time?

I stare at the letter, my fingers trembling. I return it to the box for a time when I have the courage to open it.

Thirty-six

The next week, a brilliant idea occurs to me. I ask myself why I didn't think of it sooner.

It all starts when I carry on with my attempts to repair things with Roscoe. I notice even with him working so hard to shut me out, something in his eye is pleading with me to succeed. It occurs to me that Roscoe is trapped behind his own stubbornness. I know how that feels.

Two things about Roscoe: 1) he loves his schoolwork; and 2) he's a serious Mama's boy. So if I'm serious about fixing things with him, I need to take it to the next level: I need to get to him through his moms.

It's been a while since I last saw Mrs Munsamy. She runs a shop in Braelyn, where the family stays. My best plan of action is to go there.

I go on a Wednesday after school, which finishes early that day. The shop is on the same street they live on, and it's a small building that used to be a house. All the goods are stacked behind the shop minder, and the customer has to stand on steps and look through a metal mesh partition to see the goods for sale.

I remember Roscoe mentioning his mother always needed help with balancing the books, which he takes care of, as well as manpower to pack the stock. I'm hoping to help with the latter.

The shop is a washed-out yellow colour with a blue roof. A bright red Coca-Cola sign with the words 'Vern's Shop' hangs on the front.

Mrs Munsamy's name is Vern. It's short for something longer, but I can never remember it. She herself said I would never remember it when she first introduced herself to me.

I climb up the three big steps so I can get to the purchasing window. 'Hello, Mrs Munsamy.'

Roscoe's mother is all the way at the back, facing away from me. 'Hang on a minute,' she squawks. She waddles towards me. Short solid frame. Long greying hair pulled tight into a bun at the back of her head. Red dot on the forehead. Purple-and-pink sari. Spectacles that make her look like an owl. 'Hal-looo, what I get you?'

'Hi, Mrs Munsamy—'

'No. No Mrs Munsamy. You call me Auntie Vern, right. Auntie Vern. No Mrs Munsamy.'

'Okay, er … Auntie Vern. How are you, Ma'am?'

'What I get you?'

'Auntie Vern. It's me, Bokang. Bokang Damane?'

'What you say about the money? You talk about the money, but you don't say what I get you. What you want dere, boy?'

'No, no, Auntie Vern. It's me, *Bokang*. I'm Roscoe's friend, from school. Remember?'

She adjusts her glasses. 'Roscoe's friend, you say?'

'Yes, Auntie Vern. Bokang.'

'Ooooh! Bo-*kang*! Why you not say? Ey, you boys, you make fun of the old lady, heh.' She laughs, sounding many years younger than she looks. 'What I do for you? Roscoe not here today.'

'No, Auntie Vern, I know Roscoe's not here. I wanted to know if I can help in the shop. I'm strong and I can pack boxes. And you don't have to pay me.'

'You want to work but no pay?'

'Yes, Ma'am.'

She considers me, the smile gone from her face. 'What you want, den?'

'Just to help, because you're my friend's mother.'

'Ooh. You're a good boy, den? Okay, you help the old lady, dere.'

Mrs Munsamy shows me around the shop. Small as it is, it's a neatly kept space. Many items are kept in two rooms at the back, as well as down in a basement, which has a desk and doubles up as an office.

Mrs Munsamy explains to me that she no longer enjoys going up and down the stairs to the basement, as it's bad for her back. She's been wanting to move some items from down there to the shelves upstairs, while transferring other items from the upstairs storerooms down to the basement. So that's my first task for the afternoon.

After an hour's toil, she invites me upstairs for a cup of tea. We sit on crates at the front of the store. The green tea steams on the low table in front of us.

'So, how's Mummy?'

'She's fine.'

'You keep her happy?' She takes off her spectacles and squints, inspecting me.

'Yes.'

'Good. You always keep Mummy happy. Always.' She inspects me again. Her gaze is intense but kind. 'What is it, den?'

'Er, nothing … It's …'

She watches me patiently.

'I don't see her that much any more. My parents separated a few months ago. I live with my father now.'

Mrs Munsamy puts her tea cup down. She grabs my hand in both of hers. She concentrates on my palm. She nods and ums and aahs.

'You've got a big heart, my boy. Just like Mummy. Very smart too, like Daddy. But you don't use your smart to protect your heart. Why you not follow your heart?'

'Um …'

She looks back down at my palm, as if she knows I have no response. 'Oh, I see …' She nods dramatically. What is she seeing that I'm not seeing? 'What happen with you and my Roscoe?' she asks.

'We had a fall-out last year.'

'What happen?'

'I … We … It was my fault. But …'

'My boy, he is stubborn. I know well. What make you think you fix everything?'

'He's my friend. I miss him. I want him back in my life.'

'Some things you don't fix. Some things just happen, you can't fix. You can't fix Daddy, and you can't fix Mummy. You look after you, right. The past is behind you. You let it go, right?'

'What do you mean?'

She smiles. 'Don't you worry. One day, you get dere.' She taps the centre of my palm, then releases my hand. 'Right! You finish up, den.'

I want to ask her more questions, but a customer appears at the window. I go back downstairs and do another half-hour's work before I call it a day.

When I get home that evening, our flat is full of people. Ernest is hosting the building committee meeting, which is attended by Mr Magadla and Mrs Thuso from downstairs, Mr Naidoo from the second floor, Mrs Mafanya from our floor, and Dr Stanley Abedu from upstairs. These meetings happen once a month and take place in different flats.

'Ah, Bokang is here,' Ernest says. 'Give him the pen and paper. He can take the minutes.'

I sit with them, listening. Mr Magadla informs everyone that the day the municipality collects refuse has changed from a Tuesday to a Wednesday. The plumbing problems experienced by the tenants on the third floor will be resolved tomorrow. Mrs Thuso complains about kids who do not live in the building playing inside and damaging the property.

After holding his silence for some time, Dr Abedu speaks. 'We need to address the issue we have on the fourth floor.' He sits forward, his face shining as if he uses butter for moisturiser. 'This non-stop noise must stop. The Mentoors do not follow the rules; they show disrespect for everyone.'

'Ja,' Mrs Mafanya says. 'This has to stop.'

Mr Magadla, looking nervous, says, 'Well, we have spoken to them already.'

'But they do not listen!' Dr Abedu says. 'I go there myself, to tell them. But if I go back again, I'm sorry, but I will not know what happens. This is not my issue!'

Mrs Mafanya also gets animated.

'Okay, everybody calm down,' Ernest says. 'I'm sure we can talk to them.'

'That's a waste of time!' Dr Abedu says. 'They need a notice, something harsh.'

'They're not breaking any rules,' Mr Magadla says. 'We must respect their privacy.'

'What about our privacy?' Dr Abedu is almost falling off his seat. '*Noise disturbance* is against the rules! My children cannot suffer these pornographic activities!'

Ah. I always wondered where those sounds were coming from. The Mentoors live directly above us and next door to the Abedus.

'Look,' Ernest says, 'I can go have an informal word with them. We are neighbours here; we share a space. Surely we can resolve this amicably.'

'I second that,' Mr Naidoo says. It's the first thing he's said since I joined the meeting.

Dr Abedu and Mrs Mafanya aren't pleased, but Mr Magadla is relieved Ernest is taking the lead on this. Even if the matter isn't exactly resolved, it is agreed that Ernest will talk to the Mentoors before any formal written complaint is given.

After the meeting, I go to my room, pull out the boxes under my bed and rummage through my stuff. I consider some of the things I rapped about with Auntie Vern. My love of drawing, rhyming and using my creative abilities are definitely things that comes from the old lady – all heart, as Auntie Vern said. My academic ability and love of reading are definitely all Ernest. The old lady must have a whole lot of heart to have dealt with Ernest all these years.

On the spur of the moment, I take the Suicide Manifesto and Nokwanda's unopened letter outside, along with a box of Ernest's matches. I go around to the back of the building and find a corner to squat in. It's a quiet night by Clermont standards. I can hear traffic and sounds from TVs coming from open windows. I set the Suicide Manifesto alight and watch it burn. I have to repeatedly light some pages. It burns slowly. It feels like my memories are burning, all the bad ones. I watch with something like satisfaction. Auntie Vern said I should let go and this feels like a start.

I don't burn the letter, though. I almost open it and read it but after the other pages have long burned to ash, I take the letter back inside with me and put it back in the box under my bed.

The following week, I'm back in Braelyn at the shop with Auntie Vern. This is my fourth afternoon coming to work with her in two weeks. Most of the work that needed doing is complete, but I enjoy coming here and chatting with her.

Auntie Vern makes us some green tea. When I'm here, I spend time listening to her stories about India, where she visits at least once a year. She comes from a long line of astrologers and diviners, and hearing her forecasts about almost every issue in the world is something I enjoy, even though some of it sounds mad-over-the-top.

'Let me see your hand, den, see what's happening with your love life. Right.' I give her my hand, amused at what she might find. 'Oh, my boy' – rubbing her thumb in the centre of my palm – 'you're a slippery one, like a frog! But I see a woman, young beautiful girl. Thick eyebrows, like your Auntie Vern! Maybe she have Indian blood.'

I laugh. 'And when am I going to meet this mystery woman?'

'She will be good for you. Your Mummy, she won't like. No, no, no, but she will be good for you.' She pulls my hand closer to her face. 'Yar, Mummy spoils you. Holds on too tight.'

And here I was thinking she's let me go too easily. 'What about this mystery girl?'

'Don't be so rush-rush! Ey! You youngsters, you want everything now. Just like my Roscoe. He can't wait, want everything now. Not so soon, my boy. Your heart must grow bigger first, and for that you must be alone.'

Well, that's not good news.

'But you will be happy.' She gives me a smile. 'Help people, and you find happiness.' She releases my hand, rubs hers together. 'Now, tell me about my boy.'

'Who? Roscoe?'

'Yes, yes. Who he love?'

'I don't know if Roscoe has a girl in his life.'

'Are you not his friend?'

'Yes. But things are not the same between us.'

'Yes, yes. This I know. Otherwise you don't come here and help me. So when you fix it?'

'I'm trying, I really am. He's stubborn.'

'Yar, you don't tell me. A mother knows well. So I help you, den. You help me, I help you.'

'What do you mean?'

'Ah!' She stands up without answering. 'Here he is.'

Roscoe appears at the shop window. His mother ushers him around to the back door. When he sees me, he stands stock still, with his mouth half open.

'Hal-looo, boy. Give Mummy a kiss.' She grabs him and pulls him down for a smooch on the lips. Then, hands on her hips, she says, 'Now, you two. Go down to basement and talk.'

'What are you doing here?' Roscoe asks.

'Hey! Downstairs. Now.'

I get up and move down the stairs. Roscoe tries to protest, but follows me when his moms literally pushes him.

Down in the basement, Roscoe and I stare at each other. We are alone and as close as we have been to each other in ages, but still it feels like we worlds apart. There is no point waiting for him to say anything, so I speak. 'Yo, Big Ros, I just wanna say—'

'How long have you been helping my mother?'

'A few weeks.'

'Wow.' He smiles. 'I can't believe you've spent that much time with her.'

'She's actually pretty cool.'

'Whatever.'

We laugh and embrace. We talk the rest of the stuff out, and it feels damn good to be on speaking terms again.

When I get home later that evening, I find Ernest sitting in the flat with Mr Magadla from downstairs, the one responsible for the building maintenance.

'So then what did you say?' Ernest asks, with his hands clasped under his chin.

'She must listen to me. The household needs my direction. But she refuses. I'm losing patience.'

'You cannot lose patience. Do you not understand her request of you?'

I go to my room but leave the door open so I can hear their conversation.

'No, I don't. She is so full of demands.'

'I can guarantee you, she wants the best for both of you.'

'Heh?'

'Ja, you heard me.'

I can't believe this. Ernest a marriage counsellor?

'Your wife is right.'

I can't bear it, so I close the door. I lay on my bed, staring at the ceiling. Ernest is a bag of contradictions: not only is he sober, he's now a relationship counsellor. Wow. I won't rush to give him credit, but I will acknowledge that at least he's doing something.

On Friday that same week, Roscoe sits with me during second break. We sit by the matric side of the cafeteria, watching a group of boys playing touch rugby.

'When did you last speak to Senzo?' he asks.

'Damn. I don't remember. Before he left. It's been too long. You?'

'Last week.'

'How's he doing? I miss his punk ass.'

'You should call him.'

'I did. Once. But he hung up on me.'

Roscoe laughs. 'Sorry, bra. But you kinda deserved it.'

'Yeah. Probably.'

The rugby ball comes bouncing in our direction. I pick it up and attempt to pass it, but it doesn't quite go to the person I was throwing it to.

'Have you been sketching?'

'Nah, not really.'

'No?' He swipes his fringe out of his eyes. 'No way. That's your gift, bra. The comic was your thing.'

'No, the comic was *our* thing. Yours, mine and Senzo's.'

'If it wasn't for you, there would be no comic. I'm a bloody accountant, and Senzo is not exactly a creative genius, bra.'

We laugh.

'It was always you.'

'Thanks, Big Ros. It means a lot to hear you say that.'

'So what you doing after school?'

'Nothing. Was gonna go home and chill.'

'Let's finish what we started. Bring back the Friday tradition – minus Senzo. You and me, we can do it.'

After school, Roscoe and I head to my spot. I'm a little nervous about having him come over, but he insists. It's one thing for me to have to deal with the downgrade of lifestyle, but to have a friend come over and see how I'm living (or dying) is something else altogether. I try giving him excuses, but nothing works. He's too excited about finishing the comic.

While we walk, I glance at him askew, checking his reactions. So far, he's holding up well. If anything, he seems entertained. Friday afternoon in Clermont is quite something. Students (and general vagabonds) treat the streets like a party ground. On every corner, people sit drinking or walk about with cans in their hands. Others sit on balconies or hang out windows and doorways with their drinks. Music blasts from some of the buildings. The place is a hive of debauchery.

'Some place this is,' Roscoe says.

274

'Yes, it is.'

'Lots of ladies, I see.'

Mr Naidoo is outside on the steps speaking to Mrs Thuso when I arrive at Norden Place; he greets us pleasantly, while she scowls. The lift isn't working, so we take the stairs. All the while I'm watching Roscoe's face for any signs of what he might think. He doesn't look sick enough to vomit or scared enough to run away. Either he's tougher than I give him credit for, or he's good at pretending. Or maybe, just maybe, he doesn't see anything wrong at all.

We find Ernest and Mr Magadla inside. They sit at the dining-room table, and Mr Magadla has a beer in front of him – a long tom Black Label, exactly the beer Ernest used to drink. I scan Ernest's face for signs of drinking. Even when I greet him, I scrutinise him carefully. I can't tell if he's had anything to drink. As we head into my room, I wonder if Mr Magadla has any idea how dangerous it is to have a beer in front of sober Ernest.

Roscoe and I go through the outline of the comic-book series from beginning to end. We look at all the sketches I drew a while back. We plot where we need to go from here.

I'm glad we doing this, but I'm somewhat distracted. I keep straining my ear towards the other room to figure out what's going on with Ernest and Mr Magadla. I can hear them talking about Mr Magadla's marital problems again. This time Mr Magadla seems just about ready to leave his wife. Ernest – unbelievably – is telling him to hang in there and fight for his marriage.

Some time later, the two of them leave without saying where they're going. A little after that, Roscoe says he has to leave too.

As soon we exit the flat, we bump into Ms Mentoor from upstairs. 'Oh, hello, boys.' She places a hand on her chest as if she's out of breath and gives us a broad smile. Her hair comes down to her shoulders and is dyed almost the same light golden-brown tone of her skin. She has gold rings in her nose and ears, and her neck and arms right down to the wrists are covered in gold bangles. She wears a top that reveals her shoulders and arms (and all her tattoos), and a very short jean skirt.

'Hi, Mrs Mentoor.'

'Please, call me Lucille.' She smiles again, revealing two gold-capped teeth.

'Who's this?' she asks, taking in Roscoe from top to bottom.

'This is my friend, Roscoe.'

She holds out a manicured hand. 'Lucille. Pleased to meet you.'

'Yes, Ma'am,' Roscoe says, smiling.

'Ooh, Ma'am? I like that. Such great manners. Where you come from?' She sticks her leg out like a horse at a gymkhana.

'My father isn't here, Mrs Mentoor.'

She ignores me, apparently spellbound by Roscoe's magic. Roscoe is beaming back at her with a confidence I've never seen in him.

'You're fresh. Do you always come here?' Mrs Mentoor asks.

'Yeah. This is my boy's place, so I hang here from time to time.'

'Mrs Mentoor, I'll let my father know you were looking for him.'

'Good. You can tell him it's about the conversation he had with my husband.'

'Sure.'

'Goodbye, Roscoe.'

'Goodbye, Lucille.'

'Hope to see you soon.'

She heads up the stairs, looking back at us over her shoulder. I wish she'd trip over those damn heels and tumble down the stairs. '*Goodbye, Lucille*? Now you two are suddenly friends?'

'What?' Roscoe says as we step outside. 'I can't help it if she was friendly.'

'Friendly? She's disgusting, dude! And since when am I *your boy*? More than ten years of knowing you, and only now you start talking like a nigga. Man, you're a joke!'

'Whatever. It was really great being here. We should do this again next Friday.'

Thirty-seven

Ernest and Mr Magadla are not in the flat when I return from walking Roscoe home. Where could Ernest be? Since getting the ride, he's always come home before dark. Every night he has been sober. But now it's getting to be eight o'clock, and I have a terrible feeling.

I hate worrying about Ernest; it seems like such a waste of time. It seems we kids are hardwired in our DNA to have an emotional bond with our parents, regardless of how seriously they take their parenting duties. Wherever Ernest is, he ain't worried about nobody but himself.

This is stupid. I should be worrying about Israel and Sizwe and maybe even the old lady, but certainly not Ernest. But as long as Ernest isn't there in Beacon Bay, then they are all right. And me? Well, I stopped wondering a long time ago if I'm all right or not.

> I'm made of bones, white and ashy, with chips and cracks all over them. Not quite a skeleton, not quite skinny. Normal-sized, a little hollowed out; stripped of flesh and fat tissue, definitely. Splayed out on a cold slab of concrete as if on a hospital bed. It's a counter in some sort of room. Gloomy. A little light filters through an open window above. This must be a basement (Auntie Vern's basement?).
>
> Jars in rows line the shelves on the walls on all sides of the small room. The jars are different sizes; some are empty, while others are

filled with powders; others contain liquids with dead things suspended in them. A smell of chalk dust, mixed with sour milk, hangs in the air.

The door behind me creaks open. Movement. The smell of rotten tomatoes stings my nostrils. Whoever – whatever – has entered the room is humming. Jars shuffle on the shelves, metal objects jangle inside the drawers, feet scrape the concrete floor.

She – or it – comes into view. An old hag dressed in black spiderwebs that move about her as if they were living things. She's completely shrouded in them and they cover her head like a hood. She has pale flaky hands, and a long obscene nose sticking out from the blackness of her attire. I can't move. I can't scream.

The old hag pins my hands down and straddles me. Why am I getting an erection? *No, no, no, no!* A long grey tongue with purple lesions dances out of her mouth. Snail trails of saliva drip from the corners of her mouth. She smiles; the tongue sways from side to side. Her eyes burn yellow. She leans down, and despite my best efforts, she licks me across the face. Her slithering tongue feels like soggy sandpaper. Her mouth covers my scream. One of her hard hands goes into my pants …

I'm in the back seat of a black car, speeding on a highway through lashing rain. We pass other black cars identical to the one we're riding in. I've been here before. The old hag drives the car. No, it's not the old hag, it's Tata uMfene. 'You must find it!' He laughs, that loud booming laugh. It's so loud I have to cover my ears. *'Ha! Ha! Ha! Haaa! Ha! Ha! Ha! Haaa! Ha! Ha! Ha! Haaa!'*

I sit up in bed. Eleven minutes past two. Movement in the flat. Laughter. Chattering. Clinking glasses. Footsteps. I stumble into the dimly lit lounge.

'There he is! Ha! Haa!'

'Eish, Hlathi. Why must you be so uncultured.'

'The boy is already awake.'

The light from the kitchen outlines Ernest as he pours amber liquid from a bottle into his glass. Tata uMfene sits in a chair by the dining table, with a glass half-full in front of him.

'Come say hallloooo!'

'Hi,' I say, rubbing my eyes.

Mr Magadla lays passed out on the couch (a new addition to the flat – the couch, not Mr Magadla).

'How are you, son?'

'I was sleeping.'

'Tell him the good news!'

'Oh, ja. Sit, boy.' Ernest isn't wearing his glasses; his eyes are red and unfocused, rimmed by pizza-crust eyelids.

The two of them are kids at play rather than two adults awake in the middle of the night.

'I have some good news,' Ernest says, before taking a sip that makes him grimace.

'My tip-offs always pay!' Tata uMfene holds up his glass. '*Halala!*'

'We've been talking.'

'You and who?'

'Hlathi here, and Magadla over there.'

'Young man can't handle his liquor!' Tata uMfene says.

Neither can the two of you, from what I'm seeing. Tata uMfene's eyes are rolling around in their sockets like dice in a roulette wheel.

'You should have seen your father! Ha! What a man! He knows a winning number, always has!'

'It's a gift, Hlathi,' Ernest says. 'Takes patience and skill. But it's our partnership that won for us.' He takes Tata uMfene's hand. 'I couldn't have done it without you.'

'We have been through a lot, Radebe, you and me. Since we were boys.'

'Did you see those fools, thinking they could cheat us?'

'Rha! They are crazy! Next time we shoot them! Ha! Ha! Ha! Haaa!'

'Err ... you said something about good news?'

They both turn to me as if they've forgotten I'm in the room.

'Oh, yes, son. Good news. The time has come, the time for you to be a man.'

'Your father is going to make it happen.'

'No, Hlathi, *we* are going to make it happen.'

'You mean?'

'Yes, son. Uzokoluka. We are taking you to become a man, in the Xhosa tradition.'

'When?'

'This coming June. We finally have the money.'

'Good, neh?' Tata uMfene slaps me on the shoulder.

I don't know what to say.

'Are you happy, son?'

'Yes, definitely. I didn't think ...'

'I know you've wanted this for a long time. This is my gift to you. Together with the ancestors, we will welcome you into manhood.' Ernest's bottom lip starts to quiver. 'Come here, son.'

We hug as his tears start running. Tata uMfene hugs us both from behind.

Thirty-eight

The effort Ernest and Tata uMfene put into getting me ready for the matric dance is nothing compared to the effort they put into planning my initiation into manhood. This 'project', as they call it, becomes the central focus of our lives.

Naturally, we see more of Tata uMfene now. He might as well be living with us, as the table in the dining room becomes the base of operations; on a few nights, he passes out on the new couch.

There are still over two and half months before June, but still there is plenty of preparation needed. The first step is a mini-ceremony known as imbeleko. This is something I should've done years ago, before I was a teenager. It's like this ceremony that every kid has to undergo to be officially introduced to the ancestors as a member of the family. One cannot go through initiation into manhood (or womanhood) without doing this first, Ernest explains to me. He doesn't explain why it wasn't done earlier in my life.

One Saturday, I drive out with Ernest and Tata uMfene to his village near Dimbaza, on the other side of King William's Town. This is where Ernest's family is from, and I haven't been out here in ages. This initial visit is to set up everything for the imbeleko.

Tata uMfene takes the lead out here in the rural areas. Ernest tells him what he needs, and Tata uMfene executes. He is truly in his element.

Two weeks after this initial visit, the day of the actual imbeleko comes. Israel and Sizwe drive with us. When we pick them up in Beacon Bay, Ernest stays in the ride and parks out in the street instead of in the driveway.

'Everything will be fine, Ma.'

'I know, my child.' She places a hand on my cheek, that thing she does.

'Don't look so sad.'

'Sorry. I'm just … happy for you that this is happening. But I want you to know, you don't have to do this.'

'But I want to.'

'I know.'

It's an overcast day, and the wind blows with a vengeance. Ernest hoots and holds up his hands.

'I have to go. We'll be fine.'

'Okay.' She gives me a hug. 'Always be a good child, Bobo. Don't let manhood take that away from you.'

I don't know what she means, and I guess it shows on my face. 'Ma, I'm not going to bush yet. There's still time.'

'No, there isn't. I feel like I've already lost you.'

Ernest hoots again.

Israel and Sizwe are excited to be part of this whole thing; Israel keeps his distance from the old man, though. I'm glad they're with me; after all, their time will come too. Ernest, as you can imagine, is super-excited, helped along by the brandy he's drinking (his new drink of choice).

Tata uMfene picks the four of us up from Norden Place, and this allows Ernest to be the inebriated passenger. Fortunately, he's at his joyful best.

The imbeleko is not a huge affair. A few of the old man's relatives attend. People from the village also attend, as is the custom on such occasions. A goat and a sheep are slaughtered. People eat and drink. Speeches are made. Tata uMfene speaks with great authority, with men taking their hats off and nodding as he does. Ernest also speaks with the authority of a lawyer mixed with the happiness of a man in his cups (or maybe just a proud father?).

We take Israel and Sizwe back to Beacon Bay just after ten at night. I pass Sizwe asleep in my arms over to the old lady. Israel is also half-asleep on his feet; it's been a long day.

By the time we arrive at Norden Place, Ernest is passed out in the passenger seat. Tata uMfene has to carry him – exactly how I carried Sizwe – into the building, up in the now working lift and into the flat; it's like a bear cradling a weasel in its arms. He takes him all the way to his room, and I'm pretty sure he even tucks him into bed.

Before he leaves, Tata uMfene sparks a cigarette and sits on the couch. 'You did well today,' he says, in a voice so low it's uncharacteristic of him.

'Thank you for being there.'

'Do you know what this means to your father?'

I shake my head.

'You've made him very happy. Nothing makes a man happier than seeing his son become a man.'

I'm not sure what to say. I'm also tired; there's so much about today to process.

'Are you ready to become a man?'

'Yes.'

'Good. I can see that. Your father can see that. You have to be ready and eager. That is always a good sign. We don't see that any more.' He taps his cigarette, then takes a long slow drag. He blows the smoke up towards the insects buzzing around the light. 'These days, too many youngsters want to go through ulwaluko for the wrong reasons. Some say it's a dying practice. Don't believe that, Bokang. You hear me?'

I nod.

'Western culture has influenced some things, but not our spirituality, not the way a father passes on his family name to his son. It is a blessing to you as a Damane, from your clan, as oRadebe. Everything you do with your life will be in the name of those who came before you. This is your real education.'

'Yes, Tata.'

'And always remember, no matter what: your father loves you.'

One afternoon the following week, I'm sitting in my room sketching. It's a Wednesday, so I'm home early. I get up from my desk when I hear a knock on the front door.

'Mrs Mafanya, hello.'

'Is your father home?'

'Er, not yet.'

'We have an appointment for three.' She checks her watch.

'Here or at the office?'

'Here, boy. He said he would be home early.' She checks her watch again.

'Okay, I'm sure he'll be home soon. Should I let you know when he's here?'

'Yes. Thank you.'

She returns to her flat across the hall. I call Ernest's office.

'Bhelekazi. Is my dad there?'

'No, he isn't.'

'Does he have any appointments scheduled for this afternoon?'

'He had one at twelve-thirty. But nothing else after. Is he there with you?' She sounds concerned.

'What time did he leave the office?'

'I haven't seen him since this morning. He came in late, and left again before eleven. Missed two appointments.'

'If he shows up there, call me.'

'I'm about to go home now.'

Through the window, I see Ernest's street parking spot is vacant. Downstairs, Mr Magadla isn't home either, his son tells me. I should be starting to cook supper, but my mind is restless. The phone rings, and I sprint to answer it. It's another person looking for Ernest, but they don't have any useful information for me.

It's a few hours of me fretting – going onto the street, staring out the window every time I hear a car slowing down – before Ernest eventually comes home. He gingerly squeezes the ride into the parking space. The car has a dent and scratches across the left-hand side back bumper.

I go downstairs to meet him. 'Tata.'

He's startled to see me. He sways unsteadily. His suit is crumpled and looks too big on him. 'Oh, hey, boy.'

I put an arm around him for support; the lift isn't working again, and he's not going to make it up the stairs without help. Inside the flat, I take him straight to his room, take off his shoes, and let him pass out in his clothes.

A knock on the door. 'Is your father back?'

'Not yet, Mrs Mafanya.'

She looks as confused as a buffalo that's lost its way from the watering hole. 'But we had an appointment. Tomorrow I must talk to those other lawyers. Where is he, boy?'

'At the office.'

'At the office?' She peeks over my shoulder, trying to see inside.

'Yes, it's a busy week. Um, he has to focus on things there.'

'What time will he be home?'

'Not any time soon. Yesterday he came back after twelve – I expect the same tonight.'

'After twelve? No, that's not what we agreed. He's really let me down.'

Grab a ticket and take a seat, lady; he's let a lot of people down.

In the early hours of the morning, Ernest's muffled voice wakes me. At first I'm so disoriented, I assume he's having a conversation with Mrs Mafanya, but she couldn't possibly be here at this time. From under my bedcovers, I listen intently.

'Ja, it was you who … told you … but you could never … not this day … never, never, *never* … who you …'

I climb out of bed and go to find him. Ernest is sitting slumped on the couch in the lounge, a bottle of brandy in his hand. He's alone and apparently talking to himself. He doesn't notice me. His eyes don't see more than a few centimetres in front of him.

'Tata.'

He doesn't respond to me, but mumbles again. 'You take me ... taken me with you ... why ... you don't care now ... you *didn't care* then ...'

I startle him by placing a hand on his arm. 'Let's go to bed.'

He begins to sing as I support him to his room. His singing is interrupted by tears. I lay him on his bed, still dressed in his suit. I sit by his side for a while, scared that if I leave him, he might not be here in the morning.

Thirty-nine

The following evening, I decide to call the only person I can talk to about all of this manhood business. Senzo doesn't answer himself, but his mother calls him to the phone. We get through the awkwardness pretty quickly before settling into a comfortable conversational rhythm.

'So, I'm finally going to bush in a few weeks, man.'

'Word?'

'Yeah, man.'

He goes quiet. 'All right. Good for you.'

'Yeah, I'm kinda excited. You know how long I've waited for this.'

He goes quiet again. A girl stands behind me, waiting to use the payphone. She wraps her arms around herself. 'You there, man?'

'Yeah, I'm still here, Big Bo. Just be careful out there, man. About everything.'

'I thought you had a ball out there?'

'Nah, man. It was crazy: mad-political, and mad-beef, dog. I left early; couldn't take it no more. My umgidi was a joke. Be glad you weren't there. I didn't wanna see nobody. That's why I just left East London. I couldn't even face you.'

'Nah, man, you cool.'

'For real, dog. I thought you'd lose respect for me, like everybody else.'

'No way, man.'

'I'm telling you. They got mad-rules out there. Some cats don't listen. One dude actually died, for real. They covered the whole thing up. It's crazy. His family couldn't ask nothing. It's harsh out there. Just prepare yourself, man.'

'That sounds serious.'

'Yeah. I wish I could tell you don't go, but you gotta figure that out on your own. Just don't do it for other people's expectations, whatever you do.'

He goes quiet again. The girl waiting behind me stamps her feet. Two more people wait behind her.

'Look, Bo,' Senzo says. 'I feel really whack about not being there for you last year.'

'Nah, man, we cool.'

'Hear me out. I heard about what you went through, man. That Nokwanda chick. Napoleon. Roscoe told me everything. I'm just proud that you made out okay.'

'Well, it certainly wasn't easy.'

'How do you handle the drama, though? I swear, I can't take it, man. My family's gone crazy.'

'Parents will be parents. Just remember what you once told me: one day all of this will be over.'

'I really miss you, dog.'

'Maybe I can come visit?'

'Yeah, maybe in September.'

'Cool.'

'You'll be cool with everything, Bo. Don't take any of this to your head. Follow your heart. Just do your second verse shit.'

'My what?'

'Your second verse shit. You know, the second verse of any song has to be more killer than the first. Always. The rhythm has to slap. The lyrics must be on point. The feeling intense. And the impact mad-definitive. It's just the way it is. In the same way, if you do well once in life, then you always have to be better from that point onwards. No doubt.'

'I feel you, Enzo.'

'Take care, Bo.'

* * *

The following evening, Ernest sits in the lounge with Tata uMfene and Mr Magadla, drinking and smoking. It's crazy how well the three of them get along. Ernest and Tata uMfene grew up together, and the experience of going to bush together solidified their friendship. Mr Magadla is much younger than them, but can still have a laugh with them. I wonder if the liquor has anything to do with that.

I sit in my room, doing homework and later some sketching. Roscoe put me onto the Animation School in Cape Town. I need a portfolio of artworks and a motivational letter as part of my application. The art ain't no problem, but I'm sweating over the motivational letter.

What's really stressing me out is doing law at Rhodes. Prof Titus Manqina, Ernest's friend, pulled through with that bursary for next year, so that's sorted. I'd be stupid if I didn't take it, especially combined with the opportunity to work with the old man.

By the time I go to bed, Ernest and his friends are still chatting. When I get up in the early hours of the morning to go to the bathroom, Ernest is still talking. It sounds more like he's shouting. My first thought is: what has Tata uMfene done this time?

'I don't care!' Ernest says. 'Why must I care? What do you want from me, Nolwazi?'

When I check, Ernest is alone in the middle of the lounge with the lights dimmed.

'We are Azanian Knights … Azanian … Knights … We are! Azania … ' He starts singing before pausing to take a swig from the bottle in his hand. He points at the wall as if there's someone in front of him. 'Everything I ever did, I did for you … what …yes … everything! Now I've lost it … you happy, I know … it wasn't good enough …'

He falls to his knees, clutching his chest with his free hand. He lets out a loud wail and his face contorts as sounds choke up in his throat. Is Ernest losing his mind? Who is Nolwazi? What are Azanian Knights?

He gets up in a rush. 'Never! *Never*! You will never kill me! I love you always, but you … nothing … *nothing* …' He starts singing again.

The strength leaves his body and he sags on his feet, swaying, his head drooping. He drops the bottle and its contents spill onto the carpet, leaving a spreading stain.

I step forward and lead him to his room. I strip him of his clothes and put him under the covers. As I leave his room, shutting the door firmly, I wonder if this is the manhood I am so eager to be part of.

Forty

In the third week of June, exams finish. I'm satisfied with my efforts, considering the mad-distraction of this whole bush thing. The old man and Tata uMfene have made a big deal of it all, despite my protests, and as the time draws nearer, their anxiety is palpable. Tata uMfene did say this thing is as much about Ernest as it is about me.

I visit Roscoe at his house in Braelyn one last time. I haven't been in a few weeks. Mrs Munsamy is delighted to see me.

'Bokang! Where you go?' She pulls me down by the head to give me a kiss. She does the same to Roscoe.

'Hi, Auntie Vern.'

'You look good, always. Sit, sit. Have some tea.' She makes us all green tea, and we sit by the small table, enjoying the warm drink. 'So, Roscoe tell me about your initiation.'

'Ah, yes. I leave in a few days. I'll be gone for four weeks.'

Mrs Munsamy nods. Roscoe holds his cup with both hands.

'Who do the planning?'

'My father and his friend. Also my two uncles from Dimbaza.'

'And Mummy?'

'The men take the lead in this process. The women help in other ways. It's complicated.'

Ms Munsamy isn't convinced. The truth is, since the folks separated, Ernest was never going to let the old lady play any kind of role in this.

'Hmm.' She places her cup down. 'When you last speak to Mummy?'

'Maybe two weeks ago.'

'Talk to her. A woman will make a man out of you, more than any man. You remember that.'

When I get back to Norden Place, I sit in my room thinking about the conversation I had with Mrs Munsamy about the old lady. I think of the life she lived in Sebokeng before she got married, all the community work she did, and how she sacrificed for us, especially protecting us from the wild storm that is Ernest.

All this thinking gets me started on the motivational letter for the Animation School application. I don't know how good the letter is, but I'm satisfied with the finished product, so that's something at least.

I spend my last night with the fam in Beacon Bay. Ernest is rather reluctant about this, but I insist. He only agrees when I tell him I need to say a proper goodbye to my boyhood.

'You serious?' Israel says. 'I can really have all of these?' He holds up my Oakland Raiders hoodie.

'It's all yours. And everything else.'

'Wow!'

Part of saying goodbye to your boyhood is giving away all your possessions. New ones will be bought for me once I get back.

'Which one's mine?' Sizwe asks.

'Nothing will fit you!' Israel says.

'Come on, Izzy, give her something.'

'But nothing will fit!'

'How about this?' I say, holding up a beanie. 'And this?' I hold up a cap in my other hand.

'Yes!' Sizwe snatches them out of my hands. She puts on the cap, which looks ridiculously big on her small head.

Israel isn't impressed but he relents. He sits on the bed playing with the drawstrings of the hoodie.

'Will we be able to come see you?' Sizwe asks.

'Yes, of course. Maybe not in the first few days, but after that, it will be cool.'

'Will we be able to sleep over?'

'You want to sleep in a hut? Out in the bush?'

'Yes!'

I laugh.

'*Girls* are not allowed there,' Israel says.

Sizwe looks hurt. 'Really?'

'Girls are allowed,' I say. 'But women are not.'

'So Ma can't come?' Sizwe asks.

'Nope.'

'At all?'

I shake my head.

'Why?'

'It's complicated, Sizwe.'

'What will we call you when you come back?' Israel asks.

'Bhuti Bokang, as a show of respect.'

'Bhuti Bokang! Bhuti! Bhuti! Bhuti!' Sizwe says.

I laugh. 'But between you and me, I don't mind if you guys still call me by my name.'

'I'll call you Bhuti Bokang,' Sizwe says.

'That's fine.'

'Yeah, me too,' Israel says.

We embrace in a group hug. Being so much older than them has always made me feel like I live in a different world. Moving out to live with Ernest has made that worse. Now I'm about to embark on another journey that will put me worlds apart from them. Somehow, though, this last one feels right.

I sit with the old lady at the kitchen table.

'My little boy, becoming a man.'

'It's hardly a big deal. I'll still be in school when I get back from bush. Not much will change.'

'Some things will change.'

The silence passes.

'You'll see me in a month's time.'

She wipes her nose with a tissue. The look in her eyes is hard to bear. We sit quietly for a while, then Ma takes my hand and kisses it. 'I'll worry about you.'

'I'll be okay.'

'Yes, you will. I remember when your father went to bush.'

'You knew him then?'

'Yes, of course. Boys went at an older age, back then. We were in university already, and he was almost twenty-one. They were so proud; him and his friends.'

'Do you know someone in Tata's life called Nolwazi?'

'That's his late mother. Why?'

'Well, I just heard him saying that name the other day – a few times, actually.'

'Was he talking about her?'

'No, not exactly. More like he was talking *to* her, while he was drunk. He seemed angry at her, blaming her for something.' I've never met Ernest's parents; they were both dead long before I was born.

'Your father didn't have a good relationship with her. She was a mean old woman; hard on him, expecting a lot without appreciating him for who he was. She didn't like me either – we used to fight. She fought with everyone, that woman.'

'Why didn't they get along?'

'Ag, it's hard to say. She was just demanding; a terrible woman.'

I think about this for a moment. 'What or who are the Azanian Knights?'

Ma looks at me, surprised. 'Where did you hear that, my child?'

'Tata was also saying something about it.'

'That was the name of the group your father used to sing with. Your father is a great musician.'

'*Tata?*'

'Yes! They used to perform all the time, spending long hours practising. It's your father's first love. All he ever wanted to be was a musician.'

'What happened?'

'His mother hated the music – criticised it out of him. Your grandfather was also a musician, but he died while your father was young, probably from sadness. Your father became a lawyer to make her happy, but in the end I don't think it made him happy.'

'But I thought Tata loved being a lawyer. I've seen him with people, advising them.'

'Your father is good with people because of who he is. I don't know if law was ultimately the thing for him. He had the brains for it, but I don't know if it is who he is inside. Music is what kept him alive; the absence of it in his life is what has killed him, just like his father before him.'

Forty-one

We drive to Dimbaza through the mist. The only sound is the rumble of Tata uMfene's bakkie.

I lean my head against the window, staring out at the passing shapes. The clothes I have on are the only ones I haven't given away to Israel (and Sizwe). The only other possessions I couldn't quite give away are my Walkman and CDs, safely stashed away in the shoeboxes under my bed. I'm sure the ancestors and the guardians standing at the gateway to manhood will understand.

Ernest and Tata uMfene occasionally mumble a few words to each other, but I can tell they would both rather enjoy the silence. Ernest hasn't had a drink today, and the tension buzzing through him is insane.

When we arrive in Dimbaza, I'm told to sit in a rondavel with two other boys. Everybody is busy outside with a sense of occasion. Nobody gives me any explanation of what is to happen, when and where. It's all about the wait.

'I'm Viwe,' one of the boys says to me in isiXhosa. 'My family name is Mtshemla. We stay in the village just over that hill.' He extends his hand in greeting.

'Thembelani,' the other boy says. 'This is my older brother.'

The two boys don't look alike. Viwe, the older one, is as light-skinned as me, with a friendly face, even when he's not smiling. Thembelani is slightly taller than his brother and has a little moustache waiting for its first shave.

'Bokang Damane. My father's family lives here.'

'Yes,' Viwe says. 'We know. Radebe. We too are Radebe. We share a clan name.'

Viwe, who is a year older than me, and Thembelani, who is a year younger, seem to understand everything that is happening. Some of what they explain to me is lost, though, as their rural isiXhosa is deeper than my city-speak.

A young man calls us to sit among the people gathered outside. Men make speeches and women sing.

We return to the rondavel to sleep. Tomorrow is the day we become initiates.

I don't sleep that night. I lie on the floor, wrapped in blankets that scrape against me like steel wool (I find out the next day that it was actually fleas biting me). It's not the terrible blankets or cold that keep me up, though; my mind is full of what tomorrow holds.

In the morning, a group of singing men takes us down to the river. Each of us is covered in a white blanket with two red stripes at the top and bottom ends. Beneath the blankets, we are naked. Viwe whispers that we should remain quiet and do as instructed. The morning air smells of cow dung and ash as we step onto the burnt grass covering the river bank. The men shave our heads bald and wash us in the cold waters of the river. A man with rough hands covers our bodies in white ointment. He tells us we are beings without a name now; animals in a state of transition; we are now abakwetha.

Shivering, we head further out of the village, up a small hill and into a bushy area. Thorny acacia trees grow haphazardly all over the grassy plains, while bendy wattles and narrow eucalyptus make up a thicket. We sit on long grass near the thicket, our blankets covering us all the way over our heads, with only a small gap permitted so we can see. Each of us has a stick, which we are told to carry at all times. Through the gap in my blanket, I can see a group of men of different ages, all looking serious.

One of the men steps forward, taking off his hat and holding it in his hands in front of him. He bears a striking resemblance to Thembelani, except his moustache is thicker. 'Hello, gentlemen,' he says in isiXhosa. 'Today is a special day for all of us.' Vapour escapes his mouth as he speaks. 'I am grateful to you all for being here today, on this day that my sons begin their journey into manhood.' Viwe and Thembelani's father introduces himself and his family, and acknowledges some of the gathered men by their clan names.

Ernest steps forward, next to Viwe and Thembelani's father. 'Gentlemen, I am humbled in your presence. I speak with gratitude and pride. I am Themba Ernest Damane, uRadebe, uBhungane, uMthimkhulu, iHlub'elimhlophe. Today it brings me great joy to be initiating my firstborn son in the tradition that I was initiated into by my own father. These are traditions that have come long before us, passed on from generation to generation, from father to son, as time goes forward. Each of us knows the importance of these traditions and rites. We know what it means to be a man of Xhosa.' Men nod and mumble their agreement. Tata uMfene stands behind Ernest, as serious as a bodyguard.

When Ernest finishes speaking, the men start singing. One of them, a man with thick dreadlocks and crooked teeth, comes over to us. He peels off our blankets like banana skins and tells us to sit with our legs open, shrivelled penises dangling in the biting June air. The men move forward and stand in front of us, leaning against each other, trying to get a good look. They comment, laugh and clap, no doubt remembering their own days, and the days of others that have come before and after them.

An elderly man who walks with a presence and wears headgear made of the fur of some wild animal, steps forward between the men. On my right, the man tells Viwe to say 'I am a man!' in isiXhosa. As soon as the words are out of Viwe's mouth, he winces. The elderly man stoops over Thembelani, giving him the same instruction.

Someone taps my thigh; another calls my attention from above. The elderly man tells me to say 'I am a man'.

'Ndiy'indoda,' I say.

The men raise their voices in approval. They gaze upon me with pride. Only when I look down between my legs do I notice I have already been sliced. Once I see the ring of white, then red, I feel the pain.

The dreadlocked man tells us not to touch the fresh wounds – we are to bleed out the blood of boyhood.

Further inside the thicket of wattle and eucalyptus trees stands our newly erected hut, made of acacia-tree branches, insulation plastic and rope. The three of us sit inside while the men relax outside, chatting, drinking and enjoying the roasted meat from the slaughtered animals.

Two men enter the hut and stay crouched. 'My name is Thefo, bakwetha,' says the dreadlocked man with the crooked teeth. 'This here is Faku,' pointing to the older man next to him. 'We are your caregivers. You are to call us khankatha. Listen to *everything* we say and you will be fine. Don't show weakness and you will be fine. Do you understand, bakwetha?'

'Yes,' the three of us say.

'Ey, these initiates of yours will need work,' Faku says, his wrinkled face giving him the appearance of a disgruntled chameleon.

'Give them a chance. Bakwetha, if you show respect, you will gain respect. Understood?'

'Yes, khankatha.'

'Good. Now, bear the pain. Know that this is nothing. Your pain has not yet begun.'

'Haak!' Faku exclaims through purple gums where most of his upper teeth are missing.

When I was about six, I scorched my arm badly on the stove, attempting to fry an egg in order to impress the old lady. When I was eight, I fell out of a tree and hurt my back so badly, I couldn't walk for at least a week. These two memories are the ones that come up when I think of extreme physical pain.

For more than a year now, I've been wondering how painful circumcision without anaesthesia must be. The actual snipping of the foreskin is not as bad as being burnt by a hot plate or even cracking your back against a branch before landing heavily on the ground. During this first day in the hut, I'm thinking I must be some kind of man as this isn't so bad. Compared to Viwe – the oldest of us – I'm taking this really well, while he's there wincing and clenching his jaws until tears form in his eyes.

As Thefo promised – and much to Faku's delight – the real pain starts later that evening, when they begin changing our dressings. The night is long; the pain is intense and the constant changing of our dressing prevents us from sleeping. In the space of seventeen hours, Thefo and Faku change our dressing fifteen times. Thefo does most of it, talking in a soothing voice as he works. Faku mostly watches, commentating on what is happening and cackling at any sign of discomfort. 'This is not the city, umkwetha,' he says to me. 'Your mother isn't here for you. Forget her.'

This is how it is for the first five days. Dressing change after dressing change. Holding back tears. Biting down on our tongues. Eating dry food. Drinking limited quantities of water. Listening to Faku cackle and chide, and Thefo encourage and nurture. Endless visitors coming with their two cents' worth of wisdom. Everyone has an opinion, everyone has advice, but nobody can tell you anything about the pain.

'This one is not perfect,' Thefo says, while attending to Viwe's wound. 'It was not a perfect cut. I will heal you, umkwetha, but it will take longer than these other two.'

And so it is that by the sixth day, Thembelani and I are walking about with significantly more freedom. We venture out of our camp, visiting other initiates in their huts across the valley. On the seventh day, a goat is slaughtered to celebrate our healing. Thembelani and I are almost completely healed with no need to change our dressings as often. Poor Viwe is still struggling with his wound.

'Come here, son!' Ernest says when he sees me. He plants a kiss on my cheek even though my entire face (and body) is covered in white ointment. The other men laugh. He is happy-drunk. 'Look who's here.'

'Israel! Hey, what's going on?'

'Hey, Bobo – oops!' – covering his mouth – 'Am I allowed to call you that?'

'Nah, kid. Call me umkwetha. How are things at the crib?'

'Good. We're on holiday.'

'Where's Siz?'

'She's at a friend's place, but she said she'll come see you soon.'

'Cool. And the old lady?'

'She's all right. She misses you. Do you have to stay in this blanket all the time?'

'All day and all night. It's my only outfit.'

'Whoa.'

'It's not so bad. Come meet the others.'

I introduce him to Viwe and Thembelani. From next week, we will allow some of the young village boys to sleep with us in the hut. They already spend their days with us, but they have to wait for us to heal properly before they can stay overnight. I invite Israel to join us on one of the nights.

Later, when everyone has left, we sit in the hut: me, Viwe, Thembelani, Thefo and Faku.

'You did well today, bakwetha,' Faku says cheerfully, his face like a Halloween pumpkin lit by the fire in the centre of the hut. 'Your fathers are proud! Haak!' He takes a sip from his mug. Ernest rewarded him with an extra bottle of liquor. (Ernest himself was so elated, he passed out on the grass and had to be carried to the car.) 'You have listened to us and that's why you're healing so well. You too, umkwetha,' he says, looking at Viwe. 'Thefo here knows what he's doing. You'll get there.'

Thefo licks the joint he's just rolled using a torn strip of newspaper. He rolls the longest and thickest joints I've ever seen. He lies on his side, supporting himself with his elbow, his messy dreadlocks hanging from his head like buffalo tails. He admires his craftsmanship with a crooked smile. Then he holds the joint out to Thembelani.

'I don't smoke, khankatha,' Thembelani says with a shy laugh.

'I thought you told us not to smoke,' Viwe says, sitting up.

'Yes, I told you not to smoke *cigarettes*. They are bad for the healing process. This here is medicine, medicine from the Transkei – Xhosa medicine. The best medicine you will find anywhere. You passed a test today, and now you are ready for this. It will help with your healing.' He leans forward, holding the joint closer to Thembelani. 'You are no longer a boy. What you do from now onwards will define you as a man.'

'Take it,' Viwe says, urging his younger brother with a nod.

Thembelani takes the joint, inspects it and hands it to his older brother, watching him carefully as he lights it with a stick pulled from the fire. Faku cackles as the smoke fills the hut. Something inside me rumbles as an old craving comes back. I extend my hand to Viwe, asking for the joint.

'Yes, umkwetha,' Thefo says, nodding in approval.

The heavy smoke from the newspaper makes me cough; it's definitely harsher than the stuff I'm accustomed to.

'Even the city boy smokes,' Faku says. He laughs, tilting his head backwards and revealing his bare gums.

Not to be outdone, Thembelani takes the joint and puffs. Thefo sparks another, and the two joints go around from hand to hand, filling the hut with thick smoke.

'Khankatha, what defines a man?' Thembelani asks, his eyes red rimmed and gleaming.

'A man is a man is a man is a man,' Faku sings, before laughing. 'A man is the word, he is law, he is community. The man represents what it means to be Xhosa.'

'So what do I need to do to become a proper man?'

'You need to listen to me and listen to Thefo' – spitting into the fire – 'This is spirituality happening here.'

'I've grown up here in this area my whole life, khankatha,' Viwe says, 'thinking we are all the same people, following the same practices. But what I've heard from the different men coming here doesn't make sense.'

'How?' Faku asks.

'One tells you manhood is this, another tells you manhood is that. Everyone has their own version of manhood.'

'Ja!' Thembelani says.

'Families may be different, bakwetha, but there is only one way of being Xhosa. The expectations of a man are the same everywhere.'

'What are those expectations?' Viwe asks.

'Strength. Reason. Governance.'

Thembelani shakes his head. 'That cannot be all.'

'The bush is a big place,' Thefo says. 'What happens in one corner of the forest is not necessarily the same as what happens in another.'

'Exactly!' Thembelani says. 'Everyone thinks their way is best.'

'You learn from what you see around you,' Thefo continues. 'You see other men being men, and you learn.'

'From all your elders, those that have come before you,' Faku adds.

'But wait, khankatha,' I say. 'What if your father is not teaching you good lessons? What if your father causes problems in your life?'

Everyone looks at me through the hanging smoke. Something pops and sizzles in the fire, making my nostrils twitch.

'You shouldn't judge your father,' Faku says, sounding like a teacher who discourages questions. 'Actions are not enough to decide whether a man is a man or not. If a father has been initiated as a Xhosa man, then he is a man, and that is to be accepted.'

'That's crazy! Khankatha just said how a father practises manhood is important.'

Faku gives me a look. He takes a swig from his mug and wipes his mouth with his coat sleeve. 'Umkwetha, you need to understand that our traditions are law; they show us the way. If those rites are bestowed on you, then you have the authority, and no one can question that or take anything away from it.'

'But doesn't that come with responsibilities?'

'Yes,' Viwe says. 'I agree with you, umkwetha. A man should prove himself through what he does. If you khankatha are telling us that a man has been given authority, then he should be judged on performance. No?'

Thembelani nods enthusiastically. Thefo looks down benignly at the joint he's rolling.

'You initiates don't understand the order of things,' Faku says, shaking his head. He reaches down to the plate by his feet and picks up a bone. 'You also don't understand the process. Explain to them, Thefo, before I lose my mind.' He puts the bone in his mouth and sucks, making a smacking sound.

'Do you know what ukuthwasa is?' Thefo asks.

Viwe and Thembelani nod. I wait for him to elaborate.

'Ukuthwasa is the spiritual calling a healer or psychic gets from the ancestors. Do you know the name we use for you here, umkwetha, is the same name they give those with the gift when they are training? And the name you use for us, khankatha, is the same one used for the caregivers taking care of them?' He looks intently at each of us, flames dancing in his dark eyes. 'These leaves we collect for the dressing of your wounds are medicine. This' – holding up the joint – 'is medicine. It is the way of the ancestors. You cannot get this education anywhere else.'

The only sound in the hut is the crackling of the fire. Thefo picks up a stick and stokes the coals.

I wonder what JP would think, hearing all this. He'd no doubt love the idea, and have a few theories of his own about the powers of weed. The stoner crowd at school would probably think this is absolute nonsense.

'I do agree with you, though,' Thefo says, 'that men should be accountable for their duties and responsibilities. Gone are the days when men were men by virtue of what was bestowed upon them. Boys are coming here to the bush at a young age, some thirteen or fourteen in other parts of these rural areas. What kind of man can you be at that age? Many things have changed. We can thank the whites and their ways for that.'

'Do you think being exposed to the ways of the whites makes you any less of a traditional Xhosa man?' I ask.

'Yes!' Faku says. He tosses the bone into the fire, where it sizzles as angrily as he does.

'What is happening in the cities is destroying our culture,' Viwe says. 'I see it with the boys and men from there.'

'But the world has moved on,' I say. 'Some things are good in white culture.'

'They own everything,' Thembelani says.

'Stole everything!' Faku says.

'But they challenge our traditions in a good way,' I say. 'We cannot be perfect.'

'No! Never! All they do is destroy. They are destroying your mind at those schools.'

'But what must we do?' Thembelani asks. 'We cannot live here in the rural areas forever. The world is happening out there, and if we want to be rich like them, and provide for our families, and feel like men doing their duties, then we must know their culture, and be a part of it.'

'Exactly,' I say. 'The school I go to gives me opportunities, even if I don't like to admit it. In this world we live in, you need to understand places like my school in order to have anything. Otherwise, you live in poverty, with nothing.'

'You are like this new president of South Africa,' Viwe says. 'Thabo Mbeki.'

Thembelani laughs.

'Don't tell me about that fool,' Faku says. 'That is a man who has lost himself. He is going to drive this country into the ground.' He uses his tongue to pick at something caught between his few teeth.

'The country is already in the ground,' Thefo says in a matter-of-fact voice.

'What exactly is wrong with Thabo Mbeki?' I ask. 'He is actually a great example of a man who has benefitted from different cultures. His leadership will benefit from it, surely?'

'You are foolish,' Faku says, shaking his head. 'Nothing good can come from their culture. This new president has been poisoned for years in England, while the real soldiers and revolutionaries were here, in Africa, learning from our brothers across the borders. He calls himself educated, but I ask: educated in what?' Faku's eyes are wide as he stares each of us in the face. 'Nothing can ever replace your Xhosa foundation.

If you have been initiated as a Xhosa man, then you must live the traditions and pass them on in the way you received them. You cannot abandon them and still think you are a man.'

'But who is to say he has abandoned them?' I ask. 'He could be a Xhosa man and more.'

'The white ways will never be better than our ways.'

'That's not what I'm saying.'

'Then what are you saying?' Faku places his mug down and straightens himself where he sits. Everybody else in the hut watches us closely.

'Education never stops; it comes from everywhere, not just one place.'

'So are we to be educated in our ways by one who has lived in the city his whole life?' He laughs. I don't say anything. Faku's eyes narrow as he takes the glowing joint from Thefo; the same cunning look I've seen in Ernest creeps across his face. 'You think your city ways have educated you more than us? More than me?'

'Outside of this hut, this forest, this homeland, nobody would consider you a man of note – you are just a farm worker.'

Faku stands up. I also stand. The others watch.

'Govern yourself, umkwetha' – gesturing at me with the hand holding the joint – 'and know your place!'

'What place is that, exactly? To be quiet and accept what I'm told by men who don't deserve respect, or who don't build me into a respectable man?'

Faku reaches for his stick and points at me with it. 'Keep talking, umkwetha. My stick is thirsty.'

I shake my head. 'So this is manhood: when words fail, turn to violence. The elders know better.'

Faku moves his hand to strike.

'Enough,' Thefo says.

Forty-two

Somebody is dragging my mother through the woods. I'm on their trail. It's a group of them. Men. Loud. Thirsty. Destructive. They laugh and mock (one of them cackles like Faku). She screams. Although they are a distance from me, they sound near.

I'm dressed in my Oakland Raiders hoodie (naked beneath and covered in white ointment), the one I gave away to Israel. I'm carrying a spear as I run, jumping over obstacles and bashing my way through the brush. The sun is setting fast. When it disappears, the mist descends and covers my face like something alive. I call out to her: 'Ma! Where are you?' No response. Not a single sound, except the breaking twigs beneath my bare feet. I'm creeping now.

'Over here,' a girl's voice calls. I move in that direction, even though something tells me this is not where I will find my mother. A hut stands on a lake. The moon shines high above it, and a fire torch burns outside. 'Over here, Bokang.' I follow the voice into the hut. Mashoto, Dikeledi's friend from Sebokeng, lies on the bed, dressed in a white gown. 'Come to me.'

I look over my shoulder out the door. Ma needs me ... I should be going that way, but ... Mashoto calls. I lie on the bed next to her. We kiss. It feels so ...

I wake up with a sharp pain between my legs. I grab my stick and run out of the hut, shouting. I swing my stick at the nearest tree. I lash at it until my erection, tightly bound in its dressing, loses its excitement.

Someone is laughing. 'Morning, umkwetha,' Faku says. He sits on a pile of wood, using a knife to pick his remaining teeth – it looks like he's sharpening them.

I feel like swinging the stick at him – bashing his chameleon head in – but I don't. I walk away, moving deeper into the thicket. I need air, I need space, I need to breathe. I change my own dressing; we've been trusted with this responsibility now in our third week. Only Viwe, who's healing is taking longer, still relies on the trusted hands of Thefo.

'Molo, umkwetha,' Thembelani greets, appearing from between the trees.

'Ewe, umkwetha.'

'I see you've been having good dreams again?' He laughs.

'Damnit.' I shake my head, the ebbing pain still throbbing below.

'It happens to all of us, don't stress. Do you dream of the same girl?'

'Yes.' Since I've been out here, I've had at least four dreams about Mashoto. Every time I wake up with a pain between my legs.

'We all dream of the same girl. You know what they say about that, right?' He takes a seat next to me on the rock.

'No.'

'There's a lesson in why she's in your life. She's your teacher.'

'Ah.' I wonder when (if ever) I'll see Mashoto again. What exactly did she teach me? All I know is she really liked me and I rejected her, kind of like how Nokwanda rejected me – except I didn't toy with Mashoto. After a moment I ask, 'Is your brother up?'

Thembelani looks away.

'What's going on between you two?'

Thembelani sighs. He picks up a twig and throws it in front of him. 'This whole healing thing is making him sick, if you know what I mean. I know he doesn't like that we – especially me – are healing faster than him. He's a big brother, he thinks he must always be first to do everything.'

I'm also a big brother, so I need to think about this. But I'm so much older than Israel, it's obvious I'd be the first to do most things. The gap between Viwe and Thembelani is less than two years. 'It's a difficult situation for him. Three weeks of sitting and lying down will drive anyone mad.'

'So? He must be a man about it. It's not my fault he's in that situation.'

'I'm not saying it's your fault. But try to understand.'

'It's not easy growing up in another's shadow. What does he understand about that?'

Thembelani's knowledge and confidence have grown exponentially in the past three weeks. His brother's incapacitation has released him from his shackles.

I wonder how much my troubles have cast a shadow over Israel's life. I doubt they have; after all, he excels in many things that I don't. I've sometimes thought of myself as his protector, but I have to admit all the trouble I've had has taken attention away from him. In the past year, he's become less talkative. The epilepsy has kept him away from the sports he enjoys so much, and I know the folks' divorce has made him mad at Ernest. 'Your brother is protective of you,' I say. 'He is also proud of you.'

Thembelani snorts. 'More like bossy. But I'll always respect him as my older brother. He must just understand my need for independence.' He points at me with his stick. 'Who will you stand up to when you get out of here?'

'My father.' My response is automatic; I barely think about my answer.

'Then you must do it, umkwetha. You can no longer afford to be afraid. Two men cannot live under the same roof.'

It is not an easy situation. Sure, there's plenty to be mad at Ernest for, but these days he's a sad figure who needs somebody – me – close by. I find myself having to put my grievances aside to take care of him, but I don't know how good that will be for me in the long run.

Birds chirp from the trees. Somewhere a cow moos. We will need to eat breakfast soon.

I stand up to stretch my legs. 'Come on, let's head back before Faku comes looking for us with his stick.'

We laugh. He throws his arm around my neck, and I do the same. 'You know we're brothers now,' he says. 'You. Me. And Viwe.'

I smile. I like that.

Forty-three

The discussion about the place where my umgidi, or coming-out cele-bration, will take place is contentious. The old lady (Israel tells me) suggests it should take place at the crib in Beacon Bay, since it was my home for so long, and will allow for everyone who knows me in East London to attend. The flat in Clermont is not even an option.

Ernest shuts down the old lady's idea, and suggests the celebration takes place in Dimbaza, at his family home, where it can be combined with the one for Viwe and Thembelani.

It kind of makes sense to have it in the rural area. But it's also sad that it's so far from the place I call home.

As soon as the sun is out, Faku is hustling us about, barking instructions with vigour. He's dressed smartly (by his standards), walks with a bounce in his step, and speaks with more bass in his usually shrill voice. 'Come, bakwetha! Today we will make people out of you again. Haak!' His stick whips through the air. 'Haak!'

Faku, Thefo and a few other men burn down our hut and everything in it – including the blankets we've been using as clothing and bedding – and then take us down to the river in a singing procession. Once again we are the dispossessed, in limbo, no longer what we were, and not yet quite what we will become. The men wash us and smear us in special ointment, before cloaking us with white blankets with two black stripes at the top and bottom ends.

They lead us up the grassy hill and back down another valley towards the village, back to civilisation, where we have not been for four weeks. The singing is loud, and resonates around the valley, opening the path before us. Again, our heads are covered, with only a small slit to peer out. My feet have hardened from weeks of walking in the bush. My skin is dry and accustomed to the winter wind. Today is overcast, but at least the wind is not so bad.

The voices of singing women greet us as we enter the village. They compete with the voices of the men. Children run about and watch in awe. We enter the same rondavel where our journey began. Here, we are finally dressed in the attire of men. I wear brown pants, a grey shirt, and a beige and brown checked jacket. My shoes are brown and look too big even though I know they are my size.

We sit waiting for our next instructions. Outside, men chat and drink. Women prepare the food. I'm told Ernest bought a cow and several sheep for the day. People make speeches. We sit and acknowledge the many visitors and well-wishers who come in to see us, most of them dropping money in front of us in blessing.

Ma enters the room with Sizwe by her side. 'Oh, my child.' She puts a hand across her mouth. 'Stand up, let me see you.'

I stand up, towering above her, feeling like I may have grown a few centimetres in the time I haven't seen her. I lean down to give her a hug. Red ointment rubs onto her cheek and the shoulder of her dress.

'I am so happy!' she says. 'How are you, my child?'

'I'm good, Ma. Everything's fine.'

Sizwe stands at my feet, reaching up. 'Bobo!'

I lift her and embrace her.

'Hey!' Ma says. 'You must show respect. He is Bhuti Bokang now.'

'Bhuti Bobo!' Sizwe says, giggling.

'I didn't think you would come,' I say to the old lady.

'No, today I'm allowed to see you. It's been hard.' She reaches a hand up to my cheek, not bothered by the red ointment. 'Oh, how I prayed for your safety. My prayers have been heard. Did they treat you well?'

'Everything was fine.'

Israel enters, and I introduce my family to Viwe and Thembelani. They introduce me to their visitors. Israel stays by my side, and I notice how he looks at me now. He is definitely more respectful. I don't think Sizwe gets the full weight of everything, which is cool.

'You've grown even taller,' Ma says. 'That's good.'

Ernest enters the rondavel, laughing. 'What do we have here?' He holds out his arms; he resembles a holy man in his full-length trench coat. Sizwe looks at the old lady, who nods, before she runs into her daddy's arms. Ernest makes a show of hugging and lifting her. Israel doesn't move.

'Khensani,' Ernest says. 'You look lovely.' The old lady gives him a smile and a hug. They exchange pleasant greetings.

'I see the boy is well,' the old lady says.

'Khensani, my love, this is no longer your little boy. This is a Damane man now!' He belts out a jolly good laugh.

'Yes, of course. I forgot.'

'But, yes, you are right, he is well.' Ernest is surprisingly sober and courteous. 'We did well, Khensani. Look at these three children.'

Sizwe beams. Israel doesn't smile until I give him an encouraging lean on the shoulder.

'Thank you for taking care of my son and doing this for him – for us.' The old lady gives Ernest another hug. When they part, she says, 'He looks so much like you when I first met you. That jacket is exactly like the one you wore.'

Ernest smiles, his eyes teary behind his glasses.

'If you wanna catch a bird,' Ma sings, 'then you have to learn to fly' – pointing her index fingers at Ernest – 'put your hands to the sky ... come on, Tata!' She shakes her hips in a dance move.

'Ah, Khensani,' he says, smiling. 'What do you know about Azanian Knights?'

The old lady continues singing until Ernest helps her finish the verse. They both laugh and grab hands and begin dancing. Me, Israel and Sizwe watch these two strangers in front of us.

'Come on, Khensani,' Ernest says. 'The family will want to see you. They've missed you.' They leave the rondavel, with Sizwe following.

'Ta Bobes,' Thembelani says, leaning close to my ear, 'I'd say your parents still have something happening between them.'

'I think so, too.'

'What did he just call you?' Israel asks curiously.

'Ta Bobes. Saying Ta in front of a name shows the same kind of respect as saying Bhuti. So you can call me Ta Bobes or Bhuti Bobes, or Ta Bokang or Bhuti Bokang. Whatever.'

'You can even call him Ta Mabobo,' Thembelani says.

'I like that one,' Israel says, a smile on his face.

During the late afternoon, we are given an opportunity to walk around outside and mingle with people. I walk with Israel by my side. I see Tata uMfene standing with the men, telling a story that makes them laugh. He's dressed like an Italian gangster in full pinstriped suit and hat.

Ma, Israel and Sizwe prepare to leave just before sundown. I stand with them next to the old lady's ride. Israel doesn't want to leave yet, but the old lady is not keen to drive back in the dark. I would love to leave with them and be around more familiar settings, but I have to spend this first night here.

'When will we see you again?' Israel asks, standing by the open passenger door.

'School opens in two days, so maybe next weekend.'

'You ready to go back to school?' Ma asks.

'I guess I have to be.'

She gives me a smile and one last hug. I watch them drive down the gravel road, feeling it was mad-dope that they were here today.

Forty-four

Everyone at school calls me Ta Bobes now, except the white kids (obviously). To them and all the teachers, I'm still Bokang Damane (or Bo-gang Dama-nee). But from those who will go through the same process (or have been through it), there is definitely a greater show of respect. I do question what that respect is based on, though. In a school environment, you take respect any way it comes. But I still feel you have to earn respect. I still have to figure out what it means to be a man.

On a Wednesday afternoon, two weeks after my return from bush, I'm chilling at the flat with Israel. He's been coming around as often as he can. He took a taxi from Westwood to Clermont after school.

'So how are the driving lessons?' he asks.

'Good. I've had two already, have another one tomorrow.'

'Nice. You so lucky, Ta Bobes.'

'Why?'

'You get to do all these grown-up things.'

I laugh. 'You'll get there too, big guy. Next year it's St Stephen's College for you.'

'Yeah. I wish we were there together.'

'Yeah, me too.'

Legacy is important at a place like St Stephen's College, and I can only hope I've done enough to make Izzy's passage easier. Academic performance is all I have left to claim any honours in, and I know I can do it for him.

'Have you decided what you want to do next year?' he asks.

'Law at Rhodes, here in East London. The old man hustled me a bursary, so that looks like a good option.'

He nods.

'I also applied to the Animation School in Cape Town.'

'Cape Town?'

'Yeah. It's this big fancy school, internationally recognised. Only the best go there.'

'Oh.' He looks out the window, then down at his hands. After a while, he speaks again. 'Ta Bobes?'

'Yeah.'

'I think it would be great if you were around next year.'

'Sure.'

The next day, I'm chilling with Roscoe in the cafeteria during second break. It's packed inside, due to the weather, and all the warm bodies create a fuggy heat.

'So, it's the matric dance in a couple of weeks,' Roscoe says.

'Hmm.'

'Who're you going with?'

'I haven't really thought about it.' This is, of course, a lie. How can I not think about it?

'What you going to do, bra? The dance is in two weeks.'

'I know. I'm just saying I haven't thought of a date. I probably won't go, anyways. Who you going with?'

'Harshita.'

I hold up my hands. 'And who's Harshita?'

'My parents hooked me up.'

'Wait. Your *parents* hooked you up with a girl?'

'You know how it is in our culture. My parents had their friends bring girls over, to chat or whatever.'

'Wait. *Girls?* You were interviewing prospective dates?' I laugh in disbelief.

'Something like that. You know how these arrangements work, bra.'

'Wow. I'm impressed.' Maybe I should commission Auntie Vern to find me a woman, for real.

'Anyways, don't give up – you'll find a date.' He gives me dap.

Sometimes it's not a matter of giving up. You can live in hope, waiting for things to align for you. Sometimes you can even try meddling with that alignment by pushing for things to happen. But sometimes you just have to accept things the way they are.

Sitting in Biology class, the last class of the day, I hear an announcement through the PA system: 'Bokang Damane, please report to Mr Summers' office. Bokang Damane in Grade 12R, please report to Mr Summers' office.'

What now?

As always, Mr Summers' secretary, Ms Tudhope, greets me with a smile that manages to be both angry and sad. She asks me to take a seat while she continues doing whatever important thing she was busy with on her computer. Her dyed hair is thinning, and I can see her spotted skull. I only have to wait four minutes before she points at the door with a withered hand.

'Ah. Bokang Damane,' Mr Summers says. 'Please sit. How are you?'

'Good, Sir,' I say, taking a seat in front of his large wooden desk. 'How are you?'

'Good, thanks for asking.' The suddenness with which his face goes from smiling to serious is impressive. He intertwines his hands and places them on the desk in front of him. 'Bokang, I'm not going to waste your time. We are trying – without success – to locate your father.' He lets the last word hang in the air while he scrutinises me under the stare of a lifted eyebrow. 'I believe you are living with him, correct?'

'Yes, Sir.'

'You saw him this morning?'

'Yes, Sir.' What I don't mention is that he was still passed out (in his clothes) when I left.

'And you will see him again this afternoon?'

'Yes, Sir. I think so.'

Mr Summers' hand slips into a drawer and pulls out a white envelope, which he places on the desk. 'Bokang, your school fees are two months in arrears. We have repeatedly tried to contact your father, without much success, I'm afraid.' He hands me the envelope. 'We wouldn't want to jeopardise your future when you're so close to finishing.' He gives me his George Clooney smile.

I hold the envelope in both hands, looking down at it as if I can read what's inside.

'You're excused,' he says.

On my way home, I think about what would happen if I didn't complete this year.

Absolute disaster.

I pass a group of girls in their yellow-and-brown Meredith House uniforms. Over seven hundred girls schooling just across the road, and I can't find one to go to the matric dance with me. Nice.

Margo, my driving instructor, is parked outside Norden Place. She's a bubbly woman with red hair and a weird smell of sweet perfume and stale cigarettes. She's cool peeps; her energy is encouraging to somebody trying to learn something as nerve-wracking as driving.

My lesson lasts an hour, and I appear to have regressed since the last one. That, or I'm distracted.

'Don't let it get you down,' she says as I step out of her ride after the lesson. 'See you next week.' She winks and I stand there watching her lighting a cigarette before she drives off.

I take a deep breath and huff it out before entering the building. I don't know whether to expect Ernest to be home or not. His behaviour these days is so erratic, I never know what to expect.

The flat is empty. I don't feel like being here. I'll think too much, feel too much. But I have nowhere to go.

I feel trapped between a past that won't let me go and a future crumbling down on me.

Forty-five

The next morning, I delay going to school in order to give Ernest the white envelope. He's awake and in a grizzly mood. He walks into the kitchen in his gown and pyjamas (I haven't seen them in ages). When I greet him, he grunts. He drinks milk straight from the bottle.

'Mr Summers asked me to give this to you.' I place the envelope on the kitchen counter in front of him.

He doesn't say anything, but he does open the envelope. He holds it in front of him, one hand at the top of the page, the other at the bottom, like he's some sort of messenger from the medieval days reading a royal creed. Then he picks his teeth with a corner of the page. When he's done, he tosses it on the table. 'Don't worry about this,' he says. 'These are small things. They'll get their money.'

'When?' I stand in front of him.

He slowly and dramatically reties the belt of his gown, watching me. 'When I have the money.'

'They gonna kick me out of school.'

'They won't.'

'Are you sure?'

He sneers. 'Since you such a big man, why don't you find some work and make some money?'

I don't say anything. I think about the money spent on my initiation, on the cows, the sheep, the goats, the clothes, the booze and Lord knows what else.

He laughs. 'Exactly. Let me worry about the money.'

'Are you going to work today?'

'My own son questioning me! Ha!'

'It's a straightforward question, Tata. Are you going to work today?'

'Why?'

'Bhelekazi says you haven't been showing up at the office.'

'What does that one know? I meet with clients outside the office.' He walks out the kitchen towards his bedroom. 'She's not even qualified, and she thinks she can tell me … rha!'

'Will you be there today?'

'Sure.'

'Okay. I'll come after school.'

What does something as banal as a matric dance matter when my fees haven't been paid?

Things are different in Norden Place these days. All our neighbours avoid us; greeting seems to be agony for them. Mrs Thuso leads the pack of haters, always sniffing around for something to blame us for.

Things only get worse when Ernest, returning from a drinking binge one Saturday night, bumps his ride into Mrs Naidoo's ride. It happens outside our building in the early hours of the morning. I hear the sound of crunching metal from the street and immediately know something is wrong. Ernest is too sloshed to notice or care. I put him to bed and spend the rest of the night trying to figure out what I'm going to tell Mrs Naidoo.

The knock on the door comes as early as seven on the Sunday morning. I answer with my best angel smile. 'Oh hi, Mr and Mrs Naidoo. How are you this morning?'

'Fine,' Mr Naidoo says. He doesn't look at all pleased. His arm is around Mrs Naidoo's shoulders. I can tell she's been crying. Poor Mrs Naidoo, she's one of the people in the building who's always been on our side. 'We need to speak with your father.'

Denying any of it is a waste of time. Waking Ernest up to deal with this is an even bigger waste of time, so I handle it myself. 'Here are my father's details, Mr Naidoo.' He reaches for the piece of paper I offer him, looking sceptical. We sit at the table, tea and coffee in front of us (Auntie Vern taught me well). 'We'll take full responsibility. The insurance details are right there.'

Of course, I don't tell him Ernest doesn't pay his insurance. But he'll find that out soon enough. Right now, I need to buy some time.

'My boy bought me that car,' Mrs Naidoo says, wiping away another tear. 'I don't want to cause trouble for you, but …'

'Yes, no, I understand. As soon as my father's feeling better, I'll discuss it with him. It's such a shame he isn't doing well.'

'Thank you,' Mr Naidoo says, shaking my hand.

'Oh, and Mrs Naidoo, I've found us five kids in the neighbourhood we can tutor. I've spoken to the parents and we good to go.' For the first time since entering the flat, she smiles. I press the advantage. 'We can officially start charging next week.'

Tutoring is something I should have been doing from way before, using my smarts to earn a bit of cash. This, and whatever Ernest can spare, will go a long way. I'm thinking I have to raise money to square up my own school fees cos Ernest can't be relied on. But this tutoring thing ain't just about the money. It's about doing something for the community, kind of like what the old lady did for her community back in Sebokeng when she was growing up.

Early the following week, I visit Ernest's office to find out just how bad things are. I go after school. He's not there like he said he would be. Bhelekazi is on a personal call that has obviously been going on for a while. She makes me wait until she sees my expression and then she wraps it up.

'When did he leave?' I ask.

'Before ten, like he usually does.' Bhelekazi is a third-year law student. This is not a serious job for her, just a way of making extra cash for not doing much. With nobody here to ensure she does the job properly, why would she care?

'How do you just let him go?'

She gives me a blank stare.

'You know what, never mind. Did he have any appointments today?'

She shakes her head. 'He books them himself these days.'

'Okay, so where's the finance book?' Being old school, Ernest doesn't own a computer.

She shrugs. 'He does that himself, too.'

'So what exactly *do* you do?'

Her long eyelashes flutter like butterfly wings.

'Look, you can go. Don't come in tomorrow. We'll call you if we need you.'

'I haven't been paid for last month.' She holds out a hand as if I have 'handouts' written on my forehead.

'We'll get back to you on that.'

Later that afternoon, Mr Magadla hijacks me as I enter the building. 'Can we talk?' I look at him, wondering why now he suddenly has time for me. 'In my flat. Please?'

Inside, he offers me a seat, but I don't take it, so we stand.

'How are things?' He laughs nervously.

'What can I do for you?'

'Look, we have complaints. About your father.'

'From who?'

'Other residents.'

'Who?'

'I can't say.'

'Well, if you can't say, then they are not real complaints.' I head for the door.

'Please, Bokang. Listen to me. I'm only trying to help.'

'We don't need your help. Tell Mrs Thuso and Mrs Mafanya to back off. When you finally do something about the complaints about other tenants in the building, you can talk to us. Otherwise, leave us alone.'

The nerve of the man. He was at my umgidi, having the time of his life. And all those times before I went to bush when he was all buddy-buddy with Ernest and Tata uMfene. *Now* he acts like he doesn't know us?

I call the old lady from a payphone later that evening. 'Tata hasn't paid my fees.'

'I know. Mr Summers called me.'

'Is there no way you can help?'

'Not at the moment. This is your father's responsibility. It's all I ask of him. He has to take it seriously.'

I don't say anything.

'Bokang?'

'Yes, Ma.'

'Let me speak with your father, okay? When will he be home?'

'I have no idea.'

'Don't worry. I'll speak to him. Even if I must find him. Take care, my child.'

She hangs up. Nobody waits behind me to use the phone. The streets are quiet. I don't know why, but Nokwanda comes into my mind. It's been exactly a year since I saw her that night at the dance, and nine months since she wrote me the letter, which I still haven't read.

I go home and lie on my bed, the letter in my hands. There's something about holding this envelope and not knowing what's inside it that gives me perspective. The way I see it, what is actually inside doesn't matter; it doesn't take away from what she put me through.

On Friday afternoon, the old lady drops Israel off at Norden Place. He stands outside the building with his backpack slung over his shoulder, his face and limbs hanging long. If he's this size now, I can't imagine what his Grade 10 growth spurt will do to him.

The old lady asks for a quiet word, so I lean into the passenger-side window.

'I spoke to your father,' she says.

'On the phone?'

'No, I had to go find him. He was at Albert's house.'

Of course he was with Tata uMfene – brother for life.

'He said he would have the money by next week.'

'From where, Ma? Gambling?'

She avoids my eyes. 'I don't know.'

In my head I hear *I don't care*.

'He promised he would take care of it.'

'I hope so. Thanks for trying.' I turn to leave.

'Bokang ... there's one more thing.'

I turn back.

She speaks in a lower tone. 'Your brother's in trouble at school' – peeking past me at Israel – 'He got into a fight. He beat the other child badly. It's now the second one.'

'Second one?'

'Yes. I had to go see Mr Johnstone. I don't know what's happening with him. And at home, he makes Sizwe cry. He's never been like this. Can you talk to him?'

The look she gives me makes me wonder if she's asking me because I might be able to help as an older brother, or if I might know something about what he's going through because of my own troubles. 'Sure, I'll talk to him.'

'Thank you.'

After sunset, I take a walk with Israel down St George's Road. It's a typical Clermont Friday: students out and about; cars blasting music and clogging up the streets; people drinking on street corners. We sit by the parking lot, at Malcomess Park, just off St George's. From where we sit, we can see Corner Pocket and Shooters Bar. The parking lot is filled with people drinking in their cars.

'Do you drink?' I ask.

'No way.'

'Smoke?'

'No!'

'You don't want to be like Tata?'

'Exactly.' The thought of it upsets him. After a moment he asks, 'Do you?'

'Not any more.'

I follow Israel's eyes to a couple with their arms around each other. They stand next to a car blasting music among a group of others. The way Israel watches them reminds me of his age: thirteen going on fourteen. Despite his size, he's still only a kid. Despite all the family drama, *he's still only a kid.*

'You know what one of my greatest fears is?' I ask.

'What?'

'That I'll end up like Tata.'

He doesn't say anything, but I can see in his eyes that he's thinking hard.

'Since I was small, I wished I had the strength to change him. The angrier I got, the more powerless I felt. Even now, when I get mad at him, I see it does nothing for me. You get me?'

He nods.

'Come on. I want to show you something.'

We walk up towards St James Road. The sky is black and street lights lead the way. We head up Gately, where there's been a car accident; ambulance and police lights flash. A crowd of onlookers stand on both sides of the street. Nobody appears to be seriously injured.

I take Israel all the way to Milton Mental Health Centre. We stand on Gately, looking at the bright lights of the institution.

'You don't know this place, do you?' I say.

'No. What is it?'

'They help people going through problems here. Kids, teenagers, adults. They have a bunch of psychologists, doctors and nurses helping people. It's not a cool place to be, but I guess they tryna help.'

Israel takes in everything I'm saying.

'You know I've stayed here twice before?'

He looks at me, brow creased.

So I explain to him some of the things that got me institutionalised. I'm glad to see him listening with attention.

That night, I dream about Dikeledi. I dream I'm kissing her, and Mashoto is in the dream too, mad as hell at me.

I wake up to hear a muffled shout coming from the living room. Israel.

I get out of bed. Izzy lies on the couch, under his blankets where he was sleeping. Ernest stands over him, trying to pull at his arm.

'This is my house,' Ernest slurs. 'You don't tell me what to do.'

Israel sits up. 'Just leave me alone!'

Ernest laughs.

'Tata, leave him.'

'Voetsek!' Ernest curses without even looking in my direction. He leans down again towards Israel. 'I just want to love my son.'

Israel unleashes a kick, his heel catching Ernest somewhere in the midriff. Ernest flies backwards and collapses onto the carpet in the foetal position. Israel gets up and charges towards his father.

'Izzy, no!' I step between them. 'Wait in my room. Go.'

Reluctantly, he leaves. Ernest moans on the floor, in serious pain. He gags and vomits all over himself. He rolls onto his back and gurgles. He starts choking until I turn him on his side. I watch him as he wets himself. For a moment, I don't move. I want to go to Israel and comfort him, but here I am, having to deal with Ernest.

I lift him up and drag him to his room. I do the best I can to undress him and clean him up. He passes out long before I'm finished. I leave him under the covers.

Back in my room, I find Israel sitting on my bed, crying. He looks angrier than I've ever seen him. I put my arm around him but my heart sinks when I realise the strength of his emotions. Israel struggles to control his feelings, and that means he has a very difficult road ahead of him.

Bokang Damane:	Why do bad things happen to good people?
The Supreme Khon:	There are no good and bad people, young apprentice. There are no good and bad things. The duality of any singularity in time is the nature of being.
Bokang Damane:	What does that even mean?
The Supreme Khon:	Good and bad are the same thing. One cannot exist without the other.
Bokang Damane:	I really wish I was dead.

The Supreme Khon: If you so wish, then you are.

Bokang Damane: This life is not worth it.

The Supreme Khon: Then you are missing the point.

Bokang Damane: What is the point of all of this?

The Supreme Khon: Do not feel aggrieved when the stars refuse to line your pockets. You need to see beyond your universe. I do not put blame at your feet, young apprentice. You are part of a disease. Your kind is the disease. Fear not, young apprentice, for I have the cure.

Bokang Damane: Give me the cure, please. I cannot take this.

The Supreme Khon: All you have to do is give in to my supreme will. Do you give in to the will of The Supreme Khon?

Bokang Damane: I do, oh great one. I do.

Book V
August 1999

Forty-six

My greatest fear has always been the possibility of turning into the worst of Ernest: a sightless beast, insatiable and lost, stumbling through a pitiful existence. Now my even greater fear is the possibility of Israel turning into the worst of me: a raging mess, tortured and incurable, bumbling through an uncaring world.

The matric dance looms large at the end of this week. Can't it be done already? Everyone's talking about it, which is annoying and hard to avoid. Roscoe has already confirmed that only two of us will be absent; the other kid is Brendan April, who's out of the country, touring with the national hockey team.

It might be time for my first conversation with Mr Knowles this year. Dr Mbatha is the other option but the folks can't afford it, and I prefer they know diddly-squat about my need to talk. In the end, I just can't bring myself to go see Mr Knowles, though; he's part of a system that creates half of my problems.

My only remaining option: JP at his crib in Beacon Bay. I mission after school on Tuesday, desperate to find him. His moms is mad-friendly when she lets me in, and the little dog, Rasta, barks something crazy.

JP is in the garage, wearing plastic goggles and a thick leather apron, and holding an angle grinder. He works on a piece of wood tied down to a table. The noise is deafening. When he sees me, he switches the thing off.

'Well, well, well. If it isn't the Supreme Khon. What's up, man?' He puts the angle grinder down and hugs me, dirty apron, leather gloves and all.

'Hey, I'm good, man. What up witchu?'

He can't stop smiling, and I'm glad he's happy to see me. I give him a chance to clean up, then we go out back by the pond and sit under the trees. I haven't smoked a joint in six weeks, and it feels great to hit JP's good stuff. We share a quart of Hansa Pilsener.

'You looking good, bro, for real.'

'Thanks, man. You don't look half bad yourself.'

'What's your secret?'

'I don't have a secret. Still the same old dude, dealing with the changes around me.'

'Changes, you say?'

'Yeah, some things have changed and some haven't. I just don't know if *I've* changed. Know what I mean?'

'Yeah, it's how it is, bro. Whatever happened with that Nokwanda chick?'

'Oh yeah, *her.*'

He nods right through the summary of events I give him, and when I'm finally done, he says, 'Damn.'

'I'm just tired of being unhappy all the time, you know. But it never seems to end.'

'It ends, though. You may not see it but one day, just like that, things will change. Take this, for example' – holding up the beer – 'not long ago, the parents would be freaked out if they saw me sitting here, smoking and drinking. But they just had to accept it.'

'Yeah. You know what's crazy? For the longest time I hated the changes in my life, I think cos I had no control over them. But now I want to change everything.'

He shifts his position on the bench. 'Growing up is solving problems, man. You have to try even if you not winning. Because other than that, there's only giving up and losing hope, and that never solved any-thing.'

'Word.'

'Tell me this: if you had no problems, what would you be doing?'

I take a moment to consider the question. 'I guess I'd have a chance to really figure out who I am. I would be able to breathe, not think, not feel anything but peace. I feel like I'd be able to close my eyes and smile inside. You know?'

JP grins. 'Like you doing right now?'

We both laugh. It feels good, in this moment.

Back in JP's room, we share another quart. His bed is so comfy, I could pass out. 'Yo, I better be heading out,' I say.

'Yeah, man. Listen, before you go, I have a proposition for you.' He regards me with a seriousness I haven't seen all afternoon.

I sit up straight from my slouching position, feeling woozy from the booze and the blunt.

'This is strictly business. I wouldn't be discussing it with anybody but you. You seem to carry yourself well.'

'Okay.'

'So I've come into some new product, and I'm looking for new mar-kets. Catch my drift?'

'Go on.'

'If you want a part of the action, you can come in, and we split sales fifty-fifty. It's good money.'

'You want me to sell your weed?'

'Nah, bro, I got enough people for that. Check this out.' From be-neath the bed, he pulls out a giant ziplock bag filled with different coloured pills. He tosses it to me.

'Shit, JP. What is this?'

'That there is the future. What everybody wants, and what gets us what *we* want.'

Examining the contents of the bag, it's easy to recognise some of the pills: Dr Schultz and Dr Mbatha used to shovel them down my throat.

'Zoloft, Tryptanol,' JP says, counting off on his fingers, 'Ritalin, Concerta. It's all there, man.'

'Shit.'

'So are you down?'

'Let me think about it.'

'Okay, bro, but don't take too long.'

Forty-seven

Chilling with the fam in Beacon Bay is the best way to battle the loneliness on the weekend of the matric dance.

On the Friday night before the dance, I'm chilling on the couch with Sizwe, watching TV.

'This letter came for you the other day,' Ma says, breezing into the room. She hands me a white envelope and stands there waiting for me to open it. The letter looks official, my name and address typed on the outside.

I rip it open and read it with Ma and Sizwe watching. It's from the Animation School in Cape Town.

'What is it?' Ma asks.

I don't respond; I keep reading.

'What is it?' Sizwe asks, tugging at my arm.

'Wait.' I read till the end, then read it again. My arms drop, the letter still in my hands.

'Bobo, what it is?'

'What is it, Ta Mabobo?' Sizwe asks.

'I've been accepted into the next round. They liked my portfolio.'

'Oh!' Ma covers her mouth with her hand. 'That's wonderful!'

'Yay!' Sizwe says, clapping.

'But ... they want to interview me. And both parents. In Cape Town.'

'Let me see.' Ma takes the letter from my hands. She takes a moment before she speaks. 'Do you want this?'

'Of course. But it's all the way in Cape Town.'

'Don't worry about that.'

'It's all gravy, Ma. I already have the bursary for law school.'

'What's going on?' Israel asks, coming into the room.

'Ta Mabobo is going to Cape Town!' Sizwe says.

'No, I'm not.'

'To study in Cape Town?' Israel asks, his brow creasing.

'Yeah.'

'Oh.'

'We need to respond to them,' Ma says. 'The interview's in a week and a half. There's time.'

'But Ma, how will we get to Cape Town?' JP's offer to make cash blinks on and off in my mind.

'Let me worry about that, my child.'

We travel on a Thursday, the late-afternoon flight. Ben Schoeman Airport ain't much of an airport, but it don't kill the excitement. I've never been on a plane before but I handle it without a sweat. The old lady's focused energy has a mad-calming effect. She really pulled through for me on this.

The crazy thing is that nothing has been achieved yet. It's not like I'm already in the school. We just going there for an interview. But so much comes with this. My first time on a plane. My first time in Cape Town. A journey with the old lady, like we reconnecting again.

When the plane hurtles down the runway, I'm grinning like a man selling teeth. The old lady dozes off during the flight. We fly above the clouds, following the sun. My eyes stay glued to the window, and as soon as we land, I'm harassing the old lady to pick up the pace.

'Why you in such a rush?'

'Things to do, Ma, things to see.'

We don't go anywhere that night; Ma says I should conserve all my energy for tomorrow. Being in Cape Town is a mad-trip. We stay in

Rondebosch, not far from the University of Cape Town. Nokwanda is somewhere out here on that netball scholarship – not that I care. Sleep doesn't come easily: my thoughts can't stay away from tomorrow.

The next day, we leave after breakfast, chasing our 11.00 a.m. meeting in Woodstock. Fortunately, it's not far by taxi, literally just down Main Road. Ma bought me a new shirt, which I'm wearing beneath my jersey. 'You must look presentable,' she says to me.

We stand outside the Animation School campus. Ma has a tissue in her hand, which she uses repeatedly to wipe her face. She dusts my shoulders and moves to wipe my face.

'Make sure you shine, my child.'

'Ma, everything will be fine. Stop stressing.'

Students crowd outside the building as well as inside the reception area. We are thirty-seven minutes early, so the receptionist asks us to take a seat. The waiting sucks. I'm not sure what to expect, and Ma's crazy-nervous energy ain't helping.

The students here are quite funky, with their dress styles and crazy hairstyles. I can't wait to be done with high school, done with wearing a uniform every day. The people here are living their lives their way, expressing who they are in the real world. St Stephen's College is a closed-off world compared to this.

Eventually the receptionist leads us into a room where we're welcomed by a tall man with greying hair at his temples and spectacles that make him look intelligent. With him is a woman with a blonde fringe and a black dress; she holds her chest and shoulders so high it looks like the dress is cutting off her air supply.

The man introduces himself as Tim Smith and the woman as Sophia Woods. He speaks in a deep and deliberate voice. 'It's so great that you're here. Will Mr Damane be joining us?' He smiles expectantly.

'No.' Ma and I answer at the same time.

Sophia, who is clutching a file to her chest, gives Tim a look. She must be close to thirty, while he must be creeping up on fifty. They have the same sense of twitchy eagerness, as if they've been smoking pips from the same pipe.

Tim – he insists we call him by his first name ('No need for formalities here') – takes us through the process, with a brief talk about the school. 'We have a great demand for admissions. Consider yourself good to have made it this far. We're only interviewing thirty candidates' – looking at Sophia for confirmation – 'after receiving hundreds of applications, literally hundreds, many from overseas. Enjoy this process. It's an opportunity for all of us to see if we can help you to get from good to great.' Leaning forward, he says, 'Right. Mrs Damane, what can you tell us?'

'About what?' Ma asks. The tension in her posture reminds me of the time she sat with me in Mr Summers' office. How long ago that seems now.

'About this amazing son of yours.'

'Well, Bobo … Bokang' – Sophia nods encouragingly – 'is my oldest child, but he's still my baby boy.'

Both Tim and Sophia chuckle.

'For as long as I can remember, he has always liked cartoons. I don't understand what animation is, but he said it is cartoons. Bokang could study anything: medicine, law, architecture, engineering or rocket science.'

Tim and Sophia grin at each other, and I wonder if it's genuine. If so, I wonder if they run at these energy levels all day, every day, and how they must feel by bed time.

'But he wants to follow his heart. I support him, knowing this will make him happy.'

'Wonderful,' Tim says, clasping his hands. His checked shirt is open at the collar and black hairs stick out like he's smuggling a baby porcupine. 'And what would be your wish for your son at this school?'

'To be happy, first and foremost. To enjoy his time here' – putting her hand on mine – 'to grow, and be the best he can be.'

Tim nods.

'Aw, that's amazing,' Sophia says.

'So, Bokang,' Tim says. 'You sent us a motivational letter with your portfolio and application. Can you elaborate on what you wrote? Tell us why you chose this school.'

Clearing my throat, I sit up in my chair. 'Filling blank spaces is my thing. Like my mother said, I've loved cartoons forever. My memories are built on them. The characters were my friends. All of my own characters are like that too, Sir; they're real. I believe so much in the power of stories and how they impact people's lives.'

Tim smiles. 'You don't have to call me Sir. But tell me, what do you see yourself doing in animation?'

'Creating worlds, if I can put it like that. If I can give people happy experiences through what I create, then I think I'm doing a good thing.'

He asks me some more questions, and I answer them freely. I get the sense he wants me to do well, and this makes me feel comfortable talking about myself.

'Can you tell us about a difficult situation you dealt with, and how you got out of it?'

Oh, boy. Where do I start? What do I tell them without making myself look bad? Senzo's words echo through my head: *In any song, the second verse always has to be better than the first; just as in life, if you do good once, you have to keep getting better.* I decide to go the honest route (well, semi-honest) and tell them how, against great odds, I managed to pass Grade 11. I leave out the suicide attempt and the time spent at Milton.

The whole interview takes an hour. At the end, Tim and Sophia stand up, extending their hands in unison, as if they're part of a stage production. The old lady and I head out the building, feeling great.

Our flight back to East London leaves later that afternoon. For the rest of the day and into the night, I replay the interview in my head, trying to figure out my chances. At the back of my mind, another voice reminds me of the hurdles ahead.

Forty-eight

Ernest is not impressed with my trip to Cape Town (obviously). As far as he's concerned, it was a waste of time. Since he wasn't expected to fund any of it, he had no say – just like Ma had no say in my initiation, as she reminds him.

Ernest lets me know how he feels about it upon my return, though. His irritability reaches new levels. We have petty arguments. He's full of instructions again, always needing me to do this or that. While I'm studying for my exams, he bitches about the electricity bill. He even tries to get me working at his office again, but I refuse, stating that my studies are more important. (I do spend plenty of time doing after-school tutoring with Mrs Naidoo, though; the business is pushing pretty well, and I'm trying to save as much cash as possible.)

I can't deny Ernest once the September holidays start, though. His final threat is, 'You can move out if you're not contributing towards the upkeep of this household.' So I relent.

The office has become a graveyard again. Dust and dead insects cover the floor and surfaces. Ernest is hardly ever there, and when he is, he's not doing anything to keep the business going. I figure we're back in survival mode, and what little income there is comes from gambling. Bhelekazi has done a number on us: things are missing and she destroyed some of the files out of spite, probably after realising she was never going to get paid.

I spend a few days cleaning up the mess. Ernest is there for most of the time on those days. One or two clients come in each day, but I reckon these are the pro bono ones – the look of frustration on his face says it all. Tata uMfene, loud and crass, is there every day, and it's always he who suggests they should leave early 'to attend to business'.

By the second week of the holidays, Ernest doesn't bother telling me to go to the office – he isn't there himself. So on the Tuesday of that week, I head off to Braelyn to visit Roscoe. We go to the shop to see his moms.

Auntie Vern is beside herself with excitement to see me. 'Look how you grow,' she says. 'Like a tree that drinks all the water!'

As always, she asks how the old lady is doing. She offers us tea, and we sit and catch up. I tell them about my trip to Cape Town and the Animation School.

'You can look after this one in Cape Town,' Auntie Vern says.

'You got into UCT?' I ask.

He looks at me as if I'm mad for doubting. 'Of course I did. Even got into Smuts res.'

'Nice one!' I give him dap.

He nods and looks smug. 'It will be nice to have you there.'

Very nice indeed. This reality seems to be coming together on its own.

At eleven the next morning, I'm still in bed, looking up at the ceiling. Nokwanda invaded my dreams last night for the first time since she's been out of my life. In the dream, we were in Cape Town having a good time. I wonder how she's doing.

Sounds of voices and cars draw my attention to the street below. The garbage men shout and whistle as they throw trash cans into the back of their truck. Shards of reflected light come off the metallic surfaces. A man dressed in blue overalls cycles past on an old bicycle with a yellow plastic hanging from the handle bars. A group of kids at the abandoned house next door playfully throw things at one another; three of them are students that I tutor. The old woman from across the street stands smoking a cigarette, watching them with loathing or pity.

This is such a familiar scene. This is my street, my hood, my life. Almost a year ago I could barely walk outside here, but now I'm so used to the visuals, the sounds and the smells. Next year, I might be in Cape Town. It's mad-trippy.

I reach under my bed and pull out the letter from Nokwanda. I don't even hesitate in opening it.

> Dear Bokang
>
> I wanted to say to you I am sorry. You met me in my life when I was going through some stuff. You didn't deserve to get caught up in my things. You were the nicest to me and I didn't treat you so good.
>
> I don't expect you to forgive me but I'm begging you to let me apologise properly. You are a great guy and you deserve to be happy.
>
> Please accept my apology.
> From Nokwanda

When I'm done reading, I collapse on my bed, laughing. How else does one react to something like this after all this time? Somehow, though, it feels like I'm listening to myself laugh rather than experiencing it.

Forty-nine

The letter from the Animation School eventually arrives at the end of the first week of the last school term. The old lady phones me during the evening – both Ernest and the old lady got phones in their respective cribs now; we can only receive calls and not dial out from Ernest's one.

'It's here! What should I do? Open it? Will you come fetch it? We need to know!'

'Calm down, Ma. Read it to me.'

'Okay, okay. Yhu! My child, I'm so nervous!'

Sizwe laughs and claps in the background.

'Take your time.'

I can hear the envelope tearing and the letter unfolding. Ma breathes hard through the mouthpiece. She quietens as she reads.

A loud scream forces me to pull the earpiece away. Ma is losing it. Sizwe also screams, and there's clapping.

'Yhu! Yhu! Yhu!'

'What does it say?'

'Oh, my God! Oh, my God! Oh, my God! Oh, Lord Jesus!'

'*Ma*! What does it say?'

'You got in! You got in! Oh, I'm so happy!'

I. Got. In.

The words sink in slowly, and I feel something warm in my belly.

This is happening. The dream is coming true; for once, it's a good one. For a while there, doubt had started to creep in, despite my good feelings about the interview.

I mission over to Braelyn to tell Roscoe and Auntie Vern the news: they're mad-excited for me.

I don't tell Ernest right away; I don't imagine he'll be charmed. I'll have to decide between law and animation (no-brainer), and he's not going to like my choice. I'll need to tell him some time, though.

My immediate concern is the money for my fees next year. The qualification at the Animation School is a two-year diploma, but the fees together with res are way more than what I would pay for law school here in East London. I don't expect to raise all of the fees for my first year, but I do expect to save at least half of what I need, with the hope that one of the folks will pay the rest.

Again, JP's offer comes to mind, but selling prescription drugs doesn't seem like my thing, and having those pills near me might be too tempting.

Fifty

Ernest eventually gets the news about my admission to the Animation School, sooner than I would have liked.

One day I come home from school and find him in the flat. I'm only here to change clothes, then I'm going to tutor a couple of kids in Mrs Naidoo's flat downstairs. When I walk in, the place is a mess, like it's been ransacked by vandals.

Ernest comes out of his room as soon as he hears me open the front door. 'Where have you been?'

'School.'

He looks like he wants to say something, but my legitimate answer puts him in his place.

'What happened here?'

'Nothing,' he says, sparking a cigarette.

It's obvious he's been rummaging through the place searching for something. He's left a hell of a mess in his wake. My first thought is, I hope he didn't get to my room. I rush in there and get on my knees to search in the box under my bed. I'm relieved to feel the cash I've been saving still safely stowed away.

'We're going to the office,' Ernest says, standing by the door.

I quickly push the shoebox back and get up before he can ask me what I'm doing. 'I have to study.'

'I'm not asking.'

Thembelani's words come back to me from when we were in the bush together: *Two men cannot live under the same roof.* The space Ernest and I share has been getting smaller and smaller. Next year can't come soon enough.

'I have to study.'

He scratches his beard. His eyes are swampy and distant. He's thirsty, and doesn't have the means to quench his thirst. He's a cornered beast, but one that no longer scares me. He takes a step, trying to mark his territory. 'You're coming with me.'

'No, I'm not. There's nothing there, Tata. Your business has failed.'

He squints his bloodshot eyes, trying to think of a smart comeback.

'I'm never going back there. I'm not studying law next year. I'm going to the Animation School in Cape Town. That's what I want. That's what I'm doing.'

The water level in his eyes rises. His lips writhe like a pair of slugs. His head twitches as he lets out a cackle. 'I'll never pay for that!'

'I don't need you to pay for anything.'

'You're a fool, boy. Just like your mother.'

The joke's on him. My dreams are waiting. I'm done here.

He watches me changing, sucking on his filter until the ash topples onto the floor, and still he drags on the damn thing. He eventually shuffles off and I finish my business and head out, feeling for once that Ernest will never stand in my way ever again.

Maybe that's the exuberance of youth talking, or maybe it's just the complacency of any person – young or old – after they think they've triumphed over another. Whatever it is, I should know better than to think I've outsmarted Ernest. Everything I feel good about up until now – coming back from a dark place in my life, my admission to the Animation School, my friendship with Roscoe and Auntie Vern, my tutoring business, and my daring to have dreams – has made me blind to Ernest's true nature. And boy, does he show it to me when I least expect it.

The next day when I come back from school, the flat is still a mess as neither of us has bothered to clean it up (he didn't sleep at home last night). But when I enter my room, I find a mess that was not there previously. My bed and the floor are a dumpsite strewn with debris: papers, photos, CDs and mementoes. My whole life tossed upside down, all my secrets and special memories violated and discarded like they don't matter.

That's not what distresses me the most, though.

My money is gone. Ernest has found my stash and taken it – all of it.

'No! No! *No*!' I scream.

I go to his room and search through his cupboards, under the bed, and in between the mattress and the frame. I know what I'm doing is irrational, but my mind is racing. I kick one of the cupboard doors, breaking the lower hinge.

Think.

Ernest cannot outsmart me.

I could call the police. No, that would take too long. Would they even believe the money was mine and not his? No, not them.

I could call the old lady. But what could she do? No, not her either.

Damnit! This is me against Ernest, as it always was. What would Ernest do with all that money? Where could he possibly be right at this moment?

The answer comes to me, and I bolt out the front door, still in my school uniform, my shirt untucked and my tie hanging loose. The Best Bet place in Clermont is not far. I run through the streets, blasting past people on the pavements. I dodge between cars, not stopping for anything. Ernest will try to double his stolen cash. He won't buy anything responsible with the money, that's for sure.

I enter the building still running, banging the door against the wall and startling the semi-comatose patrons. They don't look impressed but I don't care. One of them asks me what I'm doing here but I ignore him. My eyes scan the room: the men at the tables, the men in the corners, standing, sitting. Nothing. Ernest ain't here.

One of the men walks towards me, but I stomp towards the counter with the mesh partition. Behind it, the old woman with the blonde hair watches the room.

'Hey, you,' says the man approaching me.

The old woman holds out her hand to him, telling him to back off. She watches me with the eyes of someone who has seen it all.

'I'm looking for my father,' I say, putting my hands on the counter. Her name is Stella, I remember now. She looks older than the last time I saw her; her makeup gives her a fake quality, like plastic fruit. The only thing alive in her face is the directness of her reptilian gaze.

'Ernest and Albert didn't come here today.' She folds her arms.

'When did you last see them?'

Her top lip curls. 'Yesterday. Maybe the day before.'

I wonder if someone like this even has the capacity to love. She doesn't care but she's intrigued to know what happens next.

'What has your pa done?'

'Nothing. I just want him to come home.'

She smiles, calling my bluff.

This is a waste of time. 'When did he last win?'

'Your pa is a loser, like all of them' – wagging her finger at the men in the room – 'they never know when to bloody quit. I haven't seen him win anything in a long time.' She smiles (it's godawful).

Her laugh follows me as I exit the building. Ernest could only be in three other places: 1) the office (not likely); 2) Tata uMfene's house (very likely); or 3) his other gambling spot in Mdantsane (also very likely).

The office is the closest. Before I head there, I use the payphone down the road to call JP. I don't give him the details, just tell him I need his help. He reluctantly agrees only after I tell him it has to do with me selling his prescription drugs. I grab a taxi on Oxford Street.

Every time the taxi stops to drop or pick up passengers, I bite my lip. The woman next to me stares as I fidget. It takes eighteen minutes to get to Ernest's office on Union Street. I run up the metal stairs, my shoes banging. I almost knock over one of the women who works with the seamstress on the second floor. She's carrying a bundle of clothing that muffles the words she shouts at me.

The office on the third floor is locked. Ernest is not here. I head back downstairs, not too surprised, but glad I checked to make sure.

Outside, I wait on the pavement for JP. When could Ernest have taken the money? He didn't sleep at the flat, so he must have returned this morning. Was it a random search, or did he see something yesterday when he surprised me in my room? Dammit! His calculating brain must have figured out I was hiding something. How could I be so stupid?

JP arrives in his bakkie after thirty minutes and finds me smoking my second cigarette. 'Supreme, bro. I'm not so sure about all of this.'

'Listen to me, you have to help.'

'Yeah, I'm here, bro. So what's the plan?'

I would love to go to Tata uMfene's house in Amalinda first, not only because it's closer, but also because I'm praying Ernest is there. But I know we should check the spot in Mdantsane first, because it's further, and I ain't trying to be in that neighbourhood after dark. 'We going to Mdantsane,' I say turning to him. 'NU 15.'

'No way, bro! A dude like me can't go there.'

'Don't be stupid. If we move now, we can get there before dark. If we sit here arguing, we get nowhere.'

'This is swak, bru!'

We take the North East Expressway and off-ramp onto the N2 towards Mdantsane. JP drives with both hands on the steering wheel.

'Relax, JP,' I say. 'Everything will be fine.'

I don't know if it will be, though. Ernest and Tata uMfene had good reason for telling me to wait in the ride every time we ever came to NU 15. The only time I went inside the spot was that one time the old lady and I went to pay Ernest's gambling debt and carry him out with his busted hand.

When we get there, the sun is close to setting. Strong smells float from the smoking dumpsite across the street.

I tell JP to stay in the car, much to his relief. As I walk away from the ride, he pulls his beanie lower over his head and scooches down in his seat, trying to disappear.

As always, drunken zombies stagger about outside the house. None of them are Ernest. Inside, more bodies clog up the place. It's not as busy as it gets on a weekend, but still there are many people. Dust floats in the air, and I wonder how people can sit in here, drinking themselves stupid. I'm conscious of my school uniform, but then, in a place like this, nobody really cares. The room is badly lit; faces are hard to see, unless I go up close and peer. Ernest is not here either. I recognise the man we paid Ernest's debt to; he's having a laugh with two other men. Approaching him would be suicide.

This is a failed plan and I give up; JP is only too happy to drive out of here. He races to the highway, and once we're on it, he's more talkative. 'What's really going on, bro?'

So I tell him. I need to talk to somebody.

'Whoa, that's hectic. That's messed up, big time.'

'I know.'

'We gonna find him. Don't worry.'

We arrive in Amalinda, outside Tata uMfene's small-ass crib. My heart sinks when I see it's quiet. Usually there's music pumping and people sitting outside. The front door is shut.

Tata uMfene opens when I knock, and is surprised to see me. 'Bokang. What are you doing here?'

'Where's my father?'

'He isn't here.'

'When did you last see him?'

'Two days ago.'

'Where is he?'

'I'm sorry, I don't know. Don't worry about him. Go home.'

He's right. I shouldn't be looking for a grown-ass man. But I'm not looking for him for his own well-being. I'm looking for a thief who stole from me. Stole my childhood. Stole my future. Fatigue sets in. The anger peters away, and a hollowness consumes me.

JP takes me back to the flat in Clermont, which I'm now convinced will be my jail cell forever.

Fifty-one

It takes a lot for me to go to school the next day. I sit with Roscoe on the matric side of the cafeteria, overlooking the first-team cricket field.

'Go to the police,' Roscoe says, holding a sandwich that smells suspiciously of fishpaste. 'He can't just get away with this.'

'I thought of that, but what would the police do? Investigate? Arrest him? By the time that happens, he would have blown my cash!'

'But he can't get away with it. Maybe he hasn't spent the money.'

'He's blown it already, trust me.'

'It's hardly been a day!'

'Exactly. Ernest don't need more time than that to cause a disaster.'

'Nonsense, man! This is your future, bra.'

'I hear you. Right now I'm bugging about how I'm gonna raise the money again.'

Fifth and sixth periods are Art class with Mr Jenkins, who is new to the school. Looking at him, you'd never think he's the creative type. He's thin and wiry, with a long nose and slits for eyes. He must be in his thirties, but he looks older when he takes his glasses off. His passion for art is evident, which makes him a good teacher. He's very encouraging, and this year I've enjoyed art more than ever before. He knows about my application to the Animation School, and he speaks to me about it every chance he gets.

'What's going on with you today, Master Damane? You look sadder than a clown at a funeral. Hey?'

'Nothing, Sir.'

'Try transfer some of that "nothing" onto that' – pointing at the canvas in front of me – 'and let's see if it can benefit you. You know Van Gogh was a sad son of a gun. Maybe that's what genius is? Hey? Bokang the Genius. Imagine that.' He rubs my shoulder before walking off.

I feel like throwing water at the canvas and watching it run down like tears ruining a beautiful face.

I walk out the gate after school feeling like I've come so far, but not gotten close. Five years I've been at this school, hating most of it. These past few months have been different, though. Knowing I had something to look forward to next year has made the time here bearable. Now I have just over a month left. Life was supposed to begin in Cape Town at the Animation School. Now Ernest has taken it away from me. I could always take JP up on his offer and raise the cash quick-fast. I don't know, though; that just don't seem right.

Inside Norden Place, I stand alone in the lift as it rattles up to the third floor. A faint sour smell hangs in the air of the flat, and the place is still a mess, with things tossed around all over. What *is* that smell? It gets stronger with each step I take. Something must be rotting in the kitchen. The vegetable trolley is empty; though, and so is the fridge. It's not coming from the bin either. The smell is weaker in here.

I open the living-room window to create a draft. Ernest's bedroom door is half-open. It was fully open this morning when I left for school. I remember leaving it that way yesterday after ransacking his room, searching for my money. The smell is stronger in that direction. Could it be a dead rat? But it's also sour ...

Ernest lays on the bed, stiff, face-up and fully dressed. His mouth hangs open and a white crust lines his lips. His hands are at his sides, palms up in supplication. The front of his shirt and waistcoat are covered in dry vomit. His shoes are off, placed neatly by the side of the bed. That alone is out of character. The fact that he lies on his back is also off. But the most off thing is that his eyes are open, wide and staring blankly at the ceiling.

'Tata,' I call out, knowing full well he's not going to respond. I step closer, knowing now for certain where the smell is coming from. 'Tata.' I grab him by his arms and shake him. 'Tata!' His body is stiff and cold, even through his shirt; his usually light skin is dull and grey.

'*Tata!*' I shake him some more, probably more than I would need to if I was waking him from sleep. But my dad is not waking up. His eyes stare beyond, not even at me, as I fight to get his attention.

'*Tata! Tata!*' I feel like I'm six years old and powerless, asking the old man to go back to the way he was before, begging him to make everything the way it was before, pleading with him to help me. '*Tata!*'

My father needs help.

I run out the flat and into the hallway. I bang on Mrs Mafanya's door, knowing she's a nurse. When she doesn't respond, I rush up the stairs to Dr Abedu's apartment. I hammer on the door, screaming. Little Clara, the last born of four, answers.

'Is your father home?'

'He's still at work.'

'Who is it?' Mrs Abedu asks, peeking around the corner. She sees my face, and immediately puts down the plate and cloth in her hands. 'What is it?'

'It's my father! He needs a doctor!'

'Clara, call your father.' She grabs me by the shoulder. 'Where is he?'

I take her downstairs, back to our flat. Kneeling by the bedside, Mrs Abedu places two fingers on my father's neck, then on both his wrists. Her face is a mask. The smell is heavy in here, but if she smells it, she's not showing any signs. It feels as if the ceiling might collapse or the walls might come crush us. There's a heaviness in the room and inside me.

Mrs Abedu turns to me with a look that tells me what I already know. She searches through the cupboards and pulls out a fresh sheet to cover my father. She takes me to the couch in the living room, where I sit and listen to her soothing words. I don't know what she's saying, but the lull of her voice is nice.

She sits with me, her hands on mine. She stays until the others arrive. First Clara with a report: Daddy is coming; the ambulance is coming (*my daddy is not coming; my daddy is gone*). Dr Abedu arrives, along with the paramedics. There's no urgency; there's nothing to save. Dr Abedu orders the paramedics around. Mrs Mafanya from across the hallway, all friendly and concerned, suggests we say a prayer. Mrs Mentoor – Lucille – comes and gives me a hug (her skin is warm and smells like cinnamon). I haven't moved from the couch. Mr Magadla, the building caretaker, comes in and apologises to me. For what, I don't know. He is deeply troubled, almost guilty. Police come.

The body of T Ernest Damane is carried out, covered, by two men. One of them nods to me on his way out.

'Is there anyone we can call?' Mrs Abedu asks.

Anyone we can call? Who? It was just me and Ernest.

'Maybe Mama?'

Mama? Ma? Yes. We need to call her; she should know. Israel should know. Sizwe should know.

They all should know.

Tata is dead.

Fifty-two

When I was about five or six years old, back when I was an only child, I once dreamed that my father died. In the dream he fell over a cliff and kept falling, and even though I don't remember him hitting whatever lay below, I remember knowing without a doubt that he was gone.

I woke up crying and the old lady came to comfort me. My father too came to my bedside and held me in his lap. He asked what happened, and I couldn't explain; it was too much to even think about or repeat in words. He laughed at me, not in a teasing way, but in a mad-comforting way. He was trying to make me see that it was just a dream and nothing to fear.

Apart from this dream, the only death I've ever thought about is my own. I've wanted to die before, in my head. The Suicide Manifesto represented my documented thoughts about dying. I never thought I had it in me to go through with ending my own life, and then that time I lay on the tracks waiting for the train, I realised how easy it was.

That scared me. If I learned anything from that experience, it's that I'm not ready to die. I'm not ready to face death. But then death doesn't listen to anybody. Death does as death wants.

* * *

It's funny how sometimes, when big things are happening, chaos unfolding, it's the little things that bring clarity.

Sitting on the couch in the third-floor flat in Norden Place, with Mrs Abedu and a few other comforting figures, I hear a double ringing sound: *clink, clink*. It comes from the window behind me: *clink, clink*. I recognise it instantly. I don't need to look out the window at the street below to know it's the man in blue overalls riding his bicycle, coming back from work. *Clink, clink. Clink, clink.*

The familiar noise brings me back to reality.

Is there anybody we can call? That's what Mrs Abedu asked. I need to tell Ma, I need to tell Israel, and I need to tell Sizwe. They have to hear it from me. They shouldn't hear it from a stranger. Nobody should ask any of them if there is somebody who can be called for them.

'Dr Abedu!' I stand up so fast Mrs Mafanya almost loses her wig (and her Bible).

'Son,' he says, always so formal.

'Where will they take my father?'

'Don't worry, I've taken care of it. He's gone to Frere Hospital. You don't need to go there.'

'How did he die?' I look the doctor straight in the eyes.

He doesn't mess me about. 'He suffocated. Choked on his own vomit. I'm sorry.' He places a hand on my arm. 'The hospital will confirm cause of death, but I am sure, absolutely.' He squeezes my shoulder.

'Can you please take me to Beacon Bay? I need to tell my family.'

We drive in silence. All I hear is the engine of the ride humming. Dr Abedu keeps his focus on the road; he holds the silence, and I can tell it's out of respect for me and the gravity of the situation. As a doctor, I can imagine he gets a heavy dose of this kind of thing. His presence, like his wife's, is comforting.

It's not likely Ma will be home yet, but Israel and Sizwe will be there, with MaMvundla. I want to be with them for a while before I give them the news.

'How long do you think he lay there?' I ask.

'You mean, after?'

'Yes, once he was gone.'

'I can't be certain, but quite some time.'

Silence.

'When did he come home last night?'

'He *didn't* come home.'

Dr Abedu looks at me sideways, disregarding the road in front of him. 'Are you *sure*?'

'Yes. Tata did not come home last night.'

We complete the rest of the journey in silence. As we pull into the crib in Beacon Bay, a long shadow is cast over the house. I tell Dr Abedu he doesn't have to stay, but he insists and I insist more, so he leaves.

My arrival allows MaMvundla to leave early. The old lady should be home in less than twenty minutes.

I sit with Izzy and Siz in Izzy's room, the one we used to share. There's only one bed in here now, which Israel has moved to the middle of the room. Pictures of the things he likes cover the walls. All signs of me having shared this space with him are gone, including the hip-hop posters I said he could have.

I sit on the chair in the corner, with Sizwe on my lap, even though she's getting too big for this. Israel sits on his bed.

'What are you doing here?' Israel asks.

'I came to see y'all.'

'Look what I made at school today,' Sizwe says, holding up a paper crown.

'It's beautiful.'

Israel clicks his tongue. 'You shouldn't even be in here,' he says to her.

'I'm with Ta Mabobo.' She sticks out her tongue at him. 'Izzy doesn't allow me in here any more.'

'What's up with that?'

'She's a child. She messes things up.'

'You two need to stick together and support each other.'

Israel makes a hissing sound without looking in our direction.

So much has changed here since I moved out. They don't know it, but their worlds are about to change again. I watch them, thinking they're about to lose more innocence than they've already lost. For long parts of my life, all I've wanted is to protect the two of them from growing up. At other times, when I've thought of them as spoilt, I've spitefully wanted them to be exposed to the harshness of the world. But now I know that regardless of what they go through, I will always stick around to make sure they'll be all right.

When Ma arrives, I take her into the room she once shared with Ernest and we sit down. She looks nervous, as if she already knows. Mothers sense when things aren't right with their children.

'What's going on, my child?'

'Tata is gone. He passed away this afternoon.'

She gasps, putting her hands to her mouth, eyes already starting to drown in sorrow. Her head shakes as if she's trying to undo what has already been said and done.

I reach out a hand to her, and her eyes follow it in horror, as if I'm a ghost from the other side.

'Ma.' I pull her into my chest.

'Oh, my child … Oh no … No … Oh, my Lord …'

I hold her for a moment before she pulls away and looks up at me.

'When? How?'

'Today. This afternoon. We need to make arrangements.'

'But where is he now?'

'Frere Hospital.' I give her the rest of the small details. 'We need to tell Izzy and Siz.'

'Yes, of course.'

We call Israel and Sizwe into her room. Ma does the talking. Sizwe cries but Israel doesn't. My tears come again as I embrace Ma and Sizwe. The three of us cry the tears that refuse to come from Israel's eyes.

Ma says I should spend the night with them. I can take Sizwe's bed, and Sizwe will share with Ma. It's a good idea. I don't think I'll ever be able to stay in the flat again. Why would I stay there alone?

Fifty-three

Ernest's funeral is on the first Saturday of November, just over a week after his passing. We need the time to hustle everything together.

Ma and I make all the arrangements. I thought Ernest would have a quiet, modest send-off, but it's Ma who makes me aware of just how many people knew him. The turnout on the day is evidence enough of this. I guess I should have known from watching how he helped people with legal matters at the firm and at the flat in Clermont.

The sale of Ernest's few possessions pays for the funeral. Selling the ride brings in the most money, and the few other household items and office furniture bring in some useful cents to ensure he has a decent send-off. My bed is moved from Clermont back to the room I shared with Israel in Beacon Bay.

The service takes place at St Saviour's church on St Peter's Road in Clermont. Ernest was not a man of the church, but Ma is a woman of faith, and she finds a way for all of this to work. She ropes in Pastor Mzoli to run the service, which took some convincing.

Sitting in a church is awkward for me; I can't remember when I last did. Ma sits in the front row, dressed in black, her face shielded by a veil. Her face is still, very business-like. I guess she's cried all the tears she's ever gonna cry for Ernest, and I know she's mostly here for us kids. Israel and Sizwe sit on the other side of me, already looking like they wish all of this was over.

The speech I've prepared is brief. Ma told me the kids of the deceased have an opportunity to speak, if they want to, but she suggested I didn't have to. I decided I should say a thing or two in any case. Finding the right words wasn't easy; I still don't know if they are the right ones.

The church is full of serious-looking people. Some of them I've seen over the past week coming to the crib in Beacon Bay to pay their respects. (It's funny how things have unfolded as if Ma and Ernest were still together – me back in Beacon Bay, Ma making all the arrangements like a faithful wife, and people treating us as if we were one big happy family.) Many of them are Ernest's University of Fort Hare buddies; even Professor Titus Manqina, who got me the law-school bursary, is present. Many of them are grateful clients Ernest has helped over the years. I didn't know people could be this grateful. Some of our neighbours from Norden Place attend: Dr and Mrs Abedu, Mr and Mrs Naidoo, Mrs Mafanya, Mr Mentoor, Mr Magadla, and the biggest surprise of all, Mrs Thuso. You must have been quite a person when your haters attend your funeral.

All the people who speak from the pulpit say the most amazing stuff about Ernest, things that make me wonder if they rapping about the same person I called Tata. The speeches are mad-long; I almost expect Ernest himself to rise from the dead and tell them to get on with it, for real.

My turn to speak comes. Pastor Mzoli has to call me twice before I realise he's talking to me. I'm aware of the crowd behind me as I walk towards the pulpit, clutching the piece of paper with my speech on it.

A bunch of faces stare up at me. Some people fan themselves with their printed programmes. To my right, T Ernest Damane lays in his coffin, gazing up without his spectacles. His eyes are finally closed, his white hair is the same, and his face is tight, as if he longs for a drink even in death.

I fold the piece of paper and put it away in my jacket pocket. I adjust the microphone and clear my throat. 'My father was a difficult man.'

Every face focuses on me; the people fanning themselves stop. 'A difficult man, with many troubles. We all have troubles, and that makes him no different from any of us. He was difficult because he set such high standards for himself, expected so much, and tried so hard. It frustrated him when things were not done to their best. He would often tell me, "Bokang, don't bother doing something if you're not going to do it properly." He expected a lot from me, maybe even too much at times. He expected a lot of all of us.' My eyes lock onto Ma, Israel and Sizwe in the front row.

'He was often unfair in his expectations. He had a way of making you want to please him, but nothing ever seemed good enough for him.' Pastor Mzoli frowns at me from alongside. 'But the truth is, he was never good enough for himself.' At this, a few heads shake in the audience. 'He never got the opportunity to be truly himself, and this made him really unhappy.' The church is still, with a sense of anticipation.

'My father was a teacher, and that is what I loved most about him. He always had the time to show you something new, or explain something you didn't understand. He taught me to love learning. He was so good at this that many of the things I learned from him were indirect; I don't even think he was trying to teach them. But his life, to me and my mother, my brother and sister, is a lesson. He will never be forgotten. His impact in our lives was too great, and I guess in that way he will live on. I only hope that wherever he is, he finds the peace he wasn't able to find in his life.'

As I walk back from the pulpit, an overzealous woman in the choir takes up a song, and everyone stands and joins in. I give Ma, Israel and Sizwe a group hug before we take our seats.

After a few more speeches, Pastor Mzoli announces that the body will be carried out of the church. Israel and I join the men carrying the coffin. We move slowly – the coffin is heavy and I'm grateful there are enough of us to share the weight (Ernest would probably criticise our efforts).

Roscoe and Auntie Vern are among the crowd. Senzo is also here, and he gives me a salute as our eyes meet. I didn't even know he'd come all the way from Joburg to be here. Ma's brother, Uncle Katlego, and my cousin Dikeledi are also here from Sebokeng; they're staying with us in Beacon Bay.

The sunlight is bright compared to the darkness in the church. Moving down the stairs towards the hearse, I catch a glimpse of the skulking figure of Tata uMfene, Ernest's lifelong friend and partner. I'm surprised to see him outside the church, trying to be anonymous despite his size. But then I remember that, unlike most of the people inside the church, Tata uMfene is uneducated. Many folk, like the old lady, wondered about the friendship between the two. Having spent time in the bush with Viwe and Thembelani, whom I now consider brothers even though we come from different worlds, I can better understand the lifelong friendship between Ernest and Tata uMfene.

The funeral procession moves on to Cambridge Cemetery. We stand in the sun, listening to more prayers and speeches, fortunately shorter this time. The shredded clouds in the sky are similar to the ones that were out the day I lay on the tracks waiting for the train.

Ma, Israel, Sizwe and I each throw a fistful of sand onto the coffin as it is lowered into the grave. We walk away, leaving Ernest in his last resting place. I wonder if he will finally find peace, and if we will also now finally find peace.

Later that evening I'm chilling at the crib with the fam. There's a feeling around us as if something has been lifted. It's been a long day that has taken its toll on us. At the same time, we all wondering what comes next.

The old lady sits with Sizwe and Uncle Katlego watching TV, still dressed in their formal clothes. Israel sits in his room with his own thoughts. Roscoe and Senzo show up in Senzo's dad's Beemer. I ask the old lady if I can go out with them for a while, and I ask Dikeledi to join us.

Senzo drives us to the cliff by Edge Road. We sit in the ride sharing a half-nip of Smirnoff (pouring out a little liquor for the pain, according to Senzo).

'That was some speech you gave,' Senzo says, slouching in the driver's seat.

'Bloody awesome,' Roscoe says, taking a swig from the bottle, which makes him grimace. Dikeledi covers her smile.

'Yeah, you should have seen some of them peeps. Man, they was bugging out!'

'It was straight to the point, bra. Really awesome. Some of those other people talked, yho!'

'It's like you was up there, ripping scripts, dog, on the mic, blessing the crowd.'

'My mom said something interesting after,' Roscoe says. 'She said, "Looks like your friend has finally found it."'

'She really said that?' I ask.

'Yep.'

'Coming from Auntie Vern, that means a lot.'

'What does that even mean, fellas?' Senzo asks.

Roscoe and I laugh. Dikeledi watches us curiously.

'Whatever, man,' Senzo says. He snatches the bottle from me. 'So I guess you the man of the house now, huh?'

'Yeah, I suppose so. Maybe I can take tips from you two.'

'Nah, Bo, don't get it twisted. This fool here ain't no man of the house. He still got a pops.' He points at Roscoe, who gives him a fake smile back. 'Me, I'm no man of the house either.'

'But you both the only sons,' I say. 'I got a brother.'

'Yeah, maybe, but Big Ros here has a father.'

'Not only that,' Roscoe adds, 'in my family, my sisters do everything. They the "men of the house". I'm just a little prince, maybe.'

'Exactly,' Senzo says. 'And I'm the last born. You gotta head your family. You feel me?'

'Don't sound like nothing I ain't been doing already.'

'Let me ask you, Bo: what was it like living on your own with your old man?'

'Crazy. Tough. Insane. Tough. Bananas. Insane. Did I say insane?'

'Yeah, living with one parent ain't no joke, yo. I been out in Jozi with my moms, and I see how that's changed me.'

'Changed you how?'

'In subtle ways, you know. I've seen all sides of both my parents. What you said today, about your old man, made me think.'

'About?'

'How much like your old man do you think you are?'

'I know I'm like him, no doubt. And you know what? It don't scare me half as much as it used to. After all, he was my old man, and I can't deny it. I can see how I'm like my old lady too, in the good and the bad ways. It's just the way it is.'

'Yeah, I suppose.'

When Senzo drops us off at the crib later, everyone has gone to bed. I sit on the back veranda with Dikeledi.

'Your friends are interesting,' she says.

'Yeah, they're a pair of clowns. I love them, though.' After a while I ask, 'How is Mashoto?'

'She's good – happily in love.'

'For real?'

'It's been nearly a year.'

'Nice. I'm so happy for her. You must send her my shout-out.'

'I will. She really liked you, that one.'

'It was a crazy time in my life.'

'Do you have anyone special in your life?'

'Nah.' I sigh. 'I don't know what comes next for me.'

She touches my hand. 'Don't be hard on yourself. These things take time.'

'Can I ask you something?'

'Yeah.'

'How did you deal with your folks' deaths?'

'It wasn't easy, and it never gets easier. It keeps coming back.'

After a while, we go back inside. Israel is still up, sitting on his bed in his clothes, rubbing his knuckles.

'You still up.'

'Can't sleep.'

'Maybe get out of those clothes, get under the covers.'

He curls his top lip.

I undress and get into bed, my head swirling. It will be great to sleep tonight, despite everything. 'What are you doing tomorrow?' I ask.

'Don't know.'

'We should do something, you and me, just the two of us.'

'Sure.'

'Good night, big guy.'

'Good night, Ta Bobes.'

Fifty-four

There's no time, really, to mourn Ernest, not when his problems still hang over us like a bad smell. Twice people come to the house blabbing about outstanding debts. Ernest owed a huge sum for the office building he was renting, and some other things we knew nothing about. Some of these debt collectors try make it the old lady's problem, but that doesn't fly – she's not liable since the separation and pending divorce. Another guy tries to make it my problem cos Ernest put my name down as the owner of whatever he was buying. But the old lady makes sure that doesn't stick either, me being a dependant and all. Those ones go away.

A couple of days later, we receive a visit at the crib from some shady characters from Ernest's shady world. We sitting having a chicken dinner when the buzzer goes. The old lady and I exchange a glance.

'I'll get it,' Israel says.

Sizwe continues the conversation, but neither Ma nor I are listening, our ears straining instead to hear Israel at the front door. We don't have a working intercom, so to know who's outside, you have to open the door and look towards the gate.

'Who is it, Izzy?' Ma asks.

'I can't see,' Israel says. 'His bloody lights are too bright.'

'Watch your language,' Ma says, getting up. The look she gives me tells me I should get up too.

A car with a messed-up fan belt stands outside our front gate, rattling and wheezing. The lights are brighter than they need to be, and smoke rises from the exhaust, making it appear like some seething beast.

Ma walks out towards the gate, a hand held up to block the light. Israel and I walk either side of her. If I ever thought I'd be doing this man-of-the-house thing alone, I was wrong.

I put my hand on the old lady to stop her before we reach the gate. We've come close enough; whoever is in the ride should switch off the engine and step out to let us know what the hell they want.

Nothing happens for a moment, and the ride heaves, as if waiting to charge. Then the passenger door opens and someone steps out. Only the dark shape of his legs and the hat on his head show against the brightness of the lights. Two more doors open, and two more figures, including the driver, exit the ride.

Someone cackles (very much like Faku). 'Molweni!' he greets, cheerfully.

We still can't see him.

'Can you switch off your lights?' the old lady says in isiXhosa.

The man cackles again. 'Yes, of course.'

The lights go out, and for a moment we have to adjust our eyes. The man who spoke is old. He wears a coat even though it's not cold to-night. On his head he wears an old fedora.

'How are you all tonight?' the old man asks in isiXhosa, still in the cheerful voice.

'Can we help you?' I ask.

The man approaches the gate, putting a hand on it like he's holding a prison bar. 'Condolences on the passing of your beloved father of the house. We have come to pay our respects. Perhaps we can come inside?'

'Sorry, but who are you?' Ma asks.

'Call us business associates of your husband, may his soul rest in peace.' The old man tips his hat and gravely bows his head.

'Thank you for your words,' Ma says. 'But this is not a good time. It's late, and we are going to bed.'

'This won't take long, Mama. We can do it out here if you want.'

'Look, my mother said you should leave,' I say.

The old man cackles. Then the joy disappears from his face. 'uRadebe owes me money – a lot of money. I've observed the period of mourning. Now it's time to collect.'

'He's dead,' Israel says. 'There's nothing to collect.'

'Oh, but there is,' the old man says. 'What he owed, his family now owes. Which means you.' He points his crooked finger at the three of us. 'Fifty thousand.'

'We don't have that kind of money,' I say. 'Even if we did, *he* owed it, not us.'

'I'm a good man. I'll give you three days. Phone me when you have it.' He nods at one of the men. The one standing at the driver's side comes forward and holds out a piece of paper. When none of us moves to take it, he tosses it through the bars of the gate.

'I'll be waiting,' the old man says.

They all climb back into the ride and the battered engine roars to life.

We stand there, watching them drive off. It seems the curse of Ernest is still looming over our lives.

For a day and a half, we do nothing. The thought of having to do something is depressing enough. But after a while, I tell the old lady we need to speak with Tata uMfene. The suggestion disgusts her but she eventually relents.

We park a few houses down the street from his house.

'Let me speak to him alone,' I say.

The old lady nods, looking relieved she doesn't have to do it.

There's no music coming from the house but there is movement inside. The front door stands open.

I let myself in through the wire gate. A man smokes a cigarette by the front door. I ignore him when he greets, and enter the house without waiting for an invitation.

Tata uMfene sits on a couch, looking like something melting and folding into itself. When he sees me, he doesn't look surprised, just tired – and guilty. He wipes his huge face with one of his meaty hands, then he struggles to his feet.

I follow him down the short passage and enter what I assume is his bedroom. A large bed covered in a shiny maroon duvet takes up the entire space. Red curtains are pulled shut. One corner is a mess of piled clothes, bags, blankets and boxes.

'You were with Tata the night he died.' I'm not asking, I'm telling.

'Yes.'

'What happened? Tell me.'

Tata uMfene can barely look at me. He wipes his hand across his face again. 'Eish, what can I say?'

'Tell me what happened. Tata did not die in Clermont. You brought him there, didn't you?'

'It wasn't my fault, you have to believe me. It was nobody's fault. Your father showed up just after you left. He was already very happy. We were all here, relaxing, having fun, like we always do. Then your father, he just went to sleep in the other room. We thought he was sleeping.'

'Rubbish!'

'I'm telling you. You know what he meant to me.'

'You used my father.'

'I loved your father. He was my brother—'

'Then why did you let him die?'

'We didn't know.' He slumps onto the bed. 'We didn't know …'

'You were all together! Why didn't you call an ambulance? Why did you bring him to Clermont?'

'We didn't know …' A big bear of a man, reduced to a whimper.

'You let him gamble his money away. You let him gamble *my* money away! You didn't stop him. You let him drink himself stupid! What kind of friend lets his friend destroy himself? *Destroy his family*?'

Tata uMfene covers his face, trying to stifle an awful squeal. It's pathetic.

'This life you lived with him has left us with problems that are not ours. Men came to our house demanding money.'

He looks up at me. 'What men?'

'Some old man. He didn't leave his name.'

'Dukashe. It must be him. He came to your house?'

'Yes! That's what I'm telling you.'

'Wait, Bokang. We can pay him.'

'How?'

Tata uMfene reaches for his wallet. He searches through it with new energy. 'Here!' he says, holding up a folded piece of paper that looks like a till slip.

I take it from him. 'What is this?'

He folds his lips into his mouth.

'What is this?'

'Your father came to me that night you were here, after you left. That whole day he had been celebrating on his own. He told me he had placed bets with Dukashe's people, and at Best Bet. Your father won at Best Bet, but lost with Dukashe. I only found this out after he was gone. You can collect the winnings at Best Bet with his ID and a death certificate. That piece of paper, it's yours.'

Epilogue

February 2000

    'What about that one?' the man asks.

'The Canon EOS,' I say.

'Can I have a look at it?'

'Sure. It's actually the D30, the most recent model.'

'Really?' His eyes gleam as he picks it up and studies it.

'This one is the first digital SLR designed and produced entirely by Canon. It's one of a kind.'

The man smiles again.

'We got it just two days ago, by special order. It's only been on the South African market for three weeks.'

'Are there other shops selling it?'

'Definitely not in East London. I doubt anywhere else in the country either. Remember, here at Jackson's Photo Finish, we make it our duty to stay ahead of the game. We understand our customers are sophisticated, so we supply the best products money can buy and give them the service they deserve.'

'Okay, I'll take it.'

'You won't regret it, Mr Herbert. You'll be wanting this special film too.'

'Tell me, what school did you go to, young man?'

'St Stephen's College.'

'Ah. Good school.'

'Hmm. Here you go.' I hand him his plastic and till slip.

'You have a rising star here, Bob,' Mr Herbert says to Mr Jackson, who has stepped up behind the counter with me.

'Yeah, he's a real asset. Definitely. You know he also draws family portraits? Show him, Bokang.'

I point to some pictures displayed next to the front counter.

'You did these? Wow!'

'When you develop your pictures here,' Mr Jackson says, 'you can also have them as drawings or paintings. We also have these lovely frames to complete the picture.'

'Marvellous. I know Diane will absolutely love these. So will the girls. Look, what I'll do is select some family pictures and bring them over, tell you which ones you can do. Sound good?'

'Yeah,' I say.

'Absolutely stunning,' Mr Herbert says, bending to peer at the portrait in front of him. 'Such talent. I was at the Anne Bryant Art Gallery just last week. Didn't see anything as remarkable as this. You ever been there?'

'Yes, I have, Sir.'

'You should have your work displayed there. Shouldn't let your talent go to waste.'

'Bokang is going to the Animation School next year,' Mr Jackson says.

'Where's that, now?'

'Cape Town. After this gap year to gain experience and raise some funds.'

'Impressive. Talented and responsible. Well, if I can contribute towards your dreams, I'd be delighted to assist. I know people in East London, even in PE, who would be fascinated by your work. Leave it to me. I'll spread the word.'

'Thank you, Mr Herbert, Sir.'

'Nice one, Bokang,' Mr Jackson says as Mr Herbert leaves the shop.

'Nice one, Bokang,' Kelly says, winking. She's another assistant, also taking a gap year.

Later, when we locking up the store, Kelly says, 'We still on for a movie after your shift tomorrow?' Her shoulder-length dark hair goes nicely with her dark-blue eyes.

'Looking forward to it. But you still haven't said if it's a date.'

'We'll figure that out. There's your brother.' She points to the door.

Israel stands there, tall and handsome, in his St Stephen's College uniform. Everything is new; none of my hand-me-downs would fit him. He's walked from St Stephen's to Westwood Shopping Centre, where Jackson's Photo Finish is. 'You ready to bounce?' he asks.

'Yeah, but I wanna hit up Musica right quick. The new Ghostface Killah album is out.'

'*Supreme Clientele?*'

'Yeah.'

'Yo, that's dope. I heard good things about it.'

We head to Musica and I cop the *Supreme Clientele* album as well as OutKast's *Stankonia*. Buying two CDs at once is me being extravagant, but I'm in a celebratory mood. Usually I'm mad-serious about saving money. The gig at Jackson's pays nicely, and I'm still tutoring kids after school.

'Mr Summers took us for a class today,' Israel says as we sit at the back of the taxi on our way home.

'Yeah?'

'After the class he called me aside.'

'What'd he say?'

'He asked me, "Aren't you Bokang Damane's brother?" and I said, "Yes, I am, Sir." Then he said, "You've got a lot to live up to. Hope the brains run in the family. Your big brother got his full academic honours at the end of his Grade 12 year. Four distinctions. Outstanding. All the best at the college, young man." Then he walked off.'

'He really said that?'

'Yep. I didn't know you got four distinctions. Is it true?'

'Yeah.'

'And honours?'

'Yeah.'

'Wow, Ta Bobes. That's amazing. Why didn't you tell us?'

'The old lady knows. So much happened at the end of last year, it just all got swallowed up. You can do better than that, though.'

'You think so?'

'Hell, yeah. You best believe that.'

Israel and I make dinner for the fam. His cooking is already better than mine. He's even considering studying formally in chef school when he's done with high school. Still plenty of time to decide, though – he's only in Grade 8.

'We have our first recital next month,' Sizwe says.

'Oh?' I say. 'When did you go back to ballet?'

'Last week.'

'That's great.'

'Yes, it is,' Ma says, rubbing Sizwe's hair. 'I know how much you missed it.'

'What made you decide to go back after all this time?' I ask.

'Izzy.'

'Izzy? *This* Izzy?'

Sizwe laughs. 'Yes! He told me he thinks I'm better than everyone at school.'

'Wow, Izzy. You really said that?'

Israel nods, smiling.

'You see what church can do for a person?' Ma says, smiling at me. 'Maybe you can learn from your brother.'

'Eish, Ma. Maybe. Let's give this one more time.'

Israel gives me a friendly punch on the shoulder.

That night, for the first time since he passed away, Ernest pays me a visit in my dream. The two of us are in a factory, walking up and down at a fast pace. He gives me instructions; it feels like a handover briefing.

He's in a jovial mood, as if relieved to be passing things on. When we exit the factory, he shakes my hand and asks, 'Did you find it?'

When I wake up from the dream, I'm smiling.

ACKNOWLEDGEMENTS

The most heartfelt thank-you has to go to Yewande Omotoso, Doreen Baingana and the Mawazo African Writing Institute for helping me turn a huge lump of a manuscript into something more refined, with a clear direction. A special thank-you to my editors, Catriona Ross for giving this story an opportunity, and Helen Moffett for helping me see further. The team at Penguin Random House has put in a Herculean effort to get this book out there and for that I am most grateful. This book would not have been possible if it weren't for my partner, Sibongile Khumalo, who has not only given me belief, but also allowed me to pursue a dream I didn't realise I had until I met her.